Praise for Betty Webb

—— The Lena Jones Mysteries ——

DESERT REDEMPTION

The Tenth Lena Jones Mystery

"In Jones's electrifying tenth...Scottsdale, Arizona, PI Lena is approached by Harold Slow Horse, one of Arizona's leading artists...[and] gets on a trail that leads her at long last to answers about her troubled past..."

—*Publishers Weekly*

"[A] satisfying conclusion to an underrated series."

—*Booklist*

DESERT VENGEANCE

The Ninth Lena Jones Mystery

"Former cop Lena has a fine sense of justice, which she achieves in this ninth entry of a series that features a vivid sense of place, an indomitable protagonist, and a sensitivity to painful social issues."

—*Booklist*

"Webb offers fans the profound pleasure of watching Lena mature as she comes one step closer to understanding and accepting her difficult past, while providing new readers with an introduction to this strong and genuinely likable character."

—*Publishers Weekly*

"Webb, no stranger to hot-button issues, takes on child molestation in a page-turner that presents both her flawed heroine and the reader with plenty of challenges to their moral codes."

—Kirkus Reviews

"Webb's pithy first-person narration cuts to the chase without a lot of filler, making *Desert Vengeance* a pleasure to read... Lena Jones is tough yet vulnerable, irreverent and sarcastic, yet dead serious at times... The Arizona desert and its touristy towns offer up a strange bonanza of desert tropes, and Webb mines them with enough restraint to strengthen, rather than overshoot, her themes of loss and retribution."

—Shelf Awareness

DESERT RAGE

The Eighth Lena Jones Mystery

"The Lena Jones series is notable for its persistent protagonist and vivid southwestern setting; this eighth entry, centered on a gruesome crime, also is particularly sensitive to the issues of foster children and what really makes a mother."

—Booklist

"Several red herrings arise along the road to a surprising and satisfying ending."

—Publishers Weekly

DESERT WIND

The Seventh Lena Jones Mystery

"Webb uses her expert journalistic skills to explore a shocking topic that private investigator Lena Jones uncovers with masterly resolve... A must-read."

—David Morrell, *New York Times* bestselling author of *The Protector*

★ "Webb pulls no punches in exploring another human rights issue in her excellent seventh mystery starring Arizona PI Lena Jones."

—*Publishers Weekly*, Starred Review

"Webb's compelling exposé of the damage done to nuclear fallout victims (known as *downwinders*), accompanied by research notes and bibliography, makes for fascinating reading... Sue Grafton's alphabet series is a prime read-alike for this series; also consider Pari Noskin Taichert and Steven Havill for Tony Hillerman influences."

—*Library Journal*

DESERT LOST
The Sixth Lena Jones Mystery

Winner of *Library Journal*'s Best Mysteries of 2009

"Richly researched and reeking with authenticity—a wicked exposé."

—Paul Giblin, winner of the 2009 Pulitzer Prize for Journalism

★ "Webb's Scottsdale PI Lena Jones continues to mix southwestern history with crime in her latest investigation... This is a complex, exciting entry in a first-class series, and it makes an excellent read-alike for Sue Grafton fans."

—*Booklist*, Starred Review

"Webb's sobering sixth mystery to feature PI Lena Jones further explores the abuses of polygamy first exposed in 2003's *Desert Wives*... Clear-cut characterizations help a complicated plot flow smoothly. As Webb points out in a note, polygamy still spawns many social ills, despite the recent, well-publicized conviction of Mormon fundamentalist prophet Warren Jeffs."

—*Publishers Weekly*

DESERT CUT
The Fifth Lena Jones Mystery

"Mysteries don't get more hard-hitting than this... Readers will be talking about *Desert Cut* for a long time to come."

—David Morrell, *New York Times* bestselling author

★ "A compelling story that will appeal to a broad range of mystery readers—and may bring increased attention to a too-little-known series."

—*Booklist*, Starred Review

"Webb's dark tale of a clash of cultures is emotionally draining and intellectually challenging."

—*Kirkus Reviews*

"This Southwestern series has a depth that enhances the reader's pleasure."

—*Library Journal*

"As in Webb's earlier adventures—particularly *Desert Wives*, with its critically praised exposé of contemporary polygamy—the long-time journalist manages to fuel her plot from the starkest of news stories without compromising the fast-paced action."

—*Publishers Weekly*

DESERT RUN
The Fourth Lena Jones Mystery

"This thought-provoking novel is a gem."

—*Denver Post*

"Webb bases her latest Lena Jones adventure on a real episode in Arizona history: the great escape of twenty-five Germans from Camp Papago, a POW camp located between Phoenix and Scottsdale... As in the preceding episodes in the series, Webb effectively evokes the beauty of the Arizona desert."

—*Booklist*

"Webb combines evocative descriptions of place with fine historical research in a plot packed with twists."

—*Publishers Weekly*

DESERT SHADOWS
The Third Lena Jones Mystery

"This third in Webb's series makes good use of both tony Scottsdale and the small-press publishing scene. Lena makes a refreshing heroine; being raised by nine different foster families gives her unusual depth. Solid series fare."

—*Booklist*

"As the suspense builds, the author touches on such issues as consolidation in the book industry, the plight of foster children, mother-daughter relationships, animal rescue programs, and more. The glorious Southwest landscape once again provides the perfect setting for Webb's courageous heroine."

—*Publishers Weekly*

DESERT WIVES

The Second Lena Jones Mystery

2004 WILLA Literary Award finalist

"Reading *Desert Wives* is like peering into a microscope at a seething culture of toxic microbes."
—Diana Gabaldon, author of the Outlander series

"If Betty Webb had gone undercover and written *Desert Wives* as a piece of investigative journalism, she'd probably be up for a Pulitzer..."
—*New York Times*

"Stark desert surroundings underscore the provocative subject matter, the outspoken protagonist, and the 'insider' look at polygamist life. Webb's second Lena Jones mystery, after *Desert Noir*, is recommended for most collections."
—*Library Journal*

"Dark humor and thrilling action inform Webb's second Lena Jones mystery... The beauty of the Southwestern backdrop belies the harshness of life, the corrupt officials, brutal men and frightened women depicted in this arresting novel brimming with moral outrage."
—*Publishers Weekly*

DESERT NOIR

The First Lena Jones Mystery

2002 *Book Sense* Top Ten Mystery

"Another mystery strong on atmosphere and insight."

—*Booklist*

"A must-read for any fan of the modern female PI novel."

—*Publishers Weekly*

——— The Gunn Zoo Mysteries ———

THE PANDA OF DEATH
The Sixth Gunn Zoo Mystery

"I became so fascinated by this righteous heroine and caught up in the tangle of improbable events that I whisked through the pages with a smile."

—*Bookreporter*

"Jealousy, crafty zoo critters, and unintended consequences wrapped in an often-humorous mystery full of quirky characters."

—*Kirkus Reviews*

"There is one shock after another in Webb's sixth Gunn Zoo mystery, featuring zookeeper Theodora "Teddy" Bentley."

—*Booklist*

THE OTTER OF DEATH
The Fifth Gunn Zoo Mystery

"While examining some timely social issues, Webb also delivers lots of edifying information on the animal kingdom in an entry sure to please fans and newcomers alike."

—*Publishers Weekly*

"The best part here is watching Bentley's investigative juices start to flow (Webb's background as a reporter really comes to the fore here)... This one will satisfy multiple audiences."

—*Booklist*

THE PUFFIN OF DEATH
The Fourth Gunn Zoo Mystery

"Iceland's rugged and sometimes dangerous landscape provides atmosphere, while Magnus, the polar bear cub, appears just often enough to remind us why Teddy's in Iceland. Webb skillfully keeps the reader guessing right to the dramatic conclusion."

—*Publishers Weekly*

"The exotic locale, the animal lore, and a nice overlay of Icelandic culture and tradition provide an enticing frame story for this solid mystery."

—*Booklist*

"California zookeeper Theodora Bentley travels to Iceland to pick up animals for a new exhibit but must put her investigative skills to use when two American birdwatchers are killed. The fourth book in this charming series doesn't fail to please. Teddy is delightful as she copes with the Icelandic penchant for partying hard."

—*Library Journal*

"I finished *The Puffin of Death* with a feeling of regret that I have not been to Iceland... This book is the next best thing to a trip there. A good Christmas present for those friends who still suffer from itchy feet."

—*BookLoons*

THE LLAMA OF DEATH

The Third Gunn Zoo Mystery

"Animal lore and human foibles spiced with a hint of evil test Teddy's patience and crime solving in this appealing cozy."
—*Publishers Weekly*

"Webb's third zoo series entry winningly melds a strong animal story with an engaging cozy amateur sleuth tale. Set at a relaxed pace with abundant zoo filler, the title never strays into too-cute territory, instead presenting the real deal."
—*Library Journal*

"A Renaissance Faire provides both the setting and the weapon for a murder... Webb's zoo-based series is informative about the habits of the zoo denizens and often amusing..."
—*Kirkus Reviews*

THE KOALA OF DEATH

The Second Gunn Zoo Mystery

"Teddy's second adventure will appeal to animal lovers who enjoy a bit of social satire with their mystery. Pair this series with Ann Littlewood's Iris Oakley novels, also starring a zookeeper."
—*Booklist*

"The author of the edgy Lena Jones mysteries softens her touch in this second zoo mystery featuring an amateur sleuth with a wealthy background and a great deal of zoological knowledge and brain power... Teddy's adventures will appeal to fans of animal-themed cozies."
—*Library Journal*

"Teddy's second case showcases an engaging array of quirky characters, human and animal."

—Kirkus Reviews

THE ANTEATER OF DEATH

The First Gunn Zoo Mystery

2009 Winner of the Arizona Book Award for Mystery/Suspense

"I've been impressed with Betty Webb's edgy mysteries about the Southwest, so I was surprised to find she has a softer side and a wicked sense of humor in a book that can only be described as '*High Society* Meets *Zoo Quest*.' I've always been a sucker for zoos, so I also relished the animal details in this highly enjoyable read."

—Rhys Bowen, New York Times bestselling and award-
winning author

"Webb's new series combines a good puzzle with animal lore, a behind-the-scenes look at zoo operations, and plenty of humor."

—Booklist

"Webb, author of the well-written Lena Jones PI series, not only presents a clear picture of what it is like to work in a zoo but also introduces an engaging new protagonist who will appeal to mystery buffs who enjoy light animal mysteries."

—Library Journal

"Webb kicks off her new series with a bright heroine and an appealingly offbeat setting: a firm foundation later episodes can build on."

—Kirkus Reviews

Also by Betty Webb

The Lena Jones Mysteries

Desert Noir

Desert Wives

Desert Shadows

Desert Run

Desert Cut

Desert Lost

Desert Wind

Desert Rage

Desert Vengeance

Desert Redemption

The Gunn Zoo Mysteries

The Anteater of Death

The Koala of Death

The Llama of Death

The Puffin of Death

The Otter of Death

The Panda of Death

Lost in Paris

LOST *in* PARIS

BETTY WEBB

Poisoned Pen
PRESS

Published by Poisoned Pen Press, an imprint of Sourcebooks
P.O. Box 4410, Naperville, Illinois 60567-4410
(630) 961-3900
sourcebooks.com

Library of Congress Cataloging-in-Publication Data

Names: Webb, Betty, author.
Title: Lost in Paris / Betty Webb.
Description: Naperville, Illinois : Poisoned Pen Press, [2023]
Identifiers: LCCN 2022029625 (print) | LCCN 2022029626
(ebook) | (trade paperback) | (epub)
Subjects: LCGFT: Novels.
Classification: LCC PS3623.E39 L67 2023 (print) | LCC PS3623.E39 (ebook)
 | DDC 813/.6--dc23/eng/20220623
LC record available at https://lccn.loc.gov/2022029625
LC ebook record available at https://lccn.loc.gov/2022029626

Printed and bound in the United States of America.
VP 10 9 8 7 6 5 4 3 2 1

For Laurent Teichman, whose loan of a certain book made all the difference.

"The mystery of existence is the connection
between our faults and our misfortunes."

—*Madame de Stael (1766–1817)*

Chapter One

—— Zoe ——

December 1922
Paris

Despite the sudden snowstorm, Poker Friday was going well at the pretty little house on Rue Vavin. Zoeline Eustacia Barlow—"Zoe" to her friends—was almost fourteen hundred francs up. But then the marquis had to go and ruin everything.

"Too bad about Hemingway, is it not?" Fortier said, in that aristocratic nasal twang that always grated on Zoe's nerves. "His poor wife will certainly pay the price." Although well into his forties, Fortier's patrician face was clear of wrinkles, and despite the long scar on his cheek from German shrapnel—he'd fought bravely in the War to End All Wars—he was still handsome.

But handsome is what handsome does.

"What are you talking about, Antoine?" Zoe asked, trying to keep the annoyance out of her voice. She held two pairs, treys and fives, and a lonely jack, but had been counting the cards and knew Fortier held two eights and at least one ace. Her friend Jewel Johnson, lead dancer at the Moulin Rouge, appeared to be hoping for a flush, and the infamous artist's model, Kiki of Montparnasse, didn't have much of anything. Neither did Kiki's escort, Nick Stewart, of the filthy rich Boston Stewarts.

Zoe couldn't decide what to do. Raise? Hold? Draw?

Outside, a cruel gust of December wind rattled the house's tall windows, giving a twinge to her left leg, the one she'd broken as a child, but Zoe had fed enough coals into the ceramic-faced iron stove to keep the sitting room toasty. Even if a finger of chill did manage to creep inside, the excellent Montrachet they were drinking tasted robust enough to fight it off. With good friends, fine wine, and a possibly winning poker hand, all should have been well, but thanks to Fortier, it wasn't. Maybe she should stop inviting the old bore to her Poker Fridays.

Fanning away the cigarette smoke wafting toward her from his stinking De Reszke, she said, "The last I saw of the Hemingways, they were fine."

Fortier lifted one edge of his lip in a sneer, which irritated Zoe even more than his voice did. On one of her many trips to the Louvre, she'd come across a portrait of Fortier's lordly ancestor, the sixth Marquis Antoine Phillippe Fortier de Guise, who'd lost his head in the French Revolution. The current marquis's sneer was the same as his ancestor's.

Zoe tried her best to concentrate on her cards, but Fortier's comment stirred the other players, too. Count Sergei Ivanovic Aronoffsky—who had folded early—said, "You truly haven't heard of your friend Hadley's misfortune, Zoe? Why, all Paris is abuzz!"

Dominique Garron, the war artist who'd lost an eye covering the Battle of the Marne, glared at Fortier with her remaining hazel orb. "Who cares about the Hemingways? Shut up and play your cards, Antoine, so we can get started on another hand." Like the count, Dominique had already folded, recognizing danger when she saw it. Same as sculptor Karen Wegner, with whom

Dominique was finishing off a bottle of Cognac Gélas to drown her poker sorrows.

As the war artist leaned back against her chair, a glowing shred of tobacco from her Gitane drifted down to the chair's maple arm. The expensive fifteen-piece art nouveau dining set had only been delivered last week, and Zoe was quite proud of it. Trying not to think about her new chair's fate, she said to the count, "Since Fortier's so busy smirking, perhaps you could tell me what's going on with the Hemingways. I've been too busy painting to keep up with the latest gossip."

The count gave her a gentle smile. She'd always seen a touch of El Greco in Sergei Ivanovic Aronoffsky's gaunt, hollow-cheeked face. His arms and legs were thin, too, testaments to the hungry months he'd spent on the run from the Bolsheviks. "You announce you've been painting? Ha! As if we couldn't tell, dear Zoe. We can smell the turpentine and linseed oil from here. I don't understand why you can't copy the others of your kind and maintain a separate studio. It's certainly not because you're hurting for money."

At this, Kiki giggled. Zoe didn't.

Your kind?

One aristocrat at the poker table was bad enough, but whenever two of them showed up on the same evening, snobbery ran rife, and Zoe sometimes found herself in sneaking sympathy with the mobs who'd dragged her friends' lordly forebearers to their deaths on the guillotine. True, the count's woes were more recent than Fortier's. Only five years earlier, when the Bolsheviks took over Russia, the poor man lost his wife, his grand estate, and two Rembrandts. In the odd way of the world, his luck had almost immediately turned. Upon reaching the welcoming arms of Paris, he'd met and married a wealthy French widow. Shortly thereafter, he found himself widowed again. Despite the count's travails, he still looked down his nose on the untitled. One would think that Jewel's love would cure him of his snobbery, but it hadn't happened yet.

Zoe sighed, thinking it was no wonder the Bolsheviks had shot *his* kind against their tapestried walls. However, it was rumored Sergei had managed to escape the bloodbath with a small hoard of diamonds, and since he was a laughably bad poker player, she'd grown to appreciate the extra pin money his inclusion at her Poker Fridays earned her. Besides, despite his occasional bouts of arrogance, she'd grown fond of the man. Unlike other aristocrats she could mention, at least the count had a heart.

Feeling the need to defend the acrid aromas in her snug little house, she said, "Now, now, Sergei. I'm a painter, and like most painters, I keep odd hours. Two and three a.m. often find me working, so having my studio here keeps me from walking the streets in the wee hours and being confused with another sort of woman."

At this, everyone laughed, but the mischievous Kiki pretended to find more than humor in Zoe's off-color joke. "Walking the streets? But, Zoe, *chérie*, it would be fun! Perhaps you and I could do that together."

Since the raven-haired model's spat with her lover, photographer Man Ray, she'd been attending Zoe's Poker Fridays with a variety of new suitors, all of whom had loads of money. Zoe didn't mind. The young men were always good for a laugh, and wasn't that what Paris was all about? Laughter and good times? Nick Stewart, Kiki's suitor-of-the-moment, wasn't a half-bad artist himself, despite the color blindness that ran amok through his inbred Boston family. But color blindness had never hampered a Dadaist, what with the urinals, hair clippings, and other nonsense objects they hung on gallery walls and called *Art* with a capital A. Few of them bothered to paint anymore, including Nick, who was currently working on an installation combining shoelaces and chicken bones.

Kiki's outré comment begged an answer. "Walk the streets together, Kiki? Sorry, but I must decline. I don't have what you French ladies call *savoir faire* or your beauty, and I'd wind up with a less-than-top-notch clientele. And who wants to have sex with hobos?" Directing her attention back to the marquis, Zoe asked, "Now, what were you saying about Ernest and Hadley?"

Not that Zoe cared about Ernest Hemingway, having once observed the bully sucker punch an inoffensive young man in La Closerie des Lilas café just for the thrill of seeing him fall. But she did care about Hadley. She'd often wondered how such a sweet-natured woman could put up with the ill-tempered man, who remained far from the success he imagined himself to have attained. Love, probably. Love, that old betrayer. Love, that old destroyer. For the past four years, Zoe had taken pains to avoid it. One broken heart was enough.

Oblivious to his hostess's feelings, Fortier was more than happy to expound on the Hemingway scandal. "The story I hear is that Hadley lost all of Ernest's manuscripts. Every word he ever wrote, even that certain-to-be-terrible novel he was working on."

Zoe frowned. "That makes no sense. How could Hadley lose his manuscripts? She's not his secretary."

"I know the answer to that," the count said, his mournful countenance buoyed by a semi-smile. "It happened aboard a train. One of the porters at the Gare de Lyon, a Russian like myself, gave me chapter and verse of the incident."

"Do tell, since we're all agog," snapped Fortier, jealous that Sergei had stolen his place on the soapbox.

With an indulgent nod, the count cleared his throat. The story he then related was a troubling one, in which poor Hadley did indeed emerge as irresponsible. A few days earlier, while Ernest was in Switzerland reporting on the Lausanne Conference, he'd run into a publisher who asked to see some of his fiction. Thrilled, as any aspiring novelist would be, Ernest immediately telegraphed Hadley, who had stayed behind in Paris, to post him a few stories and his unfinished novel.

Under most circumstances, this would have been a sensible enough request.

But Hadley had fallen ill with the flu, Sergei continued, which is why she hadn't accompanied Ernest to Lausanne in the first place. Anxious to please her husband, she'd staggered around their tiny apartment collecting the manuscripts, and in her delirium, packed up the carbons as well. She stuffed everything into a valise. Hoping to surprise him, she hitched a ride with their landlord to the Gare de Lyon, where she bought a ticket on the Paris-Lausanne Express. Once aboard, Hadley placed the valise under her seat. Still feverish, she went back out on the platform to purchase a bottle of Evian for the long journey.

"The porter told me that when the poor woman returned to her seat, the valise was gone," Sergei finished. "So I ask you, Zoe, an important question, one for which you, as her most trusted friend, should have the most informed answer. Yes, all Paris is aware of Ernest's habit of knocking down unsuspecting men in cafés, but do you know if he is also in the habit of knocking down his wife? Given the enormity of her crime, should we worry about pretty Hadley's safety?"

Zoe was so miffed it took her a moment to answer, and when she did, she discovered she'd lost the poker hand. Kiki, the little sneak, had been holding an inside straight and had been too foxy to let it show. The sly cat was still raking in the francs when Zoe finally found her voice.

"Ernest may be a bullyboy in the cafés, Sergei, but I doubt he hits Hadley. She's the one with the money, remember. Ah, did I hear you say she packed the originals *and* carbons?"

"Everything."

As much as Zoe hated to admit it, Sergei might be right.

Poor Hadley.

Zoe had met Hadley earlier in the year, when the marquis, already a poker-playing regular, invited Zoe to accompany him to one of Gertrude Stein's famous "evenings." Gertrude, who looked and acted more like a Roman emperor than a woman, had gained fame for her foresight in championing the talents of Picasso, Matisse, and others while they were still unknowns, and now she reigned supreme in the salons of Paris. To be granted entrée into one of her gatherings signaled that your work was being taken seriously, so Zoe was thrilled to accept Fortier's invitation. A meeting with Gertrude would surely turn her luck around!

It hadn't worked out that way.

The evening had started off promisingly enough, with everyone feasting at a table spread with rare delicacies. But after the housekeeper whisked away the remnants, the mood changed. Instead of allowing Zoe to join in the conversation with the other artists and writers—all male, she noted—Gertrude insisted she join the wives and mistresses in a small adjoining room. With a condescending smile, the big woman explained, "Ladies always enjoy talking to Alice. She knows so much about running a household—sewing and cooking and such."

Sewing and cooking and such? Oh, bushwa!

Deeply offended, the only reason Zoe hadn't sloshed her wine into Gertrude's face was because she didn't want to further humiliate Fortier. The moment Gertrude made her pronouncement, he'd flushed with embarrassment, and his mouth opened and closed and opened again as he tried to find the proper words to decry their host's prejudice. Taking pity on him, Zoe stood up, and with the rest of the ladies, filed out of the room. She was spoiling for a fight, though, and was looking forward to giving Alice a piece of her mind. But once she was settled in a room overstuffed with paintings and furniture, Hadley, who sat next to her on the uncomfortable horsehair sofa, leaned over and whispered, "Patience, Zoe. It'll be ugly, but you'll survive. We all will."

Zoe had noticed Hadley earlier, her enviable porcelain skin—much smoother than Zoe's own—the glorious auburn hair cut into a flapper's bob, and the dance of intelligence in those blue-gray eyes. She appeared several years older than her husband and nowhere near as pretty, and Hadley's long, slender fingers revealed the gifted pianist she was reputed to be.

"Does Gertrude do this often?" Zoe whispered back. "Banish the females to purdah?"

"Every damned time."

"But..."

Hadley placed a beautifully manicured forefinger against her lips. "Shh. Here comes Alice."

Zoe found Alice Toklas less condescending than Gertrude. If anything, the small woman seemed a bit shy. But the following discussions of petit point and the proper mincing of truffles bored her, and only Hadley's witty asides made the experience bearable. By the time the evening was over, Zoe realized she'd found a kindred spirit. Since then, hardly a week passed when she and Hadley did not share a drink or three at La Rotonde. Sometimes Hadley would even visit the little house on the Rue Vavin and serenade her with mini concerts of Bach or Handel on Zoe's Gaveau upright. When in a particularly rebellious mood—usually after another humiliating visit to Gertrude's with her vain husband—she'd pound out jazz.

Now Zoe's friend was in big trouble.

Chapter Two

Friends do not allow friends to suffer alone, but since Hadley was still in Switzerland with Ernest, the next morning Zoe decided she could best help her friend by tracking down those lost manuscripts. After helping Madeline, her housekeeper, clear away the debris from last night's poker party, Zoe scribbled a quick telegram, then paid Dax, the most trustworthy of the waifs who lurked at the end of the street, to run it over to the telegraph office.

TAKE HEART—STOP—WILL FIND MISSING MS
    —STOP—GIVE ERNEST MY LOVE—STOP
    ZOE

The GIVE ERNEST MY LOVE bit was pure nonsense, but politesse was the wisest part of friendship. Zoe would never let Hadley know how much she disliked Ernest.

"The valise is gone, and those manuscripts have long been scattered to the wind," Madeline said, when Zoe told her of Hadley's misfortune. Today, the housekeeper's artificial arm appeared to be giving her trouble, sticking here and there when it should have been wheeling effortlessly through the required motions to finish the cleanup.

"Should Karen Wegner look at that?" Zoe asked, pointing to the offending apparatus.

The studio where Karen worked stood just off Boulevard de Edgar-Quinet, not far from Zoe's little house on Rue Vavin. After Madeline's government-issued arm proved less than satisfactory, Karen, who specialized in the new art of kinetic sculpture, cobbled together a more suitable prosthesis, a wondrous collage of steel, wire, and pullies. But nothing could have performed as well as the original muscle and bone, which had been blown off at the Somme while Madeline tended to the wounded during the Great War.

Madeline shook her head. A plump woman with features too blunt for beauty, she was richly endowed with fortitude. "A good oiling should fix it."

After fetching a bottle of linseed oil from the studio, Zoe found her housekeeper was correct. A few daubs here, a few daubs there, and the contraption moved smoothly enough for the washing-up to be finished in record time.

"You're probably right about Hemingway's valise, too," Zoe said, putting the last wineglass away. "But I at least owe Hadley the attempt."

"Hmm."

With Madeline's "hmm" still ringing in her ears—like good house-keepers everywhere, she was a devout worshipper at the Church of Minding Your Own Business—Zoe put on her weatherproof boots, the pair with the built-up heel on the left, and bundled up in layers of wool. Thus defended from whatever insult the weather might throw at her, she set off for the Hemingways' flat.

Being from Alabama, Zoe was relatively new to snow, and she didn't really mind it. If anything, the brisk walk was refreshing after last night's smoky poker game. And, truth be told, after moving from a thirty-room plantation house to a four-room pied-à-terre, the broad Parisian avenues gave her room to breathe. Enjoying the day, she took the long way to the flat where the Hemingways lived. Cutting through the hordes of shoppers, tourists, and boulevardiers, she turned north, enjoying the sounds of horses as they clip-clopped around the *grrr-grrr-grrr* of green omnibuses. Despite the cold, street singers were out. One of them, a thin girl not yet into her teens, sang "*Mon coeur est un palais de glace*," *My heart is a palace of ice*, which touched Zoe enough that she half-filled the child's bowl with francs.

Once Zoe entered Le Jardin du Luxembourg, the street noise dropped away. Above, a canopy of horse chestnut trees stretched their bare limbs to the snow-speckled sky. Come spring, they would be lush with blossoms.

Halfway through the park, she arrived at the big water basin and paused for a few minutes to study the icicle-draped Carpeaux fountain, where rays from the winter sun turned the icicles into colorful prisms. As she watched the colors dance against the gray stone, several young boys ran up to the pond and began breaking up its icy surface with long sticks. She enjoyed their energy, and their yips of happiness. Last summer she'd watched a couple of them sail toy boats in the same spot.

Zoe recognized the tow-headed boy. He was around seven years old, and his freckles reminded her of Leeanne, her younger sister. Little Lee-Lee hated her freckles and couldn't wait until she got old enough to cover them with makeup. Was she doing that now, Zoe wondered? They hadn't seen each other since Zoe's banishment from Beech Glen, although they'd managed to communicate through a complicated chain of letters. Thinking of Beech Glen, Zoe's smile faded. With her stepmother now ruling the roost, the chances of seeing Lee-Lee again weren't good. Maybe once the woman died...

No, strike that fantasy. If Anabelle died, Beech Glen would fall into the hands of Zoe's brother, Brice, who was no better.

And there was nothing Zoe could do about it.

Sometimes Zoe missed Beach Glen so much it hurt. That didn't mean she didn't love Paris—her love of the city would always win over the Alabama plantation—but that didn't mean she could forget her birth home. She remembered watching red, gold, and purple sunsets from the wide veranda. Remembered the calls of whip-poor-wills at dusk. Remembered the fireflies dancing in the night.

Whenever Zoe's mood grew glum—usually during solitary evenings—she would walk to her studio's big glass wall and look out at the gas lamps as they came alive along Boulevard Montparnasse. This fabled city was her home now, and it had embraced her as Mercy, Alabama, never would.

But, oh, the memory of those fireflies.

Zoe turned away from the freckle-faced boy and diagonally crossed the park, continuing on its gravel paths until she exited at Rue Soufflot. From there, it was only a few more blocks until she was brushing snow off her shoulders at the entrance to 74 Rue du Cardinal Lemoine. The gray limestone building, with its important-looking entryway, appeared little different than any other apartment building in Paris, despite the fact that its neighbor was a loud dance hall. Maybe lack of sleep contributed to Ernest's touchiness.

Oh, well. Everyone had problems these days, didn't they? Resisting the temptation to excuse Ernest's bad behavior, Zoe rapped on the door. It was immediately opened by the building's concierge, a kind-faced woman of about fifty. "May I help you?" she asked.

"It's rather complicated," Zoe said. What she was about to request might strike this woman as outlandish, but she had no choice.

"Complicated?" Instead of being wary, the concierge appeared intrigued and invited her into a small room filled with family mementos. Chief among them was the photograph of a smiling young man in a soldier's uniform. Did he survive the Great War? If so, did he return with his body and mind intact?

Zoe knew better than to ask. Instead, she explained the purpose for her visit.

The concierge listened carefully, then nodded. "Oh, yes, Mademoiselle Zoe Barlow! Madame Hemingway has mentioned you many times—her friend, the artist!—so of course I'll allow you access. But I assure you it's hopeless. Why, Monsieur Hemingway himself came back here only two days ago, all the way from Switzerland! He searched and searched and found nothing." She lowered her voice to a whisper. "I heard him cry, you know. He got drunk and he cried for hours. The poor man was so distraught I feared he might do himself harm."

Zoe frowned. "Is he still here, then? If so, I should probably..."

"No, no. He went back to Switzerland the very next morning. I think he is working there at that big peace conference. The one about the Turks, I think."

Relieved, Zoe said, "Then perhaps I can have a go at it. An artist's eye, you know. I might see something he missed."

The concierge nodded sagely. "A *woman's* eye."

A few minutes later, they were huffing their way up four flights of stairs made odorous by the *pissoirs* at the end of each hallway. It was so unpleasant that despite Zoe's dislike of Ernest, she found herself sympathizing with him. If there was ever a fire in her studio and she lost her paintings... It didn't bear thinking about.

Their climb finished, the concierge unlocked the door to the Hemingways' flat, and escorted Zoe in. After a moment of shock, she stared at the place Hadley called home. It explained something that had puzzled her over the past year. Although a frequent visitor to Zoe's little house, Hadley had never issued an invitation to hers. Now Zoe understood why. The tiny sitting room, little more than closet-sized, was furnished only with a couple of shabby chairs, an ancient cupboard, and Hadley's rented piano. The alcove-type bedroom looked even smaller, with its sagging bed and a two-seater dining table. Zoe found the sanitation situation even more worrying. Maybe there was a communal *pissoir* at the end of the hall for the male residents, but why should a refined woman like Hadley be forced to use a bucket in the bedroom corner for a toilet?

"It is a simple flat," the concierge said, obviously embarrassed by the lack of comfort. "But they are young, and very much in love."

Love. There was that deadly word again.

Biting back what she really wanted to say, Zoe just grunted, then began her search. After only a few minutes, having looked under the bed, the mattress, and through each drawer and shelf in the tiny flat, she admitted defeat. Not one word written by Ernest remained in this place.

Her nascent sympathy for the man fled as she recalled a recent conversation with Hadley over a glass of wine at La Rotonde. Hadley complained that Hem had begun renting a private writing room for himself in a nearby building so the sound of her voice wouldn't intrude upon his lofty thoughts. Here was a man living on his wife's inheritance, yet disallowing her even the barest of modern conveniences while he found more comfortable working quarters for himself.

As the French would say, oh *le cochon*! The swine.

There remained one more place Zoe might search. After leaving the grim flat at Cardinal Lemoine, Zoe set out for the taxi stand at the intersection of boulevards Montparnasse and Raspail. In the past, she had used the services of Avak Grigoryan, an Armenian taxi driver who, for a few francs, would ferry anyone anywhere in his 1918 black Avions Voison motorcar nicknamed the Grim Reaper. The Reaper, which did not always heed its driver's orders, had survived several accidents its passengers almost hadn't. But the price was right.

Avak and the Grim Reaper were awaiting their next victim when Zoe approached.

More of a gentleman than some actual gentlemen she knew, the man with the magnificent black mustache tipped his hat when he saw her. "Where I drive you this handsome day, Mademoiselle Barlow? To shop for the Christmas?" Although Avak was a man of the world who spoke several languages—Armenian, Turkish, German, French, and English—the structure of his French and English sentences remained creative.

"No shopping today, Avak," she replied, "but plenty of errands. First, I need to hunt up a train porter. It probably won't take long and, whatever happens after that, you'll be well-rewarded."

A smile. Due to a recent beating by street toughs, he was missing an incisor, which his mustache helped conceal. "Another night at lucky cards, Mademoiselle?"

"You could say so."

"Maybe one day you teach me this poker so I win francs?"

The request elicited another memory, this one ancient, when Zoe learned the basics of math. Because their big plantation house usually thronged with visitors, her hostess mother had no time to help with her schoolwork. But her father—a doctor, he was usually busy, too—nevertheless spent several evenings teaching her how to play what he called "draw poker." Somewhere along those odd, happy days, she'd begun to figure out the secret lives of numbers. Now she used the game to top up Beech Glen's monthly remittance checks, which only went so far.

"I'll do that someday," she promised the taxi driver. "But for now…"

Flashing a grateful smile, Avak helped her into the Grim Reaper. The car's landau top would cover her if it began snowing harder, but poor Avak would have to brave the weather in the open.

It seemed the Grim Reaper would behave itself, at first, but by the time they made it out of Montparnasse and across the Seine, its gaseous farts had caused a dray horse to rear and prompted a nun walking along the Pont d'Austerlitz to deliver a string of curses that would shame a sailor.

Hadley had boarded the train at the Gare de Lyon, a beautiful if somewhat ungainly station with a tall clock tower that threw long shadows across the immense cobblestone plaza in front. Horses, having more sense than automobiles, feared the place, as if remembering the forever goodbyes of the Great War, and the return of torn-apart bodies. But Avak's Grim Reaper did not have an animal's good instincts. It rattled along, scattering children, stray dogs, and horses in its wake. When it pulled into a space near the station's great Departure Hall, Zoe nearly fell out of the motorcar, she was so anxious to leave it.

She dropped some francs into Avak's gloved hand. "Wait here and you'll earn double that."

He bowed. "For which I grateful to the good God, mademoiselle."

And to me, she thought but did not say. After everything Avak had been through, he deserved courtesy.

The big plaza in front of the Gare de Lyon was crowded with street singers, old men and women hawking postcards, and diminutive match girls selling their sulfurous wares. Zoe loved these cheerful entrepreneurs, and she often purchased little treasures from them. But the plaza's dark side was all too real. Today, despite the chilly weather, it thronged with war veterans begging for handouts. Many of them were missing limbs, while others had been blinded by mustard gas and were being led around by one-armed comrades.

More than a million and a half French soldiers and forty thousand French civilians had died in the War to End All Wars, one thousand in Paris alone. That death toll didn't include the more than two hundred thousand who had succumbed to the Spanish flu, or the million more who'd sustained such serious injuries they would never be whole again. As Zoe made her way across the great plaza, she felt like she was walking through a freshly dug graveyard waiting for lost souls who hadn't yet finished dying. By the time she reached the entrance to the station, she'd given away a substantial portion of last night's poker winnings.

But Beauty lived here, too, because Paris was still Paris, war-damaged or not. In the Gare de Lyon's Departure Hall, she passed the elegant station restaurant with its smaller clock, which was busy disagreeing with the clock tower outside. *It is only sixteen minutes to ten, not seventeen*, Clock Minor quibbled. The Tower Clock shot back, *You are incorrect, it is now sixteen and a half. Hurry, hurry, life flies while you stand still!*

Zoe approached the first porter she saw, a twentyish, one-legged war veteran clad in a uniform now innocent of blood. Trying hard to smooth out her Alabama-accented French, she asked, "Where would I find the train to Lausanne, Switzerland?"

"You won't. It's gone." His voice was raw as his manners. *Mustard gas.* He began to turn away, not caring whether his answer had distressed her or not.

"Which track was it on?"

He kept walking, the wooden peg on his left stump giving him a stride that resembled a swagger. "Four."

Zoe limped along—her own bad leg was acting up—until she spied a friendly face. Gaston. In his sixties, he'd been too old for the military, so he still had all his limbs. A friendly man, he'd helped with her luggage only a week earlier when she visited a new male friend in Saint-Étienne. In anticipation of the meeting, she'd tipped

Gaston lavishly, and she allowed herself more wine than was wise. In the end, alas, the anticipation proved more delightful than the reality, when it turned out that her new friend liked boys more than he liked girls.

C'est la vie.

"Gaston!" Zoe called, waving down the porter.

His furrowed face creased into a smile. "Ah, the mademoiselle who traveled so happily to Saint-Étienne. Another trip to that wondrous place?" He glanced down at her empty hands. "What, no luggage?"

"I'm not leaving Paris today; at least I don't think I am. I'm here on behalf of a friend of mine who lost her valise on the Paris-Lausanne Express."

To her surprise, Gaston nodded. "Yes, yes, Madame Hadley Hemingway. Oh, what a terrible thing! The poor lady was distraught, almost fainting with despair. Oleg and I tried to soothe her, but she was beyond consolation. She'd tucked her valise under her seat, you see, then foolishly went to buy a bottle of water on the platform, but when she returned to her compartment, the valise was gone. After we calmed her sobs, we left her in the care of a kind lady and began a search. We went into the neighboring cars and asked if anyone had seen a person acting suspiciously, but no one had seen anything. At least that was what they claimed, and who was I to call them liars? The valise was truly gone, along with Madame's precious papers."

Zoe winced. "They weren't her papers; they were her husband's."

"So she told us. I pray he has forgiven her, but she should never have left the valise by itself. These days, many desperate men hang about the station; you've seen them out there in the plaza. Some are not above thievery. For all they knew, the valise could have carried jewels or gold!"

Gaston was correct. The war had torn millions of men from

their families and occupations, often wounding their minds more severely than their bodies. To consciences numbed by horror, thievery counted for little.

"This Oleg who helped you search, may I speak with him?"

"His French..." The porter smiled. "It is not good, and I am sorry to say he has no English, but since my wife is Russian, I can help."

Gaston went on to describe Oleg as a man with a common-enough story these days. Like many Russian soldiers, he had deserted the Great War's battlefields to join his country's bloody revolution. A couple of years later, he'd lost heart over the never-ending slaughter, and made his way to Paris in search of a less dangerous occupation.

Zoe and Gaston finally found him as he was helping a luggage-laden woman into a taxi, near where Avak waited faithfully in the front seat of the Grim Reaper. As soon as Oleg collected his tip, Zoe began questioning him, helped along by Gaston as interpreter.

Yes, Oleg said, he remembered the crying lady with the dark red hair. No, he did not know who'd stolen her valise. No, he could not remember who else was around at the time because there were so many people going to and fro—friend meeting friend, lovers tearfully parting—so how could they expect him to know who was who and what they were doing? Oleg was all big-eyed innocence.

But Zoe was a good poker player and recognized a bluff when she saw one.

"Fifty francs if you tell me who took the valise," she said. That amount, a pittance to her, would be enough for the man to eat, drink, and pay a couple month's rent.

Oleg flushed. His hands, which had twitched throughout his bumbling tale of know-nothingness, made grasping motions.

"Well?" She waved her purse.

"It was Vassily Popov! He said he needed the money to help

his daughter, Sophia!" Oleg couldn't take his eyes off Zoe's purse, a pretty enough thing, being encrusted with a sprinkling of beveled stones, but she doubted Oleg was a connoisseur of women's fashions.

"Where does this Vassily Popov live?"

A flood of Russian mixed with French, but Zoe recognized a name: *Mary Cassatt.*

Chapter Three

Soon Zoe, clutching the rough map Gaston had drawn, was on her way to the tiny village of Le Mesnil-Théribus, fifty miles north-east of Paris, while the trusty Avak sat up front, exposed to the elements. Despite her determination, she felt uneasy, but not from the pain in her leg; she was used to that.

Several times, the Grim Reaper attempted to more closely examine a ditch, and only Avak's expert driving kept them on the road. After a few miles, though, the car settled down enough for Zoe to study the scenery.

The countryside looked different under snow than did Paris, where too often the snow lay mixed with ashes and horseshit. At first, the clean, low hills reminded Zoe of the rare winter she'd once experienced at Beech Glen. That year, a dusting of pure white had disguised the dead grasses of winter, softening the trees sil-houetted against the steel-colored sky. To her then five-year-old eyes, Beech Glen had become a frozen fairyland, but the unusual snowfall was the only thing her memory shared with today's bitter landscape.

Thanks to the miserable weather, the road to Le Mesnil-Théribus was clear of horse traffic, but snow covered the pasturage on both sides. Zoe was well-prepared, bundled up in her sheared beaver coat and matching cloche, further protected by the landau, but she worried about Avak, who sat uncovered in the front seat of the Grim Reaper.

"Are you warm enough?" she screamed at him, over the car's noisy motor.

He waved away her concern. "Sit and enjoy scenery so pretty, mademoiselle."

Plantation-raised Zoe saw only sheep awaiting slaughter, trees standing only to be felled. As the Grim Reaper chugged along, black crows screamed and cawed after them. A few had the temerity to follow along for a few miles, now and then dipping down to proclaim their disapproval. One stayed with them all the way to Le Mesnil-Théribus, gliding away only when the car reached the outskirts of the village.

Zoe had hoped to catch a glimpse of Château de Beaufresne, the estate of Mary Cassatt, the great American Impressionist. Oleg had told them that, on the days Vassily Popov did not work, the Russian and his daughter, Sophia, lived in a woodsman's cottage near the painter's chateau. Having now experienced the long journey from Paris to Le Mesnil-Théribus, Zoe found herself admiring the thief's grit. What a horror his commute to Paris must be! And how in the world had he even found this out-of-the-way place? His was a difficult existence, to be sure, but such was the lot of a thief. Popov's poor daughter, however...

No one gets to choose their family, do they?

"There Château de Beaufresne be, mademoiselle!" Avak's voice brought Zoe out of her glum reverie.

Since the gate leading to Cassatt's château was open, Zoe was able to glimpse it as they passed by. Exquisite in its simplicity, the two-story house stood in front of a deep forest, its red brick edifice boasting two rows of white-shuttered windows in perfect alignment. Behind the château, she could see a small lake. Crossing it was a bridge that appeared to be a duplicate of the one at Monet's Giverny. Zoe mourned not seeing more of the property, but she had pressing business, so they left Château de Beaufresne behind and turned onto the rough track that led to the humbler home of a thief.

Mere yards into the forest, the track became so overgrown they had to abandon the Grim Reaper, leaving it under an oak to fend for itself. The sun briefly fought its way through the cloud cover, creating spindly shadows. What had almost seemed a carefree adventure while they were still on the road no longer felt so merry, and the moment Zoe stepped out of the car, the heavy scent of mildewed leaves rose to greet her.

This ancient odor sent a rash of goosebumps along her arms. She felt as if she'd somehow inserted herself into a time when tribal people lurked in killing parties behind the trees. What the hell did she think she was doing, hobbling along on a road that was little more than a deer run? Maybe it was only her imagination, but she could swear she heard deep grunts up ahead and the rustle of feet moving through fallen leaves. Human or animal? Peaceful or...

Stop it, Zoe!

After all, she was no stranger to forests. Beech Glen was surrounded by woodland, and during her childhood, she'd explored its miles of beech, oak, and pine. But this forest was the remainder of an ancient world, and it looked downright hostile. Had this place ever been gentled by friendly fireflies?

If so, wild boar probably ate them. The animals were known for their aggressiveness, and anyone unlucky enough to cross their path might find themselves impaled on sharp tusks. Zoe also wouldn't be surprised if wolves and lynxes roamed here, too, whereas at Beech Glen, all you saw were deer, raccoons, and, every now and then, a coyote. Back in the States, coyotes were everywhere. Her maternal grandmother, who'd once lived in New York City, had sworn she'd once seen a coyote trotting down the middle of Park Avenue.

As Zoe and Avak moved through the skeletal trees, she noticed the weather had warmed slightly. The early morning's crispness was gone, and the melting snow created a veritable swamp of mud and leaves on the forest floor. Several times she stumbled into a stand of leaf rot, burying her foot in mud up to her ankles—oh, her poor shoes!—but it was too late to turn back. According to Gaston's map, they were almost at the shack. Once confronted, Popov would peacefully hand over the valise, and she'd find Ernest's manuscripts safe inside.

Zoe had always loved fairy tales.

Eventually, Avak, who had been blazing their trail through the dense underbrush, suddenly stopped. "Look," he whispered, pointing ahead.

The so-called "woodsman's cottage" turned out to be a shack most rats would feel embarrassed to call home. It squatted several meters off the track, hidden behind scrappy brush and a stand of juniper and pine grown so close together they made an almost impenetrable fence. The only thing giving away the shack's presence was the smoke rising from its chimney.

The Grim Reaper was only half the reason Zoe had chosen not to travel here by train. The other half was Avak, who, although sweet in nature, looked fierce. In fact, given his great height and scarred face, he appeared downright terrifying. Feeling brave with this gentle giant by her side, Zoe maneuvered her way through the undergrowth up to the shack's ill-fitting door and gave it a hard rap. For Hadley's sake, she hoped the thieving Popov hadn't yet found a buyer for Ernest's valise.

"Open up!" she demanded.

Nothing behind the door; no sound of feet scurrying to hide ill-gotten gains, no cries from the thief's daughter, pleading for mercy.

For the second knock, Zoe let Avak do the honors. "Open up!" he growled, his tone ferocious. "Not open up, break door down I will!"

His threat did no good, and the shack remained silent. Avak looked to Zoe with a silent question.

She nodded.

Avak raised his massive, boot-clad foot and gave the door a good kick. It flew open. Which, in a way, was unfortunate, since the sights and smells of a freshly killed man and woman proved quite unpleasant.

Chapter Four

Zoe bent over the two bodies to determine if there was anything she could do, but she'd seen death before and recognized it here. Both had been shot in the forehead, and at close range.

If she kept thinking about it, she'd have to cry, and tears wouldn't help anyone, so she turned away. Hemingway's valise was nowhere to be seen, but she spotted a small stack of papers lying atop the kindling next to the fireplace. More pages were feeding the flames. Zoe could be single-minded when necessary, so she rushed past the bodies and pulled a page out of the fire. Giving the typewritten page a quick scan. Notes? Poems?

Taking a deep breath, she stuck her hands back into the fire.

"Be of care, mademoiselle!" Avak cautioned.

She ignored his well-meant advice and continued grabbing at the manuscript pages as sentence fragments ran by her...*and he said that he said she said...the Indian woman on the bunk...a machine is a machine is a machine... He bled like a gutted pig...lions in the high grass...life was hopeless when honestly faced... Yes, he said as he ran toward the cannons yes forever...*

Word upon word burning away to warm a piteously cold room.

As Zoe reached for another page, her sleeve began to smoke, and her hands...

Strong arms dragged her away, even as she grasped for more.

"No, mademoiselle, no!" Avak insisted, not letting her go. "You burn self! Need doctor! Gendarmes!"

Zoe watched the last of Hemingway's words curl into ash. As soon as Avak released his grip, she disregarded her blistered hands and added the scorched pages to the untouched stack yet to be used for kindling.

What now? They were standing over two dead Russians, and there would be questions. During her nearly four years living in France, Zoe never had a personal experience with the French criminal courts, but she knew the country operated under the Napoleonic Code, where a suspect was deemed guilty until he proved himself innocent. As an American with money, though, and subsequently of value to the country's ravaged economy, she figured she'd probably be treated gently. Avak's fate was more precipitous, because in France, as in the American South, crime was considered the province of the darker, lower classes. Never the gentry.

Yet there was nothing else to be done. Zoe needed to report the crime. Only minutes earlier, on their way through the village, the Grim Reaper's gaseous farts had raised more than one pair of eyebrows, and the noisy beast would eventually be tracked down. Best to sound the alarm themselves.

First, she needed to see if Hemingway's valise—and possibly more pages—was hidden in the shack, so after handing the scorched pages to Avak, she began to search. It went quickly, since the shack held no furniture other than two rough sleeping pallets on the floor. A few articles of clothing were folded neatly and stacked against the wall, but that was it. Zoe's hands throbbed as she sorted through the clothes, but she found nothing. Same with the rags used as blankets.

No valise. No more manuscripts. Giving up, she allowed Avak to lead her back to the Grim Reaper, and prepared a likely story for the police. As they bumped along the rough track, the rescued pages now wrapped in one of the less ragged blankets, she related the story she'd come up with to Avak so his version of their activities would mirror hers. It was the truth, just not the entirety of it.

They appeared to be in agreement until Avak veered from the main road and started up the long drive to Mary Cassatt's Château de Beaufresne. "What are you doing?" she asked, alarmed. "You said we needed to go to the police, and they'll be in Mesnil-Théribus."

"No doctor in village, and your hands want fixed. American painter has friendships of many doctors."

"And you know this how?"

"The wife of my brother cooks for the Madame. Veronique burned hand on big stove, and the Madame telephone—*telephoned!*—doctor for to heal. He drove all way from Beauvais!"

"But the police..."

"The Madame will telephone them also, but I not know if gendarmerie nearby. Small village is."

As the pines and oaks whipped by, Zoe's hands demanded more of her attention, so she ceased speaking. After all, she'd endured worse. *This is nothing*, she consoled herself. She was alive. A man and a young woman were not. Whatever Popov's crimes, he'd died with terror on his face, and Sophia...

It looked like Sophia had died with a question on her lips.

Within minutes, Zoe and Avak were standing at Mary Cassatt's front door, speaking to her housekeeper. Although the woman frowned at their muddy feet, when Avak pointed to Zoe's blistered hands, she motioned for them to enter. She left them in the parquet entryway while she rushed along the hall, calling loudly, "Madame! A woman's been hurt!"

Zoe was beginning to appreciate Avak's wisdom in finding the fastest help possible. But despite her increasing pain, she peered into the sitting room and beheld a treasury of delights. She was straining forward for a better look when a clatter of footsteps announced the approach of two more women, a plump maid carrying a brush to clean off their muddy shoes, and an older woman as elegant as her château. Her thick glasses couldn't disguise her cataracts.

Mary Cassatt was going blind.

While the maid was busy brushing away the mud, Cassatt leaned over Zoe's hands until her nose was mere millimeters from the largest of the blisters.

"*Est-ce douloureux,* mademoiselle?"

"Yes, it hurts," Zoe answered in English.

Cassatt looked up, her near-blind eyes searching out Zoe's. "Mississippi?"

"Alabama. But our accents are similar to those of our cousins to the west."

The corner of Cassatt's mouth twitched. "You're an artist."

Surprised as much by her bluntness as her powers of observation, Zoe asked, "How did you know?"

"There's a sliver of Prussian blue under your right index fingernail, and a smear of cadmium yellow across the cuticle of your right thumb. You came to France to paint."

Perhaps because of the pain she was trying to ignore, Zoe fell back on the truth. "Actually, my family—what's left of it, anyway—threw me out." The moment the words were out of her mouth, she regretted them.

But they didn't disturb Cassatt. "Ah, well. I know certain families, especially the aristocrats in our Southern states, do not care to have their artistic kin living within gossip range. From your lovely frock, I surmise you have found success in Paris."

Cassatt wasn't as blind as Zoe had at first thought, nor as prim. "Not because of my painting. My disapproving family sends me a monthly remittance, to which I add my poker winnings."

The twitch developed into a youthful grin, revealing that the seventy-eight-year-old woman still had most of her teeth. "Then you must be Zoe Barlow. My good friend Count Sergei Aronoffsky has spoken of your facility with cards."

Grin met grin. "Sergei is too kind. And not as good at poker as he believes."

Once the mud on their shoes was brushed away, Cassatt invited them into her sumptuous sitting room, where Zoe surveyed the furnishings: a crystal chandelier that put Beech Glen's chandelier to shame, a Grecian-legged Regency sofa an emperor could have reclined on, silk brocade draperies, Persian carpets, and paintings, paintings, paintings. Slowing her eyes' swift run, Zoe noted a Cezanne still life with pears and apples, a Renoir of a young woman in a pink dress, and two Degas—one painting was of horses at the racetrack, the other of ballet dancers whose legs were as well-muscled as the horses'. Farther along was one of Cassatt's own works, a mother bathing her child. The tenderness on the mother's face…

Don't think about that, Zoe.

"Such a joy to realize you are acquainted with Antoine Fortier, too," Cassatt continued. "I imagine the wily marquis's poker game is more expert than the count's."

Before Zoe could agree, the housekeeper returned. She wheeled a cart carrying a mound of snowy towels and a Doulton pitcher and washbasin similar to the ones in Zoe's bedroom at Beech Glen. Cassatt bade her move to that spectacular Regency sofa near the tall window where the light was still strong so the housekeeper could better attend to her. As Zoe settled onto the sofa, she examined it more closely. The marvelous thing was upholstered in a mischievous interplay of phthalo blue chrysanthemums and dioxazine purple roses, its color scheme made even more startling by the Payne's gray background. A courageous choice, dared only by the most courageous of artists.

"Cleanliness is of paramount importance when it comes to burns," Cassatt said, watching the housekeeper pour cool water over Zoe's blistered hands.

Up until this time, Avak had been standing silently nearby, but he now spoke up. "We hoping doctor…"

Cassatt raised a large-knuckled hand. Arthritis? "I've already telephoned, and he's on his way. For heaven's sake, man, sit down. I can't have you standing around like that."

Ever self-effacing, Avak chose a less elegant chair in the corner.

"We need to inform the police, too," Zoe said. Leaving out the Hemingways' names, she gave Cassatt an edited version of what had transpired: a husband's request, a sick friend's rush to the Gare de Lyon, the search along the train platform for a bottle of water, the loss of the valise, the pages burning in the woodsman's shack, and the questioning look on the dead girl's face.

A formidable woman, Cassatt didn't flinch. "I'm aware of the building you speak of, but it's not actually on my property. I was under the impression it's been abandoned for years."

Zoe shook her head. "One of the porters at the Gare de Lyon told me a man named Vassily Popov and his daughter, Sophia, were staying there."

"Without my knowledge, or I would have done something to help those poor souls. What a miserable existence they must have led during this harsh winter!" She stopped for a moment, as if trying to envision the scene, then added, "Life is cruel."

With that, she ordered the housekeeper to contact the authorities.

Zoe glanced over at Avak, who was looking increasingly

nervous. She gave him a soothing thumbs-up, because like most émigrés, he dreaded being questioned by government officials.

"Your friend's manuscripts, were they an important work?" Cassatt inquired, turning back to Zoe.

Careful to leave out her own opinion of Ernest's scribblings, Zoe responded, "To my friend's husband, they were everything."

"But not to you?"

Zoe shrugged. "You know what they say about beauty being in the eye of the beholder."

Cassatt smiled. "Indeed, I do. It means you believe the pages were rubbish and yet..." Here she motioned to Zoe's burned hands. "Yet you did that to yourself to rescue them."

The light chatter of the next few minutes helped keep Zoe's mind off her pain. As Avak sat silently in the corner, she and Cassatt spoke of the recent death of Degas and the failing health of Monet. At one point, Zoe thought she saw a tear in the old woman's eye, but then, perhaps to chase away her sorrow at these losses, Cassatt embarked upon a scowling discourse against the Cubist movement reigned over by a "deranged" Picasso. Zoe held the opposite opinion, but she wasn't about to contradict the great Cassatt, who'd painted masterpieces while Zoe was still in rompers.

Entertained thus, the time passed quickly. While they waited for the police, Cassatt had her cook, Avak's sister-in-law, serve a light lunch of cold chicken, cheese, and pickles, washed down with a lovely Pouilly-Fumé. Zoe's blistered hands, although sore, performed satisfactorily.

Hunger abated, they chatted on. Cassatt turned out to be surprisingly well-informed on local police matters, explaining why it might take a while for a detective to arrive.

The Great War had gutted the local gendarmeries, she said, and fully a third of the country's young policemen had been felled by German guns. The same death rate held sway for police officers in other departments, such as the Garde Mobile, the security force under the control of the Ministry of the Interior. Out of necessity, policing was now more loosely structured, with one department borrowing from another as the need arrived. An elderly gendarme had been dispatched from the nearby gendarmerie at Fresneaux, but more than an hour passed while they waited for a detective to make his way from Paris. God only knew which department he'd turn out to be with, Cassatt grumbled. Or how competent he'd be.

The doctor arrived first. He treated Zoe's burns with a soothing salve and wrapped her hands in bandages. She could still move her fingers, but painting would prove difficult for a while. After giving Zoe instructions to keep her hands clean, the doctor departed.

They could still hear his car motoring away when another car arrived. Its driver turned out to be from the Sûreté.

Detective Inspector Henri Challiot looked like he'd stepped from the pages of a French fashion magazine. In his early thirties, he stood well over six feet tall and wore an impeccably tailored camel-hair coat over a serge suit that probably cost as much as some of the motor cars in Paris. A cashmere scarf the same color as his blue eyes hung loosely around his neck, creating a handsome contrast against his dark hair. He smelled like a perfume factory.

Zoe hated him on sight.

The detective treated Cassatt with the respect due a legend. Not so, Zoe. Upon looking her up and down as if she were a horse up for sale, his eyes finally stopped at her built-up left shoe. He frowned, then looked away. Lame horse. Nothing for him here. But upon learning that she, not Mary Cassatt, found the dead couple, he turned his attention back to his reject.

"Who are you, Madame, and what were you doing hanging about in the woods?"

She squared her shoulders. "My name is Zoe Barlow. And I wasn't 'hanging about.' I was looking for something."

"'Something' being what, exactly?"

"A valise."

She'd been standing while the introductions were being carried out, so to give herself a moment to calm down, she moved away from him and regained her seat on the Regency sofa. *Deep breaths, Zoe. Deep breaths.*

"What kind of valise?"

"A stolen one."

The Inspector raised his eyebrows. "How do you know the valise was stolen?"

"Because the owner said it was." There was no need to bring Hadley's name into this.

"Really? And who is this mysterious 'owner'? Your house-keeper? Your lover?" Here, a quick glance at Avak.

Zoe gaped. From the look on Cassatt's face, the legend hadn't much liked Challiot's rude question, either.

Not getting an answer, Challiot tried again. "This valise you were searching for, was it of good quality?"

The truth was, Zoe didn't know, and now her hands hurt too much to worry about whether the valise was calfskin, tapestry, or mere canvas. Gritting her teeth, she said, "Inspector, are all these questions necessary? Shouldn't you be doing something about those poor people in the shack? They're dead, for God's sake! A man and a young woman hardly more than a girl, yet here you are, going on and on about a missing piece of luggage. Don't you care?"

The detective gave her a look devoid of any emotion. "During the War, I had to send my men to their deaths at Verdun, so if there is one thing that tragic time has taught me, it's that the dead are very good at waiting."

Having learned that more than a hundred and sixty thousand French soldiers had died at Verdun, Zoe could say nothing to that without appearing heartless.

The inspector nodded, satisfied at her discomfiture. "Since you seem unwilling to answer my last question, let me try a new one. Did you find anything at all of interest in the woodsman's cottage?"

Calmer now, Zoe described the rescue of several scorched pages and explained why they were so important to her friend. In her haste, she let Hadley's name slip. Oh, well. Hadley would forgive her. Whether Ernest would or not, who cared?

"That, Madame Barlow, is a highly unlikely story," he said, when she finished.

"I don't care whether you believe it or not; it's the truth."

Challiot darted a glance at Avak, who quickly nodded agreement. "True, that is!"

Ignoring this, Challiot said to Zoe, "You expect me to believe you traveled from Paris in December merely to search for some failed storyteller's manuscripts? You and that man over there?" He ended the question with a leer that made plain what he thought.

Oh, the filthy-minded bastard!

Furious, Zoe stood up. Summoning what was left of her dignity, she snapped, "It's *Mademoiselle* Barlow. And for your further information, Monsieur Avak is my driver, not my lover."

A gasp from the prim housekeeper and a disapproving frown from Cassatt. Too late, Zoe reminded herself she'd better control her mouth before she wound up in a scandal that eclipsed the one she'd left behind in Alabama. Waving her bandaged hands at the inspector, she said, "Pardon my poor manners. The pain has made me...made me..."

"Careless," he supplied blandly. "So. You say the papers that brought about this visit to the wilds of Mesnil-Théribus were not important, yet you traveled fifty miles with your driver-not-your-lover, only to wind up in a woodsman's shack with a dead man and woman you claim not to know."

"That's a pretty fancy rewording of what I said, but it's accurate enough. By the way, their names were Vassily and Sophia Popov, not 'dead man and woman.' Show them some respect."

A grunt. "Madame—or rather *Mademoiselle*—are you aware there is blood on your sleeve?"

At this, Avak finally spoke up. "Mademoiselle Barlow kneel to help woman, but death there already. There is no wrong in her."

Challiot narrowed those dangerous blue eyes at him. "You're Armenian, are you not?"

Avak lifted his chin. "Full name Avak Grigoryan. Maths teacher, once was. Live Paris since 1916, escape from Turkish massacre of my people at Erzincan. You wish see my papers?"

"I vouch for Monsieur Avak," Zoe said. "He's a good man who does great service for the people of Paris by ferrying them around at an honest price."

Challiot leveled his eyes at her again. "And who will vouch for you, Mademoiselle Barlow? I understand you are a stranger to Madame Cassatt, although she has heard *of* you."

It took Zoe a moment to recover from this verbal slap, but before she could deliver a comeback, Cassatt came to her rescue.

"Mademoiselle Barlow travels in the highest of circles, Inspector, and I am certain her friends will vouch for her. Besides being a good friend of Count Sergei Ivanovic Aronoffsky—who I'd like to remind you was a confident of the Russian royal family— she is also acquainted with Marquis Antoine Phillippe Fortier, the eleventh Marquis de Guise. And she is close friends with Béatrice Camondo, the famous equestrienne."

Despite the fraught situation, Zoe almost smirked.

Challiot wasn't impressed by the aristocrats—after their Revolution, few Frenchmen were—but he did blink at the mention of the Camondos.

"Yes, Inspector," Zoe said, trying not to sound smug. "Camondo."

Béatrice Camondo—whom Zoe frequently accompanied on

the riding trails of the Bois de Boulogne—was the daughter of one of Paris's most powerful banking families. Fabulously wealthy, the Camondos were also known for their generosity. They'd given many of their paintings to the city's museums and established more than a few parks, perhaps even a park in which Challiot's own children played. If he had children. Zoe snuck a look at his ring finger. Nothing there, not that a wedding ring meant anything these days.

Recovering from his brief moment of respect, he said, "Then you are to be congratulated on your choice of powerful friends. Let me see your papers, anyway."

More accustomed to demagoguery than Zoe, Avak already had his *papiers d'identité* out, whereas Zoe had to scramble with bandaged hands through her purse for hers. After finding them, she shoved them at the Inspector.

Was it her imagination or did she see a hint of a smile? "Madame is most kind."

"*Mademoiselle!*"

Yes, definitely a smile. He was enjoying this, the cad.

The detective studied her papers perhaps too long, then returned them, tsk-tsking. "Such trouble to go to for a valise that is not even yours. And now I must ask your driver-not-your-lover to escort me to this famous shack. We will take my car."

Avak readily complied, but as he escorted the inspector through the door, he threw Zoe an anguished look.

· · · ◇ · · ·

How long does it take a cop to examine the scene of a double murder? Somewhat short of forever, it turned out. Cassatt once again proved herself a gracious hostess by filling the interminable wait by resuming their conversation where it had left off. Zoe, no longer feeling the need to defend herself, relaxed again on the comfortable Regency sofa.

"Are the Dadaists still hanging plumbing on the walls and calling it Art?" Cassatt asked her.

"Unfortunately, yes."

"Barbarians," Cassatt huffed.

"They claim Beauty can be found in everyday objects."

"Then why bother learning how to paint at all?" Another huff.

Sighing, Zoe said, "That question has been asked, and no one appears to have an answer."

The afternoon sun had shifted enough that its golden rays colored the room with warmth. The buttery glow helped calm Zoe's nerves, and although the questioning expression on Sophia's dead face was never far from her mind, she was able to converse sensibly with Cassatt until Avak and Inspector Challiot returned. Avak looked shaken; the inspector didn't.

"Now I need to view the cause of your long drive from Paris, Mademoiselle Barlow," Challiot said. "Where are those manuscript pages you profess to have rescued from the flames?"

This was exactly what Zoe had been worrying about—finding Hemingway's lost work only to lose it again.

Avak, not as concerned about the fate of the manuscript, said, "I fetch from my car."

"I will accompany you, Monsieur."

"No need be..."

"What part of '*I will accompany you*' do you not understand?" Challiot snapped.

Defeated, Avak left the room, closely trailed by the inspector.

"Not a charming man," Cassatt said. "But handsome."

"If you care for that sort of thing," Zoe grumped.

Cassatt laughed.

Within minutes, the two were back, Avak carrying the blanket-wrapped pages, Challiot brushing ashes from his hands, which were as beautifully cared for as his immaculate coat and suit.

"Your Mr. Popov probably stole the missing valise to sell. He was perhaps observed doing so and followed here," the inspector said to Zoe, who hadn't risen at his entrance. "Then again, the villain may be a local. The townsfolk hereabouts are needy, having lost so many of their young men during the war. But we shall see. As for your friend's writings, Mademoiselle, I took a brief look at what was left of them and have come to the conclusion that he is fortunate to be married to a woman of means. However, there can be no doubt about the true beauty surrounding us."

He approached the Cassatt painting Zoe had admired earlier, the woman bathing the child. After studying it closely, he turned and bowed reverently toward its creator. Then, as if unable to leave well enough alone, the detective said, "I find 'Ernest Hemingway' to be an unwieldy name for a writer."

This slighting of an American name further irked Zoe. "Unwieldy? Compared to whom? Pierre Choderlos de Laclos? Jules-Amédée Barbey d'Aurevilly? Guy de unpronounceable Maupassant?"

Cassatt tried hard not to snicker, but she couldn't help herself.

Challiot gave Zoe a tolerant smile. "The Mademoiselle believes me to be an old—what do they call it in America—an old *fuddy-duddy*? Yes, I have read those old masters, but I am also well-acquainted with Rimbaud, Zola, and even the earlier books of Marcel Proust, who so sadly left us recently. I plan on finishing the rest of his works as soon as they are published. But don't mistake me for a nationalist. I read the American Mark Twain and find the boy on the raft to be quite amusing. I am also inching my way through *Ulysses*; not the Greek saga, but that odd novel by the wild Irishman. It was published in France, I must point out. But as for Mr. Hemingway's scribbles..." He grimaced with distaste.

Educated as well as handsome. Forcing herself to meet those blue eyes, she asked, "May I have my friend's property back now?"

Zoe expected a refusal, but to her surprise, Challiot lifted the pages from Avak's arms, then crossed the room and deposited them gently on her lap. "A reward for Mademoiselle's gallantry."

Chapter Five

Velvet night had descended on Paris by the time the Grim Reaper deposited Zoe in front of her house. Once again, she was grateful not to live in one of Paris's big apartment buildings, where nosy neighbors might sniff at her late-night comings and goings. Not that anyone should care, for she was at least as respectable as the house's original occupant, the mistress of a wealthy *parfumier* who'd transformed a twenty-horse stable into an elegant little house with a mirrored-ceiling boudoir and all the conveniences. But then the *parfumier* up and died, leaving the mistress broke. She moved out, and Zoe moved in.

The house was set back from the street by a narrow alleyway, which saved it from the noise of the nearby Métro station and the often-strange occupants of the nearby Hôtel du Blois. The hotel was the current abode of the infamous Aleister Crowley, the deranged Englishman who proclaimed himself an intimate of Satan, and who did more drugs than was good for him. While not a religious person, Zoe took care to avoid the man's company, in case whatever madness he suffered from proved contagious.

But old religious habits die hard. On the way home from

Mesnil-Théribus, Zoe had lifted up a prayer for the departed souls of Vassily and Sophia Popov. She'd also added one for poor Hadley, leaving out Ernest. He could just lump it.

When she limped into her house—two long drives had played merry hell with her bad leg—she found Madeline already gone. Fortunately for Zoe's growling stomach, the housekeeper had left her a dinner of assorted cheeses and dried fruit, plus a baguette the size of a strong man's arm. Hungry though she was, Zoe took care to hang up her sheared beaver coat in the boudoir's wardrobe, then put Ernest's rescued papers on the top shelf while trying hard not to look at her reflection in the boudoir's mirrored ceiling. So disconcerting.

Like the rest of her art nouveau furniture, Zoe's wardrobe displayed no sweet-faced cherubs—just sleek modernity with a refreshing lack of the Victorian folderol that so marred the family home at Beech Glen. She'd enjoyed choosing the furniture, especially the ash-and-maple escritoire designed by Hector Guimard, and the curved Louis Majorelle headboard in the comfy boudoir. But she was especially proud of the carpets she'd found at a nearby street market, their patterns of bright red, green, blue, and gold keeping the sitting room's color scheme from becoming monochromatic. Other pieces of furniture, such as the dark-blue horsehair sofa and its two matching armchairs, came with the house.

The first time she'd invited Hadley over, her friend had dubbed the house Le Petit Bibelot because of its small size and preciousness, *bibelot* meaning "trinket," in French. To be sure, the place was small, but it was still large enough to host Zoe's Poker Nights and Wednesday Salons. Everything she needed in life was here on this little piece of Parisian earth: a large sitting room/dining area combination, a boudoir with a modern en suite toilette, and the wonderful glassed-in studio at the northern end of the house.

What more could a woman want?

Well, to be truthful, she would rather *not* have a mirrored ceiling in her boudoir; it always made her feel as if she were onstage. But apparently, the lovestruck *parfumier* had wanted to see and see and see...

C'est Paris, so what the hell.

$$\cdots \diamond \cdots$$

Snug and safe in Le Petit Bibelot, Zoe ate as best she could with her bandaged hands. While she sipped at a mediocre sauvignon blanc, she wondered why anyone would murder two poverty-stricken Russians who lived in the middle of nowhere. Despite what Challiot theorized, there had been nothing worth killing for in that hovel. The valise was gone, and Ernest's writings were mainly ashes.

Hadley would be distressed to learn of the manuscripts' fate, so after thinking it over, Zoe decided to give her friend the comfort of a good night's sleep before telegraphing the Swiss hotel where she and Ernest were staying. Sorrow was always easier to bear in daylight.

She worried about Avak, too. The Armenians—or at least those Armenians who'd escaped into Paris after the Ottoman Turks tried to wipe out their entire race—were often used as scapegoats. Misplaced jewelry? Blame an Armenian. Unruly child? Blame an Armenian. Two dead people in a woodsman's shack? Blame an Armenian. She foresaw a hard time coming for her taxi-driving friend, but she would do what she could. Perhaps her friends the Camondos could help. Being Jews, they knew a thing or two about race hatred.

Zoe allowed herself a moment to marvel over the chance meeting of a legend. True, Impressionism was now a lowered flag, replaced by Cubism, Expressionism, Dadaism, and the creep of Surrealism. But a legend was still a legend and not to be sniffed at, even though Zoe's own work reflected the free-thinking of the present day.

This musing about free-thinkers reminded Zoe she'd promised to meet Kiki for lunch tomorrow at La Rotonde. So she went light on the wine, stopping at a half-bottle. Considering the sauvignon blanc's mediocrity, the sacrifice was not difficult.

Now, if only her damned leg would stop hurting...

· · · ◇ · · ·

August 1908
Mercy, Alabama

For Zoe's eighth birthday party, she wore a ankle-length, pink linen dress tailored especially for her at one of Birmingham's finest apparel shops. Why, it made her look almost ten! The icing on the red velvet cake spelled out her name, and she was able to blow out all eight candles with one great whoosh. Her friends were all there: Jessica from Sunny Acres, Betty Lee from Pine Haven, Nelda Joy from Turning Gate, and at least a dozen more. Overseen by their alert parents and nanas, they stuffed themselves with cake and ice cream, played Pin the Tail on the Donkey and Merry-Go-Away. It was the best day of Zoe's life.

And almost the last one.

During the third round of Hide-and-Seek, she grew tired of being pinched by that annoying Donny Ray Kingsley—MaryJo Albertson said he had a crush on Zoe—so she slipped out to the veranda and sat on the steps. Sweet aloneness!

She happened to glance across Beech Glen's vast horse pasture to the two-hundred-year-old oak shading the far end. She'd always dreamed of someday climbing to the top, so why not now, as a present to herself? *Happy birthday to me*, she hummed, and after tucking up the long hem of her dress into its sash, she set off at a run.

It was a fine August day. Hot, no wind. The sun hung high in the sky, and the oak's leaves were lush, caressing Zoe's face as she began scaling the tree. About halfway up, she stopped to let her aching arms rest. From where she balanced herself on a stout limb, she could almost see the entirety of Beech Glen spread out around her. The big white house with six ionic columns shading the long veranda, ten outbuildings, including three barns and a tight grouping of log cabins that once made up the "servant quarters" (she'd been taught to never use that other word). Surrounding the cabins were row upon row of bright-leafed cotton plants on the verge of bursting into white. Zoe was so entranced with the view that she wanted to see more—maybe even to where Beech Glen ended and the next county began. For that, she'd have to reach the top, so she left the stout limb and started climbing again.

In her haste, she wasn't careful enough.

Three-quarters of the way up, the limb beneath Zoe broke, sending her plummeting down through the face-slapping branches, and onto the hard earth below. A sickening crack and a nauseating wave of pain announced the thirty-foot fall had done something terrible to her left leg.

Dazed, she lay on the ground trying to catch her breath.

When she could breathe again, she didn't bother to scream; she was too far away from the house to be heard. The birthday crowd was too busy with their stupid games, and the workers in the cornfield on the far end of the back forty couldn't hear her. Why, even her pony, who was grazing at the far end of the pasture a half-mile away, had paid no attention to her screech as she fell, or the big thump when she landed. He wasn't a dog and only rarely came when called.

Get up, dummy, she told herself. *You got yourself into this mess, now get yourself out.*

But when she attempted to stand, the pain almost killed her, and she could hear the scraping of bone against bone. Zoe fell again, this time with her face flat against that no-good tree limb, which came darned-near close to poking her in the eye. She found a sort of relief in muttering every dirty word she knew, but being only eight today, the list wasn't long.

Finished cursing, she raised herself onto her elbows, and began to crawl.

As her left leg bumped along behind her, it hurt so much she vomited out her birthday cake, but crawling and vomiting was better than lying under the tree waiting for the crows to peck out her eyes. She had no choice but to crawl, crawl, crawl, up the slope toward the house. Thinking about the distance upset her, so she concentrated on making her way to smaller stuff, like the patch of dandelions near a small hillock. When she reached them, she'd yell and scream until some farmworker happened by. Or when the partiers finally noticed their Birthday Girl had disappeared.

Dummies! Especially Donny Ray Kingsley who'd said he loved her.

Liar! She'd seen him kiss MaryJo! And at her own birthday party!

Puffing and cursing, at least as well as an eight-year-old could curse, she finally reached the patch of dandelions. From there, she saw a pile of horse droppings a few yards farther on and decided she could probably make it there, too.

Then she'd give up and squall like a baby.

How could she ever have thought it was a pretty day? Sweat stung her eyes, and the ground felt like a campfire someone forgot to put out. She'd probably burn to death out here, crawling along like a worm. As if that wasn't bad enough, here came the bugs. Horseflies! Mosquitoes! Nipping and sucking and being bigger jerks than even Donny Ray Kingsley. She crawled and slapped, slapped and crawled, until she finally made it to the horse droppings, where she let herself just lie there and hurt for a while. After a few minutes rest, she spotted a pinkish rock with a June bug perched on top about twenty yards away. June bugs were fun. Some summer nights she'd catch one, tie a string around its middle, and let it fly circles around her. When she got bored, she turned it loose, but half the time the dumb thing didn't know it could leave, so it kept flying in circles, dumb as Donny Ray Kingsley.

She wiped the sweat off her face and began to crawl-slap-crawl again. Her leg hurt like a—what was Daddy's favorite expression?— like a *sumbitch*! That was it, but then she realized thinking about how much her leg hurt just made it hurt worse.

Twenty yards, easy peasy. *Hello, June bug, wanna fly in circles?*

The second she made it to the June bug's rock, the stupid bug flew away, which was no big deal, because somewhere along the way a red-and-black king snake had started slithering alongside her, and she was happy to make his acquaintance. Watching pretty Snakey kept her from thinking about her leg. For a long while Snakey stayed with her, slithering around a clump of milkweed, over the hurt-hurt-hurt of sharp gravel, Zoe entertaining them both by singing snatches of the birthday song.

"Happy birthday to me, happy birthday to me..."

When you were singing, she discovered, you couldn't feel a *sumbitch* anything!

But after a while, Snakey grew bored with her and slithered off to find something more entertaining than a vomit-speckled girl. So she crawled on alone, from dandelion patch to horse droppings to June bug–topped rocks, crawled and slapped, slapped and crawled through the weeds and rocks, eventually losing both shoes, both socks, shredding her pretty pink party dress, losing everything until she became nothing more than a raw, wounded creature with no thoughts, no mind, only a thing that crept along the ground with no more self-awareness than the bugs that fed on her.

Throughout the afternoon she crawled, to one dandelion, to one rock, to one lump of dung. She crawled and crawled until her head hit something hard and she found herself staring up at the horse pasture's whitewashed oak fence, where Silas Hansen, Beech Glen's crevassed-faced overseer, looked down at her and said, "Why ya crawlin' around like that, ya dumb little shit?"

··· ◇ ···

December 1922
Paris

The next morning, Zoe's left leg ached so badly she could barely make it to Le Petit Bibelot's ceramic-tiled bathroom. When she did, she sat on the commode longer than necessary, dreading the walk back to the adjoining boudoir. A long soak in the huge tub helped—the *parfumier* who'd built the house for his mistress had insisted on the latest in modern plumbing—but her limp remained more pronounced than usual. At least the bath eased the swelling on her burned hands and fingers. Now she could slip off the amber ring her father had given her to celebrate her release from traction. She'd been nine then, fascinated by the tiny bug trapped inside the ring's dark gold jewel. Unlike Zoe, the bug hadn't escaped.

During Traction Year, as Zoe now thought of it, a visiting aunt had said something about each cloud having a silver lining, which at the time Zoe thought was the biggest lie in the history of lies. But it was during that horribly confining Traction Year, when her leg hung from weights and pullies like a smoked ham, that her mother began reading her the *Babette in Paris* series. There were twenty-five books in all, printed in both English and French, and they related the adventures of a ten-year-old French girl who lived near a big museum named the Louvre. Babette's mother, Lily, was an artist, and her father, Armand, was a policeman. Babette couldn't figure out which she wanted to be when she grew up. By the time Zoe was on her feet, albeit propped up with crutches, she was speaking French and had announced to her parents that as soon as she grew up, she was moving to Paris.

Zoe smiled at the memory. The visiting aunt had been right, but not for the reason she'd meant.

While soaking in the tub, Zoe had stopped seeing the faces of the dead man and girl in Mesnil-Théribus, but the minute she climbed out and wrapped herself in a silk kimono, their faces returned. Vassily, his mouth agape. Sophia, asking some unanswerable question.

As Zoe had learned to do long ago, she forced herself to think about pretty things, such as the golden light streaming in through the boudoir's small window. This worked for a while, but soon she was wondering what sort of wordage she needed to use in the telegram she'd send Hadley.

BURNED UP—STOP
DESTROYED—STOP
ALL SHIT ANYWAY—STOP

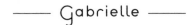

Gabrielle

February 1922
Paris

I came back to myself today.

The way the sun threw shadows to the west of my bedroom proves it to be morning, but other than that, I do not know the day or the month. Autumn? Winter? The tip of my ear—the one he liked to lick—is cold and the air feels dry.

"*Pauvre petite*," a woman says. She stands outside of my sight line, and for some reason, I cannot turn to face her. Was I a poor little thing now? *Pauvre petite*, like they say to babies, the old, the sick, the dying?

I try to open my mouth to say, *No, you are wrong, I am I, and I am in here listening to you speak of me as if I am a mere thing, not the I who I am and always will be.*

But my mouth remains closed.

I try to lift my hand to flag the woman's attention, to beg her to speak to me as one woman to another, but my hand disobeys me, too. *Be still*, it insists.

How long have I been like this?

Zoe

December 1922
Paris

There was no merciful way to describe the manuscripts' fate in a telegram, so Zoe decided to hobble over to the Café du Dôme, where a small bribe would gain her access to the office telephone. Then she'd walk down the boulevard to La Rotonde, where she had a standing Sunday breakfast date with Kiki. The model's love life, or lack thereof, was always good for a laugh.

After a liberal dusting of scented powder, Zoe applied her makeup—Precious Pearl for her face, Sensuous Scarlet for her lips—and slithered into a dove-colored dress brightened by lavish trimmings of red chenille. To match the chenille, she chose her most comfortable pair of red shoes, the built-up heel on the left cunningly constructed to be nearly invisible. Then she shrugged into a three-quarter-length coat of tan beaverette and topped off her ensemble with a red cloche. Redheads weren't supposed to wear red, but pooh to that!

Her hands, though...

Well, there was little she could do other than to rebandage them and hope for the best. Fortunately, one of the gentlemen—probably the count—who'd attended Zoe's Poker Friday had forgotten a pair of driving gloves, and although their yellow-ocher color clashed terribly with her ensemble, *c'est la vie*.

Fashionably fortified against the cold, she left the house.

Before she made it to the corner, Zoe found herself chased down by Dax, the neighborhood message boy. He handed her a *pneumatique*, one of those notes delivered through Paris's underground system of compressed air tubes linking the post offices. The message was from Kiki.

Chère *Zoe...*

I am so very, very, very ill, probably dying! Must have eaten bad mussels at Café de la Lilas last night so forgive me, chérie, *but I must remain in bed today and well into the evening. I will never eat again—too dangerous! In the event I am still alive tomorrow, let us meet at La Rotonde.*

Your dying friend, KIKI

The *pneumatique* made Zoe smile. While she believed the model was spending the day in bed, she doubted her friend's supine position had anything to do with misbehaving shellfish.

"Has Mademoiselle forgotten poor little Dax?" piped a tiny voice.

"Never," Zoe assured the message boy, pulling several francs from her purse. "And here is something extra. Return to

Mademoiselle Kiki's and tell her Zoe demands she have fun and expects a full accounting on Monday. If she does not answer your knock, slip the note under the door."

As soon as her bandaged hands had clumsily scribbled out acceptance of their delayed plans, the urchin snatched the note and the accompanying francs, then set off at a run toward Kiki's flat.

Most of Zoe's friends didn't crawl out of bed until noon, but other Parisians were not as fortunate. As she made her way down Boulevard du Montparnasse to the Dôme, she passed young postcard sellers hurrying toward lucrative corners, black-clad shopkeepers sweeping away the night's accumulated debris, and horse-drawn carts laden with offal. Set against these homely scenes was the delicious scent of baking baguettes and croissants from the boulangeries. She ignored the sharp stench of the *pissoirs;* after four years in *La Cité,* she was used to them.

Besides, walking loosened up her wonky leg.

The crowd was still thin when Zoe arrived at the Dôme, so she was able to find a table inside near one of the heaters. Dreading the telephone call to Hadley, she dawdled over her coffee while leafing through the pages of *Le Temps* someone left on a chair. Not her favorite reading material, since the newspaper was known for being serious to the point of boredom, but every now and then, Zoe found it beneficial to catch up with what was going on in the world, not just who was painting what in the ateliers of Montparnasse.

As she turned the pages—not easy with gloved hands—she learned that the Irish were killing each other in Dublin, and the Fascists were making asses of themselves in Rome. Meanwhile, back in the States, a group of women had organized the Molly Pitcher Club to promote the repeal of Prohibition. *Good luck to them,* she thought. Outlawing booze had been ridiculous in the first place, and from what Zoe had seen prior to her exile from Beech Glen, Prohibition only made Americans drink more.

She was about to start reading an editorial summing up President Harding's nasty Teapot Dome mess when she spotted her friend Jewel Johnson hurrying down the sidewalk toward Rue Vavin. The dancer dazzled in a deep sienna coat that almost matched her gorgeous skin. Tossing *Le Temps* aside, Zoe ran to the door, flung it open, and called, "Hey, Jewel! Join me for breakfast!" Seeing the fraught expression on Jewel's face, she added, "What's wrong?"

"*You*, that's what's wrong!" Jewel lamented, stopping short. "I was headed to your place as soon as I heard you'd witnessed a murder, and that you were almost murdered yourself, and your beautiful hands..." Her voice wavered as she stared down at Zoe's ugly ochre gloves.

"Shut the damn door!" someone called. "You're letting in the cold!"

Jewel, hearing this, hustled inside and gave Zoe a trembling hug as soon as the door closed behind her.

Zoe knew better than to ask her friend how she'd found out about the murders. News traveled quickly in Paris, but it wasn't always accurate. "I didn't witness the murder, Jewel," she said, leading Jewel to her table. "And as for my hands, it's just a blister or two, nothing serious."

"Pinky swear?"

"Pinky swear." To illustrate, Zoe hooked a gloved finger around Jewel's and gave a little tug. It hurt, but she wasn't about to let her friend know. Jewel tended to worry too much about her as it was.

Soon, the two were sipping coffee and nibbling fresh croissants while Zoe separated fact from gossip. It took a while, but the tension on Jewel's beautiful face began to lessen.

"Then no one tried to kill you?"

"By the time Avak and I got there, whoever shot them was long gone." Which wasn't exactly true, since the Russians' bodies were still warm on her arrival.

"Everyone's saying the dead woman was Anastasia."

"Then everyone's wrong."

The official story was that Grand Duchess Anastasia Nikolaevna Romanov had been executed with the rest of her royal family when the Bolsheviks took over Russia, but few people believed it. For the past few years, Anastasia had been seen playing backgammon in Monte Carlo, tossing rubles into a fountain in Rome, and—according to a letter from Zoe's sister, Leeanne—buying horse fodder in Mercy, Alabama.

And now in Mesnil-Théribus. Chopping wood, perhaps?

"It's simply not true," Zoe reiterated.

Jewel had been a great believer in Anastasia's escape, so some of the concern left her face. "But my concierge and the proprietor of the boulangerie next to my flat said..."

"Believe me, no grand duchess would be staying in that shack. If Anastasia's still alive, she'll be holed up in a château more along the lines of Mary Cassatt's spread. Or Sergei's apartment."

"But..."

"Just because we want something to be true doesn't mean it is, Jewel."

The dancer was silent for a moment, then said, "Yes, Zoe. I know."

At this, they both fell silent, each remembering their own wounds—and there were many—but this was Paris, where you weren't allowed to be gloomy. So Jewel lightened the mood by teasing Zoe about her gray chemise. "The bold Zoe Barlow, wearing gray!"

"What, you can't see the red trim?" Zoe teased back. "This dress fairly *screams* chic."

Jewel chuckled. "Well, you would know, wouldn't you?"

For a plantation-raised girl who'd once thought Birmingham was the Big Time, getting used to Paris hadn't been easy. Fortunately, the first day of her arrival she'd met Jewel, and within weeks, Jewel had invited her to parties attended by both the high and the low, from aristocrats to taxi drivers, to sculptors and back-alley sots. She'd also steered Zoe to the painting school of Académie Julian and told her about a precious little house in Montparnasse that had just gone up for sale.

Zoe's clothes, though...

Only time, and the studious perusal of French fashion magazines, had fixed that.

"Anastasia or not, I hope she died quickly," Jewel said, jarring Zoe back to the present.

Zoe was about to reassure her when she heard their names being called from the front of the café. She looked up to see the painter Romaine Brooks walking toward their table with writer Djuna Barnes. Djuna had a newspaper tucked under her arm. Since publishing her word-portrait of James Joyce this past March, she had become one of the most sought-after lesbians in Paris, not that this made Romaine's light shine any less brightly.

"My goodness," Romaine said, as the two took the remaining seats. "What a surprise to see you two night owls up so early."

Romain and Djuna had always been wellsprings of Paris's best gossip, and Zoe decided this was her chance to squelch the rumor about the dead woman in Mesnil-Théribus being Anastasia Romanov. But before embarking on that chore, she explained she was up at such an early hour because she had to place an international phone call.

Djuna raised her handsome eyebrows. "An international telephone call? *Ooh, la la!* You must be involved in some serious business, eh? Such as finding the Hemingways' lost valise and the shootings in a woodsman's shack."

Zoe stared at her, appalled. "What the hell...?"

Djuna raised her copy of *Le Figaro*. Never as boring as *Le Temps*, it blared the headline in sixty-point type, MESNIL-THÉRIBUS

MASSACRE! It even displayed a sketch of the shack and the insufferable Inspector Challiot standing in front of it.

Curse that paper six ways from Sunday! It was too late to squelch anything. Well, Zoe had handled gossip before and would again, since Parisians loved nothing better than to shred an American's reputation. Not that she'd had much of a reputation to begin with, since the whispers had followed her all the way across the Atlantic.

"That rag prints nothing but lies," Zoe said, slipping off the ugly gloves in preparation for the telephone call.

Jewel gasped in horror at her bandaged hands. "You said it was only a blister or two!"

Zoe repeated her earlier lie, but no one bought it.

With a frown, Romaine said, "Go ahead, make your important telephone call, then get your pretty hind end back here and tell us everything. I especially want to hear if the rumor about one of the victims being Anastasia is true."

Giving up, Zoe headed for the café's back office, where for a few francs, one of the waiters let her use the phone. However, he stood there while she spoke with the long-distance operator, as if fearing she might smuggle out a desk or a lamp. After two failures to put the call through—snow on the telephone lines?—Zoe finally reached the hotel where Hadley and Ernest were staying. The desk clerk who took the call shouted through rising static that the Hemingways were already out enjoying the slopes. All he could do was leave a message.

"Fine," she shouted back. "Tell Mrs. Hemingway I'll send a telegram later in the day."

Relieved to have avoided a sad conversation for now, Zoe left the office. As she returned to her table, she noticed her two friends could have been models for *Le Petit Echo de la Mode*. Artist Romaine, all decked out in a bold lavender dress with a matching cloche almost covering one eye, journalist Djuna in a more subtle blue. The cloud of smoke that drifted up from the table made them look like forest nymphs emerging from a mist. As for herself, Zoe was going easy on the Gitanes.

"How did that happen, the injuries to your hands?" Jewel asked.

"I had to pull Ernest's pages from the fire," Zoe answered, waving away the cigarette smoke.

"Why bother?" Djuna asked. "You know that phony can't write worth a damn." At Jewel's frown, she added, "Well, Zoe's still alive, isn't she? Besides, I want to know if the dead girl was really Anastasia!"

Romaine added, "And if Ernest is going to leave Hadley for losing his oh-so-magnificent manuscripts."

"No to both questions," Zoe answered, dabbing her lipsticked mouth with a napkin. "The dead woman was dressed in little more than rags; obviously no grand duchess. As for Ernest, I doubt he'll leave Hadley, but knowing him, he'll probably make her pay in some unpleasant manner."

Djuna scowled. "I hear he doesn't allow her to speak to him until noon. Who does he think he is? God?"

"A not uncommon belief for a man," Zoe quipped. After getting the laugh she'd aimed for, she added, "Ernest claims Hadley's voice interferes with his work."

"The brute," Romaine muttered, her sentiment seconded by Jewel.

"Poor Hadley," the dancer said. "But about that valise. Do you think the police will ever find it?"

Zoe shook her head. "Probably not. He must have sold the thing the day he found it." He'd probably been disappointed in not finding the valise filled with gold. For some time now, she'd kept hearing rumors that gold was being smuggled out of the country via the railways. Popov had probably heard the same thing.

Outside, boulevardiers swanked past the café's windows,

showing off their winter finery, their bright colors in sharp contrast to the gray stonework of centuries-old limestone buildings. They looked carefree, but Paris had taught Zoe to never judge people by their clothes. One particular boulevardier, a young beauty with raven hair and dark eyes, appeared to have been crying. Had she lost someone in the Great War? A father? A lover? Despite her red eyes, she was smiling, though, and speaking animatedly with her male escort. *La vie*, it carries on.

Putting Ernest's failings as a husband aside, Zoe described the inadequate rescue of some manuscript pages but avoided mentioning the dead man and woman.

Djuna, ever the journalist, noticed the omission. "How dead were they? Hours? Days? Where were they shot? Torso? Head? Who do you think did it, and why?"

"Oh, hell, Djuna!" Jewel gasped, having been silent up to that moment. "If Zoe'd wanted you to know all that, she'd have told you!"

Djuna pulled a face. "Zoe can stand up for herself."

"I most certainly can," Zoe said sourly. "But Jewel's right. I gave a complete accounting to the police, and I don't really feel like going through it again. I'm not a journalist like you." She brushed a croissant crumb off a bandaged hand. "However, this much I will say. They were Russians, and not aristocrats. It's my guess they were killed by a passing tramp, someone even poorer than they."

"Few passing tramps carry pistols," Djuna said. "Too expensive."

"Maybe a Bolshevik," Romaine offered. "Those madmen are passionate about their politics, and if the murdered man and woman were Russians... Well, you know how the followers of Lenin and Trotsky carry on."

"Don't exaggerate, Romaine. Not every Russian is political," Zoe argued.

Jewel rolled her eyes. "I have yet to see one who isn't."

Her friend did have a point. Zoe had once heard Sergei himself poke fun at his ever-feuding countrymen, all of whom appeared to be intent upon assassinating each other, both on the left *and* on the right. Such a strange revolution, where the only winners were grave worms.

The events at Mesnil-Théribus thus disposed of, the rest of the conversation devoted itself to the planned Trousers March in protest of Paris's continuing law against women wearing men's pants. The idea had been proposed by Fleurette Joubert, the fierce editor of *La Voix de la Femme*, who had once been arrested for wearing them. Women wore trousers on horseback, women wore trousers on bicycles, and every now and then, a rules-flaunting woman wearing trousers would sally into Café du Dôme. They just weren't *supposed* to. The law still stood, and from time to time, a cranky gendarme would arrest a trousers-wearing woman out of sheer spite.

Zoe and Jewel had pledged their support of the Trousers March, following up their pledges by purchasing men's evening trousers. But Zoe felt torn. In those days of still-suffering war veterans, heartbroken widows, and orphaned children, a woman's right to wear trousers didn't always seem that important.

· · · ◊ · · ·

After Zoe's renewed vow of faithfulness to the Trousers March, she returned home to paint as best she could, but her housekeeper's rare lapse of judgment prevented it. In Zoe's absence, Madeline had allowed Inspector Henri Challiot access to Zoe's studio, and there the bully stood, arms crossed, staring at her work. Madeline had even served him tea!

Ignoring Zoe's scowl, Madeline handed her employer a cup with her artificial hand, which seemed to be working fine today. No squeak, although Zoe would have preferred the distraction.

Challiot gestured toward one of Zoe's paintings. "I like that one. The other I do not like at all."

"Everyone's a critic," Zoe muttered.

A Gallic shrug. "My wife used to paint."

Used to. "She gave it up?"

"You could say that."

"What did she paint?"

"Flowers and such."

How like Challiot to want information but give little of his own. Zoe had learned to beware of those kinds of men, especially when they spoke of their wives.

"You do not paint flowers," he said, rather stating the obvious.

"I find human beings more interesting. Flowers never hide, they are what they are, but human beings are secretive." And she should know.

He pointed to another unfinished oil. "Why does this man have three eyes? Is he a demon?"

"A third eye can mean anything you want it to. Even insight."

He snorted. "Blacks and greens are seldom the colors of insight. In my experience, they're the colors of envy. That particular green, it is called 'Paris green,' is it not? I hear the color is poisonous because it's made with arsenic."

"I wouldn't know, since I seldom dine on oil paint." But his comment had startled her, because the painting's title was *Envy*. Perceptive of him. Then again, he was a detective, wasn't he?

"Back to my original question," Challiot said. "Is that a man or a fox? Maybe two foxes, because I see three eyes, two noses, and rather peculiar hair, which more resembles an animal's pelt, not a human's. When I look at your work, Mademoiselle Barlow, I see the evils of human nature, what the priests might call "the Seven Deadly Sins." He waved his arm around at the studio, where the finished paintings dried as they leaned against the walls. "They're all here. Envy, gluttony, greed, sloth, wrath, and pride. But not lust."

"*Lust* is up next on my calendar." Then, realizing he might misinterpret her statement, Zoe added, "Um, my *painting* calendar."

A slight smile. "Understood. But aren't you interested in the virtues? Man isn't only evil, you know. Some of us still possess virtue."

Zoe countered his smile with a frown. "I've already painted the virtues, and a dull lot they were." She motioned to the dried canvases. "I might give them another go later."

Still, she felt discomfited. When non-artists looked at her work, they inevitably asked why her apples didn't look like apples or why her people looked like circus freaks. Her invariable response was that since cameras were now commonplace and excellent at capturing a thing's exterior, why should painters continue down the same crowded path? These days, painters thought it wiser to reveal the interior of an object, not its façade. For some reason, Challiot seemed to understand.

"You don't think much of humanity, do you?" he observed.

"Do you, a police inspector, think more highly of the species?"

He awarded her a small bow. "Touché, Mademoiselle. To that effect, I have some information I would like to share with you. First, your driver. That Armenian."

"That Armenian's name is Avak Grigoryan," Zoe snapped.

"Touché again. It appears he truly was in his car when the Popovs met their ends."

"I told you so at the time."

"No good police inspector believes a witness's statement unless it is seconded by at least two other disinterested parties. Monsieur Grigoryan is fortunate in the fact that a farmer and his son happened to see him drive by at the exact moment they heard gunshots in the distance. They put the shooting down to hunters. Alas, they were wrong. Furthermore, in my search of Avak's vehicle—which, as I have learned, is amusingly referred to as the Grim Reaper—I found no armaments of any kind, nor the scent of any recently discharged pistol." Here he tapped his nose. "I am known for my keen sense of smell."

Somehow, Zoe managed to keep from laughing at this proclamation.

Challiot noticed her struggle. "Oh, I do not exaggerate, Mademoiselle. For instance, you are partial to Madame Chanel's new fragrance, the Number Five, am I correct? It is too bad the subtle scent of roses is buried beneath the less subtle scents of turpentine and linseed oil. And, of course, medicinal salves. How are your hands today? Not too painful, I hope."

"My hands are fine," she responded, allowing frost into her voice. This man noticed too damned much for her liking. Male beauty was all well and good, but add intelligence to the mix and you had a man capable of breaking hearts. "You haven't said why you're here, but now that you have two witnesses who saw Avak and me at the exact time of the murders, I assume we're finished, correct?"

"Ah, but you have misunderstood me, Mademoiselle. The farmer and his son did not see *you*. They only saw someone bundled in furs, sitting in the back of Monsieur Grigoryan's loud motorcar."

Zoe opened her mouth, but nothing came out.

The satisfaction on his face further infuriated her, so she turned and left him in the studio with only *Envy* for company.

As Zoe stalked into the kitchen, Madeline handed her another cup of tea. "Chamomile," she said. "It has a calming effect."

"A better calming effect would have been for you not to allow that man into this house."

"One does not say no to the police, Mademoiselle."

"Oh, for heaven's sake, haven't I told you a thousand times to call me Zoe?"

"Only nine hundred and ninety-nine times. Still one to go, at which point I may begin to consider it."

Besides losing her arm while nursing at the Battle of the Somme, Madeline had also lost her husband and a brother to the Great War. Given this history, there was little Zoe could say to scare her, so she just "hmphed" and made her way to the leather-and-chrome chaise in the sitting room where she could at least enjoy her tea in comfort.

Unfortunately, as soon as Zoe had settled herself, Inspector Challiot exited the studio and stood in front of her, pen and notebook in his hand. "About your presence at the murder scene, Mademoiselle..."

Chapter Six

Zoe's night was restless, with frequent appearances by Vassily and Sophia Popov. Now that she was awake, they still hung on. Vassily had been an unattractive brute with a low brow and a nose that appeared to have been repeatedly broken, but even as a corpse, Sophia looked angelic. Her golden-brown hair brushed lightly over an oval face graced with sculptor-perfect features, and her gray-blue eyes hadn't yet filmed over in death.

Commanding herself not to think about them anymore, she painted for a while. A little before noon, she took off her grimy smock, slipped into better clothes, and headed for the Café de la Rotonde.

Despite Kiki's despairing *pneumatique*, Zoe's friend obviously did not die from misbehaving shellfish, because she was sitting at an indoor table when Zoe arrived.

"Why the solemn face, Zoe?" Kiki asked, after the two greeted each other with double-cheek kisses. The model was dressed in a ragtag layering of a floral knit chemise, a red-and-white-striped vest, and despite the cold, an open woolen coat in an odd off-puce color. On anyone else, such a getup would be laughable, but on Kiki it was magnificent.

Kiki's discordant beauty helped Zoe push away the memory of the slain Russians. "You caught me remembering something I'd rather not," she said, "so let's not talk about that. Are you hungry?"

"So hungry I could eat one of your American buffalos!"

The day was another chilly one, so they made their way inside and took a table near a heating pot, only to discover they had placed themselves between two disparate groups of Russians. On their left were Mensheviks; to their right, Bolsheviks. Both sides attempted to ignore the other, but every now and then, a snide remark drifted over to the other table and faces became strained. What their particular disagreements were with one another was beyond Zoe's understanding. From the snippets of conversation she could understand—which, admittedly, wasn't much—both sides hated the White Russians, followers of the assassinated Tsar Nicholas. Now that the tsar was dead, the groups' differences appeared to be *how much* they hated aristocratic Whites like Count Sergei Aronoffsky. The Mensheviks seemed more live-and-let-live than the Bolsheviks. Or was it the other way around?

Sitting on the opposite side of the room was the young couple Zoe thought of as The Lovers. They talked only to one another, as if the rest of the world didn't exist. They always sat at the same corner table, their chairs pulled close to one another to expedite their constant cuddling. The girl looked more like an elf than any human Zoe had ever seen, with her pert, turned-up nose and ears that were slightly pointed at the top. Well, at least the one ear Zoe could see, because the girl's right ear was always covered by a red beret.

Her lover was as handsome as she was beautiful. Sleek, dark-blond hair and perfectly groomed goatee, his hands were constantly touching her, as if to remind himself that she was a corporeal being, not some playful hallucination sent by a mischievous god.

Entranced by The Lovers, Zoe proceeded to shed her ugly

yellow gloves. This elicited a shriek from Kiki. "Your hands! What happened to them?"

For a moment Zoe was surprised Kiki hadn't already heard about the events in Mesnil-Théribus. Then she remembered Kiki's new beau, and where the model was concerned, the quickest way to get to know someone was in bed. Kiki also wasn't prone to reading newspapers, so once again Zoe found herself describing what she'd discovered in the woodsman's shack. She glossed over the condition of the bodies but described the décor of Mary Cassatt's château in detail. Kiki cared about such things.

Curiosity sated, Kiki glanced around the warm café. Spotting a man at the rear of the café, she leaned over and whispered, "Isn't that Proust? I heard he was sick."

"Was. He died last month. The guy you're looking at is Blaise Cendrars. He's a poet."

Kiki heaved a sigh. "I don't trust poets. Or photographers. All they do is make promises they don't keep. The man with him, the one who isn't so attractive, he's not a poet, is he?"

"That's Antoine Bourdelle. He sculpts. You left a party with him once."

Kiki wasn't to be blamed for not recognizing either man, since the nippy wind outside had driven in a larger stewpot than usual of painters, sculptors, and poets. Such a gathering was standard for La Rotonde. In fact, its lively environment was one of the main reasons Zoe preferred it to the more refined Le Dôme. The whole free-thinking world seemed to pass through La Rotonde's doors, including political cranks of every stripe. To Zoe, her beloved café attained the pinnacle of notoriety when Ernest—in a dispatch to the Canadian newspaper he worked for—compared La Rotonde to the bottom of a bird cage. He wrote that not only had the scum of New York's Greenwich Village been dumped into the cafe, but that the aforementioned scum was "the oldest scum, the thickest scum, the scummiest scum."

So how could Zoe resist? Since as a child she'd been curious about Greenwich Village but, of course, had never made it there— few plantation-raised girls had—La Rotonde served as a substitute. Life was meant to be lived, not merely endured, and La Rotonde's "scummiest scum" added spice to the journey.

Kiki, having recovered from the ugly sight of Zoe's bandaged hands, was now working her way through a bottle of Chateau Mouton Rothschild when one of the Russians unfortunately mentioned Trotsky. In response, a Bolshevik threw a glass of white wine at the Mensheviks. The glass's path took it over Zoe's head, where it rained down its contents, so that by the time the glass reached the intended target, it was empty. At least it was a cheap white, not a port, Zoe thought. Port stained.

Not wishing to serve as the fire wall between the arguing Russians, Zoe and Kiki snatched up their own half-empty wine bottle, crawled under the table, and awaited rescue. Several Russian curses and broken glasses later, the barman and three of the larger waiters managed to throw both groups of brawlers into the street, where they continued their name-calling but spared the rest of La Rotonde's glassware.

The waiters were helping the wet pair of women out from under the table when a familiar voice rang out, "Well, if it isn't Zoe Barlow! And Kiki du Montparnasse! Could an afternoon at La Rotonde be any more perfect?"

Its owner was Bobby Crites, an artist from New Orleans, who Kiki had once posed for during the days when he was painting saleable work. Alas, somewhere along the line, he had discovered the nihilistic joys of Dadaism. Since then, he hadn't produced anything saleable. Because of this, he was no longer able to afford the rent in his old rathole of a studio and had begun sharing space in Louise Packard's studio on Rue Delambre. He often slept there, too, since with Louise's arthritis, she could no longer paint well into the night. Although Zoe found Bobby's Dadaist "installations" ridiculous, he was such a sweet little guy—freckles on a snub nose, hair so white he could have been eighty instead of twenty-five—she welcomed his company.

Bobby had missed the dustup between the Mensheviks and Bolsheviks, so his threadbare gray suit, the only one he owned, remained dry. Despite Louise's largess, he did look thin, so Zoe called to the waiter for some pot-au-feu and a baguette.

"I won at cards the other night," she explained.

"You are an angel, Zoe," he said.

"Don't thank me; thank my stepmother's monthly Stay-Away-from-Beech Glen checks." She tried to keep the bitterness out of her voice, but Kiki noticed.

"Poor Zoe," she said, patting her wealthier friend on the shoulder. "So much money, so little love. Not even from her own mother."

"*Step*mother," Zoe corrected. Gloria Monmouth Barlow had died when Zoe was ten, replaced less than a year later by the detested Annabelle Proctor-now-Barlow.

After clearing his throat, Bobby said to Kiki, "Whereas you, dear one, are beloved by the world."

Kiki pushed her lower lip out in a pout. "Not anymore. Now that Man Ray has deserted me for good, and Nick is out there partying with Nasty Nancy Cunard, I am left to suffer alone through the cold December nights."

There was a moment of silence as they envisioned poor, witless Nick Stewart, of the inbred Boston Stewarts, caught in the clutches of the infamous heiress to the Cunard Cruise Line. Nancy would use him up, then throw him away.

Breaking the silence, Bobby said, "Poor Kiki. You are always welcome to share the warmth of my corner of Louise's studio. I'm not large, so I don't take up much space."

True. Not much taller than a ten-year-old child, if Bobby hadn't decided to become an artist, he could have excelled as a jockey.

Not a fan of short men, Kiki purposely misunderstood his offer. With a laugh, she said, "Louise's garret is colder than mine. No wonder she's arthritic."

Bobby grunted an assent, then said to Zoe, "What did it look like?"

Zoe feared she knew what he meant by "it" but pretended she didn't. Maybe he'd get the hint. "I don't understand."

"The murder scene. Was it terribly bloody?"

"Have some more wine, Bobby."

He did, but his curiosity remained. "I hear they were decapitated."

"They weren't."

"But..."

Kiki mercifully recognized Zoe's distress and brought the conversation back to her favorite subject: herself. "Oh, Bobby, life is so tragic, don't you think? We artists, we feel too deeply. When Man Ray left me, I thought I would die, but look: here I am, as alive and beautiful as ever." She gestured at her famous ass and breasts. "How can he walk away from this?"

At that moment, the pot-au-feu arrived, and for the next few minutes, Bobby's conversation was punctuated by the sounds of stew being slurped. "Man will come back." *Slurp.* "He always does." *Slurp.* "He loves to photograph your beautiful behind." *Slurp.*

Kiki tilted her chin upward. "This time, he has treated me so cruelly I may decide to keep my beautiful behind to myself."

Zoe had to laugh. Man Ray and Kiki were birds of a feather, both striving to shock others, even when it rebounded into their own faces. But this was Paris, and if one didn't shock from time to time, one had failed *La Cité*. Only half-listening to Kiki prattle on, Zoe watched Bobby wolf down his pot-au-feu and wondered how long it had been since he'd last eaten. Her weekly salon, where she put out a bountiful spread for those not as fortunate as she, remained two days away. What would he do until then? Ordinarily, she and her housekeeper would shop together on the morning of the banquet, but now Zoe came up with a better idea, one that would aid her and Madeline both, as well as gaunt little Bobby.

Unlike most pieds-à-terre in the Montparnasse district, Zoe's kitchen was furnished with a modern icebox that could store generous amounts of foodstuffs, keeping them fresh for days. Bobby might have been small, but he was still stronger than the average woman, so today she would shop early, allowing him to benefit from some purposeful over-purchases.

"Bobby," she said, fluttering her mascaraed eyelashes, "you are strong, right?"

Vain as any man when asked such a question, Bobby immediately took off his coat, rolled up his right sleeve, and made a fist. A bump emerged from the area where the bicep should be. A small one, but definitely a bump.

"Excellent!" Zoe said, clapping her sore hands as softly as possible. "Now that you've finished your pot-au-feu, put your coat back on. I need someone to help carry groceries back to my house, and I was hoping..."

"Groceries? You mean food?"

"*Certainment.* I can manage one parcel, but that is all, whereas you, with your tremendous biceps, could carry two, maybe even three."

"These are things for your Wednesday Salon, right?"

"Yes. And don't worry. I expect to see you there, too. No salon is complete without you."

Bobby picked up Zoe's hand as if to kiss it, then stopped when it was halfway to his lips. "*Merde,* Zoe! What have you been doing with your hands? Welding?"

Zoe could have kicked herself for taking her gloves off earlier. "Only saving a few papers from a fire. The pain is almost gone." A bit of an overstatement there, but mostly true. The doctor's salve had eased her suffering so that now her hands bothered her little more than the enduring ache in her left leg.

Kiki, who had been listening, grumped. "Go, then, and buy your baguettes and pâtés and expensive cheeses while I sit here alone, weeping over my broken heart."

Kiki was normally a good actress, but Zoe had noticed her exchange sultry looks with a handsome young man three tables over. Unless she was wrong, he was British, and his suit probably cost as much as six months' rent in the ninth arrondissement. A young Lord-Somebody-or-Other, probably.

Paris was crawling with them.

Chapter Seven

Two hours later, a cheerful Madeline stored the makings for the Wednesday Salon, and Zoe sent a grateful Bobby away, loaded down with food that didn't need an icebox. Bread. Fruit. Tinned meat. Enough to keep him going.

The day's good deed thus accomplished, Zoe changed out of her boulevardier finery and back into her painting rags. A pair of men's trousers, purchased at an outdoor market, a huge shirt that had probably adorned some circus fat man, and a paint-spattered smock. If she worked quickly enough, she could finish *Envy* by early evening. She might even have enough time to gesso a freshly stretched canvas for *Lust*. It would be nice to add some red to her palette.

But what was that old saying? *Man plans and God laughs.*

She was in the middle of adding a curve of pure Titanium white as a glint to the *Envy* monster's third eye when she heard footsteps approaching from behind. Madeline? No, they were too self-assured for a woman. Only a man of supreme self-importance would walk like that.

"I see your hands have healed enough to paint," Inspector Challiot said behind her.

Not bothering to turn around, Zoe replied, "I would say *bonjour*, but a visit from the Sûreté is never cause for celebration. What is it now?"

"I am here to see those pages again."

"What pages?" Like her friend Kiki, Zoe could play dumb when necessary.

"Monsieur Hemingway's stories. He being a reporter and the victims Russian, my superiors believe there might be a political connection to the crime."

Zoe added a second slash of Titanium white to her canvas, then immediately wiped it away. Too much. Envy was seldom overt, being one of the subtler sins. "There was no mention of revolutions or murdered Romanovs in his pages, Inspector."

"Ah, but I would not be a good detective if I took your word on that, would I? You will either allow me to inspect them here, or I will impound them and take them away. Your choice."

Fuming, Zoe very, very slowly wiped the Titanium white off the brush, then settled it oh-so-softly-and-slowly into a linseed oil-dampened rag to keep it fresh. Only then did she turn around to face Challiot. Today his camel-hair coat was adorned with a brown-and-black plaid cashmere scarf. The only thing marring the spiffy ensemble was a pair of ugly galoshes. Since when could French policemen afford such fancy duds? Even if he enjoyed independent means like herself, Zoe disapproved. For a man to pay so much attention to his wardrobe suggested a mind focused on trivia, not depth.

But his threat to remove Ernest's papers had alarmed her, so she knuckled under. "All right. Simply in order to prevent you from becoming a thief, I will fetch them."

He spread his hands, which again were perfectly manicured. "Rest easy, Mademoiselle. Thievery is not one of the seven deadly sins."

"Really? To steal another person's property isn't proof of greed, which *is* a deadly sin? Or envy, wishing to own what someone else has?"

"Not when in pursuit of the virtue of Truth. Besides, the valise does not belong to you, and neither do those pages. I am letting you keep them here only out of courtesy."

Madeline, correctly guessing at the outcome of Zoe's set-to with Challiot, had already taken the salvaged pages out of the boudoir's wardrobe and spread them out on the long dining table. No big deal, Zoe thought. He'd discover nothing in those ninety-six pages (she'd counted) that made sense, just blood and sweat and a host of other masculine things.

For the next few minutes, Challiot studied the pages. When he finally straightened up, he looked disappointed.

"You see?" Zoe grumbled. "No dead tsars. No brooding Trotskys. Just men behaving badly."

"Mademoiselle is a harsh critic."

"Takes one to know one." After a pause, she added, "Ah, have you had any luck locating Mr. Hemingway's valise? Or the rest of his other papers? I'm certain the Hemingways would be grateful to get them back."

The detective gave Zoe an odd smile, half humor, half wince. "The Sûreté assumes the porter sold it before leaving Paris and it's now carrying around some tourist's underwear. But has it occurred to you that we are taking your friend's word that the valise and its contents were actually stolen? Madame Hemingway could have easily tossed them into a refuse container at the train station, where Mr. Popov found them."

The remark set Zoe back for a moment. "Why in the world would Hadley Hemingway make up such a story, especially one that reflects so badly on herself?"

"Many women in troubled marriages make up stories when

they are too embarrassed to tell the truth. I have been asking around, and I hear that Monsieur Hemingway frequently goes into a café, gets drunk, then for no discernible reason, suddenly attacks other men. It makes me wonder if he also attacks his wife."

Outrageous!

"Starting fights in cafés is a far cry from beating one's wife, Inspector." What irony, defending a man she didn't like.

"Possibly, but here is another theory," Challiot said, with a sly expression. "During my investigation, I learned that Monsieur Hemingway briefly returned from Switzerland to search the apartment after learning about his wife's 'loss' of the valise. Perhaps he, too, followed certain leads—just as you did, my clever mademoiselle—and tracked the thief to his home near Madame Cassatt's estate. Such a man, already known for his brutality, might find it reasonable to kill the man who fed his work to the flames."

Zoe refused to let this second outrageous accusation pass. "*I am more capable of murder than either of the Hemingways!*"

"Who would you like to kill, Mademoiselle?"

Before she could answer, *You, you Frenchified pissant!* Madeline interrupted. "May I put these pages away now, Inspector? Damaged as they are, Mademoiselle Barlow undertook great trouble to save them for her friend, and it would be sad to see them further damaged by overexposure to sunlight."

Challiot nodded. "You may return them to the darkness, Madame, and I thank you for your kind assistance." To Zoe, he said, "And I must thank Mademoiselle Barlow for bringing humor to what up until now, has been a somber day."

Then he kissed Zoe's bandaged hand.

· · · ◇ · · ·

The rest of the day was a waste. She couldn't paint, couldn't read, couldn't enjoy the music on her gramophone. She could do nothing but pace back and forth from one room to another, stewing about the inspector's gall, worrying about Hadley, wondering where the missing valise ended up. Zoe had only been able to save those ninety-something pages, but from what Hadley had told the authorities at the train station, Ernest's entire life's work was in the valise. How many more pages were still missing? A hundred? *Several* hundred?

Unable to stand it any longer, Zoe announced to Madeline she was going out for a walk along the Seine, where the booksellers' kiosks carried the current fashion magazines. Superficiality could be calming.

The day now warmer, Zoe's walk to the river was pleasant, hardly bothering her bad leg. Street singers sang of unfaithful lovers, and on the corner of St. Germaine and St. Jacques, an organ grinder played a tune while a little red-capped monkey danced. Out of pity for the poor creature, Zoe dropped a few francs into its tin cup. As she approached the river, a light snow began to fall again. It settled for a few moments onto the cobblestones, where it was quickly crushed by the wheels of green omnibuses, then trampled into a nasty muck beneath the hooves of dray horses. Fortunately, the snow shower didn't last long, and soon the sun shone down on Paris again.

The Seine glittered in the sunlight, and as Zoe crossed the Pont Neuf to the Right Bank, she looked down and saw a canal boat making its way downriver. A young man standing on its rear deck waved to her. She waved back and watched until the boat disappeared under Pont des Arts. Because the weather was relatively mild today, the booksellers were busy. After wandering alongside their kiosks, she decided to buy a few magazines to send to her recently married sister. Zoe had longed to attend Leeanne's wedding, but it had been impossible. In Mercy, Alabama, the widowed Annabelle Proctor Barlow's decrees counted as absolutes, and Zoe's brother, Brice, would have been dispatched to keep her from entering the church, so Zoe had hardened her heart and pretended not to care. She pretended so well that at times she even convinced herself.

But Paris was not Mercy, Alabama, and her stroll along the kiosks proved successful. She found a recent issue of *Le Petit Echo de la Mode* containing an article on the upcoming spring fashions. Wool was out, linen was in, the colors bolder. Zoe particularly admired the illustration of a pink silk chemise, which boasted an embroidered sash that swept diagonally down from the shoulder to tie in a bow at the hip. Racy, but still within the limits of propriety. The article also informed its readers that the dress was available at Clotilde's Boutique on Saint-Germaine-des-Prés for slightly less than two hundred francs. While the shallow side of Zoe's nature whispered, *It's perfect for Poker Night,* her less selfish side argued, *New brides can always use new clothes.*

As yet undecided, she continued her stroll along the bank of the Seine. Art students, some of them even talented, sat at their easels sketching the great Notre-Dame Cathedral, whose shadow loomed over the Île de la Cité. Zoe had done the same when studying at Académie Julian. The cathedral still exerted its pull on her, but the pull of a certain garden proved stronger, so Zoe left the kiosks behind and entered the enclave named for the legendary king, Le Vert-Galant, Henri IV. Because of him—his statue was there, mounted on a horse—the little garden never ceased to make her smile. In the late 1500s, the Protestant king took time away from his many domestic duties (two wives and fifty-six mistresses!) to encourage the addition of greenery such as this, throughout the city in order to make Paris "a wonder of this world."

The busy king had succeeded, especially here. The tiny garden may not have been as spectacular as some, but Zoe found it an island of peace among the hubbub of the city. Tall oaks stood guard over a boat-shaped lawn, which would have been emerald in a warmer season, but now lay under an inch of snow. On this white carpet, sparrows warred with wood pigeons for seeds and insects. Despite their inferior size, the sparrows usually won. Seeing the small triumph over the large heartened Zoe, so she sat on one of the benches and inhaled the frosty air. As she watched the sparrows' brave sorties, she put away the memory of the woodsman's shack and instead recalled the poet Keats's observation: "*Beauty is truth, truth beauty,—that is all ye know on earth, and all ye need to know.*"

The moment's peace didn't last. Seconds later her rebellious brain reversed course back to a Henri very different from the garden-loving king. This Henri was an overbearing, blue-eyed cop.

Disgusted with herself, she walked over to Saint-Germaine-des-Prés and bought that damned dress.

··· ◇ ···

Since Jewel never danced on Mondays, she and Zoe always used her night off to hit the jazz clubs. At ten p.m. on the dot, Count Sergei Aronoffsky's Rolls-Royce Silver Ghost pulled up in front of Le Petit Bibelot. The liveried chauffeur helped her into the back seat, where her friends awaited, bundled in furs.

First stop: Casino de Paris, to see the Jazz Kings.

The Casino had been entertaining Parisians since the eighteenth century, and given its name and triple-arched, stained-glass exterior, newcomers to Paris often thought they'd be entering a gambling establishment. But the Casino offered something even more dangerous than roulette or baccarat: a semi-naked Mistinguett, whose voice was rumored to make strong men weep. Zoe remained unimpressed by the songstress. She'd seen naked women before, so on the way over, she and Jewel had decided to head elsewhere as soon as the Jazz Kings finished their set.

"I was thinking we could try Anima," Jewel said to Sergei, who was quieter than usual.

"Mmm," he replied, staring out at the night.

"Because there we can dance!"

"Mmm."

Sergei was not noted for his chitchat, but this night Zoe's poker-playing friend seemed particularly silent. Zoe put it down to a difficult day.

In his way, the count was a good-looking man. Olive skin, deep-set eyes, black hair sprinkled with gray. His face bore the gaunt mysticism of an El Greco Christ, and he looked every bit of his forty-two years. When he gazed at Jewel, though, some of those years vanished. "If you want to dance, my darling, we will dance," he told her. "Whenever and wherever you wish."

After the count's escape from the Bolshevik's bloody revolution, he'd married the wealthy widow. When she died, he vowed never to wed again. But six months after the Great War ended, one of his Russian friends had taken him to see the new American dancer at the Moulin Rouge. She'd brought a new style of dance to Paris, the friend said, a combination of ballet and jazz.

Sergei had been swept off his feet.

Overnight, the royal Russian count became a stage-door Johnny. Every night after she danced—come rain, sleet, snow, what have you—he could be seen standing at the stage door with his roses, his El Greco face raw with longing. Jewel once confided to Zoe that she'd originally thought his behavior ridiculous, and she treated him with the amused contempt stage-door Johnnies deserved. "As if flowers could buy me!" she'd laughed. "Here in Paris, after enduring what I'd endured back home, I felt free for the first time in my life. I wasn't about to give that up."

What I'd endured back home. Jewel was from Mississippi, and

Zoe knew what Negro women endured there: the same cruelties they endured in Mercy, Alabama.

But even damaged hearts could be breached, and the count's gentle perseverance eventually won out, but only to an extent. Despite the count's pleas, Jewel refused to marry him. She enjoyed Sergei's company on her days off, but seldom her nights, when she preferred to lie alone and untouched in her own narrow bed.

"Don't you love him?" Zoe had once asked her, remembering the love of her own life, a man for whom she'd do anything. And did.

Jewel had given Zoe a pitying look. "Of course I do. But I'm not ready to give up my freedom."

··· ◇ ···

When the trio arrived at Casino de Paris, it was at first pleasant to come in from the cold. But several hundred warm bodies packed into the auditorium raised the room temperature better than a dozen coal stoves, so they couldn't divest themselves of their furs quickly enough. Sergei, as befitting his station, was dressed conservatively in white tie and tails, but Jewel astonished in a dress seemingly composed of nothing but rhinestones and feathers. Compared to her, Zoe's dark-blue chemise and silver headband looked tame.

Parched from their ride across the city, Sergei procured glasses of absinthe from the bar while they waited for the show to begin. Zoe would have been happier with a merlot, but as the saying went, never look a gift drink in the mouth. Although Sergei remained unusually quiet, Jewel's gay chatter made up for it. Louis Mitchell, the drummer and band leader of the Jazz Kings, was Jewell's cousin, and she'd been looking forward to seeing him perform again.

Like Jewel, the Jazz Kings were at the forefront of American Negro entertainers who'd discovered Paris didn't care what color you were as long as you were talented. But Mitchell, whom Zoe had met at the birthday party the count threw for Jewel, confided to Zoe that he'd been astonished at his band's instant popularity. "Back in the States I wasn't allowed to drink at most of the water fountains," he'd said to her, "but here in Paris, I can drink anything I want, anywhere, at any time, while White men can't get a drink in the States! Not legally, anyway."

Zoe had appreciated his jab at America's Prohibition Law, which had been enacted by hypocritical, hard-drinking politicians solely in order to pacify their Calvinist wives. Here in Paris, as well as in the rest of civilized Europe, the alcohol flowed, especially at the Casino. They were well into their second absinthe when they heard the Jazz Kings being announced, so they bolted back what little remained of the yellow-green concoction and made their way to their seats.

For the next hour, the band played hits like "Ain't We Got Fun" and "Oh Gee! Oh Gosh!" while Zoe's feet tapped along. Like Jewel, she was desperate to dance. When the Jazz Kings eventually turned the stage over to Mistinguett—who was wearing next to nothing again—they made a quick exit. It was only midnight, and there was fun to be had elsewhere.

Only a few minutes after leaving the Casino, they were back in Montparnasse, at Anima. Unlike the grand Casino, the jazz club was a mere a hole in the wall, but the music, performed by yet another American jazz band, was excellent. During the weekends, these musicians played separately at various clubs throughout the city, but on Mondays they reformed themselves as the Black Crows and made Anima the hot spot for Parisian jazz lovers.

"What's wrong with Sergei?" Zoe asked Jewel, as they headed off to the dance floor for a foxtrot to "Toot, Toot, Tootsie."

"He won't tell me," Jewel answered. "He has his moods."

Well, didn't they all? But tonight's music was grand, and Zoe soon forgot about the moody count and lost herself in dance as the band turned "Tootsie" into a long medley that included "Wang Wang Blues" and "Sheik of Araby." Her movements weren't as fluid as Jewel's, but they were every bit as energetic.

Dripping with sweat, the two made it back to the table after the medley ended, only to find they'd been joined by another couple— Louise Packard and little Bobby Crites. Louise's son had died at Verdun and, shortly thereafter, the Spanish flu came calling for her only grandchild. How the woman managed to carry on was a mystery to Zoe, but Louise just kept painting away her sorrows on huge Cubist portraits.

And drinking.

"You two enjoyin' yourselves?" Louise asked, her voice slurred. Her face looked more haggard than usual, making the fifty-something woman look more like sixty.

Zoe reminded herself to cut way down on the booze, but not tonight. Why rush?

Jewel stretched her arm across the table and gently squeezed Louise's hand. "Now that you two are here, we'll enjoy it even more."

"Amen to that," Zoe said. "And we'd better see you two on that dance floor!"

"Yes, there must be dance," Sergei agreed, sounding oddly morose. After ordering another round of drinks for everyone, he fell silent again.

Zoe paid little attention to him for the rest of the night, something she would come to regret.

Chapter Eight

Zoe awoke with a hangover and swore she'd never drink again. Hurting all over, she hobbled into the bathroom. A hot bath with the Dior salts worked miracles, and by the time she climbed out, she'd reversed her vow. She just wouldn't drink quite as much.

No point in overdoing things, even temperance.

Painting on *Envy* didn't go well. Zoe worked furiously for a short while, but then discovered that her hand refused to paint the shapes her brain ordered up. Some of the trouble had to do with the broken blisters marching from her fingers to her wrists, but the noise in her head bothered her even more. It just kept yammering and yammering about that damned valise. What had Vassily Popov done with the thing? Did it still contain the rest of Ernest's stories?

Zoe also couldn't help revisiting that long, cold drive to Mesnil-Théribus. Fifty miles! How had Vassily Popov endured that daily trip to the train station? After all, he was no spring chicken. True, as a porter he would have been able to hitch a free ride on whatever train stopped in the environs, but then he'd have a walk of several miles, much of that in the dark, sometimes through snowdrifts.

It made no sense.

Frustrated, Zoe threw down her brushes and paced the studio, making several circuits around the easel before deciding another trip to the Gare de Lyon was in order. She needed another talk with Gaston—the thieving porter's supervisor—but she couldn't get to it today. There was already enough on her plate.

Her mind made up, she gave her poor brushes the gentle cleaning they deserved.

··· ◊ ···

Early afternoon found Zoe at the Studio for Portrait Masks, working on a face mask she'd been painting for one of *Les Mutilés*, the Mutilated Ones, as they were called. These veterans from the Great War had endured such devastating facial injuries, that after the surgeons had done everything they could, most of them walled themselves off from the world. Reynard Dibasse, the man she was helping today, had never returned home, fearing his mother would mistake him for a monster and be felled by a heart attack. He was not over-imagining. The poor man had lost an eye, his nose, and part of his lower jaw. Like others of his ilk, he'd arrived at the studio wearing a large-brimmed hat, his wounds covered by a linen facial curtain with a hole cut out for his remaining eye.

The studio had been founded in 1917 by Anna Coleman Ladd, a sculptor from Philadelphia best known for her decorative sculptures of water fountains—nymphs, fauns, and the like. During the war, Anna's husband served with the Red Cross, so she put away her tools and joined him. Upon visiting the hospitals and seeing the horrors inflicted on human faces by shrapnel and mortar shells, she went to work. By the time she returned to America with her husband, she'd created lifelike masks to cover a hundred and eighty-five brave men's faces, leaving behind other artists to carry on her work.

For four years, Zoe had been one of them.

Reynard was a former farmworker from St. Lo, a small village in Normandy. Given the serious wound to his jaw, he spoke with a pronounced slur. Embarrassed by the sounds he made, he'd at first been loath to speak to her, but when she told Reynard he merely sounded like a man who'd just returned from a too-happy night at the cafés, he found humor in that and became downright chatty.

"I get handsome now?" he asked, his one eye twinkling. It was gray, flecked with yellow.

"Handsome enough to drink at the cafés again, so cut the gab and hold still."

Karen Wegner, a better sculptor than she was a poker player, had completed the base of Reynard's mask after making a plaster cast of his entire face. She'd used the mold to create a face-shaped sheet of galvanized copper attached to eyeglass-type stems on each side. It had been Zoe's job to make the mask appear lifelike by covering it with a liberal application of flesh tones. In Reynard's case, this called for a mixture of Titanium white, yellow ochre, umber, and a touch of vermilion perfectly blended to match the skin on the man's neck. He was a redhead, so after quizzing him, she'd added a few freckles across the mask's nose and cheeks.

That was two weeks ago. He hadn't seen his mask yet and was now back for the final fitting.

Zoe had painted the visible sides of the mask's "eyeglass" stems the same skin tone as the face, and the curved pieces behind his ears the same color as his red hair so that the stems would appear less obvious. As Reynard sat unmoving, she slipped the mask on him, hooking it behind ears miraculously untouched by German shrapnel. Satisfied with the fit, she gently tapped the mask around the top and sides to settle it onto what remained of his face.

"Does that feel comfortable?" she asked.

"Yes."

"Close your eye."

Always obedient, as he'd been while enduring the carnage at the Marne, he shut his remaining eye.

Then Zoe reached down to her worktable and picked up the mirror she'd placed there earlier. Held the mirror in front of him.

"Now look, Reynard."

He did.

Saw his beautiful new face in the mirror.

Gasped.

Then began to weep.

The happiness of others is contagious. After Reynard had recovered himself, Avak and Zoe drove him through the gathering twilight to the Gare Saint-Lazare and the train to Normandy, so that he could at last reunite with his mother. She would not mistake him for a monster now.

Cheered at having done a good deed, Zoe returned home to paint another sin.

As she entered the cobbled walkway that hid her little house from the lamplit street, she realized something. For all Ernest's bits of writing—at least the few sentences Zoe was able to save— there'd been few mentions of sex. Considering he was a young and energetic man, she found that odd. Had Hadley kept him so satisfied he no longer entertained fantasies? Impossible. What healthy young man did not fantasize about carnal love, especially when surrounded by the fleshpots of Paris, where homosexuality was open and prostitution was legal? Why, *La Cité* itself was a sexual stimulant! When not actually with a man, Zoe often dreamed about being with one, feeling strong arms around her, her tongue seeking his...

"You are looking lovely this evening, Mademoiselle Barlow."

"*Shit!*" she yelped as Inspector Challiot emerged from the shadows.

"Such a crass remark from such a delicate lady."

"I'll 'delicate' *you*, you horse's ass! What the hell are you doing lurking around my house like this? If you weren't already a cop, I'd call one."

A smile. Lord, but he was good-looking!

"There were roses in your cheeks when you walked up the pathway, roses not even the dim lamplight could hide. Were you, perhaps, thinking of me?"

"Don't be ridiculous."

"And yet, as I have moved closer, you have not moved away."

Zoe's brain ordered her to step back, but her feet wouldn't oblige, not even when Challiot came close enough for her to smell him. Tobacco and cognac. And something else. Limes? Impossible. It was December. Then she remembered she was in Paris, where even men took pains to smell sweet.

She sniffed. Loudly. "Real men don't wear cologne."

Still smiling, he stepped closer. "You are incorrect, Mademoiselle. In Paris, discriminating men wear Fougère Royale by Houbigant. It whispers of citrus, lavender, and Moroccan spices. Whereas you, Mademoiselle, smell much the same as before. Linseed oil. Turpentine. And *woman*."

"Stay away from me." Why did she say this in a whisper?

"Ask me again and I will."

But she could only stand there staring at his eyes, their vivid blue...

Zoe took a deep breath, prepared to repeat her words more forcefully, but found herself saying, "Perhaps you'd better come in."

Chapter Nine

Zoe awoke with someone's arms around her, her bed smelling of limes, Moroccan spices, and sex.

"*Ma chérie*," someone whispered, nuzzling her ear.

"Who the hell...?"

"You have forgotten me already?"

She'd gone to bed with a cop! "Listen, there's been a mistake..."

"Did I tell you last night how much I love your mirrored ceiling?" He looked up and waved at himself.

"No, this is all wrong, you should go..."

"Shhh." A warm hand briefly covered her mouth, then transferred itself to her left breast.

Startled, Zoe draped her arm over the right breast so he couldn't get at that one, too. This man had to get the hell out of her bed before Madeline arrived, or what was left of her reputation would be destroyed. "No, really, a big mistake. You need to go..."

His hand moved south. Way south. So did his mouth. She suddenly remembered he'd done the same thing last night and she'd lost her mind.

But now she had it back. "You shouldn't do *that,*" she gasped. "It's illegal."

"We are not in Alabama, Zoe."

He started doing *that* again.

"*Dear God!*"

He lifted his head for a moment. "Do you always pray in bed, *chérie?*" Then he returned to what he'd been doing.

"*Oh, Jesus!!!*"

··· ◇ ···

Henri made it out the door only minutes before Madeline arrived, but Zoe could tell by her smirk the housekeeper somehow knew she hadn't spent the night alone. Ah, well, gay Paree, and all that jazz.

Later, as she was splashing around in her big tub, Madeline opened the door a crack and announced, "Telegram, Mademoiselle. Would you like me to read it to you so you can prolong your bath?"

"Never mind. It's time for me to get out of here, anyway. The water's cooling."

As soon as Madeline closed the door, Zoe made good her word. Limbs loose—no aches this morning!—she crawled out of the tub and toweled off. After wrapping herself in the red-and-black silk kimono she'd bought at Clotilde's Boutique, she made her way into the kitchen. Madeline had already started chopping vegetables for the Wednesday Salon pâtés. There would be at least two dozen, enough so her less-fortunate friends would have one small pâté each to take home at the end of the evening, along with the "left-over" cheese, fruit, and bread.

Catching sight of Zoe's flushed face, Madeline smirked again. "Ooh, la! You must have used the new bath salts of Madame Dior. You smell lovely and look so very relaxed." Gesturing with her metal arm, the housekeeper added, "I put the telegram on the blond table near the settee."

"Did you tip Dax well?"

"Of course, with those francs you keep in the jar. He is such a dear little thing."

Like many of Paris's children, Dax was also a half-starved little thing. So many children lost parents during the war and the Spanish flu epidemic that the oldest of them had been left to fend for themselves. Even before the war, the orphanages had already been full to bursting, so there was a limit to their help, and now hundreds of orphans roamed the streets of Paris. The lucky ones like Dax were given meals and a cot in the shelter Jewel had set up—and which Zoe helped fund—but what would become of the others was anyone's guess.

Sighing, Zoe opened the telegram to find it was from Hadley in answer to the one Zoe had sent upon finding part of Ernest's manuscripts.

WILL CALL DOME 10 AM WEDNESDAY—STOP
–WANT HEAR WHAT SAVED—STOP
HADLEY

Zoe was on her second cup of coffee at the Dôme when she heard the café's telephone ring. One of the bribed waiters waved her into the office.

"So not everything was burned," Hadley said, once Zoe had described the remnants of Ernest's scribblings.

"Some were only slightly scorched, but many looked like notes or experiments, nothing that could be strung together to form anything approaching coherence." Zoe didn't comment on the poor quality of the writing. She also didn't mention she would continue to look for the valise. No point giving her friend false hope.

"Well, it's all a shame, isn't it?" Despite her words, Hadley sounded almost chipper. Or maybe the telephone line wasn't as clear today as Zoe originally thought, and a playful hiss of static lightened her friend's voice.

"Some of the fragments were attempts at word repeats," Zoe continued, "the kind Gertrude Stein has been playing with, but hers seem more...well...polished." As much as Zoe hated to compliment Stein, given their unpleasant history, truth was truth. Stein's word repeats, seeming babble at first, always made emotional sense in the end. The woman knew what she was doing, whereas Ernest...

Talk about a rube!

"You're sure none of the Nick Adams stories are there?" Still sounding chipper, and no, it wasn't static. What was going on in Switzerland that Zoe didn't know about?

"I couldn't tell. There are a couple of consecutive pages here and there, but it's hard to make out where they belonged, in a short story or in a novel. But that name didn't appear on anything I found."

The ensuing long pause made Zoe nervous. Was Hadley suffering from delayed shock, or had they been disconnected?

When Hadley finally spoke again, it sounded like she'd made up her mind to accept the worst. "Well, you did your best, Zoe, and I greatly appreciate it. Now let me figure out how best to tell Hem, and when. Let things settle a bit. You know him, no matter what's going on, whatever kind of sickness he seems to have, he recovers quickly. That's beginning to happen now. In fact, he's been so loving lately I'm wondering if the loss of his manuscripts wasn't for the best. You know, good fortune disguised as bad."

"I don't understand." How could a man losing his entire life's work, bad though it was, *ever* be considered good fortune?

"It's simple," Hadley continued. "Maybe now he'll give up this whole foolish fiction business and stop going to that stupid office of his and start letting me talk before noon. That's been hard, Zoe."

"I'm sure it has, but don't you think..."

Hadley talked over Zoe's words. "And I may have some really good news soon. When I left for Lausanne, I was so ill with the flu I forgot my 'cap,' too. You know, that little diaphragm thing the doctor gave me to keep from getting pregnant? Now, as amorous as Hem's being, there is every chance I might catch!"

Zoe frowned, remembering Ernest once stating he wanted to become more established as a writer before becoming a father. He'd been quite insistent about it. "Have you told him about this?"

"Don't be such a worrywart, Zoe. Hem will make a wonderful father, just you wait and see. He'll be so busy playing with the baby—and I just know it'll be a boy!—that he'll forget all about becoming a great writer!"

"Answer my question. Does Ernest know you forgot your cap?"

A pause, then, "He's had so much to worry about lately I decided not to tell him. Why cause the poor man even more distress?"

Knowing from her own experience how painful it was to have one's dreams dismissed as mere foolery, Hadley's attitude toward her husband's dreams chilled Zoe. Still, from Hadley's point of view, Zoe could see why she preferred him to be a husband, not a writer. That awful apartment of theirs... She hoped her friend wasn't committing another blunder. "Look, I can take those pages over to your flat so they'll be waiting when you two return. The concierge knows me now and will let me in."

"Let me think on that for a while. No use rushing into anything, is there?"

"I guess not." Zoe decided it was time to tell Hadley about the other events in Mesnil-Théribus. "Ah, there's something else. There's been a tragedy."

"One larger than the loss of Hem's scribblings?"

"Considerably larger."

To Hadley's credit, she was weeping over the fate of the two Russians when the call ended.

··· ◇ ···

As Zoe left the Dôme, she passed the count, who was just being seated with Jewel. Sergei appeared more animated than he had at the jazz club, perhaps because the morning's papers had been abuzz about Jewel's spectacular performance last night at the Moulin Rouge. He had always been proud of his lover's talent.

His dour face lightened when he saw her. "Zoe!" he called. "I just sent you a *pneumatique*! Upon reflection, I..."

He was cut off midsentence by an elderly woman in a tattered dress, who upon spotting him, sat down unasked at his table. Ignoring Jewel, she began babbling in Russian, forestalling any explanation Sergei had been about to give Zoe. Judging from the names Zoe recognized—Nicholas, Alexandra, Anastasia—the old woman was bewailing the slaughter of the Russian royal family. Zoe agreed the royal family's deaths were a tragedy, but it was over and done with, and all the wailing in the world wouldn't bring them back.

To avoid getting caught up in a conversation Zoe couldn't even follow, she waved and kept on walking. Jewel blew her a goodbye kiss; she was used to her and Sergei's time being interrupted by morose Russians. Whatever he wanted to discuss was probably in the *pneumatique* he'd sent, and it would be waiting for her when she arrived home.

Farther along Boulevard du Montparnasse, Zoe ran into Kiki, who was headed toward La Rotonde. The makeup on the model's face looked like it had been there all night, and her usually glossy black bob was dull and mussed. Her puce-colored coat was torn at the sleeve. Seeing Zoe, she blinked several times. "Oh. Zoe. I was just trying to remember what we did last night."

We? Kiki appeared to be suffering from a monster hangover and maybe something else. "We weren't together last night," Zoe answered. "The last time I saw you was when we were at La Rotonde and you were flirting with some British guy."

Kiki's smeared but still-beautiful face folded into a frown. "Gregory somebody? Is that who you're talking about?"

"I never knew his name. Just saw him. Around twenty-five. Blond. Hazel eyes. Saville Row suit."

"Oh. That sounds like Alan. We went to a party. Can't remember much after that."

Concerned for her friend, Zoe steered Kiki into a small café dark enough to hide her dishabille. "I'm going to buy you coffee and something to eat to help you straighten up. You don't want our usual crowd seeing you like this."

"You're an angel, Zoe."

"Yeah, but I think my wings are molting."

Three cups of coffee and a big bowl of onion soup later, Kiki had recovered from the worst of her hangover, and a portion of her memory had returned. "After the party grew dull, Alan wanted to go over to a place where they give you opium and a soft pillow to dream on, so I said why not, and off we went. I had some beautiful dreams about forests and water nymphs, and then some dreams not so beautiful about wolves tearing at me. I couldn't tell what was a dream and what was real. Have you ever experienced that, Zoe?"

"I can't remember," Zoe joked. This wasn't the truth. A plantation-bred girl was reared to be alert to Nature's dangers so she wouldn't get bitten by a snake or gored by a bull. Therefore, Zoe had never allowed herself to get so out of control that she couldn't remember a night's festivities. But the joke made Kiki laugh, which had been Zoe's intention.

"Paris is wonderful, is it not?" Kiki sighed. "All the fun we girls enjoy?"

Normally Zoe would have agreed, but Kiki's messed-up face and torn coat were evidence that the price paid for Parisian fun tended to be steeper for women than it was for men.

Chapter Ten

Although Zoe's poorer friends would have been happy with day-old crusts, the excellent Madeline had prepared a king's feast for the Wednesday Salon. Three large quiches, a couple dozen small pâtés, chunks of cheeses chosen for their easy portability, a small mountain of baguettes, several roast hens stuffed with croutons and spices, trays of macarons and petits fours, and enough fruit to help everyone survive until next Wednesday. To wash it all down, bottles and bottles of wine, both red and white, although not enough for her guests to take with them. The silly sots—herself included—drank too much as it was.

Zoe was so busy helping Madeline that every now and then she was able to put aside her worry over the Count's *pneumatique* and its reference to the dead girl in Mesnil-Théribus. It had read:

Dearest Zoe: It is of the utmost importance that you send me a detailed description of the young woman you found murdered near Madame Cassatt's château. While I understand the young woman's name is said to be "Sophia," and that she is supposedly the daughter of the man she

*was staying with, I have reason to doubt that. I need to
know her approximate age, the color of her eyes and hair,
and anything else which might lead to her true identity.
Perhaps a drawing from memory by your gifted hands?
In light of our long friendship, I beseech you not to tell
anyone of this communication.*

Yours in hope,
Your friend, Sergei

Long friendship? Well, in these émigré days, Zoe guessed
four years wasn't too much of an overstatement. And although
Sergei had block-printed the message instead of using script, he'd
stamped the *pneumatique* with his signet ring as if it held great
historical significance.

Sensitive to the count's desperation, she'd sent an answering
pneumatique, but had yet to hear back. Tomorrow, after the mess
from her Wednesday Salon was cleared away, she would make the
sketch and deliver it personally. As for now, her guests had begun
to arrive, each carrying an empty string bag which would be filled
to bursting when they left. Artists were never ashamed of their
poverty; they flaunted it, seeing their dire straits as proof of their
talent. These days many of them even sniffed at Picasso, who they
declared was living like a bourgeoisie with his ballet-dancer wife
and his spoiled, fat baby. Sour grapes, of course, but sour grapes
were edible.

To Zoe's delight, sculptor Karen Wegner arrived hand in hand
with Reynard Dibasse, back in Paris after reuniting with his mother.
He wore his new portrait mask, and instead of being horrified at
what lay underneath, the artists flocked around him, praising the
mask's realism. At first shy after years of self-imposed seclusion,
Reynard blossomed under this new admiration and soon felt comfortable enough to proclaim his own creativity, secret until now. After

downing a couple glasses of wine, he recited his latest poem—an ode praising Karen's strong arms and Zoe's blistered hands.

Little Bobby Crites turned up, too, and Zoe spotted him wolfing down pâté. For a moment it reminded her of the only time Hadley and Ernest had attended her Wednesday Salon together. She'd been warned about her friend's husband's behavior, but...

··· ◇ ···

March 1922
Paris

That first evening with Ernest and Hadley had started off well enough. The good-looking couple was reputedly as poor as the proverbial church mice and, like everyone else, needed a respite from dreary poverty. Ernest was nice enough when sober, and Zoe believed at the time that if she could just keep him from overindulging, everything would work out.

It didn't.

Hadley was her usual charming self. When urged, she sat down at the piano bench and began playing a series of blistering jazz rags that sent several couples fox-trotting across the floor. An admiring crowd had gathered around the piano when a tipsy Ernest broke through the throng and insisted on showing her how to play. To Zoe's irritation, Hadley obediently surrendered the bench. Although not quite tone deaf, Ernest's amateurish banging away at "Chopsticks" broke up the crowd around the piano, and the fox-trotters stopped dancing.

With an abashed grin, Ernest quit playing and stood up. "Sorry. Guess piano-playing's harder than it looks. Time to let the little woman take over again!"

The entire room sighed with relief, but all the joy had vanished from Hadley's playing, and she stopped halfway through "Toot, Toot, Tootsie." Smiling up at her husband, she said, "I guess I'm a little off tonight, Tattie."

"Everyone's allowed to get an 'off,' sweet Wicky," he said, patting her head like she was a golden retriever. "Let's get ourselves another drink. It'll fix us both up."

Zoe was dismayed to see Hadley blame herself for Ernest's party-pooping behavior, but she'd noticed his air of peacockery before. If the man wasn't the centerpiece of every evening, he would always do something to remedy the situation. The gossips blamed his strange childhood. Apparently, his mother had dressed him in girls' clothes—ruffle dresses, bonnets, and lacy underpants. *Ick!* Was that why he was a bully now, albeit a subtle one when it came to his wife?

And a not-so-subtle bully when it came to others?

But Ernest was Hadley's problem, not Zoe's, so as long as the fool didn't play any of his two-fisted café tricks, she'd put up with him. And, after all, the room was filled with artists, musicians, and poets, and although some of the people present could have used new shoes, the talent arrayed in Le Petit Bibelot was considerable. As far as Zoe was concerned, they were all stars.

Except for Ernest.

Upon seeing he was having a conversation with little Bobby Crites, his six-foot frame looming over the five-foot-three painter, Zoe relaxed. Turning her back on the buffet table, she spotted Dominique Garron, the famous war artist, telling a small group about the day a German shot her eye out. Zoe edged closer to hear the tale once more. She always enjoyed the part where Dominique shot back.

"I hadn't meant to drive so close," Dominique was saying. "When the German..."

Before she could get to the good part, Zoe heard a bang, a

scream, the sound of breaking dishes, then a thump. When she turned around, she saw Bobby Crites lying on the floor amidst a slurry of pâté and olives. He was bleeding profusely from his nose, while Ernest cock-a-doodle-doed around him.

"You see?!" Ernest yelled, flourishing his big fists, one of them bloody. "You see?! That's what happens when a man isn't prepared. A real man is always prepared!"

The smile on his face would have been more appropriate if he'd knocked out Jack Dempsey in the first round, whereas he'd only sucker punched a mere waif who hadn't seen it coming. He didn't seem to understand that.

"See?! See?! A real man keeps his guard up!" he kept yelling.

As the others stared in shock, Louise Packard fell on her knees beside Bobby and began washing the blood away with the glass of Chablis she was holding. Good enough, but as a woman who'd been bred to deal with out-of-control animals of various species, Zoe hurried over to the ruined buffet table and grabbed Ernest by the arm before he hit anyone else.

He stopped strutting. "Zoe. Wha...?"

"You're drunk, and you need to leave." Turning to poor Hadley, she said, "I'm sorry, you know how much I love you both, but this is just too much."

Below them, Bobby began to moan. "He's coming around," Louise said. "He's all right!"

"Of course the little pip-squeak's all right," Ernest growled in annoyance. "I just taught him a lesson. A real man..."

Zoe let go of Ernest's arm and drew back her hand, preparing to slap him silly, but the moment passed when Hadley released a sharp yelp. Zoe looked over and saw her friend doubled over, clutching at her stomach.

"Oh, Tattie," Hadley cried, to her husband, "I'm feeling sick!"

Ernest cut his cock-a-doodle-do-ing short. Stepping over his small victim, he hurried to Hadley's side and put a tender arm around her. "Wicki Poo! What's wrong?"

"My stomach. I... I think I need to go home." Whimpering, Hadley leaned her head against Ernest's broad chest, but not before throwing a duplicitous look at Zoe.

Hadley's act worked. The bully in Ernest vanished, leaving in its place a protective husband.

Taking her cue, Zoe called out, "Anyone have a car? Hadley is unwell and needs to get home."

Dominique spoke up. "I drove over in my Ravel."

Zoe sighed with relief. Although very much female, Dominique was almost as big and burly as Ernest, and if he attempted to create a problem on the way back to Rue du Cardinal Lemoine, she would have no trouble dealing with it. After all, Dominique had two German kills to her credit.

After they'd left, with Ernest cooing sweet nothings to his "ailing" wife, Bobby picked himself up off the floor, and the party continued as if nothing had happened.

But that was the last time Ernest had been invited to Le Petit Bibelot.

··· ◇ ···

December 1922
Paris

How quickly the year had flown! Tonight, safely *sans* Ernest, the mood remained peaceful, and little Bobby Crites had long since recovered from Ernest's sucker punch. Bobby had arrived with his motherly benefactor, Louise Packard, who immediately wanted to know what Zoe had been doing in Mesnil-Théribus.

"That nasty little paper *Le Figaro* printed a story that an 'artist'—which everyone in Paris is saying was *you*—discovered a couple of corpses there. But Mesnil-Théribus? Why? Good Lord, Zoe, there's nothing there but chickens and goats!"

"And Mary Cassatt," Zoe reminded Louise. "As to what I was doing in Mesnil-Théribus, I was chasing down a rumor that Hemingway's manuscripts somehow made their way there. You've probably heard about the train incident."

"Who hasn't?" Louise lit another Gitane, but her arthritis was acting up so much she could hardly keep the match steady. "I've always believed Hadley is jealous of her husband's work," she said, exhaling a thread of smoke. "Perhaps this was one of those purposeful kinds of 'forgetting' weak women are prey to."

"I doubt that," Zoe lied.

Louise's mention of the murder investigation elicited more questions from the others. "What was it like walking into a woodsman's cabin and finding dead people?" asked Tripp Eiger, a poet from Pittsburgh who cranked out nonsensical blank verse about machines and offal.

"Awful," Zoe answered, wishing everyone would just shut up about it. She'd been trying to forget the dreadful scene, yet here they were, dragging her back.

"Do you think the two were spies, either for the White Russians or the Bolsheviks?" This from the politically astute Karen Wegner.

"No idea. But bear in mind, I have friends on both sides, so..."

Fortunately, Tripp's next question turned the conversation away from murder. "How is the sainted Cassatt, and is she still painting?" he asked. Somehow, he'd managed to procure a pack of Camels, and the others were shamelessly bumming them.

"Cassatt is healthy, but I don't know if she still paints," Zoe lied again, knowing Cassatt wouldn't want the truth bandied about. If such an affliction as old age ever visited itself upon Zoe, she'd want her friends to keep quiet about it, too.

Kiki had to hear more about the murders, though, and asked if there was a chance Mary Cassatt had killed the Russians. "Americans can be nasty," she said, indelicately.

"I doubt Cassatt even owns a gun," Zoe bit back. But as she thought more about it, she wondered if the question might not be so foolish after all. Cassatt was American, and Zoe knew how much her fellow Americans treasured their firearms. Why, even she...

"We're running low on Chablis, Zoe," Karen grumped, breaking Zoe's train of thought. "That Burgundy is turning my teeth maroon, and Reynard doesn't like women with maroon teeth."

"More Chablis coming right up," Zoe said, heading to the kitchen.

For the rest of the evening, they ate, drank, and gossiped. It was Paris, and all manner of new things were happening, although the constant snows caused more than a few grumbles. Louise was thinking about spending the rest of the winter in the Côte d'Azur, where the weather would be kinder to her arthritis than chilly Paris. She was going on and on about the lovely hotel where she'd once stayed, when Tripp sniped, "And how do you afford such luxury? By selling your ass instead of your paintings?"

Louise took his crude joke as a compliment. Flashing yellow teeth at him—she'd drunk most of the Chablis herself—she laughed, "You're just jealous, Tripp. I was with Raymond Ashe, as you well know. You've always lusted for him yourself, you bad boy."

Tripp pretended horror. "Not true! I wouldn't sleep with him if he was the last man in Paris!"

"Oh, yes, you would!" cried little Bobby. "I hear he's almost as wonderful as his bank account."

Soon, the teasing turned to Zoe, where she learned her own recent indiscretion was no secret. "So how is the handsome inspector?" Louise asked her.

"His health is fine," Zoe said, lighting a Gauloise, which immediately elicited a coughing fit. She reminded herself to cut back to one cigarette per week, and one bottle of wine per day; moderation in all things. "Henri is quite robust."

"I'm not asking about his health, you sly fox. How is he in bed?"

Since there was no way to avoid sexual teasing in Paris, it was best to make light of it. Pretending mirth, Zoe answered, "If I told the truth, you'd demand I share him."

Karen, who'd always found this sort of banter boring, said to Bobby, "Speaking of people fleeing the Paris weather, don't you sometimes visit your relatives in the now-infamous Mesnil-Théribus?"

Bobby made a dismissive wave. Despite his minuscule stature, his hands were normal-sized. "Very distant cousins. Provincials, you know, with provincial attitudes. And since Mesnil-Théribus is north of Paris, what would be the point of visiting them in winter? In summer, perhaps, when the apartments here could roast chickens without an oven."

Karen shook her finger at him. She was one of those people whose appearance belied her personality. Plain-featured with pale, lank hair, she at first looked like one of those poor wallflowers at debutante balls praying to high heaven that someone, *anyone*, would ask her to dance. A closer look at her arms and shoulders revealed a woman who could chisel away a block of marble until it gave up its soul.

"Don't you lie to me, Bobby!" she mock-growled. "A friend of mine from there—René Thibault, he was in Paris a couple of weeks ago attending the DiChirico exhibition—and he said he saw you drinking in the Mesnil-Théribus café Saturday with your cousin what's-his-name. Abelard, isn't it?"

"Impossible," Bobby replied. "I never left Paris. And, for your information, Abelard is more like a third cousin, several times removed. Hardly a relative at all."

"Really? Then you have a twin brother in Mesnil-Théribus, who is also on speaking terms with Abelard. René's eyesight is very keen."

Bobby's face assumed an air of triumph. "How could this René of yours 'recognize' me, tell me that? I've never met the man."

"You met him at the Dufy exhibit we all attended last month. Anyway, René said when he spotted you at the café that he was thinking about discussing Dufy's work with you, but before he could walk over to your table, you and Abelard went all tête-à-tête, whispering and such, so he respected your privacy."

"Then came tattling to you!"

Most of the crowd was too drunk to notice Bobby's combative tone, but Karen did, and she backed off. "Oh, well, maybe René does need glasses. He *is* almost thirty."

Zoe was feeling her wine, too, or she would have questioned Bobby about the strange coincidence of an American from Louisiana visiting relatives in tiny Mesnil-Théribus on the day of a double murder.

By the time the clock struck two, everyone was quite drunk, and there was so much cigarette smoke in the air it smelled like the house was on fire. The crowd began to thin, with the poorer artists, poets, and musicians staggering away, their string bags bulging with food. Watching them leave, Zoe leaned on the doorjamb in order to remain vertical, and once again pledged her fealty to future moderation.

When the last of her guests vanished down the Rue Vavin, she closed the door against the night and tottered off to her bed, still wondering why little Bobby Crites sounded so defensive about being seen in Mesnil-Théribus.

· · · ◇ · · ·

Zoe suffered another hangover the next day and spent nearly an hour in the bathroom appreciating the mercies of modern plumbing. Her throat was raw from cigarette smoke, and her tummy... Well, the flush-toilet performed admirably.

"Poor Mademoiselle," Madeline commiserated, as her employer weaved unsteadily into the kitchen. "I've prepared a stomach-calming tea for you made of chamomile and fennel."

"Tastes like hell," Zoe grumped, taking a sip.

"Perhaps Mademoiselle should not drink so much?"

"Don't nag. How's your arm after all that cleaning?" The sitting room, dining room, and kitchen were spotless, as if the rabble of drunks had never visited. Blond and ebony wood glowed; chrome trim glimmered.

"My arm is like a good soldier, willing to perform whatever service is required."

"Without squeaking?"

"Not so far this morning." The housekeeper gave Zoe a gentle smile. "And your hands, Mademoiselle. How are they?"

Despite her hangover, Zoe had taken off the bandages that morning and even put her amber ring back on. Holding her hands up, she said, "See? Perfect."

"If you say so."

As Zoe carried her tea over to the long table, she realized that something had been nagging at her, something having nothing to do with last night's party. Someone had asked her to do something, but who and what? She sat there for a while, nibbling at a dried baguette crust slathered with salted butter. It went down well, but...

After another rushed visit to the bathroom, Zoe's memory returned.

The count had asked her to make a sketch of the dead girl she'd found in the woodsman's shack. An odd request, this desired portrait of a person he didn't know, but since Sergei was a close friend of Zoe's dearest friend, she'd do it. Feeling somewhat better, she wandered into her studio for a sketch pad and some pastel crayons. The morning sun was streaming onto her easel—no way Zoe could deal with that—so she propped the sketch pad up on a small table lurking in a less glaring corner and began to draw. The outline of Sophia's oval face came first, and, after that, the details. Her cheekbones had been high, her chin strong, and her forehead was hidden by curls. Her mouth? Rosebud.

Drawing the dead wasn't a pleasant task, but she'd done it many times before in Alabama. There'd been a small settlement of Negro people near the eastern edge of Beech Glen's vast acreage. None of them had enough money to buy a camera, let alone pay for the development of prints, so they'd never been able to share in the White custom of photographing their dead loved ones.

··· ◇ ···

June 1910
Mercy, Alabama

Zoe was ten when the first of them requested her services. The little boy—Amos was his name—looked to be around five and had no idea of the dangerous situation he was creating for everyone. He only knew his mother had died, and he'd seen this crippled White girl out in the fields drawing pictures of horses so realistic they looked like they'd shrunk and were trotting across the paper.

"Please, can you draw my mam for me so's I can always remember her?" Amos had asked, coming up to her while she was drawing the new Guernsey milk cow.

Looking at his tearstained face, she could hardly say no, so after making certain no one at Beech Glen saw her, she limped after him through the woods to a cabin little larger than the woodsman's shack she would one day enter in Mesnil-Théribus.

Inside, she could see Amos's family clustered around a home-made casket. At first, they wouldn't let her in the door—over the centuries they'd learned not to trust White people—but when Amos began to cry, begging for a picture of his mam looking alive again, they relented. One of the older women said, "My girl's name was Jenny Rose. You do her right, hear?"

Zoe looked down into the casket and saw a pretty woman who didn't look much different than her own recently deceased mother, just darker. So she bit her trembling lip and started to draw. Nine years later, Zoe was still drawing their dead—mothers, fathers, grandparents, children, babies—when the events happened that sent her packing to Paris and, ultimately, to the portrait of a dead Russian girl named Sophia.

Pete, shot dead by a German bullet.

That terrible basement.

Her newborn baby tossed away like garbage.

Oh, my Amber child, where are you?

In her studio at Le Petit Bibelot, Zoe added a few light strokes of violet to shadow Sophia's perfect nose, then gave it a creamy high-light on the tip. Almost finished, she smeared a pale rose on her cheeks, more on the lips, and streaked the hair with the warmth of the summer sun. Finished, Zoe sat back and gazed at the result.

Sophia, alive again.

Zoe sprayed the sketch with a fixative to keep it from smearing. Once that dried, she backed the flimsy pastel paper with a sheet of cardboard to make it more secure, then taped a flap of butcher's paper over the drawing for extra protection. Now for the Métro.

Jewel would most certainly be visiting the count, but *c'est la vie.* After dropping off the sketch, she'd visit the Gare de Lyon and talk to that porter, Oleg. He might know if Vassily Popov sometimes stayed overnight in Paris rather than make that long trip to Mesnil-Théribus.

Zoe hadn't yet given up hope of finding the remainder of Ernest's manuscripts.

Gabrielle

April 1922
Paris

Someone has rearranged this room.

My bed now faces the large windows to the south, out of which I can see Monsieur Eiffel's tower, and every now and then a sparrow as it flits about on its tiny business. This morning there were clouds, and I entertained myself by imagining shapes in them. A cow. A dog. An axe.

Whomever was responsible for this rearrangement has surrounded my bed with plants, some small, some large. Under other circumstances I might wonder about the wisdom of their placement—how does one make the bed, for instance?—but as I lie here unmoving, I thank God for that person.

Ma mere?

I close my eyes against the raw glare of the sky. *No, not Maman.* She died when I was twelve. But I remember her soft voice, tender caresses, and now that I think on it, the wondrous fact that she taught me the Latin names of every plant in our garden. Many of those plants are mirrored in this oddly configured room. To my left are two long window boxes filled with grasses, mainly green *Phormium tenax*, with sproutings of *miscanthus* and *stipa*. In front of them sit small tubs of tame kitchen herbs. *Ocimum basilicum,*

Thymus serphyllum, Origanum majorana. Everything green and glistening, as if they had just been rained on. To my right, pots and pots of *Aquilegia vulgaris* blooming in pink, purple, and yellow, all nestled together for warmth against the sharp-scented greenery of *Juniperus chinensis.*

How can this be?

As I lie here, a street singer many stories below is singing about her broken heart.

Is my heart broken, too?

Who am I, this woman who, like her mother, knows the Latin names of plants and the proper times for them to flower, yet cannot remember her own name?

Perhaps I am only a phantom in someone else's dream.

Chapter Eleven

—— Zoe ——

December 1922
Paris

After climbing into the daylight of the eighth arrondissement, Zoe took a few moments to admire the high-toned scenery. Within whistling distance of the Champs-Élysées, Rue de Ponthieu was a testament to the skills of Baron Georges-Eugene Haussmann. He'd been chosen by his cousin, the Emperor Napoleon III, to design a series of new boulevards that would bring more light into the city. Nowhere was Haussmann's brilliance more apparent than along this street. Elegant limestone buildings rose many stories high, topped by matching blue-gray zinc roofs. Below, fully grown trees added the voice of Nature to the mechanical noise of the boulevards. The neighborhood was so expensive that even Beech Glen's monthly remittance checks couldn't have afforded Zoe an apartment here.

Under ordinary circumstances, Sergei couldn't have afforded to live here, either, the Bolsheviks having confiscated his estates, leaving him essentially penniless except for that small bag of diamonds they knew nothing about. But after arriving in Paris, his title, good looks, and the fact that he was a widower with no children made him irresistible to certain society ladies. Within months, Sergei found himself married to a childless dowager who showed him the courtesy of dying not long after their ceremony, leaving him her opulent apartment, three servants, and enough money to keep him in caviar for the rest of his life. Not much more, though. Certainly not enough to keep furnishing Sergei's gambling habits (Zoe's coffers weren't the only ones he'd enriched). If the count didn't watch himself, his gambling habit might bust him, and he'd need to move to less expensive digs. That would be unfortunate, because Zoe would miss the building's doorman.

Pierre Lazenby threw her a big smile when she was still half a block away.

"Ah, Pierre, how goes the war?" she asked, once she reached him.

Pierre Lazenby laughed, as he always did, at this question. Another veteran of the Great War, he was famous for chasing down a German colonel, bayonetting him in the ass, then standing guard over the squalling officer until reinforcements arrived. The French were so delighted they awarded him the Croix de Guerre.

"The war goes well, Mademoiselle Barlow. Why, just yesterday, I captured two little thieves attempting to steal food out of the back bins."

"Did you punish them appropriately?"

"Most certainly. I sent them on their way with two baguettes and told them to ask politely next time."

"Good man." Zoe handed him several francs, much more than the cost of the baguettes. "Have you seen the count yet today?"

He shook his head. "Nor any of his household. I believe they have Thursdays off, for some reason. A Russian thing, maybe? Now that I think on it, I did see that beautiful dancer friend of his go upstairs a couple hours ago."

"Jewel Johnson."

"Yes. I saw her dance once at the Moulin Rouge." The doorman sighed at the memory. *"Elle était magnifique!"*

As he opened the gate to let Zoe into the central court-yard, she could see the building's famous fountain, where three marble horses reared up from a pool, water cascading from their mouths. In the center, a statue of Poseidon flourished his trident. Thanking Pierre, she crossed the courtyard, entered the building proper, then started up a belle epoch staircase that curved around a chandelier the size of a Renault. It was too fussy for Zoe's taste, but even an Expressionist like herself could appreciate the fine craftsmanship.

The count owned half of the building's second floor. His flat stood to one side of the grand staircase, the apartment on the other side owned by one of the lesser Rothschilds. Usually, Sergei's valet would already have the gilt-festooned door open for her when she arrived, his stiff smile in evidence, but today, no valet. And the door remained closed.

Since even a count can open a door, Zoe gave it a ladylike rap. No point in annoying the lesser Rothschild.

But she heard nothing. Not even the gasps of passion or the pitter-patter of aristocratic feet.

"C'est moi, Sergei!" she called, hoping the lesser Rothschild would survive her unladylike squawks. "It's Zoe! With the portrait you requested!"

Still nothing. Were Sergei and Jewel so wrapped up in each other they couldn't hear? Perhaps she should just leave the sketch with Pierre Lazenby, but after her long, dry Métro ride, the least the count could do was offer her some wine. She'd heard he'd recently bought an entire case of 1900 Chateau Latour, and her morning's effort was surely worth a glass.

Tasting the Latour already, Zoe rapped more forcefully. Even if her friends were making love, it wouldn't kill them to take a break for a few moments to accept her delivery, drink to her health, then go back to whatever form of sexual congress they were enjoying.

"C'mon, Sergei! I know you two are in there!"

Silence.

Worried now, Zoe tried the doorknob.

Unlocked.

Warily, she pushed the door open.

"Sergei? Jewel?"

She stepped cautiously into the foyer and, when no one answered, proceeded through to the lavish sitting room, where heavy red brocade and thick tapestries abounded. Something seemed off. As she stood there, calling out for Sergei, Zoe noticed a sharp odor in the air, the same odor she'd encountered only days before.

Death had visited this place.

At the end of a long hallway, the door to Sergei's boudoir stood open, a splash of red against the gilded oak. Part of Zoe wanted to run away, to cry out for help, but the other part remembered Jewel was probably in there. Whatever had happened in that bedroom, her friend might need help. Then again, the person—or persons— who had given Death its entrée could be hiding in there, too.

Friendship won over common sense. After putting the portrait of Sophia down on the marble floor, Zoe scrabbled through her handbag for her silver rat-tailed comb, the only thing approaching a weapon she had on her. Then, with the sharp end of the comb pointed outward, she tiptoed down the hall toward the boudoir.

She was too late.

Sergei, shot twice through the forehead, was already dead, and Jewel—her throat shredded by yet another bullet—was coughing as blood filled her mouth.

Hardly realizing what she was doing, Zoe climbed onto the

bed, and with her hand—the same hand Jewel had clasped so firmly the day they first met—tried to clear out the blood so her friend could breathe.

"Don't go!" she begged, as the blood kept coming. "Please don't leave me!"

But Jewel was past hearing.

Instead, her truest friend took one final gasp, then left this evil world.

Chapter Twelve

When the local gendarme arrived, he used Sergei's telephone to contact his superiors at the Sûreté. Among the numerous detectives sent out—a Russian count rated more than one—was Inspector Henri Challiot, who, because of his work in Mesnil-Théribus, was now considered an expert in all things Russian.

"I don't understand," Zoe said, her voice quavering. "Who could have done this, and why? Everyone loved Jewel! And why didn't Pierre…"

"What are you doing here?" Henri demanded. "Despite what you told the gendarme, one does not visit an aristocrat without invitation."

"One doesn't need an invitation to visit a friend!"

No longer trusting her ability to stand, Zoe sat on the hallway's marble floor outside the count's apartment, still holding her rat-tailed comb. Somehow, she'd found the strength to fetch Pierre, but this was as much as she could manage. Eyes shut, she leaned against the wall, wishing she could faint like women were always doing in the novels she sometimes read. But she remained mercilessly conscious, smelling the odor of death leaking out the open door, hearing the gruff voices of high-ranking officers as they walked across priceless carpets, remembering her friend's dying agony.

Henri loomed over her, not allowing her grief to get in the way of his questions. "Answer me, Zoe. Why are you here at the scene of yet *another* double homicide?"

Zoe looked up at him. "She's my friend, but she's not here anymore. She's with them." The faces of the other dead she'd drawn over the years flashed across Zoe's memory: Pete, Jenny Rose, Olive, Abraham, Lily...

"Again, I ask you—what were you doing here? If you don't answer my question, I swear I will handcuff you."

Realizing he wasn't going to let up, she pointed to the pastel sketch lying next to her on the marble floor. "Sergei asked me to draw that."

Challiot picked up the pastel, lifted the protective flap, and studied it. "Why, this is a perfect capture of the dead girl in Mesnil-Théribus!"

After losing her darling Jewel—and Sergei, who also mattered in this vale of tears—Zoe had little grief left for a stranger, but she felt the responsibility to accord the woman some dignity. "Her name was Sophia."

"She had no official identification on her."

A lick of anger gave Zoe strength. "Not every émigré makes it over the border with the proper papers. You know that."

"And you appear to know too much. Although it distresses me to say this, you must accompany me to the Île de la Cité and the Prefecture of Police, where my superiors can question you more closely. And, for God's sake, Zoe, give me that comb before you stab yourself in the eye."

• • • ◊ • • •

Being questioned in a room filled with high-ranking police and other governmental officials kept the day's nightmare going, but after the sun set, then rose again, Zoe finally managed to convince the assemblage of cops she hadn't killed anyone. Disappointed with her, they turned their attention to poor Pierre Lazenby. The doorman had been inexplicably absent from his post at the very moment when the killer must have entered Sergei's apartment.

Wearing only a baggy black dress someone found for her, and wrapped in a rough blanket—the police had kept her own bloodied outfit, sheared beaver coat and all—Zoe stepped into the sunlight. How was she going to get home? She had no desire to submit her blanket-wrapped self to the stares of a crowded Métro car, but she was too weak to make it on foot to Montparnasse. This early in the morning, there were few taxis on the Île de la Cité, so she just stood there numbly until a green Citroën pulled up and a familiar voice called, "Get in!"

Inspector Henri Challiot.

"Please, no more questions." She sounded like an injured animal.

"I promise, Zoe. But you cannot ask me questions, either."

Having no other choice, Zoe climbed into his car. He rested his hand on hers for a moment, then slid a copy of the morning's newspaper across the seat.

"You think I feel like reading now?" She wanted to slap him but knew she'd better not.

"We often have to do things we don't wish to do. Read." He steered the Citroën between two horse carts on the Boulevard St. Michel.

Although Zoe was not one to follow orders, this time she did. COMTE ET DANSEUSE ASSASSINÉS! the headline screamed. Four paragraphs down, Zoe stopped reading. "I don't understand. What's *Vosstanovit Rodinu?*"

"Keep reading."

The car stopped suddenly as an elderly, black-clad woman, her long skirt dragging against the cobblestones, stepped in front of them as if bent upon suicide-by-automobile. Fortunately, the Citroën had good brakes. Although untouched, the woman cursed at them in non-Parisian French—some of the more colorful phrases Zoe had never heard before—then continued on her oblivious way.

"Retired prostitute," Henri said. "From Marseilles, sounds like."

"Spend a lot of time with prostitutes, do you?" she snapped, immediately regretting it. Why add cruelty to an already too-cruel world? "Sorry."

"Apology accepted. Now continue reading before you ask questions I can't answer."

Still shaken, Zoe read the rest of the article.

Count Aronoffsky was a primary figure in Vosstanovit Rodinu, roughly translated as "Rebuild the Homeland," a group dedicated to the restoration of the Russian aristocracy. A member of Tsar Nicholas Romanov's inner circle, the count was active in helping other aristocrats escape the Bolsheviks. Like others in Vosstanovit Rodinu, the count believed certain members of the royal family had not perished in Yekaterinburg, but had been spirited to safety and are currently in hiding somewhere in France. The police suspect a gang of anti-Royalists to be behind the crime, most likely the Bolsheviks.

Zoe shook her head. "Sergei never discussed that organization with me."

"Are you sure?"

"I thought you promised not to ask me any questions."

A sigh. "You are correct."

The rest of the story wrapped up Jewel's life in two short

paragraphs, mentioning her ballet classes in Mississippi, her war-time years dancing at New York jazz clubs, then her emergence into stardom at the Moulin Rouge when she moved to Paris. It said nothing about her kindness.

Zoe threw the newspaper to the floor. "There's more about Sergei in here than about her."

"This world has never been fair."

"It should be!"

"Now you are sounding like a Bolshevik, Zoe. Be careful."

"Going to arrest me for it?"

He took his eyes off the street long enough to frown at her. "If duty demands."

"Then don't talk to me ever again."

"I can be accommodating when necessary. But before you freeze me out, I'm going to make sure you get your pretty coat back."

Stalemated, they continued on their silent way to the Rue Vavin, where Henri let her out without an *au revoir* or a kiss.

Zoe was too miserable to have her usual breakfast at La Rotonde the next morning, so she made her own coffee and gnawed on a mushy pear. She was wondering whether a trip to the Gare de Lyon to talk to that Russian porter Oleg would get her mind off Jewel when Madeline arrived early, bringing fresh croissants and a special edition of *Le Figaro*.

"This is your taxi-driving friend, no?" the housekeeper asked, shoving the scandal sheet at her.

Zoe stared at the headline in horror.

ANARCHISTE ARMENIEN ARRETE POUR
MEURTRE D'UN COMTE

An anarchist arrested for the count's murder! No fancy pen-and-ink drawing this time, just a raw police photograph of a manacled

Avak Grigoryan standing between two detectives. One of them was Henri.

Avak had been badly beaten.

Holding her hand over her mouth, Zoe ran into the bathroom and lost what little she had eaten. As soon as she'd gargled and washed her face, she returned to the kitchen to read the rest of the article.

The combined forces of the Sûreté and the Prefecture of Police announced they have arrested the ruthless assassin who shot Comte Sergei Aronoffsky as he lay asleep in his luxurious eighth arrondissement apartment. The comte, a former confidant of the now-deceased Russian royal family, was active in Loyalist causes. Over the past five years, his benign activities on behalf of his countrymen have elicited great animosity between Russian revolutionaries and other anarchists, one of them being Grigoryan, who was seen arguing with the comte in the plaza of the Gare de Lyon two days ago.

According to witnesses, the comte insisted the taxi driver move his car, and Grigoryan refused, stating that he was waiting for a fare. When the comte remonstrated with him, the taxi driver refused to give way. Not wishing to make a public spectacle, the more gentlemanly comte had his driver move to a parking area further from the station.

"Grigoryan was also identified by several citizens as driving his taxi around the same district the night before the comte's body was discovered," said Superintendent Maurice Narcisse, of the Prefecture of Police. "And I am sad to say that visiting the comte at the time of his death was famed dancer Jewel Johnson, who was also killed."

Upon questioning, doorman Pierre Lazenby admitted he was lured away from his post by a woman of the streets who uses the sobriquet "Zou-Zou." When questioned, the woman substantiated Lazenby's story. He was admonished for his dereliction of duty, then released.

As for Grigoryan, the police also consider him a suspect in the killing of a Russian couple in the village of Mesnil-Théribus.

"Considering the horrifying nature of all these crimes, I am happy to remind our peace-loving citizens that we still employ the guillotine for heartless assassins such as Grigoryan," said Superintendent Narcisse.

Detective Henri Challiot, of the Sûreté, had no comment.

Zoe put down the paper and, after the quickest of baths, dressed and headed for the Métro. Tracking down the Hemingways' damned valise would have to wait.

When the maid ushered Zoe into the magnificent eighth arrondissement château that was home of one of Paris's most powerful banking families, she found her friend Béatrice Camondo seated at a desk in the drawing room. Béatrice was reading the same newspaper article that had aroused Zoe to action. Although it had only been light for two hours, the flush on Béatrice's cheeks and her tweed hacking jacket, jodhpurs, and dusty boots testified that she had just returned from her daily ride on one of her horses in the Bois de Boulogne.

Good, Zoe thought. Avak needed a battle-ready Béatrice. Deciding the less she had to explain, the better, Zoe motioned for her to continue reading, then used this reading time to survey her surroundings. Zoe had always loved this house, even though a hint of sadness hung over each room. Her friend's brother, Nissim—a pilot—had died during aerial combat in the Great War, but grief hadn't dimmed the château's charm. Inspired by Louis XV's Le Petit Trianon at Versailles, the house was furnished almost entirely in eighteenth-century furniture and artwork, with the exception of a few Sisleys, Cézannes, and Manets. Normally, Zoe found such beauty calming, but not today, when it seemed surreal.

Once Béatrice finished reading, she put the newspaper aside.

"A story in a different newspaper said 'an artist' found the count's body, the same artist who discovered the murder scene in Mesnil-Théribus. Would I be wrong in surmising this was you?"

Without further ado, Zoe gave Béatrice her version of both events, and why and how she'd been unfortunate enough to be present at each.

"So they were shot in the same manner? By the same gun?" A frequent huntress in the Halatte Forest near Senlis, Béatrice hadn't winced at Zoe's graphic descriptions.

"Same-sized bullet holes in their foreheads." Except for poor Jewel, who'd been shot in the throat. Having seen the placement of the bodies on the bed, Zoe understood why. In his final moments, Sergei had attempted to shield her, but his gallantry only managed to prolong her suffering.

Béatrice didn't bother to hide her distress. "There appears to be more of a Russian connection here than an Armenian one. How could your friend Avak kill the Russian couple in Mesnil-Théribus while chauffeuring you around the countryside? Are the police insane?" Not waiting for an answer, Béatrice continued, "And yet they arrest that poor man! If what the newspaper says is true, how strange it would be for so many people to be murdered over a parking dispute at the Gare de Lyon. Or that your taxi-driving friend is an anarchist assassin with the ability to be in two places at one time? But he is Armenian, and we both know how Armenians are treated these days."

"Yes, we do."

"We used to have many Armenian friends in Turkey. Papa was born there, you know, but when the war started, the Ottoman Turks began a series of massacres. The Armenians they didn't murder outright, they put in concentration camps and let die of starvation: babies, women, everyone."

Avak had told Zoe some of this, and at the time, she'd wondered if such an outrage against humanity could possibly be true, but now

Béatrice—never been given to flights of fancy—was backing up his story.

"I heard the death toll came to a million," Zoe said.

A bitter laugh, so out of keeping with the delicate beauty of her surroundings it was jarring. "*More* than a million, yet the Turks deny the slaughter ever happened. Their goal was to exterminate the entire Armenian race, and they almost succeeded. The rest of the world doesn't care about what's going on, but isn't that the way it always goes? Before the War, the world was deaf about the Germans, deaf about the Russians—look what happened to the Royal Family!—and the world's been deaf for centuries about the pogroms against the Jews. Now the world's playing deaf about what's happening to the Armenians."

Béatrice took a deep breath and then leaned forward, her eyes narrowed in outrage. "So tell me what I can do for your Armenian friend, Zoe, and it will be done!"

——— Gabrielle ———

June 1922
Paris

When I came back to myself this morning, I found I could move my head. Not by much, but oh, the freedom! If I'd been able to produce tears, which I cannot, I would have wept with joy.

Now I can better view the framed watercolors lining the walls. Most of the paintings are of rare specimens of plants, such as *Viola hispida*, the Rouen pansy, but oddly enough, the picture that draws my eye is the painting of the *Helianthus*, the common sunflower. The artist must have been me; I vaguely remember scrubbing away chrome yellow from underneath my fingernails.

Sunflower. Wasn't that what the Dutch artist was painting the morning he killed himself?

Best to not think about Death. If he heard me call his name, he might drop by for a visit.

Shifting my head another centimeter I study the living plants surrounding my bed. Today, on one of the spiky leaves of *Phormium tenax* grass, I notice a round lump, a moving something half the size of my smallest fingernail.

A green spider.

Its green is as intense as tourmaline, almost the same color as the blade of grass it sits on. If the creature hadn't moved at that very second, I might not have seen it. But there it is, a *Micrommata virescens,* a beautiful green Huntsman spider. Female. The species is unusual in that they do not weave webs. Instead, the Huntsman lies in wait until an aphid or ant comes by and then strikes.

Hello, I think at her. *Are you here to visit me? Or eat me?*

As if appreciating my little joke, the spider stands up on her back legs and waves at me. *Hello back, Madame.*

Such a strange day, when spiders speak. But many things have seemed strange to me lately. I ask her, *Have you had any luck hunting today?*

The ants have been generous.

They sacrificed themselves for you?

It is a good thing to sacrifice oneself to Beauty, don't you think, Madame? And as for the ants, they were delicious.

How did you get in here? The window is closed.

Someone opened it when I happened to be passing by.

You are adventuresome, then, because we live on the top floor of this building.

All spiders are adventuresome. But on that particular day, I was lonely because I had just eaten my mate. Are you lonely too, Madame?

Often, but for a different reason. Since I can hardly move, the days of drawing comfort from others—or giving comfort—are over.

Trust me, Madame, those days will return. But you must learn patience.

The Huntsman spider kind of patience?

Of course. Such patience is a requisite for us. Otherwise, we would starve.

What is your name, spider?

Since spiders do not socialize, we have no need for names.

I would tell you my name if I could remember it.

Such a sadness. If you wish, I will allow you to give me a name so we can at least have one name between us.

An image comes to me, that of a childhood friend. She had eyes almost the same green as this spider, and compared to me, she was energetic and wise. *How about 'Odile'?* I ask the spider.

That is a pretty name, Madame, and I shall be happy to own it. But now that we have introduced ourselves, I shall continue calling you Madame until you recall yours. Is that permissible?

Of course, Odile, I…

I fall away again.

Chapter Thirteen

Zoe

Béatrice Camondo was as good as her word, and by evening, Paris was abuzz over the news that the arrest of Avak Grigoryan was a simple case of mistaken identity. After sending a *pneumatique* to Béatrice thanking her for her intervention on Avak's behalf, Zoe was able to pull herself together enough to do what she always did when overcome by sorrow: paint.

She started by putting a few alizarin crimson touches on the lower left corner of *Lust*. The idea was to draw the viewer's eye away from the central figures of a couple engaged in sexual congress to a much smaller image of a man dying of his wounds on the battlefield, for wasn't man's never-ending urge for war a kind of lust, too? Alizarin crimson was reminiscent of fresh blood, something she'd noticed in that woodsman's hut. Vassily and Sophia Popov hadn't been dead long enough for the alizarin to darken into Venetian red, and the blood in beautiful Jewel's mouth...

No, Zoe. Think about that later.

Straightening her spine, she added more alizarin, then more, until the only thing she could see was the blood on the battlefield.

Later, she was taking a breather by sipping a glass of chenin blanc—no more red for her on this ugly day—when someone knocked at the door. For a moment she thought about not answering, because she suspected who it was. She took another sip of her wine.

But then he called, "Zoe, please."

It would be nice to think she was an independent woman who needed no comfort from anyone, but this would be a lie.

She put down her wineglass and went to let Henri in, and when she did, Zoe saw her sheared beaver coat draped over his arm.

··· ◇ ···

Henri hadn't stayed the night, so the next morning—after Zoe wept over Jewel for a while—she walked over to La Rotonde for breakfast. Alas, none of her friends were there. The only familiar faces were The Lovers, tucked away at their corner table. In between their usual billing and cooing, they groomed each other, him picking away a bit of fluff that had the effrontery to attach itself to his beloved's red beret; her relieving his black jacket of a long strand of her own red hair.

The Lovers' antics almost made Zoe smile.

But joy was waiting for her when she arrived home and discovered Madeline serving tea to Zoe's sister, Leeanne, and Leeanne's new husband, Jack Carrolton, of the Birmingham Carroltons. The couple was passing through Paris on their way from London to Bavaria, where they would visit his paternal grandparents on their farm. After spending a good half hour hugging and crying, she and Leeanne—Lee-Lee, as she'd always been called—finally settled down enough to talk in complete sentences.

"Oh, Zoe, you look marvelous!" Lee-Lee lied, wiping away happy tears. Her sister was three years younger, and at times, her facility for telling untruths made her seem even younger.

"Nowhere near as marvelous as you, darling Lee-Lee."

Love made women glow, and her sister dazzled, from the blond hair wrapped in a loose braid around the top of her head, to her ankle-length wool dress the same shade as her blue eyes, to her high-topped Spanish leather boots. But Zoe was a mess. After she had gotten up this morning, she hadn't bothered to do much about her appearance, just bathed quickly, smeared on enough makeup to cover the worst of her grief over Jewel, then threw on a less-than-chic dress with an unraveling mid-calf hem. In retrospect, her choice of costume was unwise, because as she and Leeanne shared old memories, she caught Jack staring disapprovingly at her hemline and severely bobbed hair. He didn't seem to like her art nouveau furniture, either.

As Lee-Lee chattered on about changes at Beech Glen—new barn, new Black Angus bull, a new foreman to replace the surly Silas Hansen—Zoe searched for her memories of the Birmingham Carroltons but came up with little. Although wealthy, they were Big City types who only rarely associated with the plantation crowd.

Despite her grief, Zoe was determined to be pleasant. Jack was, after all, her new brother-in-law. Still hugging Lee-Lee, she forced a smile. "You must tell me how you two met."

"Remember Annabelle's fortieth birthday party?" Recognizing her flub, Leeanne's face reddened. "Oh, I'm sorry. Of course, you don't remember. You weren't there, you were...ah, *here*. In Paris. Studying art." Finding her footing again, she continued, "Anyway, Jack had been visiting his relatives at Oakwood—you know, the Burgesses, his third cousins twice removed?—so he came to the party with Nancy Kay and her folks. And that's how we met!" Lee-Lee clapped her hands like an excited child.

The disapproval left Jack's face and he looked at his new bride with adoration. "I knew the minute I saw her that she was the girl for me," he said. "Isn't she just the prettiest little thing?"

Little wasn't the word Zoe would have used. Lee-Lee was only a half-inch shy of Zoe's five feet eight, but Southern men liked to imagine their women as helpless little creatures. It made them feel manlier.

"So how *is* the widow Annabelle Proctor Barlow?" Zoe asked, finally getting around to asking.

Some of the joy left Lee-Lee's face. "You know how she is." Neither was fond of their stepmother, who now lorded over Beech Glen with an iron fist, even bossing around their brother, Brice.

"Is she still wearing black?"

"After nine years, no less. She likes to compare herself to Queen Victoria, who wore widow's weeds for what, forty years?"

"Annabelle always did like drama," Zoe said dryly, remembering the flowery good-versus-evil speech her stepmother delivered as she banished Zoe from Beech Glen forever. Assuming a false brightness, Zoe changed the topic. "But what a delightful coincidence, you being here today! I was about to post a package to you this very afternoon. Come, follow me into the bedroom."

Lee-Lee shot a quick look at her husband. Jack smiled and nodded, which Zoe thought odd. It almost looked like her sister was asking for permission.

The dress she'd first seen featured on the cover of *Le Petit Echo de la Mode*, then bought at Clotilde's Boutique on Saint-Germaine-des-Prés, fit Lee-Lee perfectly. The pale pink matched her naturally rosy lips and the diagonal sash ending at the bow on her hip accentuated her perfect figure, while the short length showed off her wonderfully long legs. Zoe's own legs—especially the left one—were scarred, but Leeanne's were flawless.

Cheered by her kid-sister's beauty, Zoe said, "Now let's show your new husband. I'm sure he'll love it."

She was wrong.

"Take that vulgar rag off right now," Jack commanded, rising from his seat. "It better suits your sister, not you."

Love's glow faded from Lee-Lee's face. When her mouth opened, no sound came out.

"*I said take it off, Leeanne!*"

As Leeanne fled into the bedroom, Jack turned his attention to Zoe. "Just so you know, I don't appreciate your calling my wife 'Lee-Lee.' Unlike yourself, she's a married woman, and should be addressed with the dignity befitting her new station in life. Since you seem unable to understand common decent behavior, as soon as she changes, we will be leaving. This visit was a mistake, one that won't happen again. I simply cannot believe you would put my wife in a whore's clothes!"

"But..."

His handsome face twisted into something ugly. "I've heard all about you, *Miss* Barlow."

There it was. He knew. Realizing any argument Zoe might put forth would be futile, she left him to his contempt and hurried into the boudoir, where she found Lee-Lee trying to button herself into her bulky dress. Her hands shook so badly she was making a bad job of it.

"Quick. Where are you staying?" Zoe whispered, taking over the buttoning.

"Hôtel Théâtre des Champs-Élysées," Lee-Lee whispered back through her tears. "But we're only going to be there for two more nights."

Zoe knew the hotel. It was near the Alma-Marceau Métro stop, and she could be there in fifteen minutes. "Does he beat you?" she asked.

"Oh, Jack would never do anything like *that*!"

Having seen her brother, Brice, behave in much the same way as Jack, and remembering her sister-in-law's collection of bruises, Zoe brushed aside Lee-Lee's denial. "What are your plans for tomorrow?"

Lee-Lee gulped her way through a relentless-sounding schedule, but one time period stood out. "You say he's meeting with a business associate at nine? Where? Do you know?"

She named a café Zoe avoided due to its frumpishness.

Zoe suggested a different place. "There's a short passageway behind your hotel," Zoe told her. "If you take it south toward the river, just before you reach Rue Jean Goujon, you'll see Boulangerie René. I'll meet you there at nine fifteen."

"But if Jack sees us..."

"René has a small back room with tables and no windows. He only allows certain people in there, and I'm one of them. If you arrive first, tell him you're there to meet me." Zoe didn't tell Lee-Lee of the other businesses René ran from that back room; her sister didn't need to know.

"Leeanne!" Jack shouted, from the other room. "Don't make me come in there after you!"

Her master's voice.

Zoe squeezed her sister's hand. "Tomorrow."

. . . ◇ . . .

After they left, Zoe changed into her painting togs and stowed her amber ring in her enameled jewelry box. Then she went into her studio, set the unfinished *Lust* aside, and began working on *Wrath*. If there was anything good about her new brother-in-law, it was that he'd briefly managed to make her forget about Jewel. She painted so furiously she only realized hours had passed when Madeline came in and announced that the pâté Zoe had promised to take to Jewel's wake was finished.

"Oh my, Mademoiselle!" the housekeeper exclaimed, catching sight of the canvas. "Who has angered you this time?"

Zoe had been so lost in her work she could no longer "see" the painting, so she stepped back and tried to envision it through

Madeline's eyes. In the center, broad slashes of naphthol scarlet, dioxazine purple, and phthalo emerald whirlpooled down toward a black hole, where a set of canine-like fangs lurked. Not subtle, but truthful.

"I don't much care for my new brother-in-law," she told Madeline.

··· ◇ ···

Zoe's day degenerated from rage to sorrow, as she carried Madeline's lovely pâté through the narrow hallway leading through the intricate maze of the Moulin Rouge's back rooms. Past the feather-maker's stash of bright plumage. Past the sewing room, where workers busily attached sequins to the briefest of costumes. Past the fitting room. Just as Zoe was beginning to fear she was lost, she finally emerged into the L-shaped space that singer-turned-director Mistinguett had chosen for Jewel's wake. After placing the pâté on an already loaded table, Zoe made her way around several rows of chairs to the corner where her friends were gathered.

Upon seeing her, little Bobby Crites rushed up. "I heard you found her body. What the hell, Zoe!"

"I don't want to talk about it."

But Zoe soon found there was no quenching her friends' curiosity. Reynard Dibasse, an ardent fan of Jewel's, wanted to know if she'd suffered.

Zoe took a deep breath and answered, "Shot in the head, both of them. No suffering."

Reynard lifted his portrait mask enough to wipe a tear away from his remaining eye. "Thank you," he whispered. "I was afraid…"

"She didn't even have time to get frightened," Zoe lied.

The tenderhearted poet didn't need to know the truth. Nor did anyone else at the wake, although the look she received from sculptor Karen Wegner proved she saw through Zoe's well-meant mercies. From behind, Zoe heard sobs. She turned to see Louise

Packard, who'd painted several Cubist portraits of Jewel. A costumed Jewel dancing. A dark Jewel lying across a white bedsheet. Jewel sitting...

The room blurred.

"Are you all right, Zoe?" Louise asked, putting out a steadying hand. "I know you two were close."

"I'm fine." Once a liar, always a liar.

Next to Louise stood Tripp Eiger, who was speaking with Bobby Crites. From what Zoe could hear, Bobby was still trying to convince Tripp he'd been nowhere near Mesnil-Théribus on the day the Popovs had been slain, but the very length and passion of Bobby's denials made Zoe certain that he had indeed been there. She was about to question him on this matter herself when Mistinguett clapped her hands three times.

"Mesdames and messieurs, please take your seats!"

The singer/director had eschewed her usual bright plumage, but she still looked dramatic in mourning black, from her shoes to her ankle-length dress, to the crown of black feathers sprouting from her red-gold hair. As soon as everyone was settled into their seats, Mistinguett led the roomful of agnostics and nihilists through the Lord's Prayer and a reading of the Twenty-third Psalm. Although in French, the hastily put-together ceremony reminded Zoe so much of the Sundays at Beech Glen that she found her lower lip trembling. She compressed her mouth into a hard line and held steady. Jewel was gone, and all the tears in the world wouldn't bring her back.

At the close of the psalm, Mistinguett sang "*C'est un Rempart que Notre Dieu—A Mighty Fortress is Our Lord.*" Zoe made it through that, too, but when everyone joined her in singing "*Tel que Je Suis, sans Rien à Moi,*" Zoe's will almost buckled. That hymn—which as a child she'd sung in English as "Just As I Am" in Beech Glen's tiny Baptist church—made the room go blurry again.

Then came the stories. One by one, dancers stood up to tell of Jewel's many kindnesses: the shelter she'd set up for street children; the elderly woman she visited regularly upon learning that she'd lost her entire family in the war (the speaker would now be taking over that sad duty); the kitten Jewel rescued from two cruel boys (that speaker had just adopted it); the time Jewel attended to a one-legged veteran who'd been hit by an omnibus. On and on. As if these tales of compassion weren't heartbreak enough, Reynard rose and recited a poem he had written about her titled "Black Swan," which left even the men in the room sobbing.

By the time the memorial was over, a wrung-out Zoe wanted nothing more than to go home and attack the bottle of chenin blanc she'd left cooling in the icebox. It was not to be. As they filed out along the Moulin Rouge's back corridors, sculptor Karen Wegner caught up to her. A tougher cookie even than Zoe, Karen's eyes were dry.

"Nice line of bushwa from our beloved Reynard."

"Glad you appreciate his talent. While I'd love to stay here and discuss poetry with you, I've got a date with a guy named Blanc."

"It'll keep. What I want to know is who died first, Sergei or Jewel?"

Zoe stopped, letting the others file around them. "How would I know that?"

"Maybe because that good-looking cop has been seen hanging around your house. Which leads me to ask—what were you doing at Sergei's in the first place?"

"Read the article in *Le Figaro*. It'll tell you everything you need to know."

"Not why you were there, it didn't."

"It's none of your business!" When several people turned around to stare, Zoe realized she'd been shouting.

Karen held up her palms in a back-away gesture. With any

other woman, it would have looked innocent, but given the size of the sculptor's hands, the gesture appeared threatening. "They were my friends, too, Zoe. So answer my question. Sergei died first, didn't he, trying to protect her? That would be just like him."

The sculptor seemed sincere enough, but the past few hours had taught Zoe that sincerity made for a convincing disguise. "I don't know. Inspector Challiot probably doesn't know, either. As for what I was doing there, I was just visiting. Now you know everything I do."

"You were visiting him on the one day a week Jewel was guaranteed to be there. Weren't you concerned about walking into..." Karen paused, then began again. "I mean, weren't you worried about interrupting an intimacy?"

Zoe felt herself flush. "No. Now if you'll excuse me..." Sidling around the sculptor, Zoe joined the rest of the artists and dancers as they flowed through the dark passageway and out onto the sunlit Boulevard de Clichy.

··· ◇ ···

As soon as Zoe arrived home, she went to work on the chenin blanc. She didn't remember much that happened afterward, but when she woke up the next morning, there was a man in her bed.

Chapter Fourteen

"Do I know you?" she asked him.

"I hope not," he responded. "I did something to you last night that is illegal in the noble state of Alabama, and you'd have to report me to the police."

"You *are* the police."

"Not when I'm naked, I'm not. Then I'm merely a person, like yourself."

"But a male person."

"That, *certainement*." He lifted the blanket so she could see.

"And you appear to be getting even more male as we speak."

"Does that frighten you, Mademoiselle?"

"Not being able to remember the illegal thing you did to me last night, I don't know whether to be frightened or not."

"Then I must refresh your memory."

· · · ◇ · · ·

Afterward, Zoe sent Henri home.

What the hell was wrong with her, she wondered, as she stared up at the mirrored ceiling. Her best friend had been murdered, and yet here she was, having sex with a married man—a cop, no less—carrying on as if the world hadn't stopped spinning on its axis, which it surely had when Jewel died. *I'm sorry, Jewel,* she whispered, not that it did any good, because here she was, heedless as ever, ignoring the lesson she should have learned four years earlier.

If you want to ruin your life, fall in love.

$$\cdots \diamond \cdots$$

Later, bathed and dressed in the least flashy of her outfits, Zoe arrived at the back room of Boulangerie René to find her sister already there, sipping a cup of café au lait and nibbling a croissant. The room, the repository of the usual baker's supplies—bags of flour, sugar, napkins, cutlery, and the like—often served as a hideout for secret lovers and other plotters. It was small, but not uncomfortably so.

Lee-Lee rose from her chair and gave Zoe a trembly hug. "I can't stay long. If Jack finds out I've left the hotel he'll have a fit."

She was dressed even more demurely today than yesterday, in a severely cut gray wool suit that hugged her neck and reached down to her ankles. The thing made Zoe itch just to look at it. Lee-Lee's black hat bore no ornamentation, either, other than a gray velvet band. The ensemble wouldn't have looked out of place on their eighty-one-year-old great-aunt.

As Zoe sat down, René brought her a duplicate of her sister's order, then returned to the front room to help his wife with less secretive customers. She took a sip of her café au lait and tried to figure out how best to handle the situation. First, she tried for a light touch. "Can't let Jack know the cat snuck out of the house, eh?"

Her sister didn't respond. She was keeping an eye on the door, as if expecting Jack to burst through it any moment.

Zoe tried again. "Lee-Lee, I'm worried about you. Jack's behavior yesterday was disturbing. No man should treat his wife that way. You are not his chattel."

This brought a response, but not one Zoe liked. "Jack is very old-fashioned. There was no way you could know. But that was quite the scene, wasn't it?" She grinned, as if her husband's churlishness was nothing more than a joke gone wrong.

Lee-Lee had never been comfortable with confrontation. While Zoe had openly rebelled against their iron-willed stepmother, Leeanne only pretended to obey, then did what she wanted. This was no time to let her get away with such evasive behavior. "Your husband pretty much called me a whore! And the way he ordered you around reminded me of how Annabelle always treated the household help. Worse, actually, because she knew they could quit, but we were stuck with her."

Lee-Lee looked down at her cutlery, as if examining it for cleanliness. "Jack's authoritativeness is one of the things that drew me to him. And, really, we should stop using her Christian name, because I might get into the habit of doing it, and you know how mad it makes her."

Zoe stared at her sister in disbelief. Was Lee-Lee under the impression their stepmother could eavesdrop from a four-thousand-mile distance? Their father had married Annabelle Proctor less than a year after their mother died. Immediately upon her instillation as Beech Glen's chatelaine, she insisted on being called "Mother." Lee-Lee had followed her directive. Not Zoe.

"Sorry I brought her up," Zoe said, "but you should know there's a difference between authoritativeness and disrespect."

Annoyance flitted across Lee-Lee's pretty face. "Why must you always be so argumentative, Zoe? Like Anna...like *Mother* says, you'd argue with a signpost."

"If the signpost pointed travelers in the wrong direction, of course I would. Then I'd take the sign down and fix it."

At this, Lee-Lee laughed, sounding more like the untroubled girl

Zoe remembered. "You don't have to worry about me, Sissy. Jack loves me, and he's everything I've ever wanted. Handsome, kind..."

"You call his behavior yesterday *kind*?"

"He has high standards, that's all. It's one of the things I admire about him."

"His so-called 'standards' seemed pretty lowdown to me."

Her sister's cheeks grew red, whether in embarrassment or anger, Zoe couldn't tell. As if stalling for time, Lee-Lee took another ladylike nibble at her croissant, then a delicate sip of her café au lait. Sated, she dabbed her lips with her napkin. "Well, anyway, Jack's ordered me to cut off our relationship."

"*What?!*" Zoe's voice rose so high that René, who'd returned to augment his supply of napkins, put his forefinger to his lips. Discretion was the order of the day in this back room.

She lowered her voice. "You're not going to listen to him, are you, Lee-Lee? I couldn't bear it if..."

"Nothing will ever separate us, Sissy. Not Mother. Not Brice. Not even Jack. We'll just keep on doing what we've been doing for the past few years."

Unlike their strained relationship with their older brother, the sisters had always been close, even after Zoe's banishment from Beech Glen. This had been made possible through the intercession of their paternal aunt Verla. The two would write to each other, but addressed their letters to Verla, who lived in Birmingham. Verla then transferred each letter to a new envelope with her own home address and sent it off to the intended sister.

"She'll send your letters to our new address," Lee-Lee said, sliding a sheet of paper across the table. "If there's an emergency, these are the hotels and dates where we'll be staying, plus the name and address of Jack's relatives near Munich. I've sent the same information to Aunt Verla, of course. If you need to contact me directly, say, in a telegram, use the name Maggie White, and I'll know it's from you. I've already told Jack that Maggie is an old friend from Miss Carmichael's who's now attending the Sorbonne."

Miss Edna Carmichael ran the finishing school they'd both attended. Zoe had been miserable there, but Lee-Lee had loved it. "Is Maggie one of your old cronies from Miss Carmichael's?" Zoe couldn't help but admire her sister's craftiness.

Leeanne's eyes danced. "She's a girl who does not exist."

"Ah."

When Lee-Lee had been small and their stepmother caught her in a lie, she would make up a story so complicated her intended punisher would lose sight of the girl's original sin. This strategy often worked, but when it didn't... Well, Annabelle Proctor Barlow could be harsh. Lee-Lee's lies had never bothered Zoe, but what did disturb her was the ease with which she excused her husband's boorish behavior.

In a way, it reminded Zoe of Hadley's excuses for Ernest.

· · · ◇ · · ·

The afternoon brought another memorial service, this one more formal than Jewel's.

Count Sergei Ivanovic Aronoffsky's service was held at the Cathedral Saint-Alexandre-Nevsky. It was a gloriously grand cathedral—Picasso had married his Russian ballet dancer there—but with the onion domes, the frescoes, and the life-sized gold leaf icons of various and sundry saints, Zoe thought it a bit much. The count's enormous popularity was reflected throughout the crowded cathedral where all ranks of Parisian society, from the humble to the titled, were gathered. Russians being a demonstrative people, the cathedral resounded with wails. The Parisians were mostly silent.

But some Parisians took part in the traditional Russian counter-clockwise circling of Sergei's open casket. A few even stooped to kiss him, but most of the circlers—Zoe included—simply laid flowers on his body. For a moment, Zoe found herself behind the elderly woman in the ragged coat who'd once cut short a conversation she'd been having with Sergei at the Dôme. The old woman was too blinded by tears to recognize Zoe. Despite her poverty she'd managed to scrape together enough money to place a white rose on the count's bemedaled chest.

Trailing behind were the Poker Night regulars. Dominique Garron, looking like a one-eyed Amazon, walked next to Marquis Antoine Fortier. He looked very much the aristocrat, with his black suit, black cloak, silk hat, and—for effect only—an ebony cane topped with a silver wolf's head. Behind him, Louise Packard's arthritic hands clutched her own cane, which had nothing to do with fashion; she was crying so hard she could barely stand. Nick Stewart also joined the casket-circlers, with an already-inebriated Kiki hanging on to his arm. Bringing up the rear was portrait painter Archie Stafford-Smythe, who appeared to be well on his way to inebriation, too.

By the time the casket-circlers finished their reverences, only the count's face was left uncovered by flowers, the wounds in his forehead mercifully disguised by the undertaker's skill.

· · · ◇ · · ·

After the service was over, the Poker Night regulars met inside the Closerie des Lilas, on Boulevard du Montparnasse.

"Does anyone have any idea what that priest person was going on and on about?" asked Archie, the monocle in his eye reflecting the weak December light outside.

"Not speaking Russian, I haven't a clue," Nick Stewart grumped.

Dominique, who had never liked Archie nor Nick, sniped, "If you'd paid closer attention, you'd have noticed that most of it was in Latin. 'I am the resurrection and the life, and those who believeth in me,' et cetera."

"Oh, please," Louise Packard said. She'd stopped crying and had returned to her usual prickly self. "Haven't we already been preached at enough?" Today she looked all of her fifty-plus years. And her poor hands...

Zoe could hardly bear to look at them.

But Dominique was pitiless, giving Louise a stern look. "I was surprised to see you there, considering."

"Considering what?"

"Don't act coy, Louise. You bore no love for Sergei. I remember you once saying something about taking a knife to his balls. You even..."

Before Louise could whack Dominique with her cane, Archie stepped in. "Now, now, ladies, let's not be catty." Every inch a British earl's son, he picked his monocle up off the table where it had fallen when he'd widened his eyes at Dominique's mention of the count's balls. "People will say anything when distraught. I'm certain Louise didn't mean it. One never does, does one?"

"Besides, Sergei wasn't stabbed, he was shot." This surprising defense came from Kiki, who'd stopped hanging on to Nick Stewart's arm long enough to capture the bottle of Châteauneuf-du-Pape sitting on the table. Without apology, she poured the remaining drops into her still half-full glass.

Dominique scowled at Kiki, but Archie, whose monthly remittance was large, simply ordered another bottle. When it arrived, he refilled everyone's glass and then proposed a toast.

"To our fallen comrade," he said. "Sergei might have been a poor poker player, but he always paid his debts." Among the British upper classes, no praise could be higher, because so many didn't.

"To Sergei!" they chorused.

Before they could finish their glasses, Fortier did Archie one better. "Another toast to the gallant Count Sergei Ivanovic

Aronoffsky," he said, doffing his silk hat. "May a fleet of Czarist angels carry him home!"

"Czarists angels, my socialist ass," Dominique muttered.

As they toasted again, Zoe snatched a quick look at Fortier. He and Sergei were close friends, and the stress of the past few days had affected him more deeply than the others. Although he was not as heavy a drinker as the rest of them, his eyes were bloodshot, and his hands shook so severely that his wine twice slopped over onto the table. No painting for him tonight. Despite his elegance, today he looked almost as old as Louise.

Zoe wasn't the only person who'd noticed Fortier's fraught condition. Louise saw it, too. She leaned over and whispered something in his ear. He gave her a weak smile, but it was obvious his heart wasn't in it.

··· ◊ ···

Exhausted from the day—grieving over Jewel, enduring a backroom meeting with Leeanne, attending the Russian funeral rites for Sergei, and a failed attempt to correct the problems on her latest canvas—Zoe turned in early. Henri never showed up, but she didn't care.

She had a bottle of Château Mouton Rothschild to keep her company.

Chapter Fifteen

Gluttony couldn't be saved, so the heartsore Zoe scraped the paint off the canvas and began again.

But after putting in several more wasted hours, she realized she'd approached this deadly sin from the usual clichéd angle— pigs at a trough. Although she wasn't a Realist, the thread of the cliché kept leaking through her abstractions. Disgusted with herself and more than a little hungover, she cleaned her brushes and left the studio.

While she'd been painting, Madeline had arrived, and was putting together the makings of boeuf Bourguignon.

"I was going to drink that," Zoe said, motioning at the bottle of Burgundy.

"Perhaps Mademoiselle should cut back on the drinking."

"Just because I have a hangover?"

"Because this is Mademoiselle's third hangover in one week."

"It's been a bad week."

"If I cut back on the wine, the stew will not taste as robust." But she poured Zoe a half glass, anyway.

As Zoe sipped at the mediocre wine, it occurred to her she'd heard nothing from Hadley in days. This worried her not only because of Ernest's temper, but because of Hadley's family background. Not long after that humiliating meeting at Gertrude Stein's salon, Zoe learned Hadley's father had committed suicide. As had Zoe's.

Oh, Daddy, what had made you so unhappy?

Hadley liked to pretend her father's death had made little impact, mainly because James Richardson had never been close to his children. But as Zoe grew to know Hadley, she recognized the scarring. Her friend was so afraid of being abandoned that she put up with whatever manner of unseemly behaviors her husband indulged in, from sucker punching other men, to pretending not to care when he lost their grocery money at the racetrack.

Zoe was no stranger to that kind of pretense, herself.

Now, as she sat at the long banquet table, she remembered Hadley confiding that Ernest's father had committed suicide, too.

What a fine collection the three of them made.

She wondered if Hadley had told Ernest the truth about "forgetting" to pack her birth control device and, if so, how he had reacted. Worried, she decided to telegraph her at the Alpine hotel Ernest had moved them into. The exact wording would be important in case the telegram somehow fell into his hands.

Composing such a telegram turned out to be more difficult than Zoe expected, and when finished, she found herself feeling more compassion for Ernest's scribbles. Like painting, writing was hard work.

QUERY—HAVING GOOD TIME
   QUERY ERNEST HAPPY—QUERY YOU HAPPY
   –QUERY ADVENTURES ON SLOPES
   WRITE ME—STOP
   BUNCHES LOVE—STOP
   ZOE

She didn't mention she was still searching for the rest of the manuscripts. Why get Hadley's hopes up?

Upon opening the front door, she spied young Dax loitering on the corner, cadging handouts from passersby. He came running when Zoe called to him. She handed the child more francs than necessary and told him to deliver her correspondence to the telegraph office. Even if Hadley and Ernest were out on the slopes of Chamby—they adored skiing—Zoe figured she could receive an answer by the end of the day. As Zoe watched Dax dodge horse-drawn carriages and automobiles, she had a thought she immediately regretted. Now that the worst poker player with the deepest pockets was dead—the count had regularly lost more money to Zoe than even Fortier—she would need to start watching her expenditures. But no matter how tight her budget looked, she wouldn't stop supporting the orphan shelter Jewel had founded.

And she certainly wouldn't end those monthly checks she sent to Pinkerton's National Detective Agency. The detectives would search for her Amber child until they'd reduced Zoe to penury. *Maybe even after that.*

So much love lost! After a few minutes of quiet weeping, Zoe allowed a more fruitful emotion to take its place: a dark rage that Jewel's killer was still free.

She would do something about that, and Ernest's stupid manuscripts could wait.

Ten minutes later, Zoe arrived at the taxi stand on the corner of Raspail and Montparnasse, where she found Avak Grigoryan trying to rustle up a fare.

"Want to take another trip to Mesnil-Théribus?" she asked him.

A big smile lit his face. "For Mademoiselle Zoe, I drive Hades and back. I owe life to you, so I take anywhere free forever."

"If you want to keep living in Paris, you'll need to be a better businessman than that," she said. "I insist on paying you, and besides, Mesnil-Théribus may be small, but it in no way resembles Hades."

With that, she climbed into the Grim Reaper and off they went.

· · · ◇ · · ·

The journey was not without its problems, although this time they were neither snowed upon nor dampened by a cold rain. On occasion, they even saw the sun. But as they approached the village of Bornel, the Grim Reaper got it into its head to investigate a stone wall, and it was only with strong-armed hauling upon the steering wheel that Avak managed to dissuade it. The words that issued forth from the chauffeur sounded rude, but since Zoe did not speak Armenian, she couldn't be sure.

"He is okay now, the car," Avak called back to her. "So much fine."

Doubting Avak's optimism, she didn't release her death-grip on the door handle. "Are the brakes working?" she yelled, over two loud backfires.

"Most time! But his steering is excellent!"

"Oh, good!"

They managed to reach Mesnil-Théribus alive, and as the Grim Reaper farted along the narrow main street, Zoe kept a lookout for the café where little Bobby Crites was rumored to have shared a drink with his cousin the same day the Popovs were murdered. Spotting a tiny café nestled alongside an inn, she told Avak to park. The Grim Reaper's brakes didn't want to cooperate, but Avak managed a rolling stop inches before they would have crashed into the post office.

"*Voilà*, Mademoiselle! All safe!"

"Follow me," she told him, disembarking shakily. "I'm buying the drinks." After the ride, she needed a stiff one, but Mesnil-Théribus was a small village. It would be prey to the prejudice common among such places: women don't drink alone in cafés.

The barman turned out to be a barmaid, a bosomy, russet-haired woman named Nanine somewhere in her thirties. No wedding ring. After Zoe belted down a hair-raising Chartreuse, Nanine served the two a surprisingly good merlot that she bragged was a local product. Glasses poured, the barmaid was quick to chat up Avak, and it was easy to see that with his soulful eyes and luxurious black mustache, he'd captured the barmaid's heart.

No other customers enlivened the room, which was little more than fifteen by twelve feet, with several tables crammed together. No gleaming windows showcased the passing world. The only decoration in the café was a fading poster proclaiming the health benefits of smoking Gitanes. These bland surroundings suited Zoe perfectly, since a bored barmaid could be a garrulous barmaid.

For a while, Zoe listened without comment to Nanine's skewed accounting of the recent murders. According to the barmaid, two Russian spies had been decapitated by a meat cleaver. As her tale grew more and more lurid, Avak tsk-tsked. Zoe's opening arrived when Avak, after an earlier prompting, deftly steered the conversation away from decapitations to the art scene in Paris, and then to the recent de Chirico exhibit and little Bobby Crites's cousin. "So many smart peoples there," he said. "And they talking about local artist Abelard Grigot. You know him?"

Nanine claimed to be an intimate of the artist, who'd set up a small studio in one of his farm's outbuildings. "He paints ugly things," she said. "People with terrible deformities, dead animals, drowning swimmers. *Merde!* Myself, I like paintings of flowers, tableaux to gaze upon with joy, not dread."

"All kinds, it takes," Avak said, nodding sagely.

Seizing the moment, Zoe interjected, "This Abelard sounds like one of the new Surrealists, a painting school I find interesting. Maybe you could tell us where we might see some of his work? Due to a lucky day at the races, I've found myself with

an embarrassment of money and am eager to rid myself of it."
Smile, smile.

Nanine threw Zoe a *stupid American* look. After giving directions to Abelard's farm, she poured her only customers more
Chartreuse. "On the house!" she said, beaming at Avak.

Zoe noticed his serving was more generous than hers.

··· ◇ ···

Abelard Grigot's place lay just before the turning to Mary Cassatt's
château, providing a stark contrast between elegance and hard-
scrabble existence. The farmstead comprised a few jumbled-
together stone buildings, one apparently lived in. The pasture
behind it was dappled with a few depressed sheep and two horses
that seen better days. On the sides of the lane leading to the house,
several chickens scratched along in the dirt, having given up on
the farmstead's meager offerings. In the middle of this wasteland
sat a comparatively new building. Three sides had been pieced
together by scraps of wood and rock, but on the north-facing wall
stood tall glass panes that wouldn't have looked out of place in
Montparnasse. When the Grim Reaper gasped to a stop just outside it, the door flew open, and a bearded man in a paint-spattered
smock rushed out, demanding to know what the hell she and Avak
were doing, scaring his livestock like that.

A sentence combining the words "Surrealism" and "francs"
quickly soothed him, and soon they were being shown a collection
of canvases created by a man who was probably insane, although
not without talent. Barmaid Nanine had accurately described
Abelard's subject matter, but Zoe found one oil in particular that
called to her: the figure of a small child standing alone in the middle
of an empty street. In the distance loomed a Greek temple, its stark
architectural lines contrasting with the girl's curly blond hair.

"I call it *Waiting*," Abelard said, proudly.

The girl in the painting appeared to be around four, the same age as...

No, Zoe. Don't think about that.

But she couldn't stop herself. Gesturing toward the painting, Zoe asked, "How much?"

The ensuing haggling proved that although Abelard was poor—farms frequently bestowed that word on a man—he was no fool, and they finally settled on a price for *Waiting* that stung Zoe only a little. Once the francs were turned over, the painter fairly danced with glee and invited them to the farmhouse for a celebratory glass of wine. With the small painting tucked safely under her arm, she and Avak followed as he led them through a tool-littered yard to a house that looked like it was about to collapse any moment. Once inside, they were introduced to Pascala, Abelard's beaming wife, and three grubby children of indeterminate ages.

They sat in a kitchen lorded over by a huge wooden stove that provided respite from the cold farmyard, and the wine Pascala offered them was a surprisingly excellent Beaujolais. The conversation was excellent, too, especially when Abelard started talking about Bobby Crites, his American cousin from the "arrondissement" of Baton Rouge. Bobby had met with him recently at the café, he told them. "He didn't stay long, which was a big disappointment for me. I'd wanted him to look at my recent work, but he said he had too many chores that day, although he never said what they were. You'd think him being a cousin, he would set me up with a gallery in Paris, but he was all hurry, hurry, hurry. Scatterbrained, that's Bobby all over. But what else can you expect from a Dadaist? They find a broken cup, hang it on the wall, and expect to sell it for ten thousand francs."

Zoe sympathized, saying that, yes, the Dada movement was a scandal to any decent-thinking person. Then she asked, "What exact day was Bobby here? Do you remember?"

After a swift conversation with Pascala, they agreed that the American cousin had been in Mesnil-Théribus on Saturday. Abelard added that Bobby hadn't been alone.

This information surprised Zoe. "Who was he with?"

Abelard shrugged. "Never saw the person. Not even sure it was a man. A beautiful woman, perhaps? He *was* in a great mood that day!" A grin. "He had more important things to do than helping a poor cousin escape this shithole. The only thing I can tell you is that whoever it was, he—or she—his friend drove a big black automobile."

"Kind, which?" Avak asked.

Another shrug. "All I know about autos is that they're noisy. Dangerous, too. I prefer my horses." With that, he shot a suspicious look out the window at the Grim Reaper, which—so far that day—had injured no one. Not even a chicken.

With nothing else to be gained, Zoe and Avak finished their wine and headed back to the Mesnil-Théribus café to speak to Nanine again, only to be told by the replacement barman that she had left to run some errands and would be back around three. Zoe looked at her watch. It was just after one. Two hours left to kill.

They ate a quick lunch of cheese, bacon, and baguettes, and then to pass the time until Nanine's return, climbed back into the Grim Reaper and drove to the woodsman's shack. It had occurred to Zoe that although several days had passed since the Popovs' murders, there was a chance some of Ernest's pages escaped up the fireplace's flue. When Zoe had discovered the bodies, she'd been too distraught to do anything other than snatch burning paper from the fireplace. Now, in the brightness of a sunny day, she decided to take advantage of the good weather by searching the forest for other pages. There remained a chance, albeit a slim one, they might even find the valise.

Avak didn't mind. A franc was a franc, whether driving along country roads or wading through a litter of fallen leaves.

Zoe's idea paid off to a certain extent. On the lee side of the shack she found two pages, singed and faded, but still readable. A few feet farther on, another page. Avak, who'd ventured deeper into the woods, came back with three more. A cursory glance proved that these pages made no more sense than the others, but Ernest might find something in them to build on. Zoe did like one line she came across toward the end of what appeared to be a short story. After a sad woman described a fairy-tale vision of their possible future, the man she was with said, *"Isn't it pretty to think so?"*

A further search proved the end of their good luck. No valise and no more pages. Scrabbling along uneven terrain made Zoe's leg ache, so they returned to the café, where they found Nanine back behind the bar. The barmaid's eyes lit up when she spied Avak, and Zoe allowed her the pleasure of a few minutes' conversation with him. When Zoe could stand it no longer, she gave him a gentle nudge, and he steered the conversation away from the everyday delights of provincial life to automobiles.

"I hear Monsieur Bobby in fine car be here," he said. "Cars my big love."

Nanine's face—so chirpy earlier—fell. "I never saw it."

"No car see at all?"

She shook her head.

Inserting herself into the conversation, Zoe asked, "How about the man Bobby was with? Do you happen to know him?"

"Never saw him, either. Probably too fancy for the likes of us, just like that American artist out at Château de Beaufresne."

Zoe noticed the frown on Nanine's face when she uttered the word *American,* but risked one more question. "Maybe Bobby said something about his friend?"

Apparently, that was one question too many. "Why would he do that, Mademoiselle? Was his friend any of my business?"

Frowning, she added, "Do you want to purchase another glass of wine?" She had filled up Avak's glass without even asking.

His drink was on the house. Zoe's wasn't.

··· ◇ ···

During the drive back to Paris, Zoe cataloged which of her acquaintances owned a "big black" automobile. She could simply ask Bobby who had been his traveling companion in Mesnil-Théribus, but given his earlier denials about being in the vicinity on the day of the Popovs' murders, she knew better than to waste her time. He'd certainly been there, as witnessed by his own cousin and the barmaid. Zoe didn't believe in coincidence. If Bobby's trip to Mesnil-Théribus had been an innocent sightseeing jaunt, there would have been no reason to lie. Yet he *had* lied. Several times.

Was he covering up for his driver, or himself?

Zoe knew her suspicions were too vague for the police to take seriously, which meant ferreting out the answer was up to her. Who owned that mysterious big black automobile? Artists, regardless of their varying societal positions, all tended to be acquainted with each other, thus the list of suspects was long. It began with British portraitist Archie Stafford-Smythe, whose remittance was large enough to afford a Bugatti. Then there was poet Tripp Eiger, whose elderly Citroën could have been considered "big" to a provincial. Other automobile-owners of her acquaintance included Karen Wegner and her Citroën; arthritis-stricken Louise Packard and her new Renault; Marquis Antoine Fortier, whose elegant Hispano Suiza had displaced the horses who used to live in the building behind his fancy apartment; and war artist Dominique Garron, whose wooden-sided Ravel still showed the bullet holes it had collected while ferrying her toward the Battle of the Marne.

Zoe also wondered which of them owned a gun.

—— Gabrielle ——

August 1922
Paris

The man has come to me tonight, but not in the way of long ago. Instead of covering my body with his own, he sits in the chair beside my bed, holds my hand, and weeps.

Oh, dear heart, do not cry for me, I think toward him. *Despite what's happened, I have found a new friend and she comforts me.*

Unlike Odile, he cannot read my thoughts.

I recognize this man now, as I have come to recognize myself.

I am a botanist who understands the secret lives of plants, and the beautiful watercolors on these walls were painted by my own hand.

My name is Gabrielle Beauvoir Challiot. I was born in the mountain village of Les Saisies, the only child of Claudine Lemarr and Yves Beauvoir. Both my parents were doctors, and they loved each other.

Almost as much as Henri, my husband, loves me.

Chapter Sixteen

— Zoe —

Zoe spent most of the next day painting. Because she couldn't keep the images of that mysterious black car out of her mind, the work went slowly, so she greeted her friends with relief when they arrived for her Wednesday Salon. After they helped themselves to the banquet Madeline laid out, Zoe decided to use the occasion to canvas them about the pleasures and perils of automobile ownership. Although she'd left behind her speedy King Model EE when she was exiled from Beech Glen, she pretended ignorance of all things automotive.

"I'm thinking about purchasing a car, but I don't know anything about them," she announced, once the sounds of chewing and wine-swilling lessened. "What kind do you all recommend?"

Not being an automobile owner himself, little Bobby Crites remained silent, but Karen Wegner suggested a Citroën. "I haven't had too much trouble with mine," she said.

Given the sculptor's muscular build, Zoe doubted any automobile would dare to give her trouble. "Where do you park it?" she asked. "Paris is becoming crowded with the things."

"My studio's in an old stable," Karen answered, "so I keep it there, covered with a sheet so the dust from my work doesn't get on it. Sculpting's a messy business."

"Your Citroën is black, I seem to recall."

"Yes, and it shows every speck of dust or mud or piece of horse-shit I drive through, so not only do I have to dust my apartment, I have to dust my car, too. If you do buy an automobile, I suggest you pick a lighter color."

Zoe pretended disappointment. "I adore black because it's so elegant. And since the stable that used to occupy this space was gutted to make way for my little house, I'll probably wind up parking my car on the street."

Louise Packard warned against this. Despite her age and arthritic hands, she was a member of the automobile-owning elite. "I wouldn't do that if I were you. Before I rented a garage for my Renault, someone tore off one of its headlamps, and I still haven't managed to get it replaced. So not only will you buy a car, you'll need to buy or rent a garage for it, too." She started to say more but had to pause for a brief coughing fit in reaction to the ciga-rette smoke filling the air. Throwing a dirty look at the smokers in the room, which included almost everyone, she added, "Black may have its problems, but it's nothing compared to yellow. I can't imagine why I thought that would be a sensible color choice for a car."

Bobby barked a laugh. "Axle-deep in snow every winter and mud every spring!" Earlier he'd seemed rather bored with the con-versation, but the talk about color perked him up. "Mud doesn't look any better on black, Louise. I remember the condition a friend's car..." He stopped, flushed, then changed direction. "You'd be smarter to buy a mud-colored vehicle. And what do you need a car for, anyway, Zoe? You have that handsome Armenian cab driver at your beck and call."

Alarmed at the mention of Avak—how did Bobby know she

used him so often?—she studied the little Dadaist more carefully. With his freckled-face, blond hair, and slight build, he could have been a model for one of Botticelli's angels, but he was no angel; he was a bald-faced liar. Did that make him a murderer? If she'd suspected he'd played a part in Jewel's horrible death, she would...

She would what? Take her own vengeance? Zoe's mouth went dry, and it had nothing to do with the Gitane she was smoking.

Little Bobby *couldn't* be a murderer. Zoe had seen evil before, and it wasn't in him. There was every chance, though, that the person who'd ferried him around Mesnil-Théribus in the mysterious black car was the killer. Despite his flaws, Bobby wasn't dumb, and he had to be aware of this possibility, didn't he? If so, why hadn't he gone to the police? Why the many denials?

Maybe he was involved in a different crime, one that might cause his own head to wind up—literally, in France—on the chopping block.

Steering the conversation away from Avak, Zoe said, "A mud-colored car? That's an interesting idea. Do automobiles actually come in the color of mud? Does anyone know?"

"That would be gray, I suppose, or brown," answered Reynard Dibasse, looking handsome in his new face mask. "Whatever color you choose, I applaud your decision. With cars come freedom, eh? Freedom to go wherever you want, whenever you want. Who cares about color as long as it runs?"

They discussed the pros and cons of car ownership for a few more minutes, each speculating which make and color would work best for Zoe. Eventually the cigarette smoke thickened so much that poor Louise had another coughing attack. After Zoe fetched her a glass of water from the kitchen, she opened the sitting room window a crack and asked everyone to put out their cigarettes.

"I can hardly breathe in here myself," she complained, as a cold blast of air whistled through the room.

While Zoe was in the kitchen, the subject had veered away from automobiles to the ongoing mess in Germany. Louise's niece, Myra, lived there, having married a German just before the Great War erupted. In a letter to her aunt, Myra complained that given the punitive structure of the Treaty of Versailles, she couldn't get enough meat or even bread. Since she had four children, what were they supposed to dine on?

"They can eat dirt!" Dominique growled, adjusting her eye patch. "The girl should have known better than to marry a German."

"Why doesn't she come back to Paris?" Zoe wondered aloud, settling back into her seat. Thanks to the open window, the air was breathable again. "I seem to remember hearing that Myra's husband was killed in the war?"

"She remarried," Louise answered. "Another German."

Dominique snorted. "Then I have no sympathy."

Zoe still felt sorry for the young woman. Being a Southerner, she knew what it was like to be on the losing side in a war. The stories she'd grown up with were filled with horrific accounts of starvation and lost land. In Myra's defense, she said, "None of that is the children's fault. For them to be suffering for their parent's mistakes, it's…it's just not right."

At the break in her voice, everyone turned to stare, so she pulled herself together. "Anyway, you know what I mean. The politicians who drafted the Treaty of Versailles have a lot to answer for."

Zoe wasn't alone in her opinion. In what became known as the "War Guilt" clause of the Treaty, the Allies demanded that Germany not only formally accept blame for starting a war which killed millions, but to also pay thirty-one billion dollars in reparations to the injured countries. Some economists warned the treaty's terms were so harsh they would send the already limping German economy into a death spiral.

"Not that the Germans don't deserve it, but those people are near starvation," said Karen Wegner, who despite her prickly temperament, also felt sympathy for their former enemies. "Like Zoe said, reparations should never be so severe that children go hungry"

Louise, who wished only the best for her niece, agreed, but with a caveat. "The Germans seemed to have learned nothing. Myra wrote me that they've found themselves a new hero, some bullyboy named Hitler. He leads a group called the Bavarian Fascisti and blames all Germany's troubles on everyone but the Germans themselves. He especially blames us Jews." She paused and took a deep breath of the clean air. "Mark my words. If there's another war, that's where it'll start. In Bavaria. And it'll be started by rabble-rousers like him."

A frisson of fear marched up Zoe's spine. *Lee-Lee and her husband were headed to Bavaria.* Agnostic that she was, she nonetheless said a quick prayer for nothing awful to happen while Lee-Lee and Jack visited his grandparents.

Unaware of Zoe's unease, Reynard snorted. "Don't worry, Louise. If the Huns start another war, we'll whip them like we did last time." Already horribly maimed, he was ready to fight again.

But they resided in the Paris of 1922, not the Paris of 1916, and no one wanted to linger too long on wartime memories, so the conversation veered back to automobiles. Still, for the rest of the evening Zoe continued to worry not only about Lee-Lee but about Bobby's mention of Avak. Yes, the article in Sunday's *Le Figaro* hinted that the taxi driver had chauffeured Zoe to Mesnil-Théribus, but one trip hardly deserved the phrase "beck and call." Had Bobby seen Avak dropping her off more than once at Le Petit Bibelot?

··· ◇ ···

The next day happened to be December 14, so as Zoe had done every year since arriving in Paris, she crawled out of bed early and walked over to the tiny charcuterie on Boulevard Montparnasse, where she purchased the shop's specialty: a French Opera Cake. It was ridiculously expensive, but worth it. Four layers of almond sponge cake soaked in coffee, *crème fouettée* (also coffee-flavored) between the layers, and frosted with a wickedly rich coffee buttercream dappled with a chocolate ganache.

The day was clear, but as Zoe carried her purchase home, the sun's brightness only seemed to heighten the snowy gloom of the past two weeks. Mercy, Alabama, rarely saw a White Christmas, but there was every chance Paris was going to. Zoe hoped the snow would be fresh that day, unlike the ash gray and urine-yellow stuff that now lay piled against the curbs.

Unlike back in the States, Parisians made little fuss about Christmas. Every now and then a street singer would chirp a carol or two, and maybe a store might feature a crèche in its window, but that was all. The churches probably behaved differently, but other than for funerals, Zoe hadn't been to a church since she'd left Beech Glen. She never would again, either. Not after...

Well, not after.

A few minutes later, back in the snug comfort of Le Petit Bibelot, Zoe set the table for three. Then she sang her little birthday song and cut three small slices from the cake.

She wept as she ate.

Oh, Amber.

Chapter Seventeen

Zoe painted for the rest of the day in a frenzy to forget. Applying brush to canvas worked so well she awoke early the next day, and instead of a leisurely breakfast at La Rotonde, she nibbled a few leftovers. She then went back into the studio and painted without stopping until Madeline interrupted.

"I know you don't like to be bothered when you are working, but your friends will be arriving soon," the housekeeper said.

Zoe looked at her in shock. Madeline *never* interrupted when she was painting. "Why?"

"It's Poker Night, Mademoiselle, and almost seven. I am certain they will prefer you to smell of Madame Chanel's perfume instead of turpentine. Especially the marquis. You know how he is."

"I sure do," Zoe grumped, abashed that she'd forgotten such a financially important evening.

"Then I will run the water for you. By the way, you have paint on your nose. Blue."

"Cerulean."

"Yes. Blue."

··· ◇ ···

Bathed, and no longer smelling of turpentine, Zoe dressed in a lavender serge suit, made more feminine by its flounced sleeves and hem. She had just dabbed on perfume when there was a knock at the door. Dominique Garron, always the first to arrive. The others followed quickly, apparently in a hurry to lose their money.

But they were not barbarians.

The evening began with a brief moment of silence for Jewel and Sergei, but the players were a tough lot, and as soon as the francs anted up, the game began. Zoe didn't play well, and it was with relief that during a break, she made her announcement. After all the wonderful suggestions her friends had made during the Wednesday Salon about automobiles, she wondered if any of them might give her a test ride. After all, automobiles weren't just about color. Comfort mattered, too.

Her announcement worked. Dominique Garron, Archie Stafford-Smythe, and even the snooty marquis, invited her for rides in their cars. Dominique apologized for not volunteering two days earlier. "Don't know where my mind was," she said.

You were too busy hating the Germans, Zoe started to say; she stopped herself just in time.

Tripp Eiger was the only holdout, explaining that his almost-new car had mysteriously stopped running and was now being cared for in a machinist's garage. When Zoe inquired about his color choice, he said it was light green but that he'd been thinking about having it repainted a less troublesome silver.

Zoe accepted each offer.

But she wasn't stupid.

··· ◇ ···

On Saturday, a happily cloudless day, Madeline stood waiting at the curb with her bundled-up employer when Dominique Garron drove up in her black 1915 Ravel.

"Dominique's taking me for a little ride, but I'll back in time for lunch!" Zoe called to her housekeeper. Then to the war artist she explained, "She worries about me all the time, who I'm with and where I'm going."

"Sounds like a busybody," Dominique replied. "I used to have a housekeeper like that."

"Used to?"

"She quit on me. Said I was mean."

Zoe laughed. "Gee, I wonder why."

The Ravel was a strange vehicle, more suitable for transporting hay bales than navigating Paris's cobblestone streets. Zoe wasn't certain how she felt knowing that numerous German bullets remained embedded in its sides. The stiff seats weren't comfortable, either, and as they bumped along, her derriere felt every brick.

But Dominique loved the ungainly thing and told Zoe that before traveling to the Front to make her war sketches, she'd had the sides fitted with stout oak over the metal, believing that the thick planking would protect her from any stray bullets. To a certain extent, the oak performed as hoped. Dominique was still alive, although thanks to a German's lucky shot, she'd not finished the war uninjured. The loss of her eye affected her driving, and at the crossroads of Boulevard Raspail and Rue du Cherche-Midi, she nearly hit an elderly man who'd entered the crosswalk on her blind side.

Much squealing of brakes, much screaming and cursing.

As they drove away, Zoe, still playing dumb, said, "Well, this has been wonderful, but I think I understand now how an automobile works. Maybe you could show me the kind of parking facilities it needs. I'm thinking I could remove one of the exterior walls of my house and replace it with a garage door big enough to allow a vehicle's passage."

Dominique glanced over at her in horror. "You'd breach the

walls of Le Petit Bibelot for a lousy car? Jesus, Zoe, please tell me you were joking!"

"Just a passing thought," Zoe said, gratified to see her little house so admired.

After their near-accident, the demonstration drive continued without drama, and Zoe was able to ask Dominique a series of questions. No, Dominique had never been to Mesnil-Théribus. No, she'd never met the Popovs. Yes, she'd heard rumors Grand Duchess Anastasia might still be alive. No, she knew nothing about a group named *Vosstanovit Rodinu*, but, boy, weren't those Russians crazy?

Dominique lived at 29 Rue de Fleurus, next door to the building occupied by Gertrude Stein and Alice Toklas. Although the women occasionally saw one another entering or leaving, they weren't friends. Part of the problem was Gertrude's open dislike of women, which—given the writer's sexual proclivity—Zoe continued to find strange.

"I haven't heard anything about Gertrude recently. Have you?" Zoe asked, as Dominique steered her Ravel into the small garage in back of the building. The car came within a hair's width of hitting the door. "She still holding her salons?"

"Not likely. She and Alice are spending the winter in the south. Can't take these city winters."

"Such a loss for the artists and writers of Paris. The male ones, anyway."

Dominique laughed. "That Hemingway fellow is a handsome devil, though."

"Hmm."

The former stable housed several cars, most of them black, which made Zoe worry that the idea she'd thought brilliant, wasn't. Still, she continued acting her role of presumptive car buyer.

"Do you ever scrape against the other cars when you park in

here?" she asked, unnerved by their perilous entry. The stalls may have been roomy enough for horses, but they made a tight fit for automobiles.

"I'm always careful."

The scrapes alongside the car next Dominique's space hinted that the war artist's definition of "careful" was somewhat different than Zoe's.

"Well, this has all been very instructional," Zoe said, a few minutes later, as Dominique wiggled the Ravel back out of the garage.

"Promise to give me a ride when you buy your new car," Dominique said.

"Oh, I will, I will," Zoe lied. It would be a cold day in hell before she bought another of the darned things. Driving around Beech Glen had been a snap; in Paris, you risked your sanity, if not your life.

··· ◇ ···

Zoe's next outing arrived at noon. This time, the proud car owner was the Marquis Antoine Phillippe Fortier de Guise, who was gentleman enough to wave to Madeline as they drove away. He was eager to demonstrate the wonderfulness of his dark green auto, which on a cloudy day could be mistaken for black. The automobile was as different from Dominique's bullet-studded Ravel as a thoroughbred from a dray horse.

"The Hispano Suiza H6 is the prince of cars," Fortier bragged as they sped along a road on the city's outskirts, where trees whipped by with such rapidity they blended into one. "It has a straight-six, all-aluminum engine and a seven-bearing crankshaft. The brakes have a power-assist in all four wheels. This is the car I see you driving, Zoe! Something as classy as yourself."

Classy? Oh, if he only knew.

"What's a power-assist?" she yelled, the wind blowing away her words. "Does that mean it stops well?" She'd noticed Dominique's Ravel, as well as Avak's Grim Reaper, had appeared stopping-averse.

"On a dime! See?"

With that, Fortier hit the brakes. The car stopped, but Zoe wound up having an intimate encounter with the dashboard.

"Impressive," she said, feeling her nose. "Am I bleeding?"

"Oh, dear, I should have warned you. Here, take my handkerchief." He plucked a paisley-printed piece of silk from his vest pocket.

Delicately, Zoe dabbed away the blood. Pretending ignorance of Fortier's friendship with Mary Cassatt, she asked, "Have you ever been to Mesnil-Théribus? Cassatt lives there."

"I am happy to be one of Madame Cassatt's close friends, and she allows me a visit when she's feeling up to it. She and I think as one when it comes to this new age of painting."

As a one-time member of the Académie Française before it sank into art history, Fortier painted landscapes that were formulaic to a fault. While Expressionists such as Zoe could complete a canvas in a week (or three, depending on how self-critical they were), it took Fortier months to finish a single canvas. How he found the patience, she would never know, just as she would never understand how such a cultural throwback was so often welcomed at Gertrude's hoity-toity salon. Maybe it had something to do with all that *marquis* foolishness. Gertrude had always been a snob.

Forcing her mind back on track, Zoe asked, "While you were at Cassatt's, did you ever catch sight of the Russians? Their shack isn't far from her house." The trees were whipping by again, forcing them to resume yelling at each other, but this time Zoe had the foresight to brace her hands against the dash.

"Not that I know of," he yelled back. "No reason to, although Mesnil-Théribus is a nice enough little place. Come to think of it, there is a certain hill to the west of the village that might make a nice subject for me. Soft slope, a mixture of trees—oak, pine, beech—and possibly a pond. The critics love my reflections. Next time I'm at Cassatt's, I'll take a closer look."

Having liked Cassatt immensely, Zoe envied Fortier's friendship with the legend and had to admit that he made an intriguing companion. Handsome despite that long scar on his cheek, he'd fought bravely during the war, leading his men to glory through the awful carnage of Verdun. He was a daring man, so it was no wonder he found these wild drives in his Hispano Suiza a diversion.

But intriguing companions or not, she reminded herself to stay on point.

"Do you take photographs of your landscapes before you begin to paint?" she yelled. She wasn't really interested, but talking about painting was preferable to the visions of car crashes and mangled bodies that kept running through her head.

"Of course not. If you want the reality of a photograph, then go ahead and take one," he yelled back. "But if you want to create a thing of beauty, throw away the camera."

"Reality can't be beautiful?" She remembered the Alabama sunsets, the way the sky hung orange and purple over the horse pasture. The evening calls of whip-poor-wills. The magical glow of lightning bugs.

"Beauty is an ideal, never a reality," Fortier said.

His was a bleak philosophy, Zoe thought. Divested of magic.

An hour later, when the Hispano Suiza disgorged her in front of Le Petit Bibelot, she realized she'd learned nothing. At least she had only one more test-drive to endure, and that would be in Archie Stafford-Smythe's Bugatti Type 29/30. She gave Madeline more francs for waiting around, assuring her the next ride was the day's last, and then she could go home. Madeline being Madeline, she just smiled and added the money to her already bulging pocket.

Archie—never known for his punctuality—did not turn up at

two o'clock, as per agreement. By three, Zoe had begun to worry about the lessening light. Night fell quickly in Paris, and as the sun slipped behind the tall buildings, her anxiety increased. If he didn't arrive soon, the day would be lost. Having been scared half to death by a sunlit drive in Fortier's Hispano Suiza, she could only imagine how terrifying a nighttime drive in a Bugatti would be.

But Archie finally arrived at 3:16, and one look at his vehicle tempted Zoe to run back into the safety of Le Petit Bibelot. Not only was the big black thing outfitted like a race car, it had no windshield. Only the memory of Jewel's beautiful face made Zoe approach the Bugatti. Archie had named it Gwenny, after his mother Guinevere. Giving Zoe a sly smile, he said, "Now that your housekeeper has witnessed you leaving with me, will she be going home? Or will she await your return?" Archie had always been smarter than he acted.

"I can't imagine what you mean," she responded.

Snickering, he blew a kiss at Madeline, then handed Zoe a pair of goggles. He wore some himself, and although he was nice enough looking with his sandy hair and gray eyes, the goggles made him resemble a bug-eyed frog. Zoe knew they'd do the same for her, but she was past caring. She just wanted to remain alive long enough to bring justice to Jewel's killer.

"Maybe you could drive slowly?" she suggested. "Give me time to see how everything works?"

Archie's response was a yodeled laugh, and soon they were flying along the Champs-Élysées, terrifying horses and pedestrians alike. Once they'd shot through the Arc de Triomphe and onto the Avenue de la Grande-Armée, Archie sped up, rendering Fortier's pace turtle-like. Her plans to interview Archie about the Popovs and Mesnil-Théribus fell to nothing, because to speak in a windshield-less car was inviting a mouthful of bugs, winter or no.

Several hair-raising miles later, when buildings grew sparse and pastures large, Archie shouted something she couldn't quite make out, so she shrugged a reply. He found this satisfactory, and a few minutes later, they stopped at a roadside café. Maybe he was going to treat her to an early dinner?

Alas, only a fine bottle of Montrachet.

"Well, now you've seen how beautifully Gwenny handles," Archie said, finishing his first glass. "She has an inline eight-cylinder engine, and if you're concerned about her safety, she has amazing brakes with hydraulic drums! If you wish, I could get you a deal on one of her sisters. That's if you really are buying a car."

Zoe spit another bug out of her mouth. "I'm giving it serious thought."

As they sat on the café's heated patio, the Bugatti collected a crowd of admirers. Archie didn't mind. If anything, he appeared chuffed at his car's star turn. Archie had never been a subtle man, which was only one of the reasons his family had turned on him. Like many British ex-pats, he was homosexual, which in England remained a criminal offense. After a scandal involving a stable hand, whose nude form he claimed to have been only painting, Archie's father—the straitlaced Earl of Whittenden—ordered him out of the country. But Archie's mother, a distant cousin of King George V, made certain her exiled son remained flush, unlike many young men suffering the same fate.

Thus the Bugatti.

Now that they were no longer in the awful thing, Zoe found questioning Archie almost too easy.

"Mesnil-Théribus? Oh, certainly. I've driven through there many times. The road to it is a wonderful one, with lovely hills and beautiful greenery—one gets so tired of Paris's unremitting grays—but one much prefers the drive during better weather. The mud, you see. As for knowing the Popovs, I can't say I've had the pleasure, although from the sketch in Le Figaro, Monsieur Popov looked like an interesting man, handsome in that rough way so many Russian men are."

A sly smile crept over his face. "By the way, Zoe Eustacia Barlow, it is such a pleasure watching you give Sherlock Holmes a run for his money."

Caught off guard, she stammered, "Wha...? No, no, I'm not..."

"I want to be your Watson."

To Zoe's horror, Archie sounded serious. Recognizing that further playacting was a waste of time, she said, "I already have a Watson."

"The gorgeous Armenian, right? Such eyes! Such a mustache! Think he'd let me paint his portrait? I'd pay him, of course."

"I don't think he does any...ah...modeling." Moving away from the touchy subject of artists and their models, she remarked that the Sherlock Holmes mysteries were fiction, not real life. And her interest in the case lay only in the fact that the police were treating her as a suspect. As for today's outing, she wasn't playing detective, she was simply comparing automobiles and enjoying spending time with her friends. Allowing some truth among the bushwa, she admitted she was still grieving the loss of Jewel. And the count.

He nodded in sympathy. "All Paris knows how much you cared for her, but you are still a liar, dear girl. And you've lit my fire. The idea of being a detective appeals to me—I'm sure you've noticed that the brilliant Sherlock Holmes is British—so I'd love to give it a go. One can do that sort of thing solo, of course, but one would rather have brilliant *you* as a partner."

"Thanks for the flattery, but I think it's best we both stay away from the investigation. Four people have already been murdered, and I don't think an amateur can accomplish what the police have so far failed at. Sticking your nose into a murder investigation could be dangerous."

The note of amusement left his voice. "I don't mind danger, Zoe."

How foolish of her to forget. Like Marquis Antoine Fortier, Archie Stafford-Smythe had exhibited extraordinary bravery in the war. That's why Archie was missing the pinky finger on his left hand. It had been shot away during the Battle of Ypres when he charged a sniper's nest.

"Oh, Archie, please don't be foolish!"

A few days later, Zoe would regret not taking her own advice.

Chapter Eighteen

Sunday's church bells were summoning the faithful as Henri crawled out of Zoe's bed, dressed, and headed down her cobblestone walkway, his step lighter than when he'd arrived the night before. In contrast, Zoe's conscience weighed her down. She knew she had to do something about the situation—he was married, for God's sake!—but not today. Too many other problems occupied her mind. Jewel's death. Sergei's. The Popovs'.

Not to mention her sister's unfortunate marriage.

Compared to those woes, Ernest's lost manuscripts seemed minor indeed, but she still composed another telegram to Hadley.

FOUND MORE PAGES—STOP—HOPE EVERYTHING
FINE IN CHAMBRY—QUERY—HAS ERNEST
FORGIVEN YOU—STOP
ZOE

She summoned Dax and sent him off to the telegraph office, then made her way to La Rotonde for breakfast. The day was bright and clear, but Paris weather could turn in an instant, so she dressed in a green wool chemise with matching cloche, and a wraparound camel-hair coat. Her leather boots, the left one built up to steady her uneven gait, were among the more sensible pairs of footwear she owned, but the physical stress of the last few days still gnawed at her bad leg.

Since few of her friends were awake this early, she ate quickly, and glanced at The Lovers only once. They were in their usual corner, but today their chairs weren't as close as usual, and the elfin girl's red beret somehow looked deflated. A lover's spat? The light being dim in that corner, Zoe couldn't tell for sure, but their problems weren't her business, so she paid her check and left.

Back at Le Petit Bibelot, she slipped off her amber ring and changed into her painting clothes. She lost herself in work on *Gluttony*, painting until noon, when Madeline lured her to the table to lunch on *Poulet aux Herbes*. The moist chicken tasted superb, and while Zoe was stuffing herself, a *pneumatique* arrived from Karen Wegner. Another copper mask was ready to be matched to its wearer at the Studio for Portrait Masks, so she threw her coat over her smock and headed for the Métro.

··· ◇ ···

Today's subject, Claude Pelletier, was in worse shape than even Reynard Dibasse had been, having lost most of the center of his face, a not-uncommon injury in trench warfare. When the order came to go over the top, the soldiers obeyed, and their faces paid the cost of their courage. Karen Wegner had already warned Zoe that Claude couldn't talk, so as she painted, using as her model an old photograph he'd brought in, she kept her conversation to a frothy monologue about automobiles and the worsening Parisian traffic. Every now and then he grunted, incapable of anything else. But she had noticed his eyes light up when she talked about the autos, so she delivered a long monologue comparing the motor size of a Hispano Suiza to a Bugatti. She didn't know what the hell she was talking about, but he appeared to enjoy her nonsense anyway. When she finally placed the painted copper mask on his face—both of his eyes remained miraculously undamaged—Claude was at first frightened of the mirror. Since the war, he'd learned to avoid them.

"It's all right, Claude," she soothed. "I promise you will be...will be..." She struggled for the right word and found herself quoting one of Ernest's scribbles. "I promise you will be pretty."

He straightened his back and looked into the mirror.

The sound he made was a note-song of pure joy.

··· ◊ ···

Once back at home, Zoe pulled a chair up to her escritoire and spent the next two hours writing down everything she'd learned so far. The truths, the lies, and the names of those who owned a dark car like one seen in Mesnil-Théribus the day of the murders. More importantly, she included which of her acquaintances enjoyed at least a passing knowledge of Mesnil-Théribus.

All this made her feel treacherous, but after what happened to Jewel, she didn't care.

Once finished, Zoe summoned Dax again and told him to deliver the material straight to Henri's office at the Sûreté.

She then walked down to the Dôme, where by prearrangement she met with Romaine Brooks and Djuna Barnes to discuss the plans for Sunday's Trousers March. Two privately hired omnibuses would pick up a few dozen female artists, dancers, and writers at the café, then drive them to the Place de la Concorde. There they would debark, link arms, and begin their trousered march down the Champs-Élysées toward the Arc de Triomphe. Details finalized, they stood, clinked their wineglasses together, and shouted, "*Vive les pantalons!*"

The elderly waiter nearest them scowled.

The women blew him kisses.

They knew the march would not be popular, and they would almost certainly get arrested before reaching the Arc, but they didn't care. Like Martin Luther, they would nail their demands to the door, and damned be anyone who didn't like it! Their high spirits kept them drinking for another two hours. When Zoe finally left for home, it was on unsteady legs having nothing to do with her childhood accident.

There was little traffic on Boulevard Montparnasse on a Sunday evening, and even less on Rue Vavin. Although she stumbled badly crossing the intersection, there were no witnesses to her humiliation. No witnesses, either, as she made her unsteady way up the shadowed cobblestone path leading to her little house.

And no witnesses as the door burst open and a burly man Zoe had never seen before rushed out holding something over his head. Startled and half-drunk, she fell to her knees just as whatever the man was holding—a cane? a sword?—passed above her head with a loud *whooosh*. Her purse fell to the ground.

He hissed, "You should mind your own business!"

As he raised the club to strike at her again, she struggled to get to her purse. It contained her rat-tailed comb, but she couldn't reach it. Desperate, she then lunged forward and bit his wrist. She'd always had strong teeth.

"*Putain!*" he shrieked. *Whore.*

She gnawed on his wrist as if it were a barbecued short rib, and when the salty taste of dirty skin turned liquid, knew she'd drawn blood. He tried to shake her off, but she wouldn't let go, knowing if she did, he'd have room enough to swing the club down at her head again. As he pummeled her head with his other fist, the sound of their struggles—his grunts, her yelps—finally attracted attention.

"You can't do that in public!" cried an outraged passerby. "This is a nice neighborhood! If you want to have outdoor sex, move to Pigalle."

Zoe quit gnawing on her attacker's wrist and screamed for help.

Startled, the passerby joined his screams to hers, and the gendarme stationed at the end of the long block came running. As his footsteps approached, Zoe's attacker fled, leaving her purse on the ground. Within moments, the gendarme and the passerby, a nicely dressed elderly gentleman, were helping her into the house.

Which is when they found the true victims of the attack: Zoe's paintings.

Each one had been slashed to ribbons and their stretchers splintered. The paintings named after the Seven Heavenly Virtues—*Prudence, Temperance, Courage, Faith, Hope, Charity,* and *Justice*—were no more. The same with *Greed, Lust,* and *Envy,* the Three Deadly Sins she'd already finished. Even the unfinished *Gluttony* had been slashed into unrecognizability, and it dangled in shreds from the easel. As if this wasn't horror enough, squashed tubes of oil paint vomited multicolored squiggles on the beautiful oak floor, their vivid hues rendered almost pastel under great splashes of turpentine and linseed oil.

"I am sorry, Madame," said the gendarme, a young man who looked barely out of his teens.

"Mademoiselle," Zoe corrected absently, surveying the slaughter.

The elderly gentleman whose sense of decency had been offended by what he'd interpreted as a public sexual encounter appeared less sympathetic. With horror, he eyed *Lust's* blazing red penis and muttered, "Disgraceful." Still, he was not without sympathy for the unhappy artist and assured her everything could be replaced. "If you wish to do so, that is," he added, patting her on the shoulder. "But flowers, irises and sunflowers and the like, are more suitable subjects for young ladies."

"Thank you," Zoe said, meaning it. She was so miserable even his semi-sympathy felt welcome.

"There's a brave girl! Now let me take a look at your hand."

Her inadvertent rescuer turned out to be Dr. Marcel Molyneux, a retired surgeon who lived in the apartment building across the alleyway, thus his concern for the neighborhood's reputation. His sharp eyes had noticed something Zoe hadn't; she'd been injured in the attack. A large red welt lay across the back of her hand, and as he prodded, she winced.

"Hurts?"

"Not that much." She'd probably received the blow while defending her skull.

"Nothing broken, just bruised. And these burns—they look about a week old—they are healing nicely. Did you burn yourself on the stove?"

"Something like that."

He frowned. "Then you must learn to be more careful while cooking, Mademoiselle. Perhaps also in your choice of friends."

Zoe saw genuine concern in his eyes. "No friend did this to me."

"Perhaps not. Then again, evil can hide behind a smile." With a final pat, her neighbor left.

After taking down her statement and delivering a warning about unreliable locks, the young gendarme exited too, leaving Zoe alone.

The first thing she did was run into her boudoir to check her cloisonné jewelry box. It lay on the floor empty. The sight almost made her weep, but not for the diamonds, which could be replaced. What hurt was that she'd lost her amber ring, the amber ring that always reminded her of...

Don't think about that, Zoe!

Gritting her teeth against the memory, she went to see if Ernest's scorched pages remained in the wardrobe. They did. Not even the thief wanted them.

—— Gabrielle ——

October 1922
Paris

My husband loves me, but I am not a fool and cannot pretend he has been faithful all these months—years?—I've lain here. My fear is that someday he will find a woman who will take him away from me.

Madame Gabrielle underestimates her power, Odile answers, creeping onto my pillow to ease my sight of her. *For him, there will never be another.*

You do not know men, bonne amie. *Even the best of them roam.*

One of her little legs caresses my ear. So sweet. I am so lucky have such a tender friend, even though from time to time I wonder if she might eat me. Oh, the price we women pay for friendship!

We Huntsman spiders do not let our husbands walk away, Odile says. *Besides, they are crunchy.*

I pretend shock. *Oh, Odile, if you were human, you would be guillotined for such an act!*

Then it is good I have eight legs and can scamper fast, eh?

Suddenly my lips feel strange. Why?

You smiled, Madame, which means you grow stronger.

No, that is impossible. I heard the doctors say so. I will never speak again. Or walk.

Odile does not accept this. *Your doctor is human, is he not? And a man.*

Most doctors are, I tell my little friend.

Then he is most certainly wrong.

Chapter Nineteen

—— Zoe ——

Just before midnight, while Zoe was still doing what she could to clean up the mess, a caller came knocking at her door. Refusing to be victimized again, she snatched up her goosenecked palette knife and headed for the bathroom, where she kept a more lethal weapon. The door crashed open before she reached it. Just as she raised her arm to strike, she recognized the intruder.

"Nice palette knife," Henri observed. "Pack some clothes. You're not staying here tonight."

"I almost stabbed you, fool."

A twisty smile. "Then my associates would have introduced you to Madame Guillotine."

Zoe snorted but put the palette knife down on the entryway table. "I'm not going anywhere tonight. Too much to do."

Henri's smile vanished. "Come quietly or I'll drag you out."

Not much liking the image of Henri dragging her down the Rue Vavin—probably by the hair, like a caveman—she obeyed. Seconds later, they were in his green Citroën, headed for God knew where. A hotel? A lunatic asylum?

"Kidnapping is against the law," she pointed out.

"Shut up and let me drive."

Given the late hour, there was little traffic on the streets, so Henri never once slowed down enough for her to jump out of the car without hurting herself. The drive seemed to take forever as they motored along in hostile silence, but he finally braked in front of a regal building in the seventeenth arrondissement. Outside the Citroën's window, she could see the silhouette of the Eiffel Tower several blocks south.

"Lovely view," she grumped, as he parked at the curb and leaned a SÛRETÉ placard against the car's windshield.

"My wife always enjoyed it."

Enjoyed, past tense. "What...?"

"This way," he said, hauling her out of the car.

She'd probably have bruises up and down her arm tomorrow to join the other bruises she'd contracted during the struggle with her attacker, but which was the more dangerous? A thief, or a man who demanded to do her thinking for her?

The building—possibly a former hotel for monied guests—had an elevator, and after they'd passed through a spiffy entryway guarded by a sleepy concierge, Henri shoved her toward it.

"Henri, I really don't want to..."

"Please shut up, Zoe."

Well, at least he'd said *please*.

Once Henri shut the elevator's filigreed iron doors behind them, she did shut up. What was one night? Tomorrow morning, Zoe would slip out before he woke, take the Métro home, and finish cleaning up her studio. Henri wasn't the boss of her.

The elevator rose and rose, and it didn't stop until they reached the sixth floor.

"Get out," Henri commanded, finally releasing her. "Just be quiet. I don't want you waking anyone."

She took a deep breath and stepped into the entryway of a

handsomely decorated apartment no inspector with the Sûreté could possibly afford.

His wife's money? Or treasures from a lifetime of thieving from the very populace he was supposed to be protecting? That settee, for instance. It could have cushioned Louis XVI's fat ass before the mobs came for him. And the escritoire? Possibly where the soon-to-be-decapitated king had written his apology for dining on caviar while his people had no bread.

"Finished gawking?" Henri asked. "Hope you like it, because you're spending the night here. Tomorrow we're getting your doors and windows fitted with the proper locks. Don't worry about your virtue. If—after your shock—you're not feeling amorous, I'll sleep on the sofa. We'll talk tomorrow."

Well, that was all fine and dandy, but what about his wife? Did the poor woman have no voice as to whomever or whatever her husband dragged home in the middle of the night? Or was she, like Fortier's estranged wife, living the high life in the south of France?

It was such a French thing to do.

Too exhausted to protest anymore, Zoe allowed Henri to lead her to a small bedroom so bare it could have been a monk's cell.

That night she slept on sheets that smelled like him.

Chapter Twenty

When Zoe exited the Henri-scented bedroom the next morning, she found him already up, talking to a gray-haired woman in her fifties he introduced as Madame Arceneau. His purported wife was still nowhere in evidence. Definitely gone. Maybe in the south of France, drinking Beaujolais with Marquis Fortier's estranged spouse.

"Lovely to meet you, Madame Arceneau, and many thanks for the hospitality, but I need to be going. Lots to do. Cleaning and such." Zoe made a beeline for the table where her purse rested. Now if she could only find her coat...

"Have breakfast first," Henri said. "You're going to need it." He looked like he'd spent a rough night.

"I prefer to breakfast with my friends," she sniped. "Not bullies."

Madame Arceneau made a sound somewhere between a snort and a chuckle, then exited the room. From the aroma of something wonderful, Zoe surmised she'd gone into the kitchen. Well, maybe just a few bites...

Cursing her empty stomach's betrayal, she sat down on the Louis XVI settee—God, was it comfortable!—and folded her arms. She'd eat, but damned if she'd chat.

Not that it mattered, because Henri did all the talking. "Before we eat, Zoe, there are a few things I must say. You want to return to the place where you were attacked and almost killed. Not the most intelligent decision you could make when you could remain here in perfect safety, is it?" He didn't wait for an answer. "As soon as we eat, I'll drive you home, but I'll stay with you while your windows and doors are attended to. I've already contacted one of the most trusted locksmiths in Paris."

He was having her locks changed? Without her approval? She fumed in silence.

"Apparently, I also need to remind you that Paris is not your pretty Beech Glen. You can't keep wandering around alone at night half-drunk. Now, shall we have a seat and enjoy our breakfast like civilized human beings?" He motioned to an ornate table that predated the Revolution. It was set for breakfast.

As she rose from the settee, the door opened and Madame Arceneau emerged, rolling a cart heaped with dishes. Scrambled eggs speckled with caviar. A selection of cheeses. Croissants and baguettes. A coffee carafe. A small pitcher of warm milk.

"Eating will make Mademoiselle feel better," Madame Arceneau said, using the same soothing tone Zoe used while feeding the feral cats hanging around the back of Le Petit Bibelot.

Zoe forced a smile. Henri might be a jerk, but she needn't be rude to his housekeeper. "It looks wonderful," she said, trying not to drool.

The years of training in social niceties at Beech Glen stood her in good stead, and she was able to eat politely enough not to be thought crude. It was difficult, though. Her self-control made her hyperaware, and as she ate, she noticed Madame Arceneau traveling back and forth from the kitchen into another room. From its double doors—they were almost as elegant as those at the count's apartment—she surmised they led to the master suite.

Sometimes Arceneau carried what appeared to be hot broth. Other times, linens.

Zoe's curiosity overcame her vow of silence. "What's she doing?"

Henri sat back, a grim expression on his face. "I'll answer your questions, but first finish your breakfast. There's bad news coming."

"If you're talking about my paintings, I already know..."

A sidelong look. "I'm not talking about your precious paintings. Now eat."

In reaction to his somber tone, she obeyed, but the food lost its savor.

Neither of them said anything else until they finished their breakfast, whereupon Madame Arceneau removed their plates and Henri bade Zoe return with him to the settee.

"Prepare yourself, Zoe," he said.

Jewel was dead, Hadley was in trouble with her husband, and Zoe's studio had been destroyed. What could be worse? Had the damned War to End All Wars started up again while Lee-Lee was in Germany surrounded by starving, murderous Germans?

Steeling herself, she said, "Tell me and get it over with."

Compassion replaced the sternness in Henri's blue eyes. "Yesterday evening before the call came to go to your place, your good friend Bobby Crites was found shot to death. He was killed by the same gun that killed Count Aronoffsky, Jewel Johnson, and the Russians at Mesnil-Théribus."

Bobby? Baby-faced little Bobby, with his silly Dadaist installations he called Art? Impossible! But the grim expression on Henri's face convinced her, and for a moment, the world seemed so ugly she couldn't look at it anymore. She closed her eyes and retreated into the dark.

"Zoe, are you all right?"

The only sound she could make was a hiccup of grief.

"I'm sorry, but you see, this is why I couldn't let you remain in your house last night. Too dangerous. And your locks... Hell, Zoe, they couldn't keep out a mouse." He put a comforting hand on hers.

She didn't pull away. With the world crashing around her, his hand felt like a lifeline.

"Regardless of the new locks, you would be much safer staying here with us until we find the culprit."

"Us? You mean Madame Arceneau lives here, too?"

"Madame Arceneau lives elsewhere."

"I don't understand. I know you're married, but..."

"I'm going to introduce you to my wife now, and then you'll understand."

For a moment, Zoe was shocked out of her grief. "You mean you want me to meet her? If so, you've lost your mind!"

"I won't argue that. These last few years have been hard on me, Zoe. The war, now this."

"This? I don't understand."

"Come." Without another word, he rose and led her toward the double doors, which opened into the most extraordinary room Zoe had ever seen.

She once visited Marie Antoinette's queenly bower on a tour through the Palace of Versailles, but it was nothing compared to what lay before her now. This was no stagnant, dust-covered monument to a dead queen; it vibrated with life. Plants of infinite variety reared up side by side throughout the entire room, creating a fairy-tale forest, their miraculous winter growth made possible by the warmth of the delft-tiled stove in the corner. Watercolor renderings of various plants decorated the walls, each executed by an expert hand. They reminded Zoe of Audubon's work, but instead of birds, these centered on the plants themselves and in several instances, the insects that lived on them. Her eyes were drawn to a watercolor of a long-leafed grass where an almost-invisible green spider made its home. The detail on the tiny spider showed not only brilliance, but infinite patience. Zoe could even see the creature's eyes; they were staring right at her.

Yet all this beauty was nothing compared to the beauty of the woman asleep in the four-poster bed.

"Gabrielle," Henri said, in a voice that resembled a prayer. "My wife."

The woman lay on her back, her red hair flung across the satin pillow like tongues of flame. Her creamy skin, the same color as the pillow, was flawless, as were her patrician features and rose-lipped mouth.

Henri's face was that of a man graveside. His ruddy color was gone, his eyes hollow. "Two years ago she fell while walking across a field in Normandy. She hasn't spoken or moved since."

Zoe had heard of things like this, a seemingly healthy person suddenly struck down. Her father, a doctor, said it was caused by blood vessels bursting in the brain. Sometimes the patients recovered, sometimes they didn't.

"She's never regained consciousness?" Zoe asked, her heart full of sorrow for this woman, this man.

"Every now and then, she opens her eyes, but the woman I loved—and continue to love—isn't there anymore." He cleared his throat. "When she was still with me, she was a botanist, and whenever I had the time, I helped with her work. We spent marvelous days in the fields and forests collecting rare specimens. That's what we were doing when…when it happened. And since she can't travel to her beloved plants anymore, I bring them to her. Just in case."

"Just in case," Zoe whispered.

Oh, what hell.

· · · ◇ · · ·

Henri was as good as his word. Once he delivered Zoe back to Le Petit Bibelot, he stayed with her until the locksmith arrived, a chubby, white-bearded man who could have passed for a French version of Santa Claus, but who spoke with a thick Italian accent. He introduced himself as Marco. While Henri gave him detailed instructions as to which locks should be replaced, Zoe put aside her grief over Bobby, shrugged on her painter's smock, and went into her studio to see if anything could be saved.

Nothing, as it turned out.

Lust, Envy, and *Gluttony* were beyond salvation. The attacker hadn't even spared the thick roll of unstretched canvas in the corner, cutting deeply into it with a knife. As she surveyed the damage, she had to listen to Henri's ongoing lecture about the foolishness of amateurs involving themselves in police business. He only stopped when a uniformed gendarme came by. After a whispered consultation with him, Henri left with a deep frown on his face, leaving Zoe in the ruination of her studio. As she surveyed the carnage, she decided of all the damage, she grieved the loss of *Lust* the most.

Lust, the sin. Lust, the comforter.

Was she being punished? If so, why?

Nothing she'd done had hurt Gabrielle. If a wife could no longer perform what Zoe's stepmother termed "wifely duties," it wasn't really adultery when a husband sought comfort elsewhere. So where was the sin? Henri hadn't taken holy orders, and neither had Zoe. Preacher Sorensen, at Mercy, Alabama's Baptist Church, claimed adultery was the worst thing a person could do. Worse, even, than murder. In fact, the Reverend preached against the wickedness of adultery so often and so loudly, the deacons eventually replaced him with a less frank preacher. Since Zoe hadn't been a believer even then, why should she have to follow the old goat's rules? Especially since there were so many good arguments to the contrary.

Horace, the Roman poet, had written *Carpe diem*—Seize the

day—and it made sense in a time when most people didn't live beyond thirty.

Horace had been seconded sixteen centuries later by Robert Herrick, the poet who'd written...

Gather ye rose-buds while ye may,
Old Time is still a-flying;
And this same flower that smiles today
Tomorrow will be dying...

They didn't live long in the seventeenth century, either. Not with the Black Death slithering around. Affairs—whether out of love or only need—made sense then. And in modern times, with the Great War and the Spanish flu, there was no guarantee the future would get any better. Young, old, saint, sinner, they were all cannon fodder, so why not pick a few rosebuds before that shit Death showed up?

Neither she nor Henri were hurting anyone, especially not a woman who would probably never regain consciousness.

So why did Zoe feel guilty?

· · · ◇ · · ·

By the time Madeline arrived to prepare lunch, the house and studio were tidy, if not whole, and much of the stench had been eased by throwing open all the windows, an extreme thing to do in mid-December. After Madeline finished bemoaning the studio's destruction, she said, "*Mon Dieu,* your pretty jewelry! Did the thief take it?"

Everything was gone, Zoe told her. The diamond necklace, the emerald bracelet, two sets of diamond ear studs, and even the amber ring her father had given her mere months before his death. The amber ring that reminded her of... Well, Madeline didn't need to know.

"I'm so sorry, Zoe," Madeline said, unaware she'd just used her employer's name for the first time. "So very sorry."

The thief hadn't bothered to damage the painting she'd bought from Bobby's cousin Abelard—the surrealist picture of a little girl standing alone in front of a Greek temple. Zoe had hung it on the wall facing her bed, which, considering her past, probably hadn't been wise. Yet, amidst the surrounding chaos, that one painting remained untouched.

Why?

Then Zoe had another unsettling thought. Leaving Madeline to search the boudoir for any dropped trinkets, she made her way to the bathroom and quietly closed the door. On a small enameled table next to the bidet sat a gilt-filigreed rosewood box that held the necessary feminine products. The lid was off, revealing the cloth pads and the strips of soft rice paper—so useful—but nothing inside the box had been touched. The thief had probably recoiled in horror at this evidence of female biology. Not being as delicate as her attacker, Zoe plunged her hand into the box, scrabbling through the pads and rice papers to the bottom, where her hand closed around cold steel.

Her pearl-handled Remington Derringer .41 was still there.

$$\cdots \diamond \cdots$$

While Zoe was finishing up a shopping list to take to the art supply store, Henri returned. "Can you identify this?" he asked, opening his palm.

Her amber ring glowed up at her.

"You caught the thief then!" she cried, snatching up the ring and slipping it on to her finger before he could protest.

He didn't mind. "Only in a manner of speaking. We found his body in an alleyway off Rue de Vaugirard. His name was Leonard Napier, a thief known to us for many years. He was shot to death sometime last night."

She felt a brief note of mourning at this news of one less soul in the world, but little more. The thief had destroyed nine paintings, injured her hand, and her head was still sore from his blows. Then she remembered the unharmed painting still hanging in her boudoir: the painting of a child standing alone among Grecian ruins.

"This Napier fellow. Did he have family?"

Henri gave her a curious look. "A wife and child."

"How old is the child?"

"Four, I think. A girl. But what's that got to do with anything?"

It has everything to do with compassion, she thought. But she merely said, "Poor man. I'll pray for him." Not that the prayers of an unbeliever would count for much. Maybe she'd send his widow some money. For the child.

Henri shrugged. "We also found two sets of diamond ear studs, a necklace, and a bracelet stuffed into his pocket, but I was able to sneak this away before your other jewels were impounded for evidence. I've seen you wearing the ring before and knew how much it meant to you."

For a brief moment, Zoe envisioned a bed surrounded by an indoor garden. "You're a kind man, Henri."

Misconstruing her meaning, he continued, "Napier was no art critic. There was no reason for him to destroy your work except to send you a message. Taking your jewelry was only coincidental to his main purpose. But there's something else you might find interesting. Before today's discovery, I'd already contacted Professor Balthazard of the Sorbonne—he's worked with us before—to determine if the bullets fired into the count and your friend Jewel matched those fired into the man and woman in Mesnil-Théribus. The professor said they did. Once the bullet is dug out of Napier—and out of your friend Bobby Crites—I'll ask for the professor's assistance again. But, having seen those wounds, I'm already certain there'll be a match."

"You think the same person who killed them hired Napier to scare me? Then executed him in order to keep his mouth shut?"

The tenderness in Henri's face disappeared, replaced by irritation. "Zoe, you're an intelligent woman, but not a wise one. Yes, that is what my superiors and I believe, but don't let that give you any ideas. Give up this amateurish business of searching for your friends' killer and leave it to the experts."

She refused to let him get by with this. "Experts? If it hadn't been for the help of Béatrice Camondo—which I requested, if you remember—the innocent Avak Grigoryan would still be sitting in a cell."

Henri wouldn't meet her eyes. "Even the Sûreté is not perfect."

$$\cdots \diamond \cdots$$

After Henri left, Zoe decided it was time to quit grieving over her lost work and do something about it. Unlike human beings, paintings could be resurrected, so she bundled up against the cold, picked up a roomy string bag, and headed through yet another snowfall to replenish her art supplies.

Traffic on the boulevards was slim, almost as if people had given up trying to make their way around. La Rotonde was crowded, though, with artists, poets, and writers sitting in the café's golden light, discussing Art with a capital A. As she passed, she saw Kiki, reunited with Man Ray, snuggling in his arms as they drank from the same wineglass. At another table, Karen Wegner, Reynard, and Archie laughed uproariously over some joke. Zoe wanted to sit down with them and drink and drink until she forgot about her dead friends, but resolute, she turned her face away from the café and kept on walking.

A few minutes later she reached Adam et Fil, one of the biggest art supply stores in Paris, where she was on a first-name basis with the clerks. The smell hit her as she walked through the door.

It would have been offensive to most people, but to an artist it was the scent of Heaven itself. The deep vibrancy of linseed oil. The sharper notes of turpentine. The earthiness of sable-haired brushes. And the colors! The walls were lined with glass-fronted cabinets featuring the minerals artists could grind themselves to make their own pigments. Malachite for the greens, hematite for the warm browns, burned carbon for black, calcite for white. A walk through the aisles was a walk through a garden of possibilities.

But grinding pigments was a dangerous, many-stepped mess that involved eggs and various oils, and every now and then, a careless artist was accidentally poisoned by the noxious fumes. To avoid such a fate, Zoe headed straight for the ready-made tubes and loaded up.

She tried her best to duplicate everything she'd lost, including her favorite palette knife, which the thief had broken in half. She'd valued that knife because of its peculiar shape—a stout wooden handle that hosted a flat, triangular-shaped metal "mixer" at its end. No matter how frenzied she became while working, it had stood up to her. Unfortunately, not to the thief.

While Zoe was in the canvas section comparing different textures, the store's door opened again and a wave of cold air chased filaments of dust along the aisle. When it shut, she heard a familiar voice asking the clerk where the poppy oil could be found.

Louise Packard.

Adding the tube of Payne's gray she'd been holding to her sales basket, Zoe rushed toward the counter. She and Louise could shop together, and she wouldn't feel so alone. Besides, Louise knew more about binders and extenders than Zoe, and her advice would be helpful. She'd thought about trying poppy oil, too. But when she reached the counter, she saw her friend's face was ravaged with grief. There were no tears, though, just a rigidity that wouldn't fool anyone who knew her.

Louise was grieving Bobby. Moved, Zoe set her basket on the counter and encircled the frail old artist in her arms. "I'm so sorry," she whispered.

Louise was trembling, but she didn't break down. "I'm painting him," she said.

Zoe nodded. "That's good."

"I don't know if it'll be Cubist or not. I just want to get his beautiful eyes right."

"You will."

"He was the same age my son was when *he* died. Did you know that?"

Zoe didn't.

"Too young. Too young," Louise said. She pulled away from Zoe and turned to the clerk again. "So where's the damned poppy oil?"

··· ◇ ···

As soon as Louise left, Zoe finished shopping. Once she'd checked off everything on her list, the sales clerk promised to have the supplies she couldn't carry delivered first thing in the morning, as long as it had stopped snowing by then. His promise came as a relief. Much of the relief vanished when he added up the bill.

One of the reasons artists were poor was because their materials were so expensive. In these modern times, most painters no longer ground their own colors and instead bought their paint in tubes. But the cost of even one small tube could buy several meals, if one's palate wasn't fussy, and it had taken twelve large tubes for Zoe to replace her hoard. She'd also needed new containers of gesso, turpentine, and linseed oil—she'd decided to put off purchasing the poppy oil—not to mention another roll of canvas, a stack of stretchers, and a new sketchbook, along with charcoal, pencils, conté crayons, and erasers. Thank God the thief hadn't thought to ruin her sable-hair brushes, or there would have been another couple hundred francs added to an already painful bill.

The amount was so large that on her way home she had a selfish thought. With Sergei dead, an assured stream of income had died with him, therefore she needed to do something she'd always avoided: economize.

But how?

One obvious economy was to drink less or, when she did drink, choose cheaper wine. Buying fewer haute couture dresses would also help. She could also rent out Le Petit Bibelot to a far richer American than she and move to a cheap atelier. However, the thought of sharing a toilet and washbasin with other tenants filled Zoe with horror. Why, she'd be living no better than poor Hadley! Even if she did initiate all those economies, it wouldn't be enough. The only other cutback she could think of was to let Madeline go and learn how to cook and clean for herself.

This was a definite no.

Not because Zoe was lazy; she wasn't. But Madeline was the sole support for her mother and aunt. The three women shared a tiny, one-bedroom apartment—Zoe had visited them more than once—and without the extra income she provided, they'd have to move to an even smaller place, possibly in the much-loathed slaughterhouse district of La Villette, where it was whispered some émigrés were living in buildings half-leveled by German bombs. The very idea that Madeline could wind up living like...

Zoe froze.

La Villette.

Of course! La Villette was the kind of neighborhood where a railway porter like Vassily Popov might bunk down for the night when too exhausted for a fifty-mile commute to Mesnil-Théribus. And where there was a chance—however slim—he'd stashed Ernest's valise.

Chapter Twenty-One

Deciding it was time to have another talk with Oleg, Popov's friend at the Gare de Lyon, Zoe reversed direction and headed for the nearest Métro station. The ride was a short one, and as she entered the train station's Departure Hall, she crossed her fingers in hopes Gaston—the station's head porter—was on duty. He spoke Russian; she didn't.

Zoe's finger-crossing must have worked, because she immediately found Gaston on Platform Four, delivering a dressing-down to a glum Oleg. When Gaston caught sight of her, he switched from Russian to French.

"Ah, the lovely Mademoiselle Barlow! What can I do for you today?"

Oleg began to sidle away, but Gaston called him back, the dressing-down not finished.

Raising her voice so she could be heard over the huff and screech of a departing train, Zoe replied, "I'm looking for more information about Vassily Popov."

Gaston's face fell. "We've had word he's dead, along with his daughter. And that their bodies were discovered by an American woman. Was that you, Mademoiselle?"

Zoe nodded. To forestall more questions, she said, "I'm sure they died quickly."

At this, an elegantly attired couple who'd been rushing toward one of the trains stopped and gawked.

Ignoring them, Gaston continued, "I am sorry you had to see such a thing, Mademoiselle. To have it happen in such a nice village, sin upon sin! More and more I begin to wonder why the world must be like this, country against country, men against men." Here, he lifted his shoulders in that uniquely Gallic shrug which meant, *Only le bon Dieu—and maybe not even Him—knows why men do the things they do.*

Agreeing the world was an unkind place, Zoe said, "Since we last met, I've done some thinking. You told me Monsieur Popov lived in Mesnil-Théribus, and that was correct. However, the village is quite distant from here. Could there be a place nearby where he stayed in inclement weather? Perhaps you would be so kind as to ask Monsieur Oleg if he knows of such a place. Although I've found a portion of Mr. Hemingway's papers, most of them—including the valise—remain missing."

Zoe dipped into her purse and emerged with a brand new five-franc note. When she waved it at the Russian, he bared his teeth in what was meant to be a smile.

The elegantly dressed couple moved closer, unwilling to miss the next installment. Murders! Bribes!

Gaston ignored them. "I do not have to translate, Mademoiselle Barlow, because Popov once told me of a little hidey-hole within easy travel from this station. It wasn't as cozy as his family cottage in Mesnil-Théribus, you understand, but adequate to keep him warm and dry."

Gaston's reference to that pitiful shack as Popov's "family

cottage," proved he had never seen it. "We do what we must, don't we?" she said rhetorically, handing him the five-franc note. "Now, if you could just give me his address, I would appreciate it."

A big smile. "Popov slept in the damaged building at 72 Rue Dafitte in La Villette. Are you familiar with the area?"

"Unfortunately, yes," Zoe replied.

"Then you know that if you must go, do not go alone."

The talk of murder having degenerated into a less exciting matter of addresses, the gawking couple moved on.

··· ◊ ···

Zoe awoke the next morning to discover more snow had fallen during the night. Work gangs were already shoveling off the major thoroughfares, so she decided to go ahead with her plans to visit Popov's hidey-hole in La Villette. She knew better than to wear anything that might mark her as a likely robbery victim, so after breakfasting on a croissant and some dried fruit, she rummaged through her box of old clothes—so useful for deep-cleaning sable brushes—and found a faded cotton dress with most of the seams still intact. Even better, she came across a moth-eaten wool over-coat which could have hung from one of Beech Glen's scarecrows. It was warm, she remembered, and had a roomy pocket for her Derringer, the perfect accessory for La Villette.

She was getting ready to head out when she heard a knock at the door. Although she doubted thieves knocked, she didn't open the door until a man cried out, "Art supplies from Adam et Fil! Open up, it's freezing out here!"

Red-faced with embarrassment (she'd totally forgotten about the promised delivery), she opened the door to find a deliveryman stamping snow off his galoshes. Two large cartons, one atop the other, hid his face. She recognized the store clerk's voice. "Looks like you bought out the whole store, Mademoiselle Barlow."

"Just about." She invited him in, then pointed him toward the studio. "Put everything in there."

He was polite enough not to comment on the studio's disarray, so she tipped him well before he left. Zoe didn't bother putting the art supplies away; she'd do that later. It wasn't that she was eager to travel to La Villette—few sane people would be—but she did want her visit over and done with.

With her Derringer nestled sweetly in the overcoat's pocket, she left, making certain the door was securely locked behind her.

She wound up lucky again. Avak and the Grim Reaper stood waiting for fares at the corner of Raspail and Montparnasse, the Armenian's glorious black mustache gleaming in the pale December sunlight. At first, he refused to take her to La Villette— "Too many bad mens there"—but when she told him she'd keep asking around until she found a cabbie who *would*, he grudgingly agreed. "If killed, your own fault."

· · · ◇ · · ·

La Villette was situated in the far northeast arrondissement of Paris and was the end of the line for the animals that made up the city's acclaimed menus. The smell of urine and feces rushed to greet them long before they reached the killing pens. Not wishing to inflict such a sensory affront to his beloved Grim Reaper, Avak parked it on a short street and they traveled the rest of the way on foot.

The Great War had not been kind to La Villette. Several mortar rounds from the Hun's infamous Paris Gun—its deadly missiles could travel more than a hundred kilometers—had landed within its borders, toppling buildings and killing hundreds. The Paris Gun hadn't been the only cause of the arrondissement's wartime misery. Squadrons of Gotha bombers had hand-tossed smaller explosives over the sides of their aircraft to land on multistoried apartments or in the midst of panicked crowds. Scores burned to death.

Four years after the Armistice, not all of the rubble had been cleared away, and new street signs had yet to be reinstalled, so Zoe and Avak quickly found themselves lost. They eventually came upon a building with its entire side sheared off, exposing abandoned apartments to the elements. In one, Zoe saw a ruined sofa and half a crib. At the curb in front of this sad ruin, several pieces of indefinable machinery rusted away.

Although Gaston had given her Popov's address on Rue Dafitte, the neighborhood's plethora of damaged buildings resulted in such visual confusion neither she nor Avak could identify the intersection. Possible help lay nearby, though. Given the destruction and the acrid miasma from the nearby slaughterhouses, they'd expected the streets to be deserted. But no, several unflappable Parisians were making their way through the snowdrifts and ruins, going about their daily business as if nothing terrible had happened here.

Less savory Parisians lurked in the shadows of bombed-out buildings, hoping to prey upon the unwary. A few blocks earlier Zoe had spied two such creatures watching them as they passed, but a scowl from Avak sent them back into the shadows. Still, Zoe made the rest of their trek with her hand in her coat's deep pocket. Avak's courage was fine and dandy, but the copper-nickel alloy of her Derringer felt even more comforting.

Gaston had warned her that the good people in this arrondissement were wary of strangers, so Zoe had prepared a sympathetic story. Upon seeing an elderly woman nervously eyeing them in front of the half-gone building, she took a chance. The woman wore a dusty black dress and stood next to something that might have once been an automobile. As Zoe approached, she shrank behind it.

"Madame, can you help me?" Zoe called. "I came here to find an old friend of my cousin's. They met during the war, and he wishes to know if his friend is well." This was only a partial lie, for

Stephen Barlow Browning had fallen in France. He'd been twenty-one and her aunt Verla's only child.

When the woman emerged from behind the whatever, Zoe could see the pucker of old burns on the woman's face. She looked Zoe up and down, noting the poor condition of her dress. It was little better than hers, which took some of the stiffness out of the woman's back. "Why didn't your cousin come himself?"

"The injuries he sustained make it difficult for him to travel," Zoe replied.

Suspicion still leaked from the woman's eyes. "At what battle was he injured?"

"Meuse-Argonne, Madame. He lost both legs." True, according to the letter Aunt Verla received from Stephen's captain. Stephen had died before help arrived.

"There are many veterans here. How can I be expected to remember their names?"

"I understand. I simply need instructions on how to find 72 Rue Dafitte." Not knowing the woman's politics, Zoe didn't mention Russians. Many Russians had deserted the Allied Front during the war to fight in their own Revolution, so they weren't popular with the poorer Parisians, who mistakenly interpreted their desertion as cowardice, not patriotism.

But when the old woman flicked a glance at the handsome Avak, her eyes softened.

"Directions, Madame," he said, his smile gentle. "We wish only such."

There was a long silence before the woman's eyes rested on Zoe again, and this time they were sad. "Then I regret to inform you that you are standing in front of 72 Rue Dafitte."

With this, she walked away.

Once Zoe recovered from her shock, she and Avak circled what remained of the building, carefully stepping around hillocks of broken brick and cement, desperate to find an entrance. When they reached the rear of the building, Zoe's dismay grew. The back door no longer existed, having been blasted away, and the rubble blocked all egress. She was about to turn away in defeat when she noticed another pile of debris lying against a shabby outbuilding. A supply shed? Although it no longer stood quite perpendicular to the ground, the shed's roof and walls remained intact, and a cobbled-together stovepipe poked out of the roof.

Since when did a supply shed need a stove?

Furthermore, last night's snow seemed to have dipped lower in what might have been a path leading from the street to the shed. It hinted at recent use.

Zoe made straight for it, Avak following close behind. "Careful, Mademoiselle," he cautioned. "Maybe bad mens in there."

"Then good luck to them." Once they cleared the debris away, Zoe slipped her hand around her two-shot pistol again.

The door opened easily, and the acrid smell of sweat and old fires rushed to greet them. When Zoe's eyes adjusted to the dim light, she saw a wooden crate filled with coal and kindling sitting next to a small stove empty of ashes. Across from the stove lay a stained mattress partially covered by several thin blankets. Altogether, the blankets might have equaled the warmth of one. No other furniture, just a small pile of neatly folded, third- and fourth-hand men's clothing. The very neatness of the ragged collection hurt Zoe's heart. This was a hovel even less bearable than the woodsman's shack in Mesnil-Théribus, which at least boasted a real fireplace, yet Popov had taken care to maintain some semblance of order here. Refusing to be swayed by pity, she went through the pile, checking each pocket, each fold.

Nothing.

Then, remembering what she'd found at Mesnil-Théribus, she turned to the crate of kindling. On top were several lumps of coal, dried twigs, and a few broken pieces of salvaged carpentry. But as she dug her way toward the bottom, Zoe spotted what looked like crumpled paper.

Her excitement rising, she dumped the crate's contents onto the floor and was rewarded by a flurry of pages. Some were crumpled, others were spattered with dirt, but from what she could see in the murky light, they were all readable. She picked up a page, squinted her eyes against the gloom, and read...

> *"Where are we going, Dad?" Nick asked.*
> *"Over to the Indian camp..."*

Zoe swallowed, then grabbed another page—this one displaying the blurred blue letters of a carbon copy.

> *The old man said it was a dog's life...*

A different page, this one an original, was filled with the kinds of wordplay Zoe had rescued from the woodsman's shack in Mesnil-Théribus.

> *stench lifted rose-like... an aura of shit...*

Zoe gave a whoop of victory.

"That what I think is?" Avak asked.

Zoe answered between a series of wild giggles, "Yes! Ernest Hemingway's lost manuscripts!" She fell to her knees and began gathering up the papers. Still giggling, she almost missed the fact that one of the pages was numbered 183. Forcing herself to calm down, she realized the page was part of a novel.

"*Sumbitch!*" she yelped, using her father's favorite curse word. "Oh, sumbitch and holy hell, we've hit the jackpot!"

Zoe didn't bother putting the pages in order—that could wait until she got back to Le Petit Bibelot. For now, speed was a necessity. They were in the heart of La Villette, and if some of the rough men she'd noticed earlier had followed them...

Well, it wouldn't be nice.

As soon as she gathered the last of the pages into a more or less neat pile, Zoe handed them to Avak, who placed them back into the crate. Then she turned to the mattress again. She hadn't found that damned valise yet, and it possibly contained even more pages. Taking a deep breath—the mattress smelled pretty ripe— she ripped off its thin blankets and examined the sides for any slit or tear that might hide other stolen goods. Although the mattress was ancient, it remained uncut.

There were two sides to every mattress, though, so Zoe grabbed the edge of the mattress and summoned Avak to help her flip it over...

And beheld a virtual garden of valises underneath.

Spanish leather briefcases flaunting shiny brass buckles. Dainty calfskin valises with less boastful hardware. Tapestried overnight bags depicting hunting scenes—bleeding stags surrounded by dogs, et cetera—others with gentle floral patterns. There was even a flattened doctor's bag emptied of its mysterious potions.

Eleven valises in all.

"Well, I'll be damned!" Zoe rocked back on her heels.

"Damn yes, you bet!" Avak chortled. "Thief sell for much francs, eat like sultan!"

Zoe wanted to kick herself. Why hadn't she asked Hadley what the valise looked like? But no, she'd carried on as if there was only one valise in the world, and she, Zoe, would find it all by its lonesome. *Pride goeth before a fall*, she reminded herself.

Not wanting to take the time to examine them—there were too many, and the shack's poor light strained her eyes—Zoe hurriedly threw the bags in the wooden crate, covering Ernest's precious pages. "Let's get this thing out of here before anyone happens by and puts up a fuss."

The crate's handholds made it easy for Avak to carry, and within seconds, they were back in the bright light of day, headed back to the Grim Reaper. It looked like they would escape La Villette without incident, but as they passed a narrow alleyway the two men they'd seen earlier rushed out and confronted them.

"*Arrêtez!*" *Stop!* ordered the larger of the two, brandishing a nasty-looking iron pipe. The smaller one had a two-by-four.

Their clothes were ragged, and both reeked of cheap wine. The tall man, older and robust as a wrestler, appeared to be the leader. His nose had been broken several times, and one eye was milky white, but the perky black beret on his straw-yellow hair hinted he wasn't blind to fashion.

"What's in the box?" Big Man asked.

Having grown up with Brice, her bully of a brother, Zoe knew better than to show fear. Forcing a laugh, she answered, "Nothing you'd be interested in, but if you enter the supply shack behind 72 Rue Dafitte, you'll find several lumps of coal and a stove to burn them in. Clothes, too, not that what you're already wearing isn't fetching."

Not used to such cheerful behavior from victims, Big Man blinked in surprise.

The shorter of the two, with a face not yet marred by life, blustered, "We want what you got there." Little Man's voice broke on the last part of the sentence, revealing he was little more than a child.

Father and son? Or a less filial relationship?

Big Man resumed control. "Shut up!" he said to the kid. To Avak, "Put the box down and get lost, or it's gonna go hard for you and her!" He took a few practice swings at the air with the iron pipe to illustrate. Little Man copied, not as artfully.

Avak started to put the box down, but a command from Zoe stopped him.

"Don't," she whispered. "They may have their weapons, but I've got mine."

Almost as shocked by her words as by their fraught situation, Avak obeyed, but he didn't look happy about it.

"What was that? What was that?" Big Man demanded. "Don't you two go talking to each other! Just slide that box over with your foot, and we'll let you live."

Zoe wasn't certain he actually meant his threat. Big Man stank of desperation as well as cheap wine, but if he'd had the heart of a killer, he and Little Man would have snuck up on them and clubbed them to death from behind. There would have been no conversation about boxes.

Smile still in place, Zoe pulled the Derringer from her pocket. "I think you've got things turned around. If you two vamoose right now, I'll let your boy live."

For emphasis, Zoe—whose father had taught her to shoot many types of firearms—fired a careful shot at Little Man. Her artist's eye served her well, and the bullet hit the snow-covered ground mere inches from his right foot. After a startled yip, Little Man turned tail and fled.

Big Man didn't flinch. A veteran of the Great War? He lowered his iron pipe. "What was that address again?" he asked, almost genially.

"The shack behind 72 Rue Dafitte," she said, her smile now more genuine. "We left the door open for you."

Chapter Twenty-Two

Zoe didn't stop shaking until she arrived at Le Petite Bibelot. She'd never fired a gun at a human being, much less a kid. Jesus, what would she have done if her aim had been off and she'd killed him?

Even if your aim was off, she chided herself, *it wouldn't have been by much. You'd have shot him in the foot at the very worst!*

Before returning to his taxi stand, Avak had deposited the crate in the middle of her long banquet table. Zoe took a few moments to warm up, then limped into the kitchen and bolted down a generous helping of Madeline's cooking cognac. Nerves thus calmed, she went to work, searching through each valise, hoping to discover which belonged to the Hemingways. But here her luck ran out. The thief had already robbed them of whatever treasures they'd once held. Not one coin was left, not one identification paper.

But that was okay. The valise itself wasn't important; only the manuscripts.

Ah, well. Zoe lifted the pages out of the crate and began putting them in order. Ernest had numbered the pages for his short stories and the novel—something about war—but that was it. The unnumbered pages consisted of Stein-ian word experiments, poetry, newspaper articles, and notes. Zoe did what she could with them and, a couple of hours later, had Ernest's work in some semblance of order. Once she added the scorched pages she'd fetched from her wardrobe, the page count topped six hundred.

Despite Ernest's flaws as a husband, he sure wasn't lazy.

Now that she was finished sorting, Zoe went into the kitchen to search for some twine. Unfortunately, Madeline, who knew the kitchen like the back of her mechanical hand, had already gone home, leaving Zoe without a map to this uncharted territory. Zoe searched her way through the pantry, two cabinets, and five drawers before she found the twine in the same drawer as a roasting spit and the poultry scissors. Then she limped back to the table, and one by one, wrapped the novel's pages together, then the short stories, then the poetry, and finally the articles. She tied each category up separately. Lastly, she separated the notes from the experiments, but since there weren't many of either, she tied those together.

Five bundles, all neat and tidy.

Zoe rewarded herself with a hot bath—using Chanel's bath salts, of course—and a change of clothing, so if a certain handsome police inspector happened to drop by, she wouldn't look or smell like a ragamuffin. But there was still more work to do. Now that she'd fired her Derringer, it needed to be cleaned.

One unfired bullet remained in the little pistol, so she unloaded it and laid the cartridge on the table. To her amusement, the cartridge rolled across the table's glossy surface until it came to rest against the Spanish leather briefcase with the shiny brass buckles. Stretching her arm to pick up the bullet, she saw something on the bottom of the briefcase that she hadn't noticed earlier—a piece of paper wedged underneath one of the buckles. When she wiggled it out, she saw it had been torn off the heavy kind of notepaper found only at stationers' shops in the better arrondissements. The writing was in block letters.

12 SAMEDI. MESNIL-THÉRIBUS

Noon Saturday. The day and approximate time Vassily Popov and the young woman known as "Sophia" had met their deaths.

Zoe dropped the note as if it had bitten her. She'd heard the police could identify suspects by matching their fingerprints to those collected at the crime scene. Now hers were mixed with the sender of the note and its recipient.

"Aw, shit," she muttered.

If Henri found out about her trip to La Villette, there'd be hell to pay. Zoe could hear him now, yelling his head off about interference in police work. And she could almost hear herself groveling and whining, "But I was just trying to help a friend!" Disgusting. What was she—a woman or a mouse?

So her fingerprints were on the note; big deal. No one with any sense, and that included a certain arrogant member of the Sûreté, could believe she'd murdered six people. She rose from the table and went into her boudoir, where she kept her makeup kit. Ignoring the overhead mirror—fun during sex, not much fun now—she found a pair of tweezers and took it back to the table. She carefully tweezered the note into a clean envelope. Then she added an explanatory note.

Henri,

Don't you dare ask me where I came upon this odd little piece of paper I'm sending you, but I believe it might be written by Popov's and Sophia's killer. Note the address and time. Perhaps a study of the fingerprints on the paper will help. In the meantime, enjoy a lovely day, and try not to catch a chill. It's cold outside.

She wasn't quite sure how to sign it. *Love, Zoe?* No, she didn't really love him, not like she'd loved Pete. *Your adoring Zoe?* Nah, no adoration, either; she knew his faults. *Zoe, with kisses and passion?* Too much.

She wound up signing her note simply *Zoe*, with no declarations. Henri would probably show up ranting and raving anyway, but what the hell. When she opened her door to look for valiant little Dax to deliver the envelope to Henri's office, the messenger boy was nowhere in sight. So she slipped on her coat and walked to the nearby post office, where she put the envelope in a *pneumatique.*

With the incriminating note now out of her hands, she made her way to the Café du Dôme, where she attempted to telephone Hadley with the good news. The long-distance operator informed her that the lines were down, whatever that meant, and she'd have to try again later. Zoe briefly considered sending a telegram, but maybe those lines were down, too.

Zoe drowned her sorrows with a bowl of onion soup, followed by a glass of sauternes and a fruit tart. Belly full, she walked home through a fresh snowfall.

· · · ◇ · · ·

This being Madeline's day off, Zoe spent the rest of it clearing up. She also finished cleaning her beloved Derringer and tucked it away into its usual spot. Then she put Ernest's manuscripts back into the crate, along with the valises, and dragged the crate into the far corner of her studio, where an even bigger job awaited her.

It took some time to organize her new art supplies, but by

evening, her studio was almost its former self. She'd even stretched and applied gesso to several canvases. When they dried, she would start replacing her lost work, beginning with the Seven Heavenly Virtues series.

Zoe hadn't been satisfied with the original paintings: *Prudence, Temperance, Courage, Faith, Hope, Charity,* and *Justice.* They felt timid. Surely virtue wasn't weak. In order to take arms against the wrongs in the world, didn't each virtue have to be at least equal in strength to its opposing vice? For *Justice,* this time, she'd try a stronger approach by substituting the judge's black robe with burnt sienna, the color of Jewel's beautiful skin. For *Courage,* she'd use the same blue as Bobby's eyes. After all, it had taken great courage for the little man to turn his back on classical art, which sold well, to become a Dadaist, which didn't.

Ignoring the only semi-dry state of the canvas, she began to paint. She kept painting until two in the morning, when she cleaned her brushes and stumbled off to bed.

Despite her exhaustion, Zoe slept badly. In her dreams, she kept hearing a baby crying, lost and abandoned in the forest behind Beech Glen.

Oh, Amber!

··· ◊ ···

The next day brought warmer weather, and the snow began to thaw. If you could ever call Paris unlovely, this was the time, when slush turned into gray water and ran down each street and alleyway. The runoff stank with the scent of every horse and dog that ever shat in it. People who could, stayed inside, as did Zoe. She even refrained from breakfast at La Rotonde. Instead, she made her own coffee and boiled an egg. Before she finished eating this plain repast, Madeline arrived, surprising her. The housekeeper carried several string bags filled with groceries.

"What are you doing here so early?" Zoe asked, looking up from the table.

"It's past noon, Mademoiselle Zoe. And it's Wednesday."

Zoe furrowed her brow. "What's so special about Wednesday?"

"That's the day you feed your friends."

In her concerns about other matters, murder and missing manuscripts chief among them, Zoe had forgotten this was her Salon evening. By eight, Le Petit Bibelot would be swarming with hungry artists expecting to be fed.

She left the preparations to Madeline's expert hands and went into her studio to begin the other task she'd been putting off: drawing the automobiles in which her friends had so kindly allowed her to become a passenger. Once she'd done that, she would hire Avak to drive her to Mesnil-Théribus again and show the drawings to Abelard. Bobby's cousin might be able to identify the "big black" car that dropped off Bobby the day of the Popov's murders.

There was no doubt in Zoe's mind that the driver was the killer.

Just as she was putting the finishing touches on Archie Stafford-Smythe's Bugatti, the mailman delivered a letter from her sister. Lee-Lee must have been in a terrible hurry, because her usually lovely handwriting was barely readable.

Dearest sister,

Must RUSH! Jack's grandmother is in the village, waiting in a long line at the butcher's, so must dash this off and sneak it to the clerk at the post counter. Jack's grandparents—I'm not too hurried to be honest!!! are rude people. They're always talking about the Allies being SWINEHUNDS (that means "pig-dogs"—see, I'm learning German!). They blame their poverty on the war THEY started! They see themselves as the VICTIMS, if

*you can believe that! They also blame Jews and Gypsies
and God knows who else who CONSPIRE—their word!—
to keep Germany down.*

*Mr. Hitler—I saw him at a rally with Jack—says the
same thing, only he SCREAMS IT! Oh, Sissie, everyone
here is poor and mean and ugly. At least the forest is
pretty. It reminds me of the one at home, only much, much
larger. Most of Bavaria is trees!*

*The country air is refreshing, and Jack is being so sweet.
I'm sorry you got the wrong impression of him, which was
ALL MY FAULT! I forgot he was a bit old-fashioned, so I
need to work harder at being a BETTER WIFE!!! (Jack's
grandmother is teaching me to COOK, can you believe it?)
Now I have to mail this before she notices I snuck away!*

*Tons and tons of love,
Your adoring LEE-LEE!!!*

The letter troubled Zoe. Leeanne was still blaming herself
for her husband's boorish behavior. Zoe had seen that sort of
thing before, and it never bode well for the woman. There was
nothing she could do. Not yet, anyway. Her sister was hundreds of miles away with her new family, and any long-distance
interference might make the situation worse. Over the years,
Zoe had learned that actions which seemed small at the time
could have life-changing consequences when you couldn't see
the forest for the trees.

*Such as the day she'd purchased a new dotted swiss dress at Miss
Eleanor's Styles in downtown Birmingham, Alabama. While leaving the store, she'd stumbled on the uneven sidewalk and dropped
her parcel, whereupon a dark-skinned, blue-eyed man—who looked
vaguely familiar—retrieved it for her. Zoe had thanked him, and he
said it was nothing, and wasn't it a lovely day, and she replied yes it*

was, and he said his name was Pete, and she fell in love right then and there, but the Great War began and all her dreams ended in that terrible basement...

So who was she to judge Leeanne? Like Zoe, her younger sister had no crystal ball, no way of seeing the future, no way of getting through the tangled forest of life other than one step at a time.

They were all babes in the woods.

Chapter Twenty-Three

When the Salon began, the poorest artists—along with a few starving poets—busied themselves around the banquet table, while the more successful gathered around Zoe. The news of Bobby's death had already reached them via *Le Figaro*.

"Will this evil ever end?" poor old Louise Packard asked, her eyes red from private weeping. Bobby's murder, added to those of Jewel and Sergei, had taken a toll, and her arthritic hands shook as she lit her Gitane.

"It'll end when someone stops killing us, period," answered Karen Wegner. Her own sorrow was muted because a drunken Bobby had once made fun of her kinetic sculptures, and she'd never forgiven him. For one brief moment, Zoe wondered if... Surely not! Karen held no grudges against either Jewel or Andrei or the Russian couple, and from what Henri had told her, she knew the same gun had killed them all.

Marquis Antoine Fortier shot Karen a look. "*Us*, you say? Don't tell me you think someone is out to kill all the artists of Paris!" A cloud of smoke rose from his ever-present De Reszke cigarette, overwhelming the heavenly aroma of Madeline's cooking.

"Just a select few," Karen answered, shrugging her muscular shoulders. "Look around and notice how our ranks have dwindled."

"Sergei was no artist," Zoe pointed out. "Neither were the Popovs."

The sculptor stood firm. "True. But like most aristocrats, Sergei supported the arts. He bought one of my kinetic sculptures."

"And a nice little landscape from my dealer," Fortier boasted.

"Same here," Louise said. "Although I know Sergei didn't like Cubism, he bought one of my biggest canvasses simply as an investment. What work did he buy of yours, Zoe?"

The count had bought only a small sketch directly from her since Zoe as yet didn't have a dealer—so she answered, "I don't think Sergei was a fan of Abstract Expressionism."

Fortier nodded. "Understandable. Neither am I, as a matter of fact. Such lazy painting."

Zoe felt insulted, both for herself and others of her ilk, and for a brief moment played with the notion of challenging the marquis to a duel. He owned a Derringer, too, she knew, so it would be an equal contest. She snickered at the thought.

Women had fought duels before in France, and not that far away from Le Petit Bibelot. In 1719, in the Bois de Boulogne, the very park where Béatrice Camondo rode her horses, the Comtesse de Polignac had dueled with Madame Marquise de Nesle over the affections of the promiscuous third Duke of Richelieu. Zoe remembered that Polignac had won the shoot-out, not quite killing her adversary. The flighty duke ended his relationship with both of them anyway, having reached the decision that any woman who could handle a gun was best avoided.

In modern France the survivors of such duels were severely punished, so Zoe restrained herself. Maybe someday she'd just quietly poison Fortier instead.

Reynard Dibasse seemed relieved by the lessening of tension. Despite his courage in the War to End All Wars, he was a peaceful man and didn't like to see friends argue. After straightening his face mask—he'd slipped it aside while eating—he proposed a toast to the upcoming Trousers March. Most women in the room, and even a few men, raised their glasses.

"To women in trousers!" Reynard cried, echoed by the majority.

However, by their very nature, artists are a grudge-carrying species, and although Zoe had cooled her own ire at Fortier, nothing could stem the long-standing ill will between him and Karen. In a way, their animosity was understandable. Karen had begun her professional life as a carver of large granite monuments, but later joined the ranks of the new kinetic sculptors. As a result, she held little respect for artists who worshipped Tradition. The style change dented Karen's bankbook, and these days she was barely making ends meet. Few collectors wanted to buy tiny metal pieces needing to be oiled regularly in order to perform. The resulting drop in finances made her irritable, and from time to time, she vented her spleen at everyone.

Meanwhile, Fortier's Watteau-esque landscapes were selling well. *Very* well. Just this past month, one of the Old Guard critics, a one-time member of the Académie, had written an article in the English edition of *Harper's Bazaar*, dubbing Fortier "The Painting Marquis." This sobriquet sent his sales through the roof. As the prices rose, so did his estimation of himself.

Right now, The Painting Marquis was enjoying ragging at poor, broke Karen. She'd sorrowfully mentioned missing the expensive hot mud treatments at Vichy, where she'd been a regular customer before her sales dropped.

"Bathing in mud?" he teased her. "Ah, Karen, you truly have the soul of a peasant."

The sculptor pretended not to feel the sharp end of the jibe. "*Ah* back, my dear Marquis, that's impossible. We don't have 'peasants' in America. We're all equal over there."

Zoe winced, knowing the sculptor stretched the truth. All equal? When Beech Glen's sharecroppers' miserable existence made Hadley's and Ernest's shabby apartment look like the Ritz?

Karen then went on the attack. "Speaking of peasants, last week I heard from a trustworthy source that your great-great-grandfather was a stable hand, not the blue-blooded marquis he was supposed to be..."

Fortier spat a non-aristocratic curse. "Why, you *bitch*!"

An answering sneer. "Takes one to know one."

Fortier started toward Karen, but Archie Stafford-Smythe, who'd been sitting next to The Painting Marquis, restrained Fortier before he could commit mayhem with his silver-tipped cane. "Be nice," Archie tut-tutted. "Remember we're in dear Zoe's pretty little house, and our poor girl has endured a miserable week."

Fortier had the grace to look abashed. Not so Karen, who sat there smirking.

Dominique ignored them. Readjusting the patch over her missing eye, she said, "What I want to know is why the authorities haven't been able to put a stop to this. As dear Louise said, we're losing too many friends, so please, Zoe, tell us what the Sûreté is actually doing."

Zoe wasn't happy about discussing the murders again, but at least doing so would give Karen and Fortier a chance to calm down. "I know absolutely nothing. Please remember that I came close to being murdered myself!" Several blank faces stared at her. Belatedly, she realized not everyone knew about the break-in. Apparently, *Le Figaro* hadn't thought it important to cover the destruction of an artist's studio or an attack on the artist. It hadn't even bothered to write about the shooting death of her attacker.

When Zoe finished filling them in, there was a lot of tsk-tsking around the room until Kiki said, "Yes, that's awful, but we know you've been working hand in hand with the Sûreté." Brunette bob glossy as ever, the model was cuddled in the arms of a new suitor—where the hell was Man Ray?—not caring that her date was making eyes at Archie. "Oh, don't look so shocked, Zoe. Everyone in Paris is talking about your *ooh-la-la* with a certain handsome police inspector."

"And him a married man," Fortier muttered prissily.

Hypocrite, Zoe thought. Fortier was married, not that it mattered. He was infamous for bedding any woman who would hold still long enough. Granted, he and his wife were separated—she lived with their teenage children in Aix-en-Provence—but as with his traditional painting style, Fortier held traditional expectations for women. He believed it was fine for a man to sleep around, but not for a woman. Zoe had found the improbable mathematics of this amusing until she'd met the woman in the plant-filled room and was forced to confront her own sins.

Ignoring Fortier, she said to Kiki, "Inspector Challiot does not share the details of his investigations with me."

"You expect us to believe that?" Dominique scoffed.

"Well, it's the truth."

Kiki grinned. "And you've never told a lie in your life, have you?"

Zoe scowled. "To repeat, the inspector has never told me one damn thing about *any* of his cases, but I do know this. The article in *Le Figaro* this morning stated that Bobby's funeral service will be conducted at ten tomorrow in Grigny. I'm going. Who else?"

The gaiety fled from Kiki's mischievous face. "But Bobby's

American! Why would he be buried here? The last thing France needs is another dead body taking up space in our cemeteries."

A collective gasp. Kiki seemed to have forgotten the thousands of young American doughboys interred just outside Paris. Louise passed over Kiki's lapse, explaining that Bobby's American parents had died during the Spanish flu epidemic, and now his only living relatives were the cousin in Mesnil-Théribus and an aunt in Grigny. Therefore, he would be planted in French soil. There was an edge to Louise's voice Zoe had never heard before. Louise might be more than fifty, with arthritic hands and back, but she'd won a Silver for skeet shooting in the 1896 Olympics. Yet Kiki didn't notice Louise's ire, and continued to grumble until a one-eyed glare from Dominique shut her up.

The rest of the evening passed peacefully. It ended with Dominique offering to ferry those without cars to Grigny the next morning in her shot-up Ravel. Inspired by her kind offer, both Fortier and Karen followed suit, and by the time the evening was over, fully eighteen Wednesday Salon regulars promised to attend Bobby's funeral.

As Zoe ushered out the last of them, she remembered something. There was a more than even chance that Abelard, Bobby's artist cousin, would be at the funeral. This would allow her to show him her sketches of black automobiles, not that they were necessary anymore. Thanks to Dominique's generosity, the cars themselves would be there. Surely Abelard would recognize the one that had dropped Bobby off in Mesnil-Théribus the day of the Popovs' murders.

With a mixture of sorrow and hope, Zoe grabbed a half-finished bottle of Burgundy off the table and made her way to bed. A half-bottle didn't do the trick, so she padded back to the kitchen for another glass.

When she finally fell asleep, she dreamed about a valise filled with snakes.

Gabrielle

December 1922
Paris

Oh, Odile, Henri brought his mistress into our home last night! I could say nothing, being only able to open my mouth to eat the medicinal gruel Madame Arceneau gives me. If I could have risen from this bed, I would have killed him.

Not her? the spider asked. *She is no doubt a whore.*

She is only a woman, one of his many since I fell ill.

But she is the only one he introduced to you. Surely that means even a greater danger than a whore who is used, paid, and never seen again.

I'm afraid you are correct, I answered my stalwart little friend.

If it weren't for Odile, I would lose my mind. Although Henri has created a sweet bower to enchant me, I feel imprisoned. I want to see beyond those snow-dappled rooftops lining the boulevards, see down among the chestnut trees where...

You are so sad today, Madame, Odile says. She sits on my pillow, caressing my cheek.

Such a faithful friend, to show such concern! *I was thinking about the world outside, how it must have changed. Henri and Madame Arsenault once attempted to free me from this beautiful prison, but I behaved so foolishly they did not do so again. Henri had strapped me into a chair with wheels, an ugly thing but useful for cases such as mine. He and Madame Arsenault took me down the elevator to our building's courtyard. I had hoped he might take me to the front of our building so I could watch the world go by, but no, just the courtyard.*

He made the wiser choice, Odile. It was spring, and the silver linden tree was budding. *Several species of butterflies—the brown and white* Carcharodus alceae, *the golden* Ochlodes sylvanus, *the sweet blue* Glaucopsyche alexis—*fluttered between the blooms of irises and peonies, and it was so much I began to tremble, wanting desperately to pay reverence to the beauty of life. My hands shook so they actually rose from my lap, and I wanted to say, "Look, I am alive in here, and I am touched by the beauty of this world..."*

But Henri read my trembling as fear, not joy, and at once took me back to my bedroom. Since then, the chair with wheels has remained unused.

Odile is touched. *Oh, Madame, is there anything I can do to ease your suffering?*

Odile understands, so I tell her, *Perhaps you, who experiences more freedom than I, will describe what is happening on the streets below?*

Madame, I was at the window before you woke, and I can tell you very little is going on. Just horses pulling smelly wagons and automobiles making their irritating rrrg-rrrg noise. I only hope they are a fad that will soon pass, like tight corsets on skinny women.

There are women below?

There are always women below. All day they walk up and down the street, showing off their beautiful coats and hats. They are there even at night, when they are escorted by men wearing their own hats, tall black affairs woven by my cousins.

The women's dresses? Their shoes? The colors and their shapes? Please, I beg of you, describe them for me!

Odile is silent for a moment, which makes me worry, but then I realize that in my excitement, I asked too forcefully. Huntsman spiders do not like to be ordered around. Besides, what could a spider know about fashion?

But Odile is forgiving, and now she crawls down from my pillow and scampers to the window ledge. She leans her tiny head against the glass.

Madame, from what I can see when the wind blows their coats open, the young women are wearing dresses that end halfway between their knees and their ankles. This morning I saw one whose dress was even more daring. It ended at her knees, and she looked cold, even though her coat was a heavy one.

What colors are the dresses, the coats?

Colors, Madame? What do you mean—colors?

Foolish me. Spiders do not recognize words such as "red" or "blue," let alone variants of those shades. But no one has yet proven that they are color blind, so I tell her, *Blue is what we call the color of the sky on a cloudless day.*

Then that is the color of the dress she's wearing. Her shoes, too.

The coat?

The coat is the color of the sky just before it rains.

Gray. And her hat?

The same cloudless-sky color, but a touch darker, and she wears it very low on one side, almost as if she does not want the man she is with to see one of her eyes, which I noticed are both ringed in the darkest of colors, as dark as an unlit alley at night.

That would be black, I explain. *She is wearing kohl, a pigment we women use to make our eyes look bigger.*

Odile gives a celebratory hop. *Madame is teaching me a new language! Blue! Gray! Black! Tell to me the color of the rose your husband brought you this morning. What is that called?*

Red, I say sadly, knowing he left the rose out of guilt.

Chapter Twenty-Four

—— Zoe ——

Located thirty-two kilometers southeast of Paris, Grigny wasn't much. Zoe couldn't even call it a village since it comprised only a few businesses and homes spread out between pastures filled with goats and dairy cattle. Grigny's cemetery looked forlorn, too, soggy from the recent thaw. At least Bobby wouldn't be sent to his final resting place unheralded. As promised, the Wednesday Salon regulars showed up (nineteen, counting herself), and Bobby's aged aunt, Camille Levey, brought along several of her neighbors to say goodbye. Thus, a respectably sized crowd stood shivering as a bribed priest—Bobby had been an atheist—sprinkled holy water over the plain wooden casket as it was lowered into hallowed ground.

Bobby's cousin Abelard did not show. According to Madame Levey, word had come that one of Abelard's children had been ill, and out of concern for her welfare, that line of the family would be staying home. As the group trudged through the mud back to their cars, Zoe realized Abelard's absence meant she needed to take yet another trip back to Mesnil-Théribus. Then, partially because of her inattention and a loose bit of gravel that rolled under her foot, she stumbled. Her sketchbook—which she'd brought along to show Abelard—fell out of her hands. The pages flew open. When the sketchbook came to rest on the gravel walkway, everyone could see the drawings of Louise's Renault, Fortier's Hispano Suiza, and Archie's Bugatti.

"You're drawing cars now?" Kiki exclaimed. "Are you going to be like Karen and forsake humans for machines?"

Thank God for Kiki! She had given Zoe the excuse she needed. Hastily picking up the sketchbook and making a great show of brushing off gravel and mud, Zoe said, "Well, when you're thinking about buying a car, you'd be surprised how intriguing they become to the eye. I'll probably do more sketches like this before I make up my mind. Maybe I'll paint them, too."

"I notice you didn't draw my Citroën," Karen said, offended.

"I'll get to it. Such a pretty car, especially in that bright yellow. Whatever car I wind up with, I do want a nice color." She threw a look at Archie. "And maybe a windshield."

Archie, being an easygoing sort, laughed. "A wise move. In summer I have to bring along a toothpick to scratch the bugs from between my teeth."

They piled into their various automobiles and headed to Fortier's pied-à-terre at 23 Rue de la Boëtie, where The Painting Marquis had graciously offered to host an après-funeral luncheon. By the time they arrived, they were starved, so without bothering to amuse themselves at the sight of Picasso arguing on the sidewalk with his Russian wife, they bypassed the two brawlers and rushed upstairs to Fortier's flat. After shrugging off their coats, they gathered around the long banquet table where the housekeeper had set up a fine feast.

Unlike Fortier's main residence, a battle-scarred seventeenth-century château in Picardy, his Paris flat was relatively small. Whereas Picasso's place had a more elaborate setup—two different floors, one for living, one for working—Fortier's studio and apartment were combined into one, like at Zoe's own Petit Bibelot. As they ate, she smelled a potpourri of herbs and baking spices, and a slight scent of turpentine and linseed oil. This was a familiar and comforting combination for her, but she was surprised the scent wasn't stronger. Perhaps he hadn't been painting lately. Other than three paintings he'd held back from sale, his last exhibit had sold right down to the smallest sketch. Maybe the excitement had exhausted him.

While Zoe did enjoy the aroma of linseed, she less admired Fortier's furniture. The pieces were so ornate they verged on Rococo; the last time she'd seen so much gilt in one room was at Versailles. So much wasted money, but she had to admit that the curlicued cabinets and outlandishly elaborate sofas perfectly suited the man's fussy landscapes. The oils he'd kept hung on the brocaded walls, hymns to an idealized beauty of Nature. He liked painting willows. Here a willow, there a willow, everywhere a willow willow. A few oaks, a few chestnuts, but willows, willows, willows, all over his canvases. And a few ponds.

Disgusted, Zoe stopped looking at them and concentrated on the food, which was excellent, but no better than Madeline's. The wine was a surprise, too, a cheap Languedoc from a bad year. They drank the stuff anyway, but as cheap wine tends to do, the swill shifted the prevailing mood from sorrow to irritation.

"I blame the Sûreté for not doing more," mourned Louise, her throat raw from crying. In the short space of a week, she'd not only lost a good friend in Jewel, but now her surrogate son was gone, too. Seeing her friend's grief reminded Zoe of her own, so she did what she could to comfort her, which wasn't much. What could you truthfully say to a person at a time like this? That life is shit, but now the people you love are in a better place?

For a brief moment, she remembered the call of a whip-poor-will, remembered her father hanging from a barn rafter, remembered the amber...

She shook the vision out of her head. *No, Zoe! Don't think about that!*

Surprisingly, Fortier was taking Bobby's death hard, too. As he helped his housekeeper rearrange some of the table's offerings, his hands trembled. The shadows under his eyes were darker, too, and as he fussed around, he smoked one De Reszke after another. Zoe had always been aware Fortier was a chain smoker, but despite the doctor's advice that cigarettes were good for you, such constant smoking couldn't be good for his lungs. She'd once told him it might be wise to cut back, but try telling a man—especially a marquis—anything.

Like Louise, Fortier accused the Sûreté of inaction. "You'll notice that when Sergei was killed, police inspectors buzzed around like bees in a hive," he grumbled. "Not so with Bobby. One lone inspector, that's all the poor little man got. What does this tell you about today's state of affairs, when only the wealthy and titled can capture the authorities' attention? Why, people could be murdered in their beds, and they'd hardly notice. Paris just isn't what it used to be."

Such a speech, delivered by a landed aristocrat, sounded ridiculous to Zoe, but judging from the roomful of nodding heads, it didn't to the others. Still, she refused to let the slighting of the "lone inspector" go undefended.

"Inspector Challiot cares as much for the poor as he does the rich," she said. "You've obviously forgotten he was originally called upon to investigate the murders of those penniless Russians in Mesnil-Théribus. He's still working that case as diligently as Jewel's and the count's."

"Little good it's done!" Fortier snapped.

The Painting Marquis was correct. "Investigations take time," Zoe replied, weakly.

In this sense, Paris wasn't much different than Mercy, Alabama. The county sheriff's investigation into Zoe's father's supposed suicide had taken months. Yet it turned up no reason why a healthy, well-to-do plantation owner would kill himself, and in such a way that his thirteen-year-old daughter would be the first to find his body.

··· ◊ ···

Work didn't go well for Zoe the next day; she couldn't capture the pain in Jewel's terrified eyes or do justice to the color of her beautiful skin.

Giving up, she left her studio and wandered into the sitting room, where she sat down on the settee and stared off into space. An overnight snowfall hushed the traffic on the street. Nary a car horn beeped, nor horse neighed. Even the pedestrians walking by kept their complaints about the weather to themselves. Zoe wished for noise, any noise, to divert her sorrow over losing Jewel—and Bobby—but Paris wouldn't cooperate. Zoe didn't even have Madeline to talk to, since the housekeeper was attending the baptism of a grandniece.

It had been days since Zoe had heard from Hadley. Zoe supposed Switzerland was snowed in worse than Paris, but when you were a skier, snow was a boon, not an obstacle. They might still be out on the slopes. Was this avalanche season? Was Hadley in any danger there? Or had Ernest—not realizing his manuscripts had been found—lost his mind and done something dreadful to her? With so much death around, Zoe's imagination was running away with her. She had to remind herself that Swiss hoteliers were good about warning visitors when the slopes were unsafe, and that Ernest had *never* harmed his darling Hadley. If anything, the boor was overprotective.

But Ernest's manuscripts were like an albatross, bringing bad luck and misery wherever they went. It was time to get the damned things out of her house.

Resolute, Zoe went back into her studio and stared balefully at the crate. She could hardly carry nine valises and six-hundred-and-something pages all the way to the Hemingways' apartment on Cardinal Lemoine. Bulk was a problem, too. Even squashed flat, the valises took up considerable room. She'd have to hire Avak again. Muttering with irritation, she slipped into her coat and galoshes and trudged through the snow to the taxi stand.

Avak wasn't there. After a ten-minute wait, he still hadn't shown up, so Zoe went home.

Now what?

As she fixed herself some tea, the answer came to her, so after drinking it down, she went into the studio and laid the valises out on the floor.

Which piece of luggage would a man be most likely to own? Her eye immediately went to the leather briefcase with the shiny brass buckles. She could easily see Ernest carrying the handsome thing around. Then again, if the briefcase had been his, why hadn't he carried it to Lausanne? She set the briefcase aside. The next choice was easier. Zoe knew Hadley's taste, and one of the tapestried valises almost shouted, *Me, me, me!*

She stuffed manuscripts into the briefcase, then put on her sheared beaver coat. After some thought, she picked up the tapestried valise and slung it over her left shoulder—less weight for her bad leg—then she hauled the much heavier briefcase onto the other shoulder.

Sensibly laden, she set off.

Thirty hard minutes later, Zoe knocked on the of 74 Rue du Cardinal Lemoine. Her leg hadn't enjoyed the walk and was punishing her for it.

The door to the first floor flat opened, and the gray-haired concierge immediately spotted Zoe's unlikely luggage. Her mouth made a perfect O. "Is one of those the famous missing valise?"

"*Infamous* missing valise, would be more accurate," Zoe said, trying hard not to wrinkle her nose at the smell of boiling cabbage permeating the entryway. At least the slimy vegetable disguised the stench of the building's *pissoirs*. "The leather briefcase holds Monsieur Ernest's manuscripts, and I brought the other one along to keep it company. There are nine more valises back at my house, any one of which might belong to him or Madame Hadley. I thought it was best to leave the manuscripts with you so the Hemingways will have them when they get back from Switzerland."

The concierge shook her head. "Italy, a little town on the Mediterranean called Rapallo. That's where they're headed now. From snow to beach, a nice vacation for them after the hard work Monsieur Ernest did in Lausanne."

Surprised at this news, Zoe said, "You've been in touch with them?"

"Oh, yes. Monsieur Ernest telegraphed, telling me he'd be back any day now to pick up some less weighty clothing for Italy." Her careworn face took on a wistful expression. "They say it's warm in Rapallo."

And here Zoe had imagined her friend either strangled by her husband or flattened by an avalanche! She gave a relieved chuckle. In fairness, all that worry was her own fault, not Hadley's.

As Zoe stood there bemused, the concierge reached for the bags. "I'll take these upstairs straightaway. No point in letting them clutter up my place."

Zoe glanced down at the woman's swollen ankles, not quite hidden by the long black skirt. It pained her to think of those old legs tromping up four flights of stairs, then back down again. "I'm more than happy to carry them if you'd loan me the key?" She turned her offer into a question.

The concierge beamed. *"Certainement,* Mademoiselle Zoe!*"*

Four flights later, an out-of-breath Zoe stood in the middle of the Hemingways' flat, trying to figure out where best to leave the heavy briefcase and its smaller partner. Chair? Table? On top of that stack of books? Then she caught sight of the sagging bed Hadley had so carefully made up before setting off on that ruinous train ride to Lausanne.

Zoe stepped into the bedroom and placed the two bags in the center of the bed, opening the briefcase to spill out its contents onto the bed. Before walking away, Zoe couldn't resist a final look. Those bothersome pages lay there smugly, oblivious to the trouble they had caused everyone. During her walk, the briefcase's former gloss had fogged over, and now, with the string-tied manuscripts trailing out, the whole affair looked like cheap presents someone hadn't bothered to wrap.

Well, that's fitting, Zoe thought, because the briefcase's contents were amateurish and useless. Except, maybe, for that one sentence she couldn't get out of her mind: *Isn't it pretty to think so?* Yes, there was something there.

And someday pigs would fly.

· · · ◇ · · ·

At six, Zoe hurriedly straightened up Le Petit Bibelot in order not to shock her Poker Night regulars, but only a few showed up. Looking around at the half-empty seats, she realized that if attendance continued to dwindle, she'd soon be out of business. Not even Louise and Fortier, both inveterate gamblers, showed up. During the entire evening, the ghosts of Jewel and Sergei hovered over the card table, keeping the bidding timid. The only salvation for the night was Archie Stafford-Smythe's lousy playing. In one hand, Zoe had two aces showing against his semi-flush although he continued to raise. The more sensible Dominique Garron folded early, but Archie proceeded to make more foolish wagers throughout the night. By the end of the evening, he'd lost almost as much as Sergei usually did.

"You feeling okay, Archie?" Zoe finally asked as he helped Kiki into the tweed coat he'd bought to replace her ruined one.

"I'm feeling fine," Archie responded, "but thanks for your concern. I didn't need that two thousand francs, anyway."

It might have even been true, because Kiki acted more disturbed about his losses than he did. "Sometimes you take advantage, Zoe," she grouched, as if she hadn't established a history of doing the same with her own male acquaintances.

Zoe didn't bother arguing with the truth.

While the rest of the players trooped off into the night, Dominique hung back, a troubled expression on her face.

"You're not really thinking about buying a car, are you." she said, making it a statement, not a question.

"I'm rethinking it."

Dominique narrowed her remaining eye. "You didn't ask the right questions, you know."

Of all Zoe's friends, Dominique was the smartest, which had often made Zoe curious as to why she had so willingly followed the fighting on the Marne merely to draw a few sketches. Yes, she had lost an eye during one of her insane forays, but Dominique could have just as easily lost her life. As soon as the doctors fixed her up, she'd slapped a patch over her missing eye and drove her wooden-sided Ravel right back to the Marne, leaving two dead Germans behind her before she returned to Paris.

You crossed Dominique at your own peril.

"I didn't *know* the right questions to ask," Zoe admitted.

"Which one of us do you think did it?"

Zoe pretended to misunderstand. "Who mixed up the cards in that second hand? Maybe Kiki. You know what she's like.

Hardly pays attention to what she's doing half the time, even when she's dealing."

"Don't play dumb with me," Dominique snapped. "It doesn't suit you. Which one of us do you suspect of killing Jewel, Sergei, poor Bobby, and those Russian wretches in Mesnil-Théribus?"

Her directness left Zoe stammering. "I...I'm sure I don't know what you're talking about."

When Dominique closed the distance between them, Zoe could smell the tobacco on her breath. For the first time she realized how tall Dominique was and how muscular. Only the awareness of the Derringer in Zoe's nearby purse kept her from taking a step back.

The war artist looked down at her with a chilly smile. "You'd better be careful, or someday soon you might wake up dead."

$$\cdots \diamond \cdots$$

The next morning, Zoe was in her studio reworking *Wrath*, when a *pneumatique* arrived, a note from her friend Béatrice Camondo. In her beautiful script, it read...

> *Dearest Zoe—I have some information about Count Sergei Aronoffsky you might be interested in. Can you stop by at one today for lunch?*
>
> *Béatrice*

$$\cdots \diamond \cdots$$

Three hours later, Zoe was enjoying the luxuries of the Camondo residence again.

This time, lunch was served in the Blue Drawing Room, possibly because Béatrice knew it was Zoe's favorite room in the house, where nothing—not even the brass doorknobs—had proved too unimportant for her father's flawless taste. A small Louis XV table. An exquisite wing chair designed by Noël Poirier. A writing desk attributed to the famed cabinetmaker Claude-Charles Saunier. While the wealth of Beech Glen was nothing to sniff at, the plantation manor couldn't hold a candle to Moïse Camondo's collection.

Whether by plan or by coincidence, Béatrice was dressed in the same subtle blue tones of the room in a pale, ankle-length silk chemise trimmed with ecru lace. Zoe felt like someone's poor country cousin.

The conversation remained light while they ate a lunch of crepes and hothouse greens, and a dessert of raspberry sorbet. When the maid took away the empty plates, Béatrice began to share a conversation she'd overheard between her father and one of his banking associates.

"It was about a month ago, and they were in his study," she said. "I only heard a bit of it before Papa saw me standing there. I was going to ask if they required more tea. After telling me no, he closed the door, and I heard nothing else. I'm embarrassed to say that I forgot about that conversation until we were at Count Aronoffsky's funeral service, and I've been mulling it over for days, trying to decide whether or not it would be ethical to tell you. Promise me you'll never reveal to *anyone* where you heard this."

"I promise."

As if afraid she might change her mind, Béatrice hurried on. "Well, Papa and this man were talking about the count's financing of the counterrevolution in Russia. He'd approached them for help with his cause, but they appeared to see it as a dubious proposition, especially in these turbulent times, when everyone is arguing with anyone about absolutely everything. Anyway, the last thing I heard before Papa closed the door was that the count had recently become frustrated with the difficulty of getting funding to his friends in Moscow. Something about diamonds versus gold."

To a certain extent, this information came as no surprise. Pretty much everyone knew of the count's Royalist beliefs. His connection to *Vosstanovit Rodinu*—Rebuild the Homeland—even headlined *Le Figaro* the morning after his murder. Zoe had never given much thought as to how it all worked. She'd heard the rumors Sergei escaped the Bolsheviks with a pouch of diamonds, but turning diamonds into a currency acceptable between unfriendly countries was an iffy affair these days. Gold, however, despite its bulk and weight, had been deemed acceptable for millennia.

"You're certain they used the word 'recently'?" she asked Béatrice. "When exactly did this conversation take place?"

"Several weeks ago, maybe a month. Do you think it might have had something to do with the murders? Myself, I suspect jealousy. One of *Le Figaro*'s articles mentioned the count was killed while he was in bed with that beautiful dancer at Moulin Rouge. Maybe she had a husband or another lover, and he..." She shrugged her delicate shoulders.

"No, Béatrice, she didn't. She loved Sergei." As a fresh wave of grief washed over Zoe, she leaned back in her chair. Béatrice was Paris-born, thus her attitude was French, and with the French, it was always a case of *cherchez la femme*. But, as an American, Zoe *cherchezed le money*.

After thanking Béatrice for the information, she took the Métro home and picked up her sketchbook. Resolute, she headed for Avak's taxi stand at Raspail and Montparnasse. There were still three hours of sunlight left, and with any luck at all, they could make it to Mesnil-Théribus, then home, before dark.

··· ◊ ···

The roads being clear, the trip was uneventful, and for once, the Grim Reaper behaved itself. When they arrived at Bobby's cousin's farm, Abelard Grigot took one look at the drawings and readily identified the car that dropped Bobby off the day the Russian couple was murdered.

The problem was, it made no sense.

By sunset, Zoe was back at Le Petite Bibelot, warm and snug after the cold journey. Too tired to paint or visit the cafés, she reheated the quiche Lorraine Madeline left for her, and spent the rest of the evening attempting to read Mr. Joyce's new novel, *Ulysses*.

That didn't make sense, either.

Chapter Twenty-Five

The day of the much-anticipated Trousers March dawned sunny and clear. After bathing and dressing in her new trousers and comfortable shoes, Zoe left the house and walked to Café du Dôme, where two rented omnibuses stood outside waiting. Considering her masculine getup, she counted herself lucky not to have been arrested on the way.

When she arrived, the other trousered women were already filing on to the buses. Among them she spotted Karen Wegner, hand in hand with Reynard Dibasse, the *Mutilé* who'd become so comfortable around them he wasn't even wearing his face mask. Or maybe he was making his own political statement, that terrible things happened to people during war. Also in trousers and ready to march were mischievous Kiki, the Amazon-esque Dominique Garron, and even arthritic Louise Packard, who was already leaning heavily on her cane. It was understood she might not make it to the Arc de Triomphe, but everyone applauded her grit.

When Zoe finally boarded one of the buses, she saw journalist Djuna Barnes and painter Romaine Brooks sitting behind the driver, a morose-looking Frenchman. Every time another trousered woman passed him, his scowl grew deeper. But the driver's displeasure proved to be in the minority, for Reynard wasn't the only male on the bus. Archie Stafford-Smythe—wearing a red satin evening dress, silver fox stole, and a sparkling tiara—grinned mischievously at Zoe from the back of the bus. Standing next to him was Avak Grigoryan, his black mustache gleaming in the early morning light. He looked so handsome that several women on the bus were throwing him coquettish looks. So much for the belief that wearing trousers unsexed women!

"Mademoiselle Zoe, pleasure it is see you today," Avak said.

"It's a pleasure to see you here, too. After all this time, you might as well dispense with the formalities and start calling me Zoe. But how did you find out about this?"

"Drive for many womens. They talk, I worry. This, I can help. *Vive les Pantalons*, eh?"

This brought a spontaneous cheer of *Vive les Pantalons!* from everyone on board, and with that, the omnibus chugged off down the wide boulevard. While they bumped along, the conversation settled into a murmur of French, English, Spanish, Russian, and Armenian. The trip—north up Raspail, west along St. Germain, then across the Pont de la Concorde—was a short one, and within minutes, the bus drew up to the curb at the end of the Jardin des Tuileries.

Debarking, they saw the great Place de la Concorde with its Obelisk thrusting up toward the sky. To their backs stretched the great gardens of the Louvre, while facing them was the long Champs-Élysées. On their right sprawled the Palais de l'Élysée, with its glorious Hall of Mirrors, then the Grand Palais, with its four bronze horses rearing on the roof. In the distance rose the imposing Arc de Triomphe, planned by Napoleon himself, through which the Great War's conquering armies had marched.

They fell silent for a moment, realizing the magnitude of what they were about to do. Not only did the vast Place de la Concorde throng with automobiles, horse carts, and gawking pedestrians, but there appeared to be a battalion of gendarmes waiting for them. Someone had bragged about the March to the wrong person.

A ripple of uncertainty ran through their ranks, but then Fleurette Joubert, the fiery editor of *La Voix de la Femme* who'd organized the Trousers March, cried out, "*Mes amies, liez vos bras et marchons!*" My friends, link your arms and march!

So off they stepped, marching together down one of the world's most magnificent thoroughfares, steadfast in their hearts, brazen in their trousers.

At first one lone soprano lifted in song, then her voice found another, then another, and soon sixty-three women and two brave men chorused "La Marseillaise."

> *Aux armes, citoyen!*
> *Formez vos bataillons!*
> *Marchons! Marchons!*
>
> Grab your weapons, citizens!
> Form your battalions!
> Let us march! Let us march!

They made it halfway across Place de la Concorde before they were arrested.

··· ◊ ···

Jail was a new experience for Zoe.

Once the men had been chased away—they hadn't committed a crime by wearing trousers, and the gendarmes were so impressed by Archie Stafford-Smythe's red dress that they let him go, too—the pants-wearing women were crammed into several trucks.

Then they were driven, still singing "La Marseillaise," to Saint-Lazare, the prison for women.

Here the singing stopped.

There were worse places than Saint-Lazare, such as the notorious men's prison Maison d'Arrêt de la Santé. Given the somewhat gentler French attitude toward women, Saint-Lazare had a better reputation than la Santé, but prison was still prison. Founded in the twelfth century as a leper colony, Saint-Lazare now housed females of all ages, from infants to grandmothers. Since it was run by the Sisters of the Order of Marie-Joseph, prayer and religious instruction were mandatory, and as the matrons herded them down the hall, Zoe could hear the *Hail Mary* being repeated over and over. Once the marchers changed into the dreary, black-and-white prison garb—skirts, not trousers—they were taken to the Prévenues Dormitory. This was a vast room set aside for women accused of various crimes, but not yet convicted. The matrons left them there to take their place along with women accused of "unsanctioned" prostitution, pickpocketing, and even murder.

Although no vicious Santé, Saint-Lazare was no picnic. For starters, it stank. The odor of sweat, urine, and spoiled milk hung about the long room, oblivious to the constant scrubbings of lye-smelling water, which only added to the foul miasma. Near one small window, a woman holding an infant huddled on a cot. Her face was bruised, as were the faces of the two toddlers clinging to her. Zoe wondered who'd beaten them and why they were here instead of in a hospital. Near this unfortunate little family, a lone woman lay on another cot, her eyes vacant. She was pregnant and near the end of her term.

During what was now being referred to as his Blue Period, Picasso had visited Saint-Lazare when his friend Germaine Gargallo was imprisoned there. He'd come away with sketches of hell. Zoe had seen his *Woman with Bonnet*, which showed a prisoner suffering from syphilis. Another of his paintings, *The Two Sisters*, portrayed two women grieving over their fates. The most intimate painting of all, *Melancholy Woman*, showed Germaine herself sitting by a small window, her face bereft of hope. Remembering those sad and beautiful works, Zoe felt a moment of panic, wondering if she would wind up looking like them after a month in this place.

Noting the anxiety on her friends' faces, Fleurette Joubert climbed onto a cot, the better to address the room. In a commanding voice, the stern Trousers March organizer assured them her solicitors were already working with the examining magistrate to get them released, and their stay would be short.

"Have no fear, sisters! We will prevail!"

Although some of the older *prévenues* hissed in contempt, the strains of "La Marseillaise" began again, drowning out opposing *Hail Marys*. This time, Zoe did not join in, the wretchedness she'd encountered having shocked her into silence. She separated herself from the singers and found a spot against the wall. On a bench across from her, underneath a barred window looking out on a leafless chestnut tree, a small child wept in her mother's lap. The little girl was the same age as Amber would be now, unless...

Don't think about that, Zoe!

"Not patriotic?" asked a nearby woman. A red-headed *prévenue*, she was still pretty, even in her ill-fitting dress. Individual tailoring wasn't an entrée on Saint-Lazare's carte du jour.

"I just don't feel like singing," Zoe answered.

"Ah, you are an American," she said, noting Zoe's accent. "How did you and your fancy friends come to be in this place? And why were you all dressed like men?"

When Zoe told her, the woman chuckled. "I would have enjoyed seeing that. How far did you get before the cops nabbed you?"

"About halfway across the Place de la Concorde."

At this, guffaws almost bent the *prévenue* double. "Two hundred meters? Some march!"

Despite Zoe's surroundings, she laughed, too, and before long, they were sharing easy conversation. The woman's street name was Fey, and she had once dreamed of being an artist, she confided, but then she fell in love with the wrong man. Next thing she knew, she was working the streets with him as her pimp.

"But you were arrested?" Zoe said in surprise. "I thought prostitution was legal in Paris."

"Not our kind," she winked. "Sometimes a little pickpocketing here, a little *chantage* there."

Chantage. Blackmail.

Sensing a good story, Zoe asked, "Putting the squeeze on important men straying from their wives?"

"It served them right. But we did other things, too." Proud of her adventures, Fey launched into an account that, minus the sex, sounded like the plot of a Charles Dickens novel.

Not to be outdone, several other prostitutes crowded around, relishing the chance to one-up Fey and shock the American *prévenue.* By the time the last chorus of "La Marseillaise" died away at the other end of the room, Zoe had heard tales about men climbing out of windows to avoid being caught, wealthy women hiring male prostitutes when their husbands "ran dry," and story after story of extraordinary sexual adventures. It made her rethink her now-destroyed version of *Lust,* one of the paintings in the Seven Deadly Sins series. She'd just begun to imagine a new version when one of the women mentioned a name that sounded familiar.

"...and then Zou-Zou said, 'Might as well fuck off, then, since you've already paid for it.'" This was followed by a roar of laughter.

Zou-Zou. Where had Zoe heard that name before?

She turned to this storyteller, whose name she'd learned was Bibi. Despite the sores on her face, the woman maintained an overripe prettiness, with her long dark hair and even darker eyes. "Who's Zou-Zou?" Zoe asked.

"You just missed her," Bibi said. "She was in here for a week, then they released her. Now *she* had a mighty tale to tell!"

Zoe remembered now. Zou-Zou was the name of the "woman of the streets," so-called by *Le Figaro*, who'd lured doorman Pierre Lazenby away from the entrance to the count's apartment building, leaving it accessible to a killer. "I'd like to talk to this Zou-Zou."

Bibi grinned. "Your type, is she? Well, if you have the francs, she'd be willing."

When they were through laughing at Bibi's joke, Zoe said, "I'm sure we'd have fun, but I'd love to speak to her about something other than woman-on-woman pleasures. We may have a friend in common."

"Zou-Zou doesn't have the pox, if that's what you're worried about." For a moment, the merriment left Bibi's eyes.

"Excellent news, but honestly...I just want to talk."

"Then you're out of luck," Bibi said, recovering her good cheer. "When she left here, she said she was going to visit relatives in Cannes, that Paris was so cold men were even keeping their peckers buttoned up."

Zoe tried not to let her disappointment show. "I wish I had relatives in Cannes, too, because... Look, it's snowing again."

At this, everyone turned to stare out the barred window to see big fat flakes tumbling down. When they finished lamenting the weather—the subject being standard conversational fare with everyone from nuns to incarcerated prostitutes—Zoe pressed onward, "Anyway, you were saying Zou-Zou had some good stories. Maybe you could share them?"

Eager to keep the entertainment going on what had heretofore been a dull afternoon, the group wasted no time relating *The Further Adventures of Zou-Zou, Lady Prostitute*. As each woman talked, the stories got wilder and wilder. Zoe played along, pasting appropriate expressions of horror or glee across her face, hoping that at some point, one of them would get to the true adventure that had landed Zou-Zou in the newspapers. The wait was worth it because Fey herself finally related this story. A week or so ago, she said, a man had paid Zou-Zou big francs to lure a doorman away from one of the fancy apartments in the eighth arrondissement.

"Zou-Zou said he told her she didn't even have to have sex with the doorman, just to keep him occupied for a few minutes," Fey related. "But Zou-Zou being a friendly sort, she did, and she enjoyed it, too. Said his pecker was enormous."

Before the others could join in with tales of other enormous peckers they had known, Zoe quickly asked, "Did she say what he looked like?"

Fey nodded. "Well, this is the sad part, because he wore a cloth mask to cover his face." She paused for a moment, out of respect. "Zou-Zou said the poor man was one of *Les Mutilés*."

Chapter Twenty-Six

Fleurette Joubert's announcement that their prison stay would be short proved overly optimistic. Their stay at Saint-Lazare lasted several days, during which Zoe's new prostitute friends kept her entertained with salacious stories about the Parisian elite.

Four full days after their incarceration, an intercession by some excellent solicitors and several bribes won the women's release, but it was a Pyrrhic victory. Several of them had lost their jobs; others, their boyfriends. To make matters worse, none of the newspapers smuggled into the prison by certain visitors—Madeline and Béatrice Camondo among them—mentioned the Trousers March. The Parisian press remained silent, as if a story about women wearing trousers would be too shocking for their readers' delicate sensibilities.

Therefore, it was a disgruntled group of women who walked out of Saint-Lazar. As they emerged en masse into a snow-flurried day—oddly enough, their illegal trousers had been given back to them—Zoe noted a familiar car standing at the curb. A green Citroën, with Sûreté Inspector Henri Challiot at the wheel.

He leaned over and opened the passenger's side door. "Get in, criminal."

Not relishing the idea of riding the Métro in her trousers and possibly getting arrested again, Zoe climbed in.

"Adulterer," she snapped.

He grinned. "That makes two of us. So where to, m'lady?"

"Home, James."

··· ◆ ···

Once back in Le Petit Bibelot, Zoe let Henri divest her of her masculine attire, and they spent a pleasurable hour in bed. But even enveloped in the warmth of his arms, something kept her from sharing what she'd learned at Saint-Lazare.

"One of Les Mutilés," Zou-Zou had said.

Zoe refused to believe Reynard Dibasse was a murderer. He may have killed in combat, but that was far different than murdering a dancer in her lover's bed or killing a young woman in a shack who might have been—but probably wasn't—the Grand Duchess Anastasia. Or killing a young artist who turned away from what had once been a lucrative career in landscape painting to follow his own odd dreams. While preparing Reynard's portrait mask, Zoe had looked into his one remaining eye, and she'd seen only gentleness.

"You seem distracted, *chérie*," Henri said, rolling off her. "Does your experience in Saint-Lazar weigh heavily on you?"

"Something like that."

He leaned on his elbow, facing her. His hair stood awry, and his face was flushed, but he remained outlandishly handsome. "Be careful, Zoe. Saint-Lazare isn't the proper place for a woman like you."

A woman like me? What does that even mean?

Zoe remembered the faces of the women in the big dormitory—the prostitutes, the accused murderers. They were all women sharing the same problem: men. If you opened your heart to a man, his love became the most dangerous weapon in the world. Now here she was, fresh out of prison and in bed with a married man, something she'd once sworn never to do. But that had been last year, when she'd been more innocent than now.

Hating herself, hating him, she said, "You should leave."

He did.

. . . ◊ . . .

At two in the morning, unable to sleep, Zoe broke another promise to herself. She fetched the thick packet of letters she'd hidden away in her escritoire and took them into her boudoir. She read only the first one, which was all she could bear.

April 1918. New York

Dearest Zoe,

My love, my light, my wife, my darling. How I miss you!

I miss your laughter, your love, your warmth! You are my island of calm in this whirlwind world.

New York is stormy this week. I have never felt such a punishing wind, and yet it's supposedly spring! But enough of my complaining. Thanks to my music studies at Oberlin, I've found steady work. Upon hearing me play at a small club down the street, the famous bandleader James Reese Europe hired me on the spot to play second trumpet in his Clef Club Society band.

This is a great thing, my darling, because I will soon be making enough to afford a place for us. Then I will send for you and we will never be parted again.

Oh, Zoe, keep yourself safe until that happy day!

All my love,
Your adoring Pete

Zoe fell asleep holding her husband's letter.

Chapter Twenty-Seven

Zoe was so bleary-eyed the next morning, she couldn't even make her way to La Rotonde for breakfast, but Madeline, bless her, had planned ahead. To celebrate her employer's release from prison, she'd purchased two hothouse pears and put them in the kitchen icebox to keep fresh. The fruit, along with a fresh croissant and a pot of coffee, made a decent breakfast. It gave Zoe the strength to start what would prove to be a grueling day.

After chasing away dark memories by painting for several hours, she felt ready to face the boulevards of Paris. Wiser now, she put on a dress. A drab one, and longer than she preferred.

While she was dressing, a thought occurred to her.

Hemingway, who'd been expected to return to Paris to select warmer clothes for his and Hadley's trip to Italy, hadn't stopped by or sent her a note professing his gratitude for her rescuing his manuscripts.

Zoe frowned. Why not? Was it just Hemingway being his usual rude self? Or, as she suspected, had he taken one look at his gibberish and been horrified?

Then again, his lack of gratitude might reveal a darker motive. If

Hadley didn't know her husband's manuscripts had been rescued, she would continue to be mired in guilt. And guilt, Zoe knew from experience, could be easily manipulated. It could make a woman accept myriad flaws in a man without complaint, a trait Zoe had already noticed about Hadley. Hadn't she'd already accepted Hemingway's drinking? His gambling? His fisticuffs? What other—as yet unnoticed—sins would a guilt-ridden Hadley accept?

Merde! It didn't bear thinking about. Hemingway wasn't a perfect husband—what man was?—and Hadley wasn't a perfect wife. And to be truthful, Zoe wasn't perfect, either.

Because in a perfect world, she would already have told Henri about the *Mutilé* who'd paid Zou-Zou to lure away the doorman at Sergei's building, but in a perfect world, there would also have been no Maison d'Arrêt de la Santé awaiting men suspected of murder. Now that she'd experienced firsthand the female version of incarceration, she could only imagine what horrors might befall a *Mutilé* in la Santé. Instead of letting that happen to Reynard, she decided to do some snooping of her own to prove he wasn't the masked figure in Zou-Zou's story. If he turned out to be...

Well, she'd cross that bridge when she came to it. Just in case, she put her Derringer into her purse, and put all thoughts of Hemingway and Hadley's strained marriage out of her mind.

There was a more immediate problem to attend to.

Reynard was now bunking full-time at Karen Wegner's flat. It was only a short walk along today's happily sun-drenched streets, so Zoe planned that as her first stop. As she approached Karen's building, she saw the couple returning from a boulangerie, a baguette tucked underneath Reynard's arm. No trousers for Karen today, just a long skirt that wouldn't shock a nun. In deference to passersby and the boulangeries, Reynard wore his mask. The two were so deep in conversation they didn't spot Zoe until she'd almost reached them, but when they did, Karen smiled. Zoe imagined Reynard did, too, but couldn't see what was left of his mouth underneath his handsome mask.

"How nice to see you again after our recent adventures!" Karen said. "And such a lovely coincidence! I have a new piece I'd like your opinion on. You might even like it."

The sculptor was teasing, of course. She knew Zoe enjoyed her wind-up kinetic sculptures; it was the bourgeoisie who didn't. Not that Karen cared.

"Will this one tell me I'm the most beautiful woman in Paris?" Zoe asked.

"No, but it might sing you a happy song."

"I could use a little 'happy' right about now." It slipped out before she could stop it.

The smile left Karen's face. "Has someone else been killed?"

"No, no. I'm just..." Zoe thought for a moment. "Sorry. I'm just in a mood."

"So is she," Renard said, gesturing toward Karen. "One of the women in Saint-Lazare spit on her, and she's still mad."

As they walked up the stairs to the third-floor apartment, Karen told Zoe she'd mistaken one of the women—a many-times-arrested pickpocket—for a former model of hers when she was still working in stone. "She thought I was calling her a whore," the sculptor said and went on to recount the many insults heaped upon her by other thieves.

Zoe counted herself lucky to have wound up with the prostitutes, a more amiable group.

Like most apartments in Montparnasse, Karen's flat consisted of a tiny bedroom and a larger living area. The north wall was mainly glass, and if she'd been a painter instead of a sculptor, the flat could have served as an excellent studio. The bits of junked machine parts, gears, and wires strewn about on a long worktable by the windows showed how Karen sometimes fiddled with her little kinetics here instead of at her studio a few blocks away. The apartment was chaotically furnished with two maroon horsehair sofas from the Victorian era, two densely patterned chairs that were vaguely Chinese, and a burled walnut dining table that looked Jacobean, surrounded by unmatched chairs in wildly clashing styles and colors.

Zoe loved it.

"Here's the new kinetic clock I was talking about," Karen said, motioning Zoe over to the worktable.

Pale light streamed down on what Zoe had mistaken for a pile of junked machine parts, revealing a foot-high sculpture. The parts that weren't metal were wood. Ash, perhaps? Whatever, the piece looked like a clock that had endured a hard life. Its second hand was missing, and the wooden panel housing the broken glass clockface looked like termites had been at it.

"Now watch," Karen ordered.

She reached behind the pile of metal and did something Zoe couldn't see. Immediately, the wooden panel revealed itself as a door. When it opened, out popped a toy rabbit, yodeling, "Cuckoo! Cuckoo!"

Reynard sniggered. "It tells time, too. More or less."

When Zoe finished laughing—*could this sweet man possibly be a murderer?*—she asked Karen, "Are you going to put this one in the show?" She'd heard Marcel Duchamp had invited Karen to join with a group of other painters and sculptors to take part in a spring showing titled *Devenir Sérieux*. Getting Serious. He'd asked Zoe, too, and before the break-in, she'd planned to propose one of her Deadly Sins paintings, probably *Wrath*. But *Wrath* had been destroyed with the others.

"I call it *Lost Time*," Karen said, cradling the little clock. "Do you think it's good enough for the show?"

"Absolutely," Zoe replied.

They spent a few minutes talking about the difficulty of women obtaining serious representation in the better galleries, and as they sipped the spiced tea Reynard had brewed, Zoe finally got around to the real reason for her visit. When she asked the two if they remembered where they were on the day Sergei and Jewel were killed, Karen frowned.

"Still playing detective, Zoe? Your handsome inspector should teach you how to be less obvious."

"You misunderstand me," Zoe lied. "It's just that, while we were locked up in Saint-Lazare, I kept thinking how strange life is, that terrible things can be happening to some people while others are having a wonderful time. Like me, for instance. You know how close I was to Jewel. Yet, on the morning of her death, I'd been doing a pastel sketch and humming as I worked. Irony, don't you see? Like 'Getting Serious,' the title of Duchamp's exhibition."

The expression on Karen's face revealed she didn't believe this tortured explanation. After a tense silence, Reynard said, "I don't remember what we were doing."

Karen shot him a look. "Oh, stop playing the gentleman, Reynard. You know damn well we were fucking."

··· ◊ ···

Zoe's next visit proved more pleasant. Antoine Fortier was at home in his fussy apartment, and as soon as she arrived, he expressed his desire to take her to lunch.

"Tell me all, dear Zoe! I'm dying to hear the sordid details about life in a women's prison." An unlit De Reszke drooped from the corner of his mouth.

Relieved to find the fussbudget in a cheerful mood, she responded, "Prepare to be shocked."

The Painting Marquis hadn't been painting today, and no Eau de Turpentine scented the air—just the stench of tobacco. The studio section of the big sitting room was closed off by a drape, and instead of being clad in a painter's smock, Fortier was already dressed for the boulevards in a deep gray suit with a maroon silk handkerchief peeking coyly out of the breast pocket. Smiling— the marquis obviously knew how dashing he looked—he threw a heavy black cloak over his snazzy outfit, then picked up his silver-headed cane and gave it a quick twirl.

"Let us now partake of the wonders of La Cité, my lovely Mademoiselle."

Zoe took Fortier's proffered arm, and off they went.

Within minutes they were seated inside Café de la Paix, at the corner of Boulevard des Capucines and Place de l'Opéra, where they lunched on oysters and watched the boulevardiers strut by on the other side of the café's big glass windows. As she sipped at a fine Vaillons Chablis, she noted how much more fashionably everyone dressed on the Right Bank, as opposed to the riotous glad rags of Montparnasse. Even the sounds were different here. On these elegant boulevards, you heard only the purrs of fine motorcars, whereas on the Left Bank, the grump-and-growl of cheaper vehicles competed with the neigh of sway-backed cart horses. Inside the Café de la Paix, the customers spoke in more moderate tones, too. No thrown wine glasses. And certainly no Bolsheviks.

"Now tell me, sweet Zoe," Fortier said, after finishing his last oyster and lighting up another De Reszke. "What's it like to be a jailbird?"

Well-groomed heads turned their way. Delicate eyebrows raised.

When Zoe finished grinding her teeth, she forced a note of careless gaiety into her voice. "It's been most amusing, Antoine. You would have loved it!" Then, lowering her voice somewhat— she did want him to open up—she repeated some of the stories Fey and Bibi shared at Saint-Lazare. She did, however, leave out

Zou-Zou's adventure with Sergei's doorman who, because of his laxity, was currently in danger of losing his job.

Once Fortier's salacious interest was sated, Zoe changed the subject. "But enough about prison life. So much grief and horror going on around us, yet half the time we don't notice until it's too late. It damn near kills me to think that while Jewel and Sergei were being murdered, I was just living my happy life, thinking only about myself. The same for little Bobby." She made a motion to brush an imaginary tear from her eye, only to discover that the tear wasn't imaginary.

Sympathetic, Fortier patted her hand. "Poor Zoe. Such a generous heart. I, too, was painting when Sergei and Jewel died. When the news came, I was devastated. Sergei and I were quite close, you know. Why, I remember when he first arrived from Paris, having barely escaped that benighted country of his. Revolution! Regicide! Communists!" For emphasis, he tapped his ebony cane against the floor.

Zoe didn't remind Fortier that his own country, as well as hers, had experienced revolutions only a couple of centuries earlier, although in America's case, they hadn't decapitated a king. Not that they hadn't wanted to.

For the next few minutes, she let Fortier hold forth about introducing Sergei to the wealthy dowager who became the count's second wife. The match had been advantageous for both of them, with Sergei reentering the luxurious lifestyle he'd once enjoyed, his new wife receiving the delicious title of Countess.

"Advantageous, maybe, but was the marriage happy?" Zoe asked.

Fortier stubbed out his cigarette. "Of course it was. She was a delightful woman, once you got past her looks."

"Ugly, was she?" Zoe hoped her sour tone would forestall any more cutting remarks about a woman's physical shortcomings. It didn't.

"She had a face that would, as you Americans so amusingly say, stop a clock. Her nose..." He made a face and took another sip of Chablis.

"What did she die of?" Zoe interrupted.

He thought for a moment. "You know, I really can't remember. A tumor? Tuberculosis? Anyway, since she had no other heirs—careless of her, right?—she left him all that lovely money, which, I might add, he put to foolish purpose." He fumbled in his pocket for a moment, took out a silver cigarette case, and lit another.

Zoe moved her chair slightly so as not to be downwind. "Are you talking about his gambling habit or his support of the counterrevolution?"

"Both," Fortier said. "Most of his money went to Russia, which was useless, because I have it on good authority everything he sent wound up in the Communists' hands. The man may have been a dear, but he was an idiot."

"His money never got to his friends?!" In her surprise, Zoe almost knocked over her wineglass. "Are you serious? I was under the impression you helped finance that group, too. Rebuild the Homeland, or whatever it's called in Russian."

"*Vosstanovit Rodinu.* I did support them—*past* tense—as would any right-thinking person. But when I found out what was happening, I stopped. I told Sergei what was going on, but he wouldn't listen. Anyway, these days when Russians come begging for money, I say *nyet*, Comrade. Paint has become too expensive as of late."

Remembering her recent bill from the art supply store, she said, "Yeah, I noticed."

His handsome face fell. "Oh, my dear! I am so, so sorry! I forgot about what happened to your studio, that you had to replace..."

Zoe hated pity. "Don't shed any tears for me, Antoine. I've already restocked, and my studio's back to normal."

An approving smile. "So independent! That's what I've always loved about you, Zoe. Losing all your work must have put you through hell, yet you are still working. Indomitable!" Fortier pointed a shaky, unstained forefinger at her right hand.

She looked down and saw a rainbow mess under every one of her fingernails.

··· ◇ ···

After thanking Fortier for lunch, Zoe bade the marquis goodbye and took the Métro back to Montparnasse, where a very different kind of conversation awaited her.

Louise Packard's studio was on Rue Delambre, and when Zoe arrived, she found the Cubist working on a large portrait of Bobby. The old artist's gaunt face looked almost skeletal, but it brightened at Zoe's entrance.

Something else had changed, too. Louise's palette usually consisted of bold primary and secondary colors, but the portrait was awash in muted grays, browns, and near-blacks, almost the same palette as Picasso's heart-wrenching *Guernica*. Zoe knew how painful Louise's arthritis had to be, but she was painting through it. To use Fortier's word, Louise was *indomitable*.

"I was just ready to take a break, so why don't we have some tea?" she said. "It's already brewed. You like mint, I hope?"

Before Zoe could reply, the painter poured a dark liquid into mismatched cups. As they took their places at a small table, Louise said, "Do me a favor and let's not talk about Bobby, okay?" She motioned to the mattress that still lay in the corner, waiting for a little man who would never return.

Zoe was no sadist, so she picked the first topic that came into her head, which was, oddly enough, their shared time in prison. "What a time we had, eh?"

The old woman managed a grin. "I grew especially fond of the woman accused of killing her husband. Pauline the Poisoner, they called her. Delightful person, quite bright. You, I seem to remember, were a big hit with the prostitutes. Must have been your Southern charm."

Zoe grinned back. "Like my Alabama relatives, they had interesting stories."

A bark of laughter. "So did Pauline!"

Since Louise's living quarters were elsewhere, her studio was pretty much bare bones. Tall windows, one large easel, a couple of cheap chairs, a coal stove, and a rough, raised platform for her models to recline upon. The sun being out, light streamed through the windows, rendering the austerity cheerful. It was rumored that Louise was supported more by an inheritance than her painting sales, but Zoe had no way of knowing. Finance was such a taboo subject. People who openly discussed their sexual proclivities clammed up when it came to money.

While sipping at her tea, Zoe continued sharing stories about the more colorful characters at Saint-Lazare until she thought Louise was ready. After one final story about another suspected murderess, she segued to the real reason for her visit. "Except for our vacation in merry Saint-Lazare, this past week has been pretty awful, hasn't it?"

The old Cubist stared down at her teacup. It looked as fragile as she did. "*Awful* isn't a strong enough word."

"We've lost dear friends."

Guarded eyes met Zoe's. "You might as well go ahead and tell me why you're really here, because I know it's not just to chat about dear old Saint-Lazare."

Caught, Zoe took a deep breath. "All right. Who do you think killed Bobby?"

A grimace. "Didn't I tell you not to bring him up?"

"Yes, you did, but dammit, Louise, I'm trying to find out who killed him. And Jewel."

"You're better off leaving such things to the cops."

"If you'll remember, they were much too quick to arrest the wrong person."

"Are you talking about that Spanish taxi driver?"

"Avak is Armenian. And you didn't answer my question. Who do you think killed Bobby?"

A blade of sunlight lit up the artist's gray hair, revealing every crevasse and wrinkle on her face. For a brief moment, Louise glanced over at the bare mattress. "If I knew the answer to that question, I'd gouge out the bastard's eyes with my palette knife." Louise opened and closed her hands several times, as if to ease an ache. Besides being paint-stained, they were an angry red and so swollen that applying paint to her big canvases had to be a painful process.

Meeting Zoe's eyes once again, she said. "You need to be more careful. Everyone in Paris knows you've been running around, talking to this person, that person, and asking questions. Do you expect the killer to confess, to say something like, 'Oh, yes, Zoe, I killed them all? Why? Oh, because I woke up in a bad mood and felt like killing someone, and once I started killing, I just couldn't stop?" The frown on Louise's face grew deeper. "You keep carrying on the way you are, whoever killed poor Bobby and the rest of them might come after you!"

Refusing to accept this non-answer, Zoe said, "Who, Louise? Who do you think killed them? You must at least have a suspicion."

Louise set down her teacup, rose from her chair, and walked to her easel. She picked up a goosenecked palette knife similar to Zoe's favorite. However, instead of holding the knife in her fingers like an artist, she clenched her fist around it like a street thug. "We're done here. I've got work to do."

Since Zoe's Derringer was in her purse, the veiled threat didn't scare her. "I'm not leaving until you answer."

Silence for a moment, then a bitter laugh. "Jesus, Zoe, what a bitch you are! But you've got balls, I'll give you that. All right, here's my answer, although I don't think it'll satisfy you. I think the Bolsheviks killed them all. I just don't know which particular Bolshevik. There are so many of the awful creatures running around Paris these days. Like rats!"

"But would Bolsheviks kill anyone in France? Other than Sergei, of course. Oh, and those two Russians in Mesnil-Théribus."

"Because that murdered girl in Mesnil-Théribus really *was* the Grand Duchess Anastasia, that's why! She was the last Romanov, so of course the Bolshies would kill her and anyone else to prevent another Romanov from claiming the throne."

Zoe didn't know whether to laugh or cry. "If that's true—and I don't think it is—I can see the murderer killing her and the man with her because he was a witness, just like poor Jewel. But why on earth would the Bolsheviks kill Bobby?"

"To draw attention away from themselves and their heinous plot," Louise said. "And it worked, didn't it?"

Chapter Twenty-Eight

On the way back to Le Petit Bibelot, Zoe stopped at La Rotonde, but she found no Kiki, no Archie, no Dominique. Frustrated, she ordered a glass of merlot, but once it arrived, she hardly touched it. She just kept thinking about what she'd been told, the truth and the lies. She was staring at her glass, the door to the café opened and The Lovers walked in, heading straight for their usual corner table.

No. She was wrong. Not The Lovers, *plural*.

Because only the male Lover was there, the blond man with the pencil mustache. The woman he was with wasn't his usual elfin partner.

She was someone new. Blond, like him. No beret.

With the same smile he'd bestowed on his former lover, he drew their chairs close together and nuzzled her neck.

Sickened, Zoe threw down money for the check and left.

··· ◇ ···

When Zoe finally made it home, she felt like a limp paint rag, so she was delighted to find her pretty little house sparkling clean, the scent of chicken and herbs wafting through its rooms. She followed her nose into the kitchen and found Madeline busy at work, her artificial arm performing with nary a squeak.

Might as well ask her, too.

"Madeline, who do you think killed Count Aronoffsky and all the others?"

A long curl of black-and-gray hair escaped from the housekeeper's tight chignon and dangled against her flushed cheek. Without slowing the savage chops she was delivering to a large shallot, she answered, "The Bolsheviks."

The Bolsheviks. Again. "Because?"

"I don't know what's in their black hearts, but most assuredly, they'll even kill *you* if you give them the chance!"

··· ◊ ···

The early supper Madeline prepared proved excellent. Chicken *casserole à la Normande*, redolent with the aromas of bacon, apples, and thyme. The wine wasn't bad, either, a Château Grillet Rhône.

Madeline left as soon as her duties were fulfilled, leaving Zoe free to drink half the bottle. Then, encouraged by Louise's own steely determination, she went into her studio, threw on her smock, and began to rework one of the ruined Seven Heavenly Virtues canvases. This time, she chose *Temperance*. For some reason, maybe too much Château Grillet, her first strokes failed, and almost as soon as paint touched the canvas, she'd wipe it away with her palette knife. The shapes—whether soft, hard-edged, or serpentine—didn't thrill. The colors—burnt sienna, yellow ochre, even blazing Chinese red—fell flat. Zoe threw down her brushes and left the studio.

Who needed temperance, anyway?

After finishing off the Château Grillet, she sat in her big Bergère chair—the only non-Nouveau piece of furniture in the sitting room and therefore the most comfortable—and stared out the small window. While she'd been in the studio, the gaslights had come on outside, encasing Rue Vavin in a buttery glow. Ordinarily, this was her favorite time of day, when automobile traffic lessened but the clip-clop of dray horses' hooves still sounded against the cobblestones.

She closed her eyes, remembering the horses at Beech Glen, remembered her father teaching her how to ride. That led to an even earlier memory, her very first. She must have been around three when he'd taught her how to count using a deck of cards. "Ace, two, three, four..." Years later, he had honed her math skills by teaching her poker and how to read the other players' faces. If only he'd taught her to read his despair. Maybe then she could have...

No, Zoe. You were just a child. There was nothing you could do.

Her heart twisted, remembering how she stood there in shocked silence, as she watched her father's body swing ever so slowly from the barn rafter.

Maybe if she'd screamed for help...

Guilt. Always the guilt.

Knowing that she shouldn't, Zoe walked over to the escritoire and took out the packet of letters.

May 1918. New York

My darling Zoe,
Less than a week has gone by since my last visit to you, but it seems like forever. How can I live without my Zoe? I can still taste your lips and feel the embrace of your arms. Oh, how I wish I could have stayed with you longer, but I must continue to play with the Clef Club Society. Rest assured every song I play, I play for you.

And now I must confess that I have done something which will make you unhappy. Mr. Europe, our band-leader, has proposed we take our music to our brave American soldiers fighting in France. To do this, we must join a new army regiment, which I have done. We will soon be headed for basic training.

The next time you hear from me, I will be wearing the olive drab uniform of the U.S. Army, but my weapon will be my trumpet, not a gun.

Do not cry, Zoe. I will be safe. When this war is over—and it will be soon, I promise—I will send for you, and we will begin our life together in New York City as husband and wife and child.

> *Loving you forever and ever,*
> *Your husband-of-the-heart,*
> *Pete*

As if reading Pete's letter hadn't caused enough pain, Zoe then went into her bedroom and stared at the surrealist painting she'd bought from Abelard Leveque.

A little girl.

Standing alone.

Abandoned to a dismal world.

Where was their Amber girl now?

—— Gabrielle ——

December 1922

Last night I heard him calling her name.

Odile was right. That Zoe person means more to my husband

than any other woman, perhaps even me. For what am I? Nothing more than a lump of flesh, of no use to anyone, especially not a man with Henri's passions.

Will he kill me before I can kill him? He is an inspector, and he knows how to disguise a murder. He could put a pillow over my face, and there would be nothing I could do about it. Then he'd be free to do what he wishes to do even now—replace me with her.

So I will kill her, too.

I must work hard to get well enough to take my revenge. I must make my hands and arms move again, my legs... The illness that sent me helpless to my bed is wearing off. Last night I discovered I can move my index finger, and all day I have been tap-tap-tapping it against the sheets. Tomorrow, another finger. Then another.

My will is strong.

And I am not without my own wiles. A few of the plants in this room are poisonous: hemlock, arum lily, cherry laurel...

Madame frowns. Is she in pain?

Sweet Odile, who'd been at the window, describing ladies' fine wear, has scrambled back to my pillow. Can she read my mind?

No, I tell her. *No pain at all.*

Suddenly I feel tired, and Odile can sense it. As I fall away again, the little Huntsman spider is stroking my cheek.

Chapter Twenty-Nine

Undone by exhaustion—from work, from sorrow—Zoe at first wasn't going to let Henri in when he came scratching at her door. But she was tired of being strong.

Still filthy with paint, she let him lead her into the mirrored-ceiling boudoir. Stood unmoving as he undressed her. Remained silent while he did what he did. Embraced him only once, at the height of her pleasure.

When she could breathe again, she finally said it: "This was the last time."

Taking it for a joke, he said, "Was I that bad?"

She didn't answer immediately, and he drew back to read her face. "What's wrong, Zoe?"

"Everything. Especially this."

Her studio was at the other end of the house, but she could smell notes of turpentine underneath the closer scents of sweat and sex. Was the wild beauty of these moments worth the damage?

Oh, Pete! If I truly loved you, would I be doing this?

"Talk to me, Zoe."

He was leaning on one elbow now, gazing down at her. In the

mirrored ceiling above, she could see the spatter of shrapnel scars blossoming on his right shoulder, the round pucker of a long-gone bullet near his spine. When she'd come, Zoe had been clutching the largest wound of all, the six-inch-long furrow dug in his butt-cheek by a German bayonet as he'd sheltered a gut-shot lieutenant with his own body.

This man had courage, so what she was about to do wouldn't kill him. "You're married," she said. And so was she, really. She would always be Pete's wife, although she'd done her best to forget that, refusing even to use the title *Madame*.

"You've known I was married for some time now, *chérie.*"

"But now I understand." *Pete's blue eyes gazing down at her with love that first time, asking her if he'd hurt her. Yes, she'd whispered, but it was a hurt she'd desired, and when it was over, she realized she had said goodbye to her separate self. She and Pete were one now, and not being fools, they knew how hard that was going to be. Yet out of that dangerous oneness, maybe something wonderful would happen.*

She would never feel like that with another man.

"I love you, Zoe," Henri said.

She refused to look at him. "You don't love me. You need me, and that's not the same."

"Always have an answer for everything, don't you?"

"It's not that..."

He grasped her wrist hard but stopped just short of the issuance of pain. He wasn't that kind of man. "What happened to make you like this?"

Too heartsick to struggle, she told him.

It took a while, because it had begun with a stumble on the sidewalk in downtown Birmingham, Alabama...

Her leg was hurting that day, and the rain had just started up again, which made it worse, and she was half blind with pain anyway, didn't see the loose board, the fall forward, until her swift rescue by a beautiful

man with blue eyes, and on and on, and on and on, until it ended with
her locked, bleeding, in a filthy basement.

She searched Henri's eyes for disgust but saw nothing but tears.
Damned emotional Frenchmen.

"My poor, sweet girl." He sounded as if something had torn
loose inside him.

"I survived."

"Oh, *ma chère bébé.*"

As Henri rocked her back and forth, she wondered why whenever someone comforted you, they spoke to you as if to a child?
Those things that happened to her were over and done with, and
they'd taken place in a different world. Before Paris, before Mesnil-
Théribus. She was a grown woman now.

"It doesn't hurt anymore," she lied.

But Henri kept on rocking her, rocking her, until comfort turned
into something else, and before she could react in any other way,
he was working his way down her body with his tongue, raising
goosebumps from her breasts to her thighs. She thought about
pushing him away, but her body didn't care what her brain wanted;
it was too far gone. Losing control, she raised her legs until they
wrapped around his neck and squeezed in rhythm until he slid
forward out of their grasp and entered her and rocked her in a
different way until they both cried out together.

Then everything went straight to hell.

Henri, smug with the satisfaction he'd given her, smiled up at
their reflection in the ceiling. "Do you love me, Zoe? Even a little?"

"Don't ask me that."

He stopped looking at himself, but the smile remained. "Still
playing the tease, *chérie*?"

Tease? What about him? He was admiring his reflection,
preening, proud of the way he'd made her lose herself in him.
Given everything she'd been through, she should have known

better, but she was a fool. She'd probably always been a fool, and now look at the ammunition she'd given him. She pulled out of Henri's embrace and sat up, her back leaning against the bed's wooden headboard. It wasn't comfortable, but his embrace was no longer comfortable, either. She remembered The Lovers, the girl in the red beret.

Replaced.

Just like she would be. To Henri, love was nothing more than a game, while to her, love was the most tragic thing ever.

Oh, Pete!

"It's time you left, Henri," she said, her voice as cold as she wished her heart could be.

"But, Zoe..."

"Get dressed and go."

He did.

See?

She meant nothing to him, nothing at all.

··· ◇ ···

Zoe dressed extra warmly the next morning, bracing herself for yet another long trip to Mesnil-Théribus. Snow was still falling, and a polar wind blew in from the north. But she had to get this over with before someone else died. After last night, she couldn't expect any help from Henri.

Half blind from sorrow and snow, Zoe almost walked into a woman leading a dog with one hand, a small child with the other. The dog, a greyhound mix, was doing fine, the animal's long legs fairly leaping over the drifts, but the child—he couldn't have been any older than five—was struggling. As they swerved out of Zoe's way, the boy went down, landing on his backside, which was fortunately well-padded under a bright blue snowsuit. Although he couldn't have been hurt, he shrieked.

Instead of telling him to be a brave boy, his mother leaned down and embraced him.

"*Pauvre petit.*" Poor little one.

Leaving them behind, she trudged on until she found Avak parked at his usual spot on Boulevard Raspail. As he spoke, snow-flakes accumulated on his marvelous mustache. "Again to Mesnil-Théribus, Mademoiselle Zoe? Or new someplace hot, like St. Tropez, where always sun shines and children sand castles build?"

"I hate to disappoint you, but..."

"Ah. Go we to merry Mesnil-Théribus."

With a chuckle, he helped her into the Grim Reaper. Once underneath the Landau top, she wrapped herself in the blankets he'd placed there for his fares, leaving only her eyes exposed to the elements. Then they set off on what would hopefully be their last visit to merry Mesnil-Théribus.

The first part of their journey went well. Horse and automobile traffic had kept the road more or less clear with the exception of a few snow-covered potholes. They didn't run into trouble until about six miles from the village, when a large black-and-yellow Renault tried to pass them. Because the road was so narrow, the other vehicle wound up running them into a ditch. The driver didn't stop to render aid, just kept plowing toward Mesnil-Théribus, kicking up a trail of snow and frozen mud until the Renault disappeared over a low rise.

"Mademoiselle Zoe be well?" Avak, whose nose was bleeding, reached out a hand to assist her. The blankets she'd been wrapped in had cushioned her, and unlike him, she remained unhurt. But the poor Grim Reaper now law on its side.

"I'm fine," she said, scrambling to find footing on the topsy-turvy floorboard. With another great heave, Avak hauled her out of the car. "But if we run into that louse in Mesnil-Théribus, I'm going to have a few words with him." Maybe more than words, since before leaving, she'd tucked the Derringer into her purse.

Back on firm but snowy ground, she examined Avak's nose. Nothing seemed to be broken, so she took the edge of a blanket and wiped the blood away. Then she sealed the injury by patting it down with fresh snow. Partner-in-crime thus attended to, she dusted herself off and rewrapped the blankets around her trembling body. As a Southern girl, she wasn't used to wind this cold, nor snow this deep. What was it? Three inches?

"What should we do now?" she asked Avak. "Freeze while we wait for help?"

He looked up and down the empty road. "Walk, we could."

"And leave the car?"

"Who steal? No one that crazy."

Avak had a point. The Grim Reaper was an ugly beast, even more so now that it lay on its side with its pornographic undercarriage exposed.

Zoe sighed. "They say exercise is almost as good for you as smoking."

So off they went, bundled up like two Eskimos on a polar bear hunt, Avak keeping his long strides short to accommodate her shorter ones. Fortunately, Zoe was wearing her custom-built shoes, and the cobbler's skill served her bad leg well until she stumbled into a snow-disguised pothole. When she managed to extricate her foot, it came away shoeless. By the time she'd retrieved the built-up shoe and shaken the snow out of it, Avak had been treated to a fine collection of American curse words. His ears were flaming, and not from the cold.

A half hour on, Zoe's leg felt like tiny demons were stabbing it with tiny pitchforks, but her misery was cut short when a horse-drawn wagon approached from the rear. It was stacked with hay bales covered by a tarp.

"Would that be your overturned automobile back there?" the farmer asked. His face was lined with age and outdoor work, but his voice was youthful. He could have been anywhere from thirty to sixty.

"I'm afraid so," Zoe answered. "Maybe you wouldn't mind giving us a lift into Mesnil-Théribus?"

"Climb aboard."

There not being enough room on the bench seat for both of them, Avak gallantly settled himself among the bales.

Their rescuer's name was Gerrard Macron, and he owned one of the farms they'd passed several miles back. In the way that country folk are raised to do, he was delivering hay to another farmer on the other side of Mesnil-Théribus who'd run short. "Can't let the livestock starve, can you?" he said, to which Zoe replied, "No, you can't."

"Your husband back there, quiet type, is he? Hasn't said a word."

"Oh, Avak isn't my husband. He runs a taxi service in Paris, and I hired him to drive me to Mesnil-Théribus. I have business there."

Like most rustics, he didn't pry, and after that, they sat in companionable silence while the steady clip-clop of the horses' hooves sent her back to the gentle winters at Beech Glen.

When her small chores were done for the day, she would slip out of the house and run back to the barn to visit Puff, her Welsh Mountain Pony. He was stabled next to Caliban, her stepmother's evil-tempered black thoroughbred. Caliban always tried to nip her as she passed his stall, but she was quick on her feet, and he never quite managed to make contact. Puff, however, enjoyed her visits, and at times even lay down next to her with his head resting in her lap while she basked in the earthy scents of hay and horse.

Remembering those easy days, an almost physical pain shot through her, so she forced herself back to the freezing present. "Will you be heading back to your farm after you deliver the hay?" she asked Gerrard.

He laughed. "If I don't, my wife will send the dogs after me."

"Then maybe you and your team could help pull our automobile out of the ditch?" She didn't mention money, which he might find offensive.

"Winters like this, I always carry a set of chains since them automobiles tend to slide off that stretch of road. Me and my horses'll get your car out of the ditch, no trouble."

"Uh, we didn't exactly 'slide off.' We were forced off by a speeding car."

He gave her a sidewise glance. "Would that be a big black-and-yellow thing?"

"A Renault, and yes, it was black and yellow."

A grunt. "Driven by Mathieu Lambert, a big man in this department, or so he thinks. He's always running people off the road. Almost got this wagon a few miles back. Don't be surprised if you run across him in Mesnil-Théribus. On the way to his fancy château, he likes to stop at the café there and remind everyone of his great importance." With that, Gerard spit over the side of the wagon. The egalitarian spirit of the French Revolution was still alive, at least in the French countryside.

By the time they made it to Mesnil-Théribus, Zoe had learned the horses' names—Pierrot was the chunky pinto, and Rafe the handsome bay—and that Gerrard had raised them from colts. Their dam had been Sault, long gone to Horse Heaven, and their sire was Roget, who followed Sault last year after siring half the horses in the area. She also learned Gerrard's wife's name was Marian, and his children were Odette, Justine, Herbert, and Ricard. They hadn't yet decided on a name for the new baby, another girl.

When Gerrard reined in across the road from the café, Zoe and Avak climbed off the wagon and waved goodbye to their savior, who promised he'd be passing back through town in about two hours. Return trip guaranteed, Zoe studied her surroundings. Two Citroëns and a dray cart and its team sat alongside the road, but she saw no sign of a black-and-yellow Renault. Monsieur Mathieu Lambert must have already tippled, bragged, and left. Disappointed, since she'd been looking forward to the confrontation, Zoe brushed the snow off herself before she and Avak entered the warmth of the café.

Nanine—the russet-haired barmaid who'd been so taken with Avak on their last visit—still stood behind the bar, and the place was as empty as before. She beamed when she saw him and, without being asked, poured two glasses of the local merlot. The summer-like heat from the stove in the middle of the room allowed her to slip off her black woolen shawl to reveal the low-cut peasant blouse that fit as tightly as did her knee-length black skirt. She had also helped Nature along with a touch of rouge on her cheeks and lips.

Avak's face lit up. He was, after all, a vigorous man with the usual urges, and when the barmaid noticed his interest, she played up her charms for all she was worth.

Zoe, she ignored.

But Zoe had planned on this before leaving Paris and schooled Avak on the right questions to ask. As she sipped her merlot, he chatted genially with the barmaid about the many attractions of Mesnil-Théribus. Then, with considerable dexterity despite his clumsy French, he steered the conversation around to the reason for their trip. "As must know you, our friend Bobby now with angels. We grieve so. He short, but good man, him."

Nanine nodded in consolation. "I hear his parents wanted him to be a jockey, but horses scared him."

"Big things, horses."

"Very big." She leaned over the bar so he could get a good look at the globular treasures under her low-cut blouse.

"Miss his paintings also. His studio, it close? Can look, us?"

Nanine's face closed down. "Who told you he kept a studio here?"

"Bobby," he lied.

Zoe had taught Avak how to lie, too, for which she figured she would probably wind up in hell. With the atmosphere now warmed in more ways than one, she said to the barmaid in a woman-to-woman voice, "Not long before he was killed, Bobby told us about a new oil he was working on, and we thought we'd take a look at it, see if it was in good enough shape to speak to a dealer about an exhibition of his work. That would be a wonderful way to remember him, don't you think? To remind people that he really could paint?"

"I promised to keep it a secret," Nanine said. Her voice wavered, though.

Noting this, Avak added, his brown eyes eloquent, "Understand, us. But be kind thing do for him. For our little Bobby."

Nanine stared into those beautiful brown eyes. After a quick look around to see if any other customers had come in—they hadn't—she reached under the bar and rattled around for a moment. Her hand emerged holding a large key. "You won't tell anyone I let you in?"

"Will never, Mademoiselle Beauty." Avak took the key from her, holding her hand longer than Zoe thought necessary.

Ten minutes later, Zoe and Avak were standing in the middle of Bobby's secret studio in an abandoned storehouse, where six big oils sat around the room in various stages of completion. Five leaned against dirty gray walls; one work-in-progress remained on the easel. The air was thick with the scent of dust and turpentine. For a moment, Zoe could hardly breathe, but she quickly recovered and touched the painting on the easel. Not completely dry.

"Pretty," Avak said, looking at the paintings. "Make home me miss."

Zoe found no *pretty* in any of them, just an overwhelming sadness.

· · · ◇ · · ·

Farmer Gerrard proved as good as his word. Hay delivered, on the way back to his farm he stopped at the café and picked them up in his empty wagon. By then Zoe was tipsy on the local merlot, and Avak—who'd wisely stopped after the first glass—had to help her onto the wagon. This time she forsook the seat next to Gerrard and chose the back of the hay-littered wagon instead, where she lay thinking about the young woman whose life ended in a woodsman's cottage in Mesnil-Théribus. She thought about the woman's smooth, unworked hands, her unblemished face. She thought about Hadley and Ernest and the damned valise that had embroiled her in this mess to start with. She thought about Jewel, about the count, about Bobby, about the cold heart of a person who would slaughter other human beings just to keep a secret. Then she thought about Henri, and how he would react when she told him what she'd found out. And how.

He wouldn't be happy, but few people were happy these days, regardless of the jazz leaking out of the dance halls onto the wide boulevards. Jazz was nothing more than a disguise for the world's howls of grief.

By the time they reached the Grim Reaper, the snow had let up, and Gerrard's strong horses made short work of hauling it out of the ditch. Good man that he was, he refused Zoe's proffered francs, then waited until the car started up before re-hitching his team to the wagon. The Grim Reaper, its sturdy self unshaken by its misadventure, responded to Avak's urgings with a growl and a mighty fart.

Then Avak pointed its ugly nose south, and they headed back to the City of Light, the City of Lies.

Chapter Thirty

Zoe now had enough information to give Henri without sounding like a hysteric, so first thing the next morning, she headed off into another full-blown snowstorm to his office on Quai de Orfèvres, only to be told he wasn't there. Disappointed, she handed the envelope containing everything she'd discovered to the young officer seated at the front desk. "Please give this to him as soon as he returns."

"That may not be until tomorrow, Mademoiselle," the officer told her. His face displayed several shrapnel scars, probably earned during the Great War, but they hadn't damaged his manners. "He is consulting on a..." He cleared this throat. "Well, Inspector Challiot is consulting."

"I understand." She didn't, really, but that's the sort of thing civilized people said when they'd rather throw themselves down on the floor and kick and scream.

Once outside, while carefully picking her way down the snow-covered stone steps, she decided that as long as she was already on the Île de la Cité, she might as well visit her favorite park, the Vert-Galant. It never failed to calm her.

There were no little sparrows in the park today and no wood-pigeons to bully them, just naked oaks reaching their arms into the snow-flurried sky. As she sat on a bench, the noise of the city fell away. Had the long-dead king's many mistresses been happy, she wondered. She hoped so. She envisioned Henri IV's fifty-six mistresses lying on satin sheets with smiles of satisfaction on their faces. What a man! What a time! But here she was, in the twentieth century, witness to maimed war veterans begging for francs at the Gare de Lyon. Yet they were the lucky ones.

The people they loved had not received the letter she had, the letter that began, *We regret to inform you...*

The letter she read once and never again.

She must have sat in the Vert-Galant for at least an hour, because when she arose, a blanket of snow slid off her lap. Regardless of the sorrows in her past, she was still alive and living in the most beautiful city in the world. All she had to do to enjoy it was ignore her heart.

Which wasn't likely. To remind herself of this, when she arrived home, she reread Pete's last letter.

> *August 1918. Somewhere in France*
>
> *My dearest Zoe,*
> *So now we will be three!*
>
> *You have made me so proud, my darling! I've been awake all night thinking of names. Jennifer? Harold? Samuel? Elizabeth? Moira? Perhaps I should leave the naming to you, my precious one!*
>
> *Now, I know this may worry you, but today we heard the sounds of German gunfire—and we returned it! Yes, the days of playing music at rear bivouacs are gone, and we have joined our French brothers in the trenches.*

Do not be afraid for me, my darling. Instead, be proud of the history I will make with Harlem's Hell Fighters, be proud of your Pete, who will prove today he is a man equal to all other men.

Oh, Zoe, how much I love you! I pray for the swift end of this War so I can meet our child and hold you in my arms once more.

I must hurry now. Our lieutenant is calling out our orders.

Your heart-husband,

Pete

That night, Zoe lay sleepless in her lonely Paris boudoir, remembering.

Remembering the day that was supposed to be her last at Beech Glen, the day she learned that human beings can make whatever plans they wanted, but that Nature had its own agenda.

It was December, three months after Dorothy, her mother-in-law, shared the letter that began, *"We regret to inform you..."*

· · · ◇ · · ·

December 1918
Mercy, Alabama

After learning of Pete's death, Zoe spent the next few months roaming Beech Glen like a fleshless wraith, hiding her heartbreak, hiding her changing body, taking a hard solace in the fact that the waiting was almost over. Before Pete left for France with his regiment, he'd leased an apartment for the three of them in Harlem, leaving instructions for his sisters—who shared an apartment in the same building—to help with whatever Zoe needed. She was now eighteen, a White woman secretly married to a Negro man, secretly pregnant, secretly widowed.

There was no future for her in Beech Glen.

Nature had been kind, at first. Although tall, she was small-boned, and even at the beginning of her eighth month, she'd gained little weight. The small bump that rose at her middle was contained by tight cotton wrappings underneath dresses a size larger, bought secretly in Birmingham and paid for by the monthly stipend from her maternal grandmother's will. True, every now and then, Annabelle would give her a puzzled look, but she mainly concentrated on Zoe's face, on the blue shadows beneath her eyes. If her stepmother bothered to think at all, she probably attributed Zoe's wraith-like state to grief over her cousin Stephen, who'd died at Meuse-Argonne.

Then one day Nature, which had once been so merciful, turned on her. On a chill morning, as she slipped into another too-large dress, she felt a brief tightening around her middle. She frowned. The baby wasn't due for another month. Besides, there was no actual pain, just pressure, as if Nature was getting her ready.

Another twinge. Then another, and another. After they finally went away, Zoe decided it might be wisest to put her plan in action now, not in a month. Tonight, after everyone was asleep, she'd go to Dorothy's.

Because of his job delivering feed to outlying farms, Henry, Pete's younger brother, had access to a delivery van. Once Zoe gave birth at her mother-in-law's house, Henry would drive her and the baby to the railway station in Birmingham. Then she'd ride the train north to join her sisters-in-law in New York.

No one in Mercy, Alabama, would ever dream that a White woman was being sheltered in a Negro's house.

Zoe spent the rest of that meant-to-be-the-last day at Beech Glen careful to avoid her stepmother's scrutiny. Although her back hurt something fierce, she managed to pack a small suit-case with just enough to get her through the next few days. Three more dresses in her unpregnant size, some underwear, the cash she'd managed to put together over the past few months, and several pieces of salable jewelry. Not a fortune, but enough to get started in a new city, with a new little life to care for. A sweet new life who would help heal the wound inflicted by a German gun.

That evening, Zoe sat at the dinner table pretending not to be hungry. With only family present, there was no Spode dinnerware laid out before them and no Sunday silver, but the crystal chande-lier still sparkled, tossing tiny dots of light across everyone's faces. They looked like they'd been sprinkled with diamonds.

Not that the chandelier's magic had any effect on their stepmother.

"Zoe, I insist you eat more of that ham; you're looking wan," she said. Annabelle Proctor Barlow appeared especially elegant that evening. She was clothed in a black silk dress—she'd famously never emerged from mourning for Zoe's father—and her onyx necklace and earrings dramatically offset her pale skin. Annabelle almost seemed to be flirting with Brice, Zoe's brother, but that had to be Zoe's imagination. Brice had a wife, and although she was away visiting her mother, surely...

At least Zoe would never have to watch this charade again.

"I didn't hear your answer, Zoe!"

"You didn't ask me a question," Zoe answered, pushing the food around on her plate.

Annabelle gave her a stern look. "Don't get smart with me."

"Sorry, but I don't feel well." It was the truth, for once. Zoe's spine felt like it was about to snap.

"Of course, you don't, keeping yourself cooped up alone in your room, painting all day, as if such a wasteful pastime ever accounted for much. You need to get out, get more exercise. That poor horse of yours..."

"I get plenty of exercise." Well, that used to be true, but no longer. Now Zoe was more careful. She had to keep her body safe for the baby, and Bright Star—who'd replaced the elderly Puff—galloped unridden in the pasture.

Annabelle fluttered her eyelashes at Brice. "Isn't that right? Hasn't Zoe been looking poorly of late?"

"Mmm," Zoe's older brother non-answered, not really paying attention to their conversation. Like her father had done while still alive, Brice focused his mind on more important things, such as how much seed should be ordered for the next planting, what field should be harvested first, and whether Silas Hansen, their foreman, should be fired or given another warning.

"You see, Zoe? Brice agrees."

Annabelle hadn't bothered to ask Leeanne, because what Zoe's little sister thought didn't count.

As dinner progressed, Annabelle told Lee-Lee to eat more ham. Lee-Lee did. Annabelle told her to eat more slowly, so Lee-Lee did. Annabelle told her to use her napkin, not her hand, to blot away the dribble of redeye gravy on her chin. Lee-Lee did. Lee-Lee only ever disobeyed when Annabelle wasn't looking. She was the good stepdaughter, but Zoe loved her anyway, and would miss her.

The rest of the evening passed slowly, almost peacefully, except for the frowns Annabelle kept throwing Zoe's way, but that wasn't unusual. While her stepmother chatted breezily with Brice—who only ever answered in one or two syllables—Zoe pretended to be engrossed in embroidering the hem of a silk pillowcase, a pastime which usually bored her. This night, however, it helped fill the time until she could decently excuse herself and go upstairs.

Soon. Soon.

At eight thirty, Annabelle ordered a protesting Lee-Lee to bed, and it was all Zoe could do not to follow the girl into her room for a final goodbye. Zoe knew better. If pressed, Lee-Lee would tell their stepmother everything, and she and Brice might be able to get the train stopped before it left the state and...

"Goodbye, Lee-Lee," she whispered.

"What was that you said?" Annabelle asked, a puzzled look on her flawless ivory mask of a face.

"Just telling her good night."

"Oh. I see."

No, you don't.

At nine, Brice excused himself and went into his office to finish some paperwork, which was the signal Zoe had been waiting for. Annabelle didn't like being alone with her.

"Good night," Zoe said, rising from her chair, the half-finished pillowcase in her hand.

Annabelle merely nodded.

Once in her bedroom, Zoe began to pace.

Downstairs, as per her stepmother's standard nighttime routine, Annabelle put a record on the gramophone, and the strains of "My Sunshine Jane" drifted up the stairs. Zoe hated the song, thought it overemotional and whiny, and she suspected her stepmother only played it to annoy her. Not that it mattered anymore. Soon she'd be in New York City, beginning a new life. The yowls of the Sterling Trio finally stopped, leaving nothing but blessed silence until Zoe heard her stepmother's footsteps on the stairs, and the soft clicks as the door to the master bedroom opened and closed. Annabelle had a long, drawn-out beauty regimen, and Zoe knew it would be at least another hour before she could leave.

At midnight, Zoe slipped down the stairs, across the darkened rooms, and out the back door. Nightbirds ceased calling to one another as she lugged her suitcase across the moonlit barnyard, headed for the edge of the forest that marked the eastern border of

Beech Glen. One lone owl fluttered by as she cleared the yard and slipped through the trees' long shadows. The sharp, clean scent of pine replaced the musky odor of manure, and from somewhere close by, a bird gave voice.

Quee-ah, quee-ah! Yellow-bellied sapsucker.

Zoe's original plan had been to drive her King Model EE to Dorothy's small farmstead, but she'd decided the noisy automobile would awaken everyone in the house. Besides, as the crow flew, Dorothy's house was little more than a mile through the woods, and even though Zoe's left leg ached, she'd learned to handle discomfort. Freedom was less than an hour away. Then no more hiding, no more lying.

But only yards along the trail, what felt like a giant hand grabbed her around the middle, its grip stronger and longer than the grasp she'd experienced that morning. It happened so suddenly that she dropped her suitcase in shock, spilling her clothes across the leaf-covered ground. She fell to her knees, waiting for release. When it finally happened—it seemed to take forever—she decided her misery was caused by the cotton wrappings around her stomach. In her rush to leave she'd fastened them too tightly and was now paying the price for her over-zealousness. Gasping against the pressure, she remained doubled over until the pain eased enough for her to unbend. Then she lifted up her dress, stuffed the hem into her mouth, and unknotted the wrappings. It dropped onto the fallen leaves, eliciting a small sound of scurry nearby. Eased, Zoe gathered up her things and began to repack the suitcase.

Had it rained before she'd started her trek?

If so, it must have happened just before she left the house. Her packed clothes had been dry, of course, but now were cold and wet, and smelled like something earthy and animal-like. The insides of her legs felt wet, too. Maybe she'd somehow damaged herself? But, no, she'd been careful, and with the aid of moonlight filtering through the pines, she checked her thighs and saw no blood on her skin. Just that strange moisture...

The sapsucker called out again. *Quee-ah, quee-ah!*

She'd drawn sapsuckers many times in the past. They were handsome birds, dark-brown, almost black, with red heads and yellow bellies, but their calls were shrill, not pretty. Sapsuckers were also known for defending their territory with noise-making, and as Zoe straightened, she heard it tap-tapping against something metal, perhaps the posted sign marking the beginning of Beech Glen's vast acreage. She had to hurry. The bird's warning might even be heard back at the house.

Abdomen eased and suitcase repacked, Zoe struggled to her feet and set off again, this time paying greater attention to her surroundings. But regardless of her caution, only several steps beyond where she had fallen, the pressure around her middle returned, this time winding itself not only around her stomach, but across her back, her hips, and down both thighs. Her weak leg gave out, and she fell to her knees again as a great rush of liquid spilled down her thighs.

She knew what this was. She'd once seen it happen to a broodmare about to foal. She planted her hands in the wet leaves, bracing herself against the next wave of anguish. Then another.

Oh, Jesus!

She couldn't move. Couldn't continue forward.

But she had to, because now she heard voices calling her name.

"Zoe Barlow! Get back here now, you stupid girl!"

Annabelle.

Even though Zoe's body told her she couldn't possibly do more than lie there amongst the leaves, she remembered her long-ago impossible crawl through the pasture with a broken leg. Heartened by the memory of her courage, she started another slow crawl forward. If she could do it then, she could do it now.

A fluttering of wings, and the sapsucker rose to the sky, leaving her alone to face the following voices.

Annabelle. Brice. Silas Hansen.

Zoe had believed she'd been careful, but the farm's overseer, probably starting off on another of his shameful nighttime adventures, must have seen her cross the barnyard and alerted the house, hoping that by revealing her great sin, his own sins would appear minor in comparison.

She tried to rise to meet them with dignity, but she could not. The pressure in her stomach and back had not been eased one bit by untying the wrappings. If anything, the pressure had increased, and she could rise no further. Gasping, she clutched at the leaves for balance and listened to the scampering of tiny creatures as they fled the footsteps that thundered ever closer.

Suddenly not even Zoe's knees could support her, and the next wave of pain threw her face down into the mud.

I'm so sorry, Pete.

Hands grasping at her. Hauling her up. Carrying her back through the woods and into the dank Beech Glen basement, her anguished body no longer worthy of the grand rooms upstairs.

The three of them stood watching until she lay bloodied and gutted on an old horse blanket.

Then a baby's cry. Annabelle's gasp. Silas's whoop of laughter.

In a fit of rage, Annabelle slapped Zoe once, twice, three times, until Brice stepped in to stop it. But he didn't stop their stepmother's mouth, though, and in a voice dripping with ice, she leaned over Zoe and whispered, "You will never see this little nigger bastard again."

Annabelle then issued harsh orders to Silas, who received them with delight.

Make this thing disappear!

Zoe wanted to die, but she didn't.

··· ◇ ···

December 1922
Paris

Our baby wasn't a bastard, was she, Pete? As was your people's custom, you and I jumped the broom at Dorothy's house before you left for New York. And our daughter wasn't ugly, she was beautiful. Underneath the birth mess, her skin glowed the color of the amber ring my father once gave me.

Oh, God, does our Amber girl still live?

Half-sick from remembering, Zoe rose from her bed in Le Petit Bibelot and padded barefoot into the studio. She stared at a newly finished canvas leaning against the wall. One of the Seven Heavenly Virtues series, she'd titled the painting *Hope*. It showed an amber-colored child gazing with innocent eyes upon a sinful world.

Zoe fell to her knees and sent out a howl of despair into the raw Paris night.

Chapter Thirty-One

The next morning, Zoe was putting the finishing touches to *Hope* when a knock at the door announced the arrival of a *pneumatique*. Apparently, while she'd been in Mesnil-Théribus, her friends had been busy.

In honor of the memory of
ROBERT LEVEQUE CRITES
you are invited to a special one-day-only
exhibit of his early and later works
at LE PASSAGE GALLERIE
43 Rue de la Gaité
6 p.m. Saturday, December 16
For view only, no sales.
REFRESHMENTS WILL BE SERVED

As soon as Madeline arrived, Zoe put down her brushes and went into the kitchen, waving the *pneumatique* at her. "Did you know about this?"

She nodded. "Of course. I even helped."

"You're telling me you helped arrange a retrospective art exhibit?"

Madeline continued mincing the poor carrot she was working on, her mechanical arm bending silently. "Two of your artist friends, the mademoiselles, came by yesterday pleading for the use of the sketches you bought from Monsieur Bobby last year. Since their need was immediate and you were far away in Mesnil-Théribus, I gathered them up, content that you would do the same if you were here. They promised to return them as soon as the exhibit was over. A one-day special event, you understand. You didn't notice the sketches missing when you went to your studio this morning?"

No, Zoe hadn't noticed much of anything other than her own unhappiness.

"I left a note," Madeline said, finally looking up from pea-sized carrot pieces.

"Where?"

"On your easel."

Zoe turned on her heel and went back into the studio. The note was there, thumbtacked to the top of her easel, right above the painting.

People only saw what they wished to see, didn't they? All Zoe had wanted for the past four years was to see her daughter's face again. That being impossible for now, she'd painted her, and the light from her Amber child eclipsed a mere note.

"Did I do wrong?" Madeline asked, when Zoe went back to the kitchen.

"You were absolutely right to loan them the sketches. As you said, I would have done so myself if I'd been here. I'm sorry I yelled at you."

"You did not yell, Zoe."

Madeline's use of her first name again proved that all was well between them, so Zoe went back to work. For the rest of the day, nothing mattered but brush on canvas and her daughter's glowing face.

••• ◇ •••

Le Passage Galerie was a minuscule space tucked between a small hotel and a stationer's shop. The large crowd made movement difficult, and the miasma of tobacco, marijuana, and sweat didn't help, either. After Zoe availed herself of a glass of low-level merlot and a marijuana-filled Lucky Strike cigarette handed to her by Smokin' Sammy Ramsey—a jazz musician she'd dated a few times—she looked around at the gallery walls. They revealed what she considered to be the downward slide of Bobby's talent. He had started his career painting beauty and ended it nailing kitchen utensils to the wall. His Dada friends strutted around, muttering things like, "Revolutionary," and "Snubbing the Académie overlords."

"Bobby would be so happy with this," Louise Packard said, approaching Zoe as she pondered a fog-hung landscape. The painting might have been straight from the outdated Romantic Realism school, but it contained the power to haunt.

"He'd be thrilled just to be in a gallery," Zoe answered, taking another hit of not-tobacco.

"I'm sure he'd rather it be under different circumstances," Karen Wegner said wryly. "As a Dadaist myself, I prefer his later work. Let the past stay in the past."

Archie Stafford-Smythe, half-drunk on cheap merlot, begged to differ. "Some of us prefer the innocence of the past to the reprehensible present. I've seen that cuckoo-squalling rabbit of yours, Karen, and didn't much like it."

To Zoe's relief, Karen merely laughed.

Perhaps her friend was mellowing with age. How old was Karen now? Thirty? Thirty-five? Unlike the more dignified Louise, she was dressed in a jarring outfit of green boots, a red velveteen skirt, a lavender silk shirt, and a long, tapestried vest over which hung a necklace made up of screws and nails. It had to be hellishly uncomfortable, but artists didn't mind suffering for their art, did they?

After a while, Zoe caught sight of Dominique in conversation with Antoine Fortier. They were discussing one of Bobby's Dada pieces, an assemblage of kitchen cutlery framed by a toilet seat. Zoe jostled her way through the crowd toward them, stopping first to refill her wineglass. The merlot tasted less raw the more she drank.

Once she reached Dominique and Antoine, she took a closer look at Bobby's odd assemblage. It was titled #49-F.

"What's that supposed to mean?" she asked Dominique. The war artist was dressed in muted tones of grays and browns, but her red-sequined eyepatch made the outfit look less drear.

"Damned if I know," Dominique answered, "This is one of those times I'm glad I only have one eye."

There came a "Harrumph!" from Fortier, the standard De Reszke hanging from his lip. He looked good in a black suit, accented by a black cravat and his silver-crowned cane. "From what I hear, he originally titled it *Winter in Cannes*, God help us all."

"I didn't know you were religious," Zoe said.

"Just a saying which means nothing." He sniffed, then frowned. "What in the world are you smoking, Zoe?"

"Lucky Strikes. Want a puff? *Très* American."

He gave her an untrusting look and shook his head.

It occurred to Zoe, then, there was something she needed to know, and Fortier was the perfect person to ask. "Since you're an expert on Romantic Realism, tell me what you think of Bobby's early landscapes. Are they as good as I think they are?"

Fortier pursed his lips for a moment, then said carefully, "They're pretty."

Well! When an artist called another artist's work "pretty," it was an insult of the highest order, and Dominique didn't miss it. "My, my. How charitable of you." She could be insulting, herself.

The Painting Marquis lifted his patrician nose and stalked on to the next painting, leaving them behind.

"What a prig," Dominique said, not caring whether he heard her or not. "Give me a hit of that Lucky Strike, Zoe."

Zoe did, then moved along to another Dada piece, where it appeared Bobby had—as the Brits say—rather fallen down on the job, because it *was* pretty, just not in the insulting sense. A brown egg sat on a pedestal cobbled together from an assemblage of twigs. Above the egg floated a golden halo, held up by sliver-thin silver wires. The title card below read, in capital letters, THE MEANING OF LIFE.

Since Zoe had already experienced enough hurt for the day, she left it for a soothing landscape of autumn-tinted trees, where she ran into Kiki. After another dustup with Man Ray, the model hung on to the arm of a new man. She looked spectacular in a red, gold, and green Japanese kimono draped over an ankle-length green skirt, and her thick, matte makeup mostly hid the shadows under her eyes. After she finished hugging Zoe—good Lord, the woman was strong—Kiki introduced her to Boyfriend No. 15 (or was it 16?). His name was Karl Bauwens, and he was studying art at the same school Zoe herself once attended. Judging by his beautifully cut suit, he was not poor.

"I hear you're an Expressionist?" she said, phrasing it as a question.

"It seems so," he answered warily, in Dutch-accented French.

She smiled. "Same here. I've found we can see more that way."

His eyes lit up. "Yes! Painting the interior of a thing instead of its exterior." They then began the de rigueur discussion about the purpose of Art with a capital A, but within seconds, Kiki grew bored.

In a voice loud enough to be heard in the nineteenth arrondisse-ment, she yelped, "Zoe, I've heard you've been pestering the inhabitants of Mesnil-Théribus again! Tell us what so fascinates you about that tiny place. I was there once and found it boring." To Bauwens, she added, "The village's only worthwhile inhabitant is Mary Cassatt, another American." Turning back to Zoe, she said, "Is that its attraction? An old lady who can't even paint anymore?"

Zoe wanted to tell Kiki that Cassatt's work would survive when the rest of them were food for worms, but there was no point. Wishing Bauwens good luck, she moved away and talked to Smokin' Sammy again. The conversation was not, refreshingly, about Art with a capital A. Sammy—real name Samuel Pershing Ramsdale IV—was from Cosby, Tennessee, and his mountain twang made his stories about speakeasies and backwoods stills sound hilarious. Zoe was listening to his account of the cops raiding one such cottage enterprise when the gallery manager announced it was time to close.

She bade goodbye to Smokin' Sammy and collected the three sketches Madeline had loaned the exhibit. After wrapping them carefully, she tucked them under her arm and began the short walk home. Despite the lateness of the hour, Zoe felt safe, having put her Derringer into her purse before leaving the house. Not that she would need it on such an enchanted night. It was snowing again, but she didn't care. Still enjoying the high from her Lucky Strike, she basked in the golden light from gas lamps that turned the snowflakes into golden Spanish doubloons, and reveled in the moan of the wind along Boulevard Montparnasse. It sounded like a woman at the height of her pleasure.

Upon crossing Raspail, she waved to the young gendarme keeping watch under a streetlamp. The gendarme waved back. He was about the same age as Bobby.

Poor, foolish Bobby.

But who was she to judge? Bobby had been no more foolish as she'd been during that long-ago December.

$$\cdots \Diamond \cdots$$

December 1918
Mercy, Alabama to Paris, France

After she gave birth to her Amber child, Anabelle, Brice, and Silas Hansen kept Zoe locked up in the dank basement for a full week as she bled and called in vain for her baby. Once every evening, the overseer brought her food and a jug of water, and once every morning, he emptied the slop jar she used as a toilet. At least he never touched her.

On the fifth day, Anabelle and Brice descended the basement stairs and told her what was going to happen. The ship. The accounts. The rules. And no, Brice spat, she couldn't say goodbye to Leeanne, because nigger-loving whores weren't allowed contact with innocent girls.

Two weeks later, chaperoned by her brother, Zoe arrived in Paris, where Brice checked her into the Hôtel des Grandes Écoles. After leaving their luggage on the bed, he walked her down the street to the Banque 6 Nationale de Crédit.

"Your account's already set up," he said, not looking at her. "All they need now is your signature."

He stood there as she was escorted into a small office where she was introduced to a rotund Frenchman with a large mustache who told her he'd been appointed her guardian. After giving her his card, he left. The bank manager stayed on as she signed one paper after another. When she finished signing—it took only minutes—she exited the office to find that not only her "guardian" had left, but Brice, too. Bidding the bank manager a hasty adieu, she rushed through the lobby, where well-dressed people milled about, speaking in a dozen languages. They paid no attention to her rising panic.

When she hobbled onto the crowded sidewalk, she couldn't see Brice anywhere. He had vanished, and somehow, she understood that when she went back to the hotel, she would find he'd already checked out.

Eighteen years old, lost and alone in a strange country with her milk-filled breasts straining against her dress, Zoe broke. She stood there in the middle of a busy sidewalk, her face turned up to a foreign sky, and wept without shame. Tears and snot streamed down her face, but she hurt too much to care. She was missing Pete, missing her baby, missing her sister, missing Beech Glen, missing everyone and everything she'd ever loved.

Clumps of pedestrians parted around her, too intent on their own business to notice a girl falling to pieces.

Zoe only stopped wailing when a beautiful woman exited the bank and placed a hand on hers. "Qu'est-ce qui ne va pas, Mademoiselle?" What is wrong?

When Zoe answered in her poor French that everything was wrong, that she was still bleeding and her milk was still leaking, and she didn't remember the way back to the hotel, the woman switched to Mississippi-accented English, "Don't worry, honey. I'll take you there, and we'll get you all fixed up."

Her name, she said, was Jewel Johnson, and she was a dancer.

Chapter Thirty-Two

December 1922
Paris

The cruel wind had increased by the time Zoe finally reached Le Petit Bibelot, so she rushed inside and slammed the door behind her. After depositing her purse and Bobby's sketches on the table, she shrugged off her heavy coat, then hurried into her studio. She pulled her smock right over her fancy dress and went straight to work. As they said in Mercy, Alabama, *Time's a-wastin'*.

This time, her labors proved more fruitful, and soon she'd laid down the base coat for a new and better-informed version of *Greed*. Just as she was swishing a sable-hair brush through a cleansing jar of turpentine, Zoe became aware of a change in the room. A lessening of pressure, a fading of warmth. Before she could investigate, she smelled the distinct odor of expensive tobacco.

"Locks don't work unless you engage them, Zoe."

She spun around to see Marquis Antoine Phillippe Fortier de Guise bundled into a Persian lamb coat and hat. His cheeks may have been chapped with cold, but the gloved hand holding the pistol—a nasty utilitarian thing—remained steady. The lit De Reszke dangling from his mouth didn't move, either.

Oh, Zoe, how could you be so careless?

Her Derringer was unreachable, in her purse in the sitting room, and as useless as an unengaged lock. Although appalled by her heedlessness, she wasn't about to let him know it and pretended a confidence she didn't feel. Continuing to whisk her brushes through the turps, she said brightly, "Oh, come on, Antoine. Shooting me isn't going to solve your problems. I've already handed over proof of your guilt to the Sûreté; regardless of what happens to me, they'll be paying you a visit."

"You think I don't already know that?" A sneer turned his aristocratic face into a vicious mask. "If I'm going to be guillotined, I'll at least have the satisfaction of knowing I killed the bitch who ruined me."

"You ruined yourself. Take a look." Zoe motioned at her new version of *Greed*, which she'd turned into an almost-lifelike portrait of Fortier, exaggerating his narrow eyes, his too-thin nose, the grasping hands being slowly destroyed by arthritis, that all-too-common bane of aging artists.

"You know nothing of the trials I've faced!"

Keep him talking, Zoe.

"I beg to differ. Yes, it's probably difficult to know that whatever remains of the Académie will strike your name from the roster once they find out Bobby painted everything in your last exhibit, but since the arrangement was working great, why'd you kill him?" As if she didn't know, but as long as he was talking, he wasn't shooting.

His sneer turned even uglier. "If you're so smart, you tell me."

After pretending to be deep in thought, Zoe said, "Oh, I get it! Bobby's cousin said he'd been in a great mood the last time he visited, so I'm betting he'd made up his mind to stop wasting his talent working for you, and to start painting for himself under his own name."

The sneer faded a bit. "You're not as smart as you think you are. You're just another dumb American with more money than you know what to do with."

Not an inaccurate insult, but still. "Dumb? Is that the best you can do? Let's see if I've got this right. You started your little killing spree with the Russians, correct?"

"Popov was a thief, no loss there."

"And you weren't?" She continued sloshing the brushes through the turps. Slowly. Carefully. *Good artists always take care of their tools.* "You were the one who was stealing from the count, not the Bolsheviks."

An artist himself, Fortier saw nothing unnatural in Zoe's obsession with brush-cleaning, and he enjoyed basking in what he saw was his own cleverness. "Zoe, Zoe! Ever since biblical days, money changers have been allowed to profit from their skills. In case you aren't aware of it—and there's no reason you should be— exchanging diamonds for gold isn't easy. First, I had to get Sergei's diamonds assessed by the proper expert, then I..."

"But why didn't the count just wire the money?" she interrupted, pretending not to know.

"Because Sergei lost everything when the Bolshies nationalized the Russian banks, you idiot! And you know what your countrymen are always saying, 'Once bitten, twice shy.' But unlike rubles or francs or even dollars, gold has no politics." His face took on a wounded look. "Then there was the problem of bribing the right people and getting the right man aboard the train. It was time-consuming work, so why shouldn't I hold back a little for myself? No crime there, although that ignoramus Popov thought there was."

His left hand began to shake. A delayed reaction from the cold and wind? Unfortunately, Fortier's gun hand held firm.

But she was almost ready. "It wasn't ignorance on Popov's part. From what I hear, he was genuinely devoted to the old regime. Once he realized you were skimming off the top, he confronted you, didn't he? Did he threaten to tattle to Sergei?"

A disagreeable laugh. "Popov was no angel. He was tired of living in poverty, which is why he'd started stealing luggage from train passengers in the first place—people he considered fair game. And that's what your pretty little friend Hadley turned out to be, didn't she? Fair game! She left that valise within snatching reach of what were probably a dozen other thieves operating out of the station that day. But you're right about one thing. Unfortunately, besides being a thief, Popov was just another dumb idealist who believed the Romanovs would one day return to the throne, and he would help it happen. That woodsman's shack in Mesnil-Théribus? It was actually a waystation where titled Russians hid until better accommodations were found. He was being well paid for it, so in his own way, he was as greedy as you accuse *me* of being."

Zoe remembered Popov's bombed-out hovel in La Villette. If he'd been well-paid, she was a monkey's aunt. She sloshed the brushes again. *Almost ready.* "But you didn't answer my question. Was he going to tell Sergei what you were doing?"

"Of course he was. So I killed him."

"What about the girl?" The aristocrat with the smooth hands and unblemished face, the woman Sergei believed was the Grand Duchess Anastasia Nikolaevna Romanov.

"I couldn't exactly leave a witness alive, could I? Same with your friend Jewel. She picked a bad time to disport with the count. But alas, I made a sloppy mess of it. Both my hands were giving me trouble that day." He raised his shaking left hand to illustrate.

"You don't deserve to even speak her name."

"She was such a wonderful dancer, and I truly regret having to kill her." He pulled a long face.

"Well, at least you're sorry."

He mistook her sarcasm for truth. "See? I'm not the monster you think I am, Zoe. And you have to admit it was clever of me to hide behind a Mutilé's mask to disguise myself when I hired that prostitute to lure the doorman away from the count's building."

"Oh, yes, that was clever. It put the suspicion elsewhere, didn't it?" As he preened under her praise, Zoe shifted her weight from her damaged left leg to her right. "But there's one thing I haven't figured out. Did Bobby know you killed those Russians?" She hoped not, but it was a wicked world, one where supposedly good people did bad things.

"Do you think I'd be fool enough to tell him? I left him at the studio in Mesnil-Théribus to finish a landscape and said I was getting a glass of wine at the café."

Good for you, Bobby! You were only a forger, not a parasitic blackmailer.

Fortier heaved a great sigh. "Well, Zoe, I've always liked you, which is why I hired that miserable little thief to scare you off, but you ignored..."

Zoe threw the jar of turpentine in his face.

The second the turps hit Fortier's lit De Reszke, it exploded into flames. As Fortier screamed and danced, she snatched up his dropped gun and ran out the front door—he hadn't bothered closing it all the way—and fired two shots into the air. The gendarme she'd seen earlier might still be in the neighborhood, but if not...

She'd put The Painting Marquis out of his misery.

"Help! Police!" she yelled, for good measure, then ran back to the house to fire the mercy shot. But once inside, she realized something.

She was no Fortier.

So she put the gun down on the table, grabbed her coat from the long banquet table, and ran into the studio, where Fortier was still burning. Still screaming. Still dancing. Using her shoulder, she knocked him to the floor and threw the coat over him. As he howled and howled, she knelt down and snuffed out the fire, even though the dying flames licked hungrily at her already-scarred hands.

Chapter Thirty-Three

As it turned out, Zoe had only melted Fortier's face, not killed him. And nothing else in her studio caught on fire. She was lucky there.

But she was lucky, too, since her gunshots were heard by the young gendarme on Raspail, who wasted no time in summoning the authorities. When the Sûreté arrived, the head of the squad was Inspector Henri Challiot, who proceeded to deliver another lecture to Zoe as soon as he stopped kissing her.

In front of everyone.

Not that his fellow officers were shocked. After all, they were French.

$$\cdots \diamond \cdots$$

After the unconscious Fortier was carted off to the hospital, Zoe spent the rest of the night at police headquarters being grilled by Henri and the rest of his wolfpack. It wasn't pleasant, and the word "foolish" was tossed around as often as the word "luck," but she was a good poker player and was able to hide her feelings. Let them call her a fool; fine. Let them called her unwomanly; fine.

None of it mattered, just as long as they didn't know how guilty she felt about burning a man alive.

"Why didn't you come to us?" asked Challiot's captain—his name was Naize.

Forcing herself to sound strong, Zoe answered for what had to be the fifth time. "I did. But Henri, er, *Inspector* Challiot wasn't in, so I left that."

She pointed to the envelope lying on the captain's desk. It contained six full pages describing everything she'd discovered, right down to the reason for the forged paintings. But Henri hadn't opened the envelope until late at night, when he'd taken it home with him.

He'd thought it was a farewell letter, and he didn't want to be seen crying at the office.

· · · ◇ · · ·

The sun rose on a sparkling morning when Captain Naize allowed Henri to return Zoe to Le Petit Bibelot.

As the Citroën pulled to the curb, Henri asked, "Would you like me to help?"

"This is something I have to do by myself."

"You're sure?"

"Yes."

"Get some rest, Zoe. After almost being...being..." He cleared his throat and began again. "You've been up all night."

Yes, she had, and she hoped she didn't look as bad as he did. A tinge of yellow stained his usually ruddy face, and his mouth—the mouth she'd kissed with such abandon—was so drawn his lips almost disappeared.

"I'll be fine, Henri."

"You're certain?"

"Yes. Now please go home."

"This isn't a forever farewell, is it?"

She kissed him. "Don't be foolish."

After giving her a grateful look, he drove away.

For once, Zoe was relieved to have to go through so many locks to enter Le Petit Bibelot; it put off the moment she'd been dreading. But all too soon, she was inside, smelling a combination of turpentine and burned flesh. Since she was still wearing her painter's smock, she strode straight through the sitting room and into the carnage of her studio.

During Fortier's tortured dance, he'd knocked over several paintings, but none were damaged. *Hope* leaned unharmed against the wall, and *Greed* still sneered from the upright easel. True, the old china plate Zoe used for a palette had shattered into a dozen rainbow pieces, and flames had singed the leaves of her sketchbook, but both were replaceable.

The charred oak floor, though...

Choking back bile, she left the studio in search of Madeline's cleaning supplies. There was no way Zoe was going to leave this horror for her.

In short order, she found the rags stuffed into a bucket at the far corner of the kitchen pantry, anchored by a stiff brush. Next to the bucket sat a large jug of vinegar. Zoe had no clue about that mysterious white powder she'd seen maids use for scouring. Salt? Flour? Baking soda? Zoe's ignorance of everyday domesticity made her regret not paying more attention to the housekeepers at Beech Glen. She did know that Madeline used lemons for cleaning while they were in season, and vinegar when they weren't, because she'd smelled them above the stringent odor of turpentine.

God bless turpentine.

Forcing herself to stay on task, she noticed a sack of salt nestled next to the vinegar, so she put it into the bucket. After toting everything into her battle-scarred studio, she began to scrub.

An hour later, she was still scrubbing.

Her hands, which hadn't completely healed from the fire at the woodsman's shack, were again blistered from dousing last night's flames. Constant scraping along the charred oak worked up splinters, and many of them made their way into her hands. The combination of salt and vinegar in the wounds set them on fire again. But Madeline was due any minute, and Zoe didn't want her to be faced with this—she'd found a few pieces of Fortier's burned flesh amidst the splinters—so she kept scrubbing. She scrubbed and scrubbed until drops of blood joined the mess on the wood, yet she still kept scrubbing.

When the door opened at ten and a pale-faced Madeline stood in the doorway, the stain was still there.

"I heard," Madeline whispered. *"Oh, ma pauvre petite."*

At this, Zoe flung herself into Madeline's arms and began to bawl.

Chapter Thirty-Four

When Zoe finally staggered out of bed, Madeline informed her she'd slept around the clock. A farm-raised girl, Zoe had never done that before.

"I stayed the night with you, *mon amie*," Madeline said, gesturing toward the front door with her metal arm. "After that article about you appeared in *Le Figaro*, it was one reporter after another banging away out there. No respect for anyone."

Amie, Madeline called her. Jewel had called her that, too. *Friend.*

Tears of gratitude at Madeline's generosity prickled at Zoe's eyes, but refusing to be a blubberpuss, she didn't let them fall. Besides, she'd cried enough yesterday to last her entire life, not that she hadn't had reason. In the space of two weeks, she'd lost three good friends to murder—four, if she counted Fortier—which in a strange way, she still did. But it was Jewel's loss that hurt the most.

It always would.

Those damned tears prickled again.

Mon amie.

Madeline had a good fire going in the big ceramic stove, but the house still felt cool, so with her messed-up hands, Zoe pulled her robe close around her. As she followed Madeline toward the kitchen, an unusual sight stopped her.

"What's all this?" she asked, staring at a heap of beribboned objects piled on the dining table. "You clean out Bon Marché?"

Madeline chuckled. "Read the gift tags."

A tall vase filled with hothouse roses bore a tag announcing it was from Avak Grigoryan. Next to the roses sat a king-sized box of Belgian chocolates from Béatrice Camondo. Kiki had donated a small enameled box filled with marijuana. Not to be outdone, Louise Packard contributed a home-baked orange-and-cream gâteau, and Dominique Garron, the bottle of Bärenjäger Liqueur she'd famously swiped off a dead German during the Great War. From Karen Wegner and Reynard Dibasse, she'd received a timbale of honey-glazed fruit, and from doorman Pierre Lazenby, six bottles of smuggled Budweiser.

As Zoe dug through the pile of gifts, she found a dozen apples and a small brochure on the healing of burns from Dr. Marcel Molyneux, the best neighbor in the world. Making her drool was a priceless bottle of 1907 Chateau Lafite Rothschild Bordeaux Rouge from Archie Stafford-Smythe. But, in a blessed surprise, Djuna Barnes and Romaine Brooks had contributed a bottle of Courvoisier and an invite to Natalie Barney's acclaimed lesbian salon.

For the first time in days, Zoe laughed out loud.

"Besides the reporters—the little cockroaches—your friends kept dropping by with gift after gift, asking if there was anything they could do for you," Madeline explained. "So, of course, I allowed them to come in from the cold just as long as they didn't disturb your rest. We sat by the fire and whispered to each other for the longest time. Such nice people, they are, and so worried about you." Noticing Zoe's lingering look at Archie's 1907 Chateau Lafite Rothschild Bordeaux Rouge, she added, "It's too early for wine, Zoe. Let me make you a nice omelet. Besides the roses, Avak also brought you a dozen fresh eggs."

Recognizing Madeline's superior common sense, Zoe sat down at the table, and while waiting for the omelet, thought about the way the smallest action could result in huge consequences. Two weeks ago, Hadley had lost Ernest's manuscripts. Meaning to help, Zoe had traveled to Mesnil-Théribus, and then…

Poor, dear Hadley. So terrified she was about to lose her husband's love, hoping against hope that a pregnancy would stave off the inevitable.

How could a woman be so foolish?

But maybe Hadley was right and Zoe was wrong. Maybe Hadley and Ernest would stay together and raise a large, happy family. Maybe he'd realize he didn't have the talent needed to become a successful writer and would find happiness in a more realistic profession. Maybe the dead woman in the woodsman's shack had *not* been the Grand Duchess Anastasia Nikolaevna. Maybe the heir to the Russian throne was still alive out there, plotting a counterrevolution that would end the Bolsheviks' bloody reign.

And maybe, one fine day, Pinkerton's National Detective Agency would locate Zoe's Amber girl.

As Ernest had written on those useless pages, *"Isn't it pretty to think so?"*

Upon finishing breakfast, Zoe dressed in a plain gray-and-tan plaid chemise and a brown pair of her built-up shoes. Warmly wrapped in her coat—after its throw-down on Fortier, it was only slightly singed—she set off for the seventeenth arrondissement. The day was splendid, even though the pale sun exposed the rows and rows of soot-topped snowdrifts. Even at its worst, Paris could never be anything other than glorious.

She'd hoped the reporters had given up, but the pests followed her down the alleyway, waving their notebooks, yelling out her name. One of them, a baby-faced American who kept calling her "Girlie," made the mistake of grabbing her sleeve. After Zoe kicked him in the balls, he fell into one of the drifts and lay on his back, arms and legs flailing. Why, he *did* look like a cockroach! After that, the reporters didn't dare follow as she descended into the underworld of the Métro station.

··· ◇ ···

Fifteen minutes later, she knocked on Henri's door.

When Madame Arceneau answered, she informed Zoe that Henri was at his office, attending to the paperwork required to send a man to the guillotine.

French justice was swift.

"I'm not here to see Henri," Zoe said.

Arceneau took a moment, then nodded and opened the door wide. "Please come in, Mademoiselle Barlow."

"Zoe."

"Of course. Zoe. And I am Hélène."

The evening Henri brought her here, Zoe had been too upset to take much account of the sitting room's furnishings, but as she entered now, she saw a collection which must have taken several lifetimes to amass. An eighteenth-century settee upholstered in yellow-on-yellow damask. A mahogany George III corner arm-chair fronted by a matching ottoman. A Louis XVI breakfront inset with Sèvres porcelain plaques. A Georgian glass-fronted armoire stuffed with books bound in leather and gilt.

Beauty a bedridden woman could no longer enjoy.

Hélène gestured toward the half-finished glass of pale liquid that sat on a sixteenth-century Portuguese table. "Would you like to join me in a glass of Chablis? I usually enjoy one around this time."

"Perhaps later. But for now..." Zoe looked toward the double doors leading to Gabrielle's bedroom. "May I visit with her?"

After a long pause, in which Hélène searched her face for any hint of guile, the woman stood up. "Most certainly, Zoe." When she opened the doors, the scent of grass and flowers rushed out in welcome.

Hélène stepped away, leaving the door slightly ajar.

The other time Zoe had been in this indoor garden, her artist's eye noticed that Gabrielle's head was turned to the left, as if she'd been studying a nearby pot that held a miniature forest of tall grasses. Yet the visitor's chair, a Chinese-lacquered beauty, sat on the right-hand side of the bed. The chair was heavy and hurt her sore hands, but Zoe picked it up and carried it around to the other side, setting it down in front of the small forest. No movement there today, no flash of tourmaline. Perhaps she'd only imagined it before.

From the catch in Gabrielle's breath when Zoe sat down, she realized Henri's wife was conscious. As sorrowful eyes met hers, she saw a thin thread of moisture trailing down her cheek.

Gabrielle was not only awake, she suffered.

Zoe knew all about that kind of thing. Forsaking the ease of the chair, she slipped to her knees and took Gabrielle's perfect hand in her own scarred one.

What had Jewel once told her? First in jest, then another time more seriously? *We're amies, now, Zoe. Friends! Like my Grannie used to tell me when I was a little girl, a friend is God's way of bringing hope to the hopeless.*

Silently thanking Jewel for showing her the way, Zoe leaned toward the woman on the bed and said, "Hello, Gabrielle. My name is Zoe, and I'm going to be your friend."

Author's Note

A couple of decades ago, someone at a party asked me where—
and when—I would like to have lived. After giving the question
some thought, I answered, "Paris, during the 1920s." As an artist
and a writer, I already knew pretty much who was living in Paris
between WWI and WWII and relished the air of excitement
that danced down the Parisian boulevards during the Roaring
Twenties. I still wish I'd been there to experience it. In essence,
Lost in Paris is my love letter to an era and a place whose creative
delights we will never see again. But we always dream. It's true that
Hadley, Ernest Hemingway's first wife, did lose all his early manuscripts, quite possibly because she was too ill with the "Spanish"
flu to be as careful as she should have been. But it is probably *not*
true that the manuscripts emerged in the same manner as they do
in this book, nor that Hemingway kept their being found a secret.

But we'll never know for sure, will we?

Acknowledgments

So many people helped to bring *Lost in Paris* to fruition. First, of course, is Barbara Peters, founder of the famous bookstore and Poisoned Pen Press, who saw an early incarnation of *Lost in Paris* and encouraged me to continue. The same goes for Diane DiBiase and Beth Deveny of Poisoned Pen Press/Sourcebooks, who made certain *Lost in Paris* was as good as it could be.

I would be remiss in not thanking author David Morrell, who is not only a marvelous writer, but whose master's degree thesis centered around Ernest Hemingway, and who was kind enough to share with me his encyclopedic knowledge of the man. Kudos also to Laurent Teichman of Le Studio, who loaned me the marvelous book, *KiKi's Paris: Artists and Lovers 1900–1930*, and who urged me to visit the extraordinary Paris estate of the noble Camondo family (which I did).

Thanks to all the other books and authors who shared their knowledge with me. They include (among others too numerous to mention) *When Paris Sizzled* by Mary McAuliffe; *Expatriate Paris: A Culture and Literary Guide to Paris of the 1920s* by Arlen J. Hansen, and *Harlem's Hell Fighters* by Stephen L. Harris.

Many, many thanks to the hawkeyed Sheridan Street Irregulars: Sharon Magee, Eileen Brady, Art Kerns, Charlie Pyeatte, Ruth Barmore, and Donis Casey. Last, but certainly not least, a million thanks and kisses to Paul Howell for his never-flagging encouragement.

About the Author

© Paul Howell

Betty Webb is the author of the bestselling Lena Jones mystery series (*Desert Redemption, Desert Wives*, etc.) and the humorous Gunn Zoo mysteries (*The Panda of Death, The Otter of Death*, etc.). *Lost in Paris*, released in spring 2023, is the first in her new mystery series set in 1922 France; *Found in Paris* will come out in spring 2024. At the beginning of her career, Betty worked as a commercial artist in Los Angeles and New York City. She eventually became a journalist who wrote about the fine arts. Her popular feature articles expanded her beat, and she spent twenty years interviewing everyone from U.S. presidents, astronauts who'd walked on the moon, Nobel Prize winners, and polygamy runaways. In between Betty's frequent trips to Paris, she lives in Scottsdale, Arizona, with her family.

See bettywebb-mystery.com for more information.